Praise for *A Woman of Inte*

Named a Best Book of Summer 2021 by *Good Morning America* •
BuzzFeed • *POPSUGAR* • *Book Riot* •
LifeSavvy • *Connecticut Post*

"There is so much punchy dialogue and funny-sad humor in this novel. . . . This is a mid-twentieth-century period piece, but oh, how familiar it all seems. Most radically of all, Tanabe writes spot-on about something many men and women are still loath to talk about: that women can love their children but still crave and need a life outside the home."
—*The Washington Post*

"Layered and engrossing." —*Publishers Weekly* (starred review)

"Tanabe crafts the historical setting convincingly [and] the novel moves at a brisk pace. . . . Perhaps the most subversive thing about the twinned stories is this: how well the masks and performances Rina puts on as wife and mother prepare her for the world of espionage."
—*Kirkus Reviews*

"The kind of historical fiction you can get lost in." —*POPSUGAR*

"A smart thriller with heart . . . and some simmering sexual tension, too."
—*Book Riot*

"This book works on so many levels. . . . Domestic suspense is often like a spy novel—vast undercurrents and power differentials underpinning a superficially close but in fact exploitative relationship—and nowhere is that point made more clear than in this novel."
—*CrimeReads*

"The glitz and glamour of 1954 Manhattan come to life in this captivating novel."
—*Woman's World*

"If you're into fast-paced classic spy thrillers, with plenty of twists and turns, this one's for you." —*Westport* magazine

"What a delicious skein of secrets Karin Tanabe has spooled in *A Woman of Intelligence*, somehow entwining the lies it takes to sustain the fiction of happy motherhood with the lies it takes to work as a covert operative for the FBI in 1954 at the height of the McCarthy hearings. Katharina Edgeworth's awakening into the gray area of patriotic action is prescient, relevant, and above all, deeply satisfying. I loved diving into this world." —Sarah Blake, *New York Times* bestselling author of *The Guest Book*

"Tanabe has long delighted readers of historical fiction with her beautiful writing, compelling plots, and sumptuous historic details. In *A Woman of Intelligence*, she gives fans a heroine to root for in the strong, complex, and spirited Katharina Edgeworth. This is the story of a woman who dares to dream beyond the gilded cage and stifling social mores into which life has boxed her, and who proves the indelible power of women to change the world in the process." —Allison Pataki, *New York Times* bestselling author of *The Queen's Fortune*

"Karin Tanabe delivers her most complex heroine yet in *A Woman of Intelligence*. Katharina Edgeworth, a former UN translator, unfulfilled in her role as wife and mother, finds herself leading a double life as an FBI informant during the McCarthy era. Filled with intrigue and wit, [*A Woman of Intelligence*] takes readers on a meticulously researched journey through post-WWII New York. This is a novel for fans of thrillers and historical fiction alike." —Renée Rosen, bestselling author of *The Social Graces*

A
WOMAN
of
INTELLIGENCE

———◆———

KARIN TANABE

ST. MARTIN'S GRIFFIN
NEW YORK

Published in the United States by
St. Martin's Griffin, an imprint of St. Martin's Publishing Group

www.stmartins.com

The Library of Congress has cataloged the hardcover edition as follows:

Names: Tanabe, Karin, author.
Title: A woman of intelligence / Karin Tanabe.
Description: First edition. | New York : St. Martin's Press, 2021.
Identifiers: LCCN 2021006924 | ISBN 9781250231505 (hardcover) |
    ISBN 9781250231529 (ebook)
Subjects: GSAFD: Suspense fiction.
Classification: LCC PS3620.A6837 W66 2021 | DDC 813/.6—dc23
LC record available at https://lccn.loc.gov/2021006924

ISBN 978-1-250-23151-2 (trade paperback)

Our books may be purchased in bulk for promotional, educational, or business use. Please contact your local bookseller or the Macmillan Corporate and Premium Sales Department at 1-800-221-7945, extension 5442, or by email at MacmillanSpecialMarkets@macmillan.com.

First St. Martin's Griffin Edition: 2022

10 9 8 7 6 5 4 3 2 1

I Have a self to recover, a queen
Is she dead, is she sleeping?
Where has she been,
With her lion-red body, her wings of glass?
—SYLVIA PLATH

A
WOMAN
of
INTELLIGENCE

CHAPTER 1

Mother.

Only one word cut through the noise of a New York afternoon.

The rest of my neighbor Carrie's monologue was lost to me as a Packard ambulance raced past us along Fifth Avenue, siren screaming and bright red gumball light flashing. On its oversize tires, the Packard looked like a white scarab beetle, slicing a path through Manhattan's congested Upper East Side.

Our view of wide and pulsating Fifth Avenue was flanked by a parade of elms now in full leaf. When the shriek of the sirens had faded, we turned our attention back to each other, two women seated on a wooden bench at the playground near the Metropolitan Museum of Art's Egyptian wing.

Carrie, a red-headed, doe-eyed girl with a pin-up body and an alabaster face, scrunched up her pretty features. "Those ambulances are awfully loud, aren't they?" she noted.

"Indeed."

She glanced uptown, as if they might suddenly start rolling down Fifth Avenue by the dozen, like the tanks during the Victory Parade in '45, nine years back. "Is it just me or did they get louder after the war?"

"Could be," I said.

"I think they have, and it's really too much," she replied decisively, her heart-shaped chin rising a pinch. "The noise scares the children." She pulled on the large diamonds clipped to her earlobes as if to adjust her eardrums back to softer sounds. "They shouldn't let ambulances take this route to Lenox Hill, so close to the park. But I suppose, if someone dies on Fifth Avenue, someone dies on Fifth Avenue," she said with a sigh.

"Even the rich have to meet their maker," I replied.

"I suppose that's true," Carrie said, sounding doubtful. As a woman made of sunshine, never clouds, Carrie was the type of uplifted soul who always focused on life, not death. Part of her seemed quite sure that her husband could simply make a large bank transfer to the grim reaper in exchange for eternal life for the whole family—that is, the moneyed New York sort of life that they were already living. If eternity meant being a farmer's overburdened wife in one of the Dakotas or that state shaped like a mitten, then Carrie would surely take her last breath in that ambulance to Lenox Hill instead. At least she'd die in the correct postal zone.

"What were you saying before the ambulance came?" I asked. "The sirens drowned you out."

"Oh," Carrie replied, frowning as she thought back. "I was saying that our children are at a perfect age. Don't you love it? Don't you just love being a mother?'"

She looked out at her daughter, Alice, and my son Gerrit, trying to climb up the metal slide, squawking happily, their faces a mix of dirt, mucus, and joy. Next to us on the bench, my one-year-old, Peter, was tucked in a white cashmere blanket, sleeping with his head on my lap, wrapped up as tightly as the mummies in the Egyptian wing a few yards away.

"Being a mother," I echoed, thinking how the sirens had seemed to amplify the word's impact. "And yes, of course," I added quickly. "Of course I do. I love it. There's nothing I love more." I stretched as much as I could in my heavy coat. April was proving no breath of spring. "We *all* love being mothers."

"We do," she said firmly. "It *is* the greatest gift."

In her teal green dress and matching coat, a child-friendly one-inch heel on her beige shoes, Carrie was a vision of a certain kind of femininity, her whole being screaming of spryness, full of the vivacity that I lacked. At twenty-seven, she was a full decade younger than I was, and suddenly she seemed even younger.

"I remember when I was pregnant with Alice," Carrie continued, touching her flat midsection reflectively. "I was at the opera with Matthew, just a human beach ball taking in *Tosca*," she said, grinning, "and during intermission, a woman patted my stomach with a hand covered in diamonds—yellow diamonds, very large—and said, 'Isn't it so wonderful? To be having a baby? Just think, when it's born, you'll never be alone again.'" Carrie cocked her head and moved her pretty red hair—shampoo advertisement hair—to the other side of her neck. "For the rest of my life I'll always have someone at my side, or at least somewhere roaming the earth, who I've created. Never alone again," she repeated. "Isn't that just the most wonderful sentiment?"

"Wonderful," I replied quickly, adding an overly emphatic nod of the head.

"You can rid yourself of a husband, or friends, and your parents die, but as long as you live, your children will always be tethered to you. The rope may get longer, but it never breaks."

"Never," I repeated, digging my nails into the bench's wooden slats.

"I wasn't expecting a revelatory moment at the opera," Carrie went on, patting baby Peter, still sleeping soundly between us. "Frankly, I was a bit unnerved to be pulled to the theater in my eighth month of pregnancy, but the Maximillian Millses had invited us and we couldn't say no to that, could we?"

"Absolutely not," I replied. My own husband would have made me accept an invitation from the Maximillian Millses even if I had been in active labor, the baby coming into the world as everyone howled at their jokes and nodded yes, please, for more canapés. No one ever declined an invitation from the Millses.

"But that woman's words made me feel . . . I don't know, exactly." Carrie looked up at the gray sky as if waiting for God to deliver the right adjective. "Peaceful. More peaceful than I had felt my whole pregnancy. It was a beautiful, comforting thing to think about. Never alone again."

She eyed me to make sure I was still listening.

"I've thought about it every day since, and Alice is two already," she said, giving a wave to her daughter, her diamond bracelets clinking. Alice's flaxen hair was in her eyes, but she didn't seem to notice, too busy playing in the dirt that stuck to her as if she were made of flypaper.

"I never quite thought about motherhood that way." I loosened the gray silk scarf around my neck, one of the last presents I remembered receiving from my own mother. After I married, she told me I had enough money to buy my own scarves.

"That woman was my own angel Gabriel of sorts. It was the best moment of my pregnancy."

"Lovely," I muttered again. My own pregnancies had only been heaven-sent during conception. The rest had been highlighted by vomiting, tears, and an excessive consumption of desserts from Glaser's Bake Shop.

I continued to pull at my scarf, suddenly conscious of feeling rather like Nathan Hale on the gallows as the executioner tightened his noose. "It is all such a blessing, isn't it?" I said brightly, glancing over to see my older son poke himself in the face with a stick. As I watched, he stopped, pulled up his coat sleeve, held the stick out in front of him, and then turned to Alice. With a single precise movement, he jabbed her right in the eye. She screamed and fell backward, her little legs straight up in the air like a tipped calf's. "A gift," I added before we both jumped up.

I sprang forward ahead of Carrie, since my child was the offender, but remembered I had a sleeping baby on the bench and went back to pick him up before I scolded Gerrit. My motions were jerky, and Peter woke up abruptly. He blinked in surprise a few times, then howled. I left the toddlers to Carrie, who gently took the stick away from Gerrit while trying not to let her daughter bite his face in retaliation. I attempted to comfort Peter, holding him as tightly as I could manage, and took off my scarf with my other hand. It would be better off in my purse than around my neck.

I hoisted the baby up, then went to yell at my other son as etiquette required when one two-year-old tried to maim another. I bent down to get closer to him.

"Gerrit! No hitting! No poking! No sticks!" I shouted. "No violence!" What else could I add to make Carrie think I was the right kind of mother? "No mischief! No roughhousing! No moving at all!"

Gerrit looked up at me, his face pink from the cold and the excitement of trying to murder his playmate, and said, "No." He picked up another stick before I could lunge at him, and poked me hard in the leg, ripping my stocking.

I clutched Peter even tighter, glad that I hadn't ended up like a tipped calf myself.

"Oh, Rina, your stockings," Carrie said, gripping Alice's hand. I waved her off and peered at Alice. The child had emerged from the fray still fully sighted, but as I looked at her blue eyes I noticed the sky behind her had darkened by several shades—gone the color of concrete.

Before I could panic, the baby panicked for me. A huge drop of water hit his fat cheek, surprising him. He started to howl and wiggle out of his folded blankets, like an animal under attack. As I hung on to him, I heard sharp little dings. Hail was bouncing at my feet. I clutched the baby to my breast and grabbed Gerrit's hand. "Carrie!" I screamed, though she was only two feet away.

"What should we do?" she said, looking from me to our bags open on the bench, food and toys strewn everywhere. "Go inside the museum?"

"With my monsters? We'll end up in prison. Let's try to get a taxi."

We threw our things into bags and purses while the toddlers cackled with glee and the baby wailed. As we rushed to Fifth Avenue, one of Peter's blankets fell to the ground. Carrie turned back for it, as I could barely hold my children, and I yelled at her to leave it.

"There will be no taxis left!" I shouted.

At the corner of Eighty-fourth, we shot our arms up, but we were among dozens doing the same.

"Watch it, kid!" a man barked as he tried to get to the curb. I looked down. Gerrit was stepping on the back of his shoes, perhaps accidentally, most likely not.

"I'm terribly sorry," I apologized as my purse slid down my arm. Some of its contents spilled out, a glass jar shattering. He stepped over the shards and whistled for a cab. As I kicked the glass off my feet, he muttered obscenities, then darted into the road and threw himself into a taxi, nearly upending an elderly woman.

"I'll cross the street!" Carrie shouted as she flung herself across Fifth Avenue, Alice's hand in an iron grip. "Whoever hails a cab first, the other runs across and climbs in!"

For ten minutes we tried, without success. I almost dropped the baby, and in my efforts to keep him off the pavement, flipped him horizontally and tucked him under my arm like a salami. A living, breathing, angry salami. Across the street, Carrie finally appeared as desperate as I felt.

"Subway!" she shouted.

We rushed to Lexington, then nearly rolled down the steps of the 86th Street station, barely able to squeeze through the turnstiles as the crowd surged toward the arriving train. Right before the car's double doors opened, Gerrit squirmed free. I stuck out my leg to keep him from sprinting away, and in one swift motion, Carrie yanked him onto the train. With all three children wailing, food dripping in our expensive handbags, my stocking torn, our lipstick smeared, and our hair ruined, the subway doors shut in front of us.

"I love being a mother," I whispered as the train groaned to a start.

CHAPTER 2

During my childhood and through my twenties I had taken the subway constantly, loving it even in the sweltering summer. Subways were a microcosm of humanity, and the New York slice of it was the most intriguing in the world, I was sure. But since I'd had children, I almost never burrowed underground anymore. "Leave that to the rats," Tom had said jokingly when I was rearranging my bronze subway tokens in my purse a few days after we'd returned from the hospital with Gerrit. He had taken them from me and placed them in his doctor's bag with the intention of giving them to the drunks who wandered into his hospital, Lenox Hill.

I looked around the subway car as I clutched Peter to my chest, trying to muffle his sobs. Carrie was shushing Alice and Gerrit with little success. I grabbed Gerrit's coat collar and pulled him to my side, trying to ignore the judgmental stares, focusing on the conversations around me instead of my inconsolable sons. Rants about the weather dominated.

"Those ice cubes nearly took my eye out."

"Why did the papers not predict this?"

"Surely it's a sign of the apocalypse."

"I thought it was raining bullets. Thought I was back in Normandy."

"You're in Manhattan, darling. You're safe here."

I turned to see the woman who had tried to calm the shaken former soldier, but people had started crowding the doors, ready to exit at Seventy-seventh.

I'd always found comfort in crowds. I missed being part of the throng. I missed being a rat. When I was a rat, even if I was surrounded by fellow commuters, I was alone. The only salami under my arm came from Carnegie Deli, to be devoured with my roommates, and the only hand in mine belonged to a man, with the promise of a very good good-night kiss, or more. A man who was not my husband, and would never be my husband, because he had no prospects or common sense. That was the best kind of man to have attached to you in a subway. To kiss you passionately when you were the last two in the car. Maybe they were the rats my husband was talking about.

"Rina! This is our stop!" Carrie cried out.

We managed to get our children above ground at Sixty-eighth Street, drag them past Hunter College, then pull them down Park Avenue. Peter had been steadily wailing since we'd left the museum, but on Park, he went from a baby crying to an animal crying. I held him close, I bounced him, I kissed him, I sang in three languages. Nothing worked. My sanity was ebbing fast as we walked in front of the consulate of Pakistan, when suddenly Carrie stopped in front of me.

"Rina. It's not hailing," she said without turning around to look at me. "Finally!" She reached her arms up to the sky and grinned.

With Carrie elated and Alice quieted, but my body still pumping with adrenaline and my boys still screaming, we made our way to 820 Fifth Avenue.

Our doorman, Sam, a transplant from the Dominican Republic, rushed over to us and took our bags, ignoring the food glop oozing out of mine. He reached for Gerrit, who took his hand without even considering biting it. Sam slipped Gerrit and Alice candy wrapped in yellow cellophane and led us all toward the beige awning of our limestone building. Even if you were drunk and disorderly and tumbling out of a taxi, Sam would dote on you. He treated all residents of 820 as if they'd just stepped out of a brushed-up Bentley.

"Are you all right, Mrs. Edgeworth, Mrs. Kirkland?" Sam asked. "Can you believe that hail? I thought the sky was falling."

"Oh, we're all right," Carrie said brightly. She and Alice were all smiles now that they could see the luxurious building they called home. Alice may have been only two, but she already seemed to sense the transformative power of money.

"I've been better," I murmured, and thanked Sam for taking Gerrit in hand.

Sam walked us through the lobby and whisked us into the elevator, where he chatted with Ronald, the elevator man. Like Sam, Ronald's black hair was perfectly slicked back, with a maroon cap perched on top. When the elevator dinged, Sam stepped out to accompany each of us to our apartments—Carrie first, as she lived on the fourth floor. In 820, there were only twelve apartments, ten of them full-floor sprawls.

"Tomorrow, let's just go to the zoo across the street," Carrie said with a grin as she stepped out.

"I may never go to Central Park again," I said dryly.

Carrie laughed, evidently sure that I was kidding. She tossed her red hair, patted the baby on the head, and gave me a kiss on the cheek before the door slid shut. Ronald pushed the button and we shot up to our private world on the seventh floor.

"Sam, I can't thank you enough," I said as he put my bag down on the kitchen counter and helped take off Gerrit's coat while I kept rocking the whimpering baby. "I am not made of the same stock as Carrie," I admitted. "I was about to give up."

"No," Sam said, smiling. "I don't believe it. You're different from Mrs. Kirkland, but you're not the type to throw in the towel. And I'm happy to help. Anytime." He slipped Gerrit another piece of candy. I should have protested, a vision of Gerrit with one wobbly yellow tooth and a mouth full of gray gums flashing through my mind, but I was too tired. And I liked Sam too much to ever embarrass him.

Instead, I walked over to my handbag, found my wallet, and handed Sam a few dollars, which he protested, I insisted upon, and he finally tucked into the pocket of his gray wool pants.

"See? You never give up," said Sam, smiling and inching toward the elevator.

"Repaying someone for their kindness is a lot easier than being hailed on while holding a baby," I said.

He pushed the button, then turned to look at me again, his dark skin seeming to glow in the late afternoon sunlight, which was finally winning out over the clouds. "In this city, you'd be surprised."

I nodded as Sam stepped into the elevator.

Exhausted, I put the baby on the floor and leaned against the counter for a minute, trying to find my strength. I closed my eyes until I felt small hands pawing at my legs, then opened them again and picked up both children. I bathed us, fed us, dried tears, changed diapers, kissed bumped knees, scolded Gerrit, apologized for scolding Gerrit, dried more tears, and then let the boys watch hours of television—*The Funny Bunny, The Adventures of Danny Dee*, the evening news—before they fell asleep on top of me, a pile of puppies on my marital bed. The same was certainly not happening three floors down. Carrie was always playing educational games with Alice. Flash cards with Impressionist paintings, Greek poetry, Polynesian fruit. And she had her housekeeper, Mrs. Flores, to help her. She had certainly not made baked chicken with shaking hands, tears mixing into the marinade, muscles exhausted from carrying a baby for nearly an hour.

I extracted my body from the pile and looked at the time. It was ten o'clock, and my bed was as it usually was, minus one husband. Tom Edgeworth. Chief of pediatric surgery at Lenox Hill. The nature of his work—surgeries were usually scheduled, after all—should have allowed him to make it home for dinner with his wife and children, but Tom Edgeworth was not choosing steak, potatoes, or family. He was choosing the hospital. It had run in operating debt for years, never saying no to the sick who could not pay, but it could no longer survive that way. They wanted to add an intensive care unit, and Tom wanted to be able to admit children to the intensive care unit. He wanted to help raise money for the hospital. And one day, he wanted to lead the whole place. So every night, his dinner was made and put into the refrigerator, not consumed until midnight.

The hospital fed his soul, and also provided us with our sliver of a social life. The only dinners we didn't eat at home were at the homes of potential hospital donors. Four-story town houses on Madison, apartments on Sixty-ninth Street with marble everything and a view of the park so sweeping you could count the pigeons. The inhabitants were the people Tom could convince to give generously. People he had known all his life. Those running Lenox Hill were fully aware that a man who was a surgeon, handsome, and an Edgeworth was a horse they wanted to bet on. Tom didn't mind at all. He had one destination in mind for his future and it was not the operating room, not full-time anyway. The donations that Tom brought in, the relationships he cultivated, would not only help save the children, they would also propel him to the executive level. Chairman of surgery, hospital director. Hence the dinners, the conversations, the pleasantries, and political talk. For those dinners, in those palatial homes, we were allowed to stay well past midnight.

Tonight, I was not going to make it to midnight.

I managed to doze restlessly for a few hours, then, startled by a bad dream, woke up covered in a layer of sweat, my heart racing. I checked to make sure the boys were breathing, then wandered into the long hallway, which my husband called the gallery. I'd copied him when we'd first moved in three years ago, when I was pregnant with Gerrit, but I quickly realized that I sounded, and felt, ridiculous, so I returned to calling it the hallway. I, unlike him, had not been raised in the ivory towers of one of Manhattan's best buildings, the San Remo on Central Park West. I'd grown up in a fourth-floor walk-up near Washington Square with pockets full of subway tokens, the competing smells of immigrant food wafting into the apartment windows, and the sounds of my upstairs, downstairs, and sideways neighbors screaming, making love, sneezing, wheezing. I'd even heard Mrs. Kuznetsov, our upstairs neighbor, die. She tripped on the hall carpet while carrying a large cooked ham and smashed her head against a side table. No one at the San Remo ever heard anyone die. And no resident of the San Remo would have dared die such an undignified death.

I walked through our very dignified hall to the library, and my favorite spot in the apartment—a window seat barely long enough for me to sit sideways, but just right if I jutted my knees up like a bridge and craned my neck a bit. From that perch, there was an unrivaled view of the Central Park Zoo to be had. But even better, there was a perfect view of the sidewalk in front of it. I wouldn't admit it to my husband, because I'd rhapsodized about the animals when we'd moved in, but I actually far preferred the life on the sidewalk to the sad creatures behind bars. I loved all the sidewalks in New York, but especially the ones by the park.

Before becoming a mother, I'd had a job, but it felt as if I had all the time in the world to do what I liked best, observe. Now I had no job, and no time. So, whenever my children were safely asleep, I went to the window to observe the life swirling below. Don't let it be said that Dr. Tom Edgeworth gave me nothing. My perch above the city came courtesy of a dwindling, but still very ample shipping fortune, of which Tom was a prime beneficiary. He was never home, but he was indisputably the provider of said home.

I pressed my face to the glass until I could smell the cold, wiping away the tears that always seemed to fall when I sat at the window seat in the middle of the night.

The hail was long over, but the night remained wet, dominated by a thin rain. Almost too thin to call a drizzle. As I looked down, I still had the sound of hail in my ears. That dreaded clicking. If I had been alone by the Met, I would have gone in when the hail started, or ducked into a coffee shop, a bookstore, any place where I could stay dry and watch the commotion from the inside out. But with small children, that was no longer a possibility. The books would have been thrown from their shelves, the coffee spilled. The baby would have howled, the toddler would have rampaged, my sanity would have fled. A woman with young children moves in a ring of chaos, inspiring murmurs, eye rolls, or grumbling reprimands when her circus troupe blows into public spaces. Where I used to spark smiles, maybe a hungry, carnal look from less subtle men, I now sparked dread.

I hugged my knees and surveyed the people free to walk calmly at night in the rain. A brown-skinned man in a beautiful orange turban was crossing the street and another man, wearing a beige raincoat and hat, was standing across from my building. The hat dipped down unnaturally, the elements too much for it. A palm tree in the snow. The man was lighting a cigarette, which he managed to do with one stroke of a match despite the weather. He then flipped the brim of his hat slightly up, looked at the match for a moment, blew it out, and put it in his pocket. The only man in Manhattan who wouldn't carelessly throw it onto the sidewalk. I watched him take a few satisfying puffs of his cigarette, until a woman with a red umbrella crossed his path. It was an unusually large umbrella, and she was a slight girl, so it looked more like a beach parasol. When her umbrella tilted back, I saw that she was laughing.

As she laughed, my tears fell faster. I dug my fingers into the flesh around my hip bones, hard enough to bruise, enjoying a strange jolt from the pain, a reminder that I owned my body and could do with it what I willed. At least when the hands of children and the eyes of the world were off me. The bruises that would appear tomorrow would join other finger-sized bruises. The marks from my nights by the window.

The girl with the red umbrella was alone. I was not. Even in this dark corner of the apartment, I wasn't alone. I desperately missed being alone.

"Never alone." I hugged my knees tighter to my chest as I remembered Carrie's words. My knees stopped short of where they used to, my thighs far from vertical. My breasts were too large to hug my legs in tight, the breasts of a nursing mother. "They'll go away when all *that* is over," Carrie had told me one afternoon. "Then they'll look nothing like they did before."

The woman under the red umbrella was almost out of view, just a flash of red and her legs underneath. She looked like a woman who had the freedom to walk in the rain in the middle of the night, the time to carefully consider the color—if not the size—of her umbrella, and whose knees fit perfectly under her chin. She didn't look anything like me.

CHAPTER 3

Katharina Edgeworth, the woman who haunts the gallery in the dead of night. Even after all these years."

Tom walked over and kissed the top of my head. I'd haunted many other hallways before 820 Fifth.

Tom was wearing the blue and yellow striped pajamas I'd given him two Christmases ago that, worn by someone who was six foot three, looked a bit like the Swedish flag. I hadn't heard him come in.

"You're home. I didn't realize," I said, turning toward him. "What time is it?"

"About five, I think," he said, pointing outside. "It will be light out soon."

"I didn't hear the door," I said, turning my hips to make room on the window seat for him. He didn't take it.

"I came in an hour ago. I didn't want to bother you. I saw the boys asleep on our bed, so I went to the guest room. I'm so tired I think I could have fallen asleep on the bathroom floor."

"I think that's what you do when you're drunk, not tired."

"That's frowned upon in surgery. Now, *after* surgery, it's very much applauded," he said, smiling. Before we were married, he'd been described in the society section of the *Times* as having "the most electrifying smile in all of Manhattan." It was true, even when he was exhausted. I'd asked him on one of our first dates if his teeth were real.

"Nah, marble. Descendant of Michelangelo's carved 'em. Did a pretty good job, don't you think? You should see me tear through steaks, a side of ribs. Gravel," he'd said, grinning as widely as he could. Tom Edgeworth had been a very easy man to fall in love with. I was just surprised that he'd fallen in love with me.

"Would you like me to make you a drink?" I asked.

"No, it's too late, but thank you," said Tom, stretching out his long arms. "I think gin would keep me up. And I very much need to be down. As in horizontal."

He put his hand on my shoulder and gave it an affectionate rub.

"Did you have an interesting day?"

I let myself enjoy the weight of him against my body. The first purposeful touch from an adult that I'd had all day.

"Sure, I did. Though the hail wasn't the easiest to navigate with the boys."

"Did it hail today?" he asked, peering out the window, as if frozen golf balls might still be strewn around the park like a wintry Bethpage Black.

"A bit."

"Well, tomorrow is Friday," he said, taking a step back from the window. "Then we can spend the weekend together."

"You're not working?"

"Not for one minute," he replied, his smile showing off his tired eyes.

"How wonderful."

"And tomorrow, don't forget," he added, his expression brightening a bit. Tom Edgeworth loved issuing reminders. "Jilly is going to come watch the boys for a few hours. She said three o'clock, but maybe just telephone to jog her memory."

"Is she?" I asked, astonished. I remembered Tom mentioning some such arrangement a few weeks back when New York was still frozen over, but I had completely forgotten about it. Jilly, Tom's parents' long-time housekeeper, sometimes came to lend a hand with the boys when we were in a pinch. Tom called it a pinch. I called it something else.

"That's very kind of her," I said, suddenly elated. "And a lovely co-incidence, as Christine Allard—do you remember her? The French girl I used to work with?"

"You worked with so many French girls," he replied, leaning against the wall. "The exuberant one?"

"You're thinking of Marianne. Christine, well, she's just lovely, in-telligent . . . French."

"Fine then, the French one. Yes, I remember her," he said, though he clearly did not.

"There's a van Eyck exhibit at the museum and it's supposed to be divine. She's been wanting me to see it with her and invited me to go tomorrow—or today I suppose—as she finishes early on Fridays like I used to. I said no, because of the boys of course, but I'll call and tell her I can make it after all. I'm thrilled. I haven't seen her in over a year and I haven't had an afternoon out in ages. Really, it is awfully nice of Jilly to come."

Tom pushed off the wall, as if he'd just woken up again. "But the reason Jilly's coming is because of the gala."

He looked at my face, clearly hoping for a sign of excitement. Or at least recollection. I didn't have either.

"The Medical Association gala at the Plaza. You forgot," he said.

The gala. An annual affair that got duller every year. Of course I'd forgotten.

"Maybe I did," I admitted. Or I'd conveniently pushed it into the dark recesses of my mind to grow cobwebs.

"Well," he said. "Luckily I'm here to remind you. Also, that you have a hair appointment at Jean-Pierre's at four. That's at Fifty-eighth and Madison, in case you've forgotten that, too. Your appointment is why Jilly is coming early. You're having your hair . . . what is it that women do to their hair? Colored, curled, pulled up, let down, and brushed and such."

I touched my shoulder-length black hair, which wasn't any of those things and certainly needed all of them. It was straight yet frizzy, more scarecrow than surgeon's wife.

"Perhaps they can paint your nails, too," he added, looking down at my unvarnished nails. "That will be even more relaxing than pushing through tourists at the exhibit, won't it? An afternoon of pampering?"

I thought of the reds and greens of van Eyck's paintings. The marble-like skin. I thought of the way my father, an art history professor, used to put little strips of paper between the pages of my secondhand edition of Helen Gardner's *Art Through the Ages*, marking paintings he thought I should learn about. He'd picked the *Arnolfini Portrait*, *Portrait of a Man*. Their greens and blues so deeply pigmented that I was convinced van Eyck's eyes just worked differently than mine.

"Equally relaxing," I said, tears threatening again.

"Good," Tom said, reassured. "Then I'm off to bed. If I don't see you in the morning—the official morning—then I'll see you at seven tonight. Kiss the boys for me," he added. He picked up my hand and pressed his lips to it. I wasn't sure if the kiss was for me or if I was supposed to transfer it to the boys. I watched Tom's tall form disappear down the hallway, then put my face against the window again. The mist had stopped. Of course it had. It was fine for the heavens to throw hail on unprepared mothers, but the powers that be would never allow it to rain on the day of the medical gala.

CHAPTER 4

I used to be the first one in the door at a party. If it started at eight, I was there at 7:59. I didn't care about being fashionably late; all I cared about was having a grand old time. Especially after the war ended. Simply to be free and alive—knowing how many other people would now remain free and alive—felt like a party. It was a party to walk down the sidewalk, a party to see young men home again, a party to catch them looking at your bare shoulders, imagining what the rest of you looked like bare. It was an honor to feel full of life, and even better, life as a wild young thing.

In 1945, I was working at City Hall, along with my roommates, Patricia and Ruby, recent Smith and Swarthmore College grads. Monday through Friday we tapped our heels up the building's grand marble stairs, our skirts rubbing our hips with enough vroom to make it feel like we were walking arm in arm with the mayor. Then, eight hours later, when the clock struck five, we'd run straight back down those stairs to taste our freedom, and our dinner. At wobbly tables or chipped countertops we'd eat the cheapest, most filling food we could find, which usually meant something foreign and enormous. Paella for an army at Sevilla on Charles Street in the West Village, practically sitting on top of one another in our itchy stockings, sweating right onto the seat, or pierogi in the East Village, folded by the expert hands of Ukrainians and Poles. On paydays we'd have steak, still giddy from the end of meat rationing, grinning goodbye to endless macaroni and welcoming the return of marbled New York strip. We'd knock back two cheap beers, not wanting to spend our meager salaries on the gin martinis we actually craved. Instead, we'd find some men to buy us real drinks. If we were in the mood for artists, we'd pretend to be sulky and profound at the Hotel Albert, but if our tongues were begging for expensive cocktails, and plenty of them, we'd go to the Hotel Astor in Times Square.

Sometimes, we'd meet men who would sweep us off our feet and we wouldn't be home for hours, or days, but sometimes it would all be a bust and we'd leave together and head back to our apartment on Mercer Street, crossing through Washington Square Park. If we were drunk enough when we left, we'd knock on the door of the Poetry Mender, an odd duck of a man who never slept. In his garret at 25 West Third he'd write poetry for fifteen cents a line and we'd tuck it in our skirt pockets, rush to the benches in Washington Square Park, stand on them, and compete for best drunken poetry reader. One of us would get a heel caught and fall down, all of us would inspire hungry whistles from virile young men, then we'd laugh until we cried happy, drunken tears. How long had it been since we hadn't immediately felt guilt while feeling joy? We'd place the winning poem in the fence around Washington Square, to give the verse some visibility, then throw the rest in the trash and be on our way, running past the buildings and the remaining revelers to collapse into bed and sleep it off.

We'd be up again Monday morning, zipping past the Woolworth Building in all her eight-hundred-foot crowned glory as we returned to work, feeling as tall and important as that majestic pile of terracotta.

Patricia, Ruby, and I were together the day after the war ended. When we read the morning papers together, I circled the *Times* headline and held it in front of their faces: "All City 'Let's Go.'" So we went. We hopped through the city as if it had just been erected yes-terday, because that's how it felt. New York City was officially reborn on August 15, 1945.

While we'd managed our fair share of fun in the waning days of the war, everything changed once peace had officially been declared. Silk dresses were selling, sugar was being sprinkled like snow, and optimism and money abounded. Because of that money, there was a feeling that America, especially Manhattan, was going to shine again. It all seemed to pump extra oxygen into our young lungs, but the best thing that happened was that the pool of men expanded overnight. They brought with them the delicious scent of testosterone. The second-best thing that happened was that I didn't stay at City Hall much longer. In the middle of 1946, a girl I knew in passing, Elisabeth Braun, stopped me in the hall after hearing me speak French to a visitor I had escorted in.

"Rina, I didn't realize you speak French? I thought just German and Italian," she said when we were alone in the hallway with a sunny view of Centre Street.

"Just?"

She smiled, and shook her head. "Sorry, in my family, if you don't speak at least four then something's not quite right."

"I'm Swiss, my family is from Fribourg, so I understand that per-fectly. And I do speak four."

"Well, did you know that the United Nations is hiring French in-terpreters? English to French and French to English. But you have to be really good."

"The United Nations?" I felt my world grow larger simply saying the words.

She nodded. "It's headquartered, for now, on Lake Success in Nas-sau County. Long Island. But the General Assembly meets at the New York City Building in Queens. It's all a hike, but it's the United Nations, so it's worth the shoe leather. Or the Long Island Rail Road ticket."

"Nice of you to tell me," I said, already feeling the excitement, ready to bound out of City Hall and into the world. "I'm interested."

"It's actually extremely self-serving," said Elisabeth quietly. "I'm only telling you because I want your job. I can't work for Braden anymore. He thinks my backside is fair game. I'm sick of having it grazed and pecked at. I'm about to put a book in my skirt. And I'm afraid it's going to get worse than grazing and pecking. The other day he . . ." She closed her eyes and shook her head. "Anyway, I want your job. And your boss."

"I'm sor—"

"My cousin Marianne is there," she said, cutting me off abruptly. "She grew up in France with American parents and worked as a secretary for the French embassy. She told me about the job opening. But you have to be able to translate as they're speaking to you. Simultaneous interpretation they call it. Are you good enough in French to do it?"

I had an aunt who had done simultaneous interpretation. And I'd spent my life rotating languages, easily, fluently.

"*Mais bien sûr,*" I replied, rolling my R until it bounced off my tongue.

"I'm good enough in French to say *mais bien sûr,*" said Elisabeth skeptically.

"I'm good enough," I assured her.

"Meet my cousin after work?"

Marianne Fontaine walked into a café across from the New York World Building, wearing a little black beret of all things, declaring herself in love with every single delegate at the UN but also with a *World* reporter named Frank (who insisted she call him Frisco). Instantly, I knew I had to work with her. I wanted to be wherever she was. More than that, I wanted to live just like her. The next morning, I dialed Fieldstone 7-1100, the Lake Success information office, and asked how to apply. A month later, I was exiting the Long Island

Rail Road at Great Neck, boarding a bus to Lake Success to go say a lot more than *mais bien sûr*.

Before I started, I'd written to my aunt Hanna, the simultaneous interpreter, and told her about my plans. She was thrilled, I was thrilled, my entire family in Switzerland was thrilled. I'd asked Aunt Hanna for advice and she'd replied, "Anticipate. Just as you can anticipate someone's physical moves, you can anticipate someone's words. You need to learn to hear what's coming."

It was hard to hear what was coming, much harder than I thought, but I kept up. Even though French and English were the official UN languages, every day I spoke Italian and German to people who had them as second, third, even fourth languages, though neither country had been admitted to the UN. I even tried my hand at Mandarin when a Chinese delegation visited, the representatives all wearing thin black ties and sharp double-breasted suits. In 1947, I listened in awe as the Arabic-speaking translators clicked through the halls as fast as possible when the United Kingdom delegation raised the question of the independence of Palestine. The translators scurried to the Egyptian representative, who then had to revisit the application of the Hashemite Kingdom of Trans-Jordan, and then we all had to take a break to welcome Siam as the newest member of the UN. If that wasn't reason to celebrate, what was?

I took the train to either Lake Success or the United Nations stop in Queens every workday for six years, going through books of commuter tickets faster than the delegates went through cartons of cigarettes. It was exhausting, exhilarating work, and I never stopped loving what *The New York Times* had dubbed "United Nations patois," a conversation made up of many languages, plus the hand gestures that accompanied them.

That LIRR train left Pennsylvania Station on the half hour for Great Neck, passing the United Nations stop on the old World's Fair grounds in Queens. Then it would squeak into Nassau County and the shiny United Nations buses would be waiting there to take us to headquarters.

I adored walking off the bus and into the Lake Success building with fifty-five proud, high-flying flags in front of the wide, squat thing, which had once been the Sperry Gyroscope company. How could a person not feel awash with success at a place with such a name? But it wasn't just the name, it was the sights and sounds. My brain felt alive speaking an endless circle of English to French, French to English, with the interpreters from France and Belgium. I adored greeting the Indian girls in saris serving as secretaries and file clerks and watching them float in their magentas and blues down the hallway, or smiling hello to the tall, elegant Ethiopian girls as they hurried to put carbon paper and letter paper in the rollers of their typewriters.

Almost weekly, I'd stop to gawk at Eleanor Roosevelt, one of five American delegates to the General Assembly, or admire the formidable presence of Andrei Gromyko, the Soviet delegate of the Security Council.

I loved having picnics on the sloped lawn at Lake Success with Marianne and interpreters and translators from all over the world, or having cocktails after work at the UN restaurant, sneaking up to the Delegates Lounge, which was closed to the public. It felt like the world had descended on Long Island for the best possible reason— peace, the kind that might endure—and somehow, I had snatched up an invitation to join. Working at the UN made us feel like the world was trying extremely hard not to repeat its mistakes.

As good as the work was, it wasn't the best part. How could it have been when it was "All City 'Let's Go'"? From the day I started in 1946 to the day I met Tom in '48, I didn't go to sleep before midnight once, except for a bout of the flu in January 1947, which had me in bed at 11:59. The rest of the time, I was busy soaking in the new city.

At the end of the workday, I'd fly back to Manhattan on the express, exit at Union Square, and start running around town searching for conversations to be had and drinks to be sucked down. Gin martinis, gin and tonics—anything with gin would do. After the war, young women could have three eyes and they'd still be taken to bed.

But if you were decent-looking and spoke French, it was watch out, world.

The first day I saw Marianne at work, her blonde curls were tamed to perfection, and her hazel eyes outlined with kohl. She took my hand and pulled me straight to the spot where we could spy on the delegates in their private, prestigious cafeteria. Like most of the other young female interpreters, Marianne lived downtown with roommates who were working girls, at least until they found the right man. But Marianne was looking for all the wrong men, and I was thrilled to join her. For years, there had been very few men our age left on the island of Manhattan. Now they were back, and we were ready to bask in the light of their adoration.

"Just say it like it is, Katharina," Marianne declared to me one night at a party at the Betty Parsons Gallery. "There are few things better in the world than being a young, beautiful woman."

"I turned thirty this year, and I should be all upset about it, but I'm not," I said, throwing down another gin and tonic. In summer, they were all we drank.

"Why should you be? You look twenty, so who gives a damn? And you're too smart to get married. Marriage and babies are for women who are perfectly comfortable performing their own lobotomies," she said, angling her head as she took in the new big thing, Abstract Impressionism. "Come on, let's go talk to those men over there. Insinuate that we're good at removing our clothing. I could use another drink."

Marianne didn't have a French accent when she spoke English. Having American parents will dilute anything, but when she was out fishing for compliments, or a bedroom companion, she dialed it up so high that the roll of her Rs could have cut glass.

We inched over to some good-looking suits at the bar, and Marianne started babbling to me in French about the who's who of the art world. Half the names sounded made up, but I just nodded and said, *"Ah oui, j'ai entendu parler de lui."*

"Des Françaises!" the man to our left exclaimed in perfect French.

"*Merde,*" Marianne murmured.

"No, we're Swiss . . . Belgian. Swiss Belgians," she said, putting her drink on the bar. "Come on, Rina," she said, pulling me out of the gallery and onto East Fifty-seventh Street. "I'm in no mood to flirt with my own kind. The charm of my accent is completely lost on them. Let's go somewhere safe from French people."

"New Jersey?"

"That's no good. We'll go way downtown, find some terrible jazz. It's only two o'clock!"

By the time we got to a place where Marianne was sure no French people would turn up—Battery Park—the music was cheap, and the rats were out, as was our cleavage.

"Being around you ladies is like traveling without having to buy a steamer ticket. What else you got to show me? You've got the Eiffel Tower in your pocket?" one very cute rat said to Marianne as we listened to some of the worst jazz New York had to offer that year.

"Sadly, no. Only lint," she proclaimed.

"Well I've got the Eiffel Tower for you in my pan—"

"That's enough of that!" I said, holding up my hand and laughing. "Where did you learn to talk to a woman that way?"

"Way downtown, baby. You speak French. I speak downtown. I also speak dockworker, factory worker, porter, washman, and soldier."

"Are those Latin languages?" Marianne asked, flapping about her eyelashes like she was ready to take flight, right into that man's bunk bed or sleeping bag or wherever he slept.

"More like prison dialects," he said, laughing. "Come on, ladies. I grew up on Lung Block. Cherry Street. That's between the Brooklyn and Manhattan bridges for you foreigners."

I rolled my eyes at Marianne, but I was grinning like a girl on a homecoming float.

"It's a shock I never got tuberculosis. Hell, it's a shock I can speak at all. But us tenement kids have charm for days. Raze our apartments but can't raze our ways, you know? Helped me better than anything else would have during the war."

"Were you overseas?" I asked.

"Germany. Came back blind."

Marianne stared at his two brown eyes. "You can't see!" she exclaimed, suddenly not understanding where his Eiffel Tower was springing from if it was not from her angelic face and thirty-six-inch bust.

"Only in my right eye. Trust me, my left can see all of that," he said, waving his hand near her chest. "And the rest of me works just fine."

She seemed contented.

"Let's get out of here, kids," Marianne said. "You too, Downtown. Back up we go." She looked at our half-blind friend and kissed him on the cheek. "You may have lost half your perspective, but we'll help you regain a new one."

The UN and Marianne Fontaine certainly gave me a new one.

Even when we ventured to the edges of the island, we always ended up at Café Lafayette in the Hotel Lafayette with its chandelier that looked brought over from Versailles and a dirty floor that looked brought in from Rikers Island. It was packed with French speakers, but after three a.m. Marianne no longer cared. It was one of the only places that still spilled out onto the sidewalk at that hour, even when the cold came in. Plus, it was in the heart of Greenwich Village and was equal parts blue-collar and French aristocrats.

"I've always wanted to swing on a chandelier," I said to our foul-mouthed, blind, yet somehow still charming new friend.

"Give me five bucks and you can swing on the chandelier. Or, take off your dress, and I'll give you five bucks to do it," the bartender, Pierre-Henri, said laughing at me.

"I don't need your five dollars," I said, letting him take me to the back, slide his hand up my dress, kiss me, and then kiss me some more. "I work at the United Nations, remember?"

"A man dropped a stick of dynamite on the building today. You're lucky we're even alive," said Marianne as the sun started to come up, which was actually true.

"To imply how dynamite-looking you all are?" asked Pierre-Henri.

"I think it had a lot more to do with tension in North Korea."

We'd sleep it off on Sundays and be fresh as daisies on Monday, shuffling between the cafeteria, offices, meeting rooms, and press and radio rooms, peeking in on the delegates' dining room before taking up our perch in the interpretation booth, *mais bien sûr*. I was still living with Patricia and Ruby, but my City Hall days, and friends, were feeling more and more domestic. We were still tied together in some ways—eating rushed breakfasts together, sharing stories of our escapades, the rent, and the magic of making our own money. But as much as I loved Patricia and Ruby, and as smart as they were, neither could compete with Marianne. They were like two perfectly charming Moulin Rouge dancers who got demoted to extras when Jane Avril walked in. Running around Manhattan with Marianne and our band of linguistically gifted foreigners made it feel like a different city altogether—and I was the delegate from New York, ready to sell what we had to offer.

Who needed parties at the Plaza back then? Who cared whether the ceiling was gilded or chipping apart, as long as the bar was open and the drinks were flowing? All of us, no matter which language we were speaking, were New Yorkers. The great city was alive again, and I couldn't see an end in sight.

But it's always when you're not looking that someone starts looking at you. And in 1948, the man who started looking was Tom.

CHAPTER 5

D r. Tom Edgeworth. Harvard undergrad. Yale medical school. Surgical residency at New York-Presbyterian. Only forty-three years old and already a highly regarded surgeon. He smiled as he gestured to the audience to stop their applause, which kept going. His dark brown hair was as thick and well styled as ever, his green eyes sparkling. His tuxedo was so perfectly tailored that it barely creased at the elbow when he gestured again for the applause to stop. He gave a speech. I listened intently, nodding my head as my newly cut black hair, with painstakingly placed Elizabeth Taylor–style waves swished against my neck. The speech was laced with genuine humility and passion. It was true, Tom Edgeworth was a very good physician. "My calling. The reason I wake up in the morning . . . and go to bed just four hours before I have to get up again." Laughter. Excited whispers among the women. ". . . the addition of an intensive care unit, more research dollars for childhood diseases, a commitment to curing leukemia, better treatments for bone malformations and congenital heart disease . . . never turning away a sick child whose family cannot pay." The sight of men shuffling in their chairs, straightening their spines because their wives were about to press them to give the hospital larger checks. Who could say no to an impassioned plea from such a man?

When the applause died down, Tom began thanking people for supporting him, for enabling his work. His mentor, a tall bald man named Jack Armstrong, was thanked first. His parents received a long mention, though they weren't present. ". . . just returned from a trip around the Orient for their fiftieth wedding anniversary." Coos from the crowd. Of course, the father of this man was a romantic. "Oh, but he's William Edgeworth's son. You didn't know? How could you not know? Look at those hands. Just like his father's. Bedroom hands." Half the women in the room had probably felt William Edgeworth's hands on them. "And of course," Tom said loudly, interrupting the wave of female murmurs. He looked out at me and smiled. I smiled back.

"And, of course, my loving wife, Katharina." He paused. His smile turned to a grin. He waited as a collective "aww" was let out by the women in the room. I smiled, the corners of my mouth quivering, exhausted.

I felt my table companion, Mrs. Morgan, reach for my arm, the cold metal of her rings waking up my warm flesh. She gave my right forearm a light squeeze and then went back to her Chablis.

"I'm humbled and hope I can . . ."

I let Tom's words trail off, though the rest of the audience was still enraptured.

"Isn't that nice," Mrs. Morgan leaned over to me and whispered in her raspy alto, a voice redolent of years of smoking L&M cigarettes.

"It really is. He's always so thoughtful 'My loving wife,'" I said with a half smile, my voice cracking slightly. Mrs. Morgan was too many drinks in to notice.

"We all said he was one of the best catches in Manhattan when he was young. I think we started saying that when he turned thirteen and switched to long pants. Mrs. Henry van Asletson desperately wanted him for her daughter Charlotte. You know that, of course." She leaned back in her chair as if to take in my reaction from the level that her eyes worked best.

"I don't know much about it," I whispered, not eager for this conversation. Everyone in Tom's circle, including myself, knew that Charlotte van Asletson was ready to rip her Paris-made underpants off for Tom and suction cup her body to his the day she turned eighteen. All the girls from his set were.

"She has a lovely face," Mrs. Morgan said reflectively, "but the hips. Too wide to reel in a boy like Tom. Van Asletson hips. Her aunt Marjorie has them too. Marjorie Delaney now. Married again. Third time. At least she found someone who doesn't mind a bottom the size of a sea vessel."

"I'm not acquainted with her," I whispered, shifting my weight in my gray silk column dress designed by Hubert de Givenchy himself. It was probably meant for women to sashay rather than sweat in. I watched my husband at the podium, nestled comfortably among the Grand Ballroom's white and gold columns, still holding everyone's attention.

"Don't lose any sleep over that." Mrs. Morgan reached for her glass of wine and polished the remainder of it off. "Little Charlotte is a pretty girl," she continued, still in a loud whisper, "but I dare say that her right eye seems sadder than the other, as if only that side of her face can see the misery in the world. And then there's the drunk uncle on the Cheverly side. Her mother's people. Miles, was it? Or Easton? Something that sounds more like a direction than a name. Rumor has it that he put a firecracker in Mrs. Wooton's alligator purse at the Fourth of July picnic in 1952 at the Chasesford estate in Tuxedo Park and it nearly blew off her nose. Singed her eyebrows. They fell on the ground like caterpillars tumbling from an oak. So, you can see why Tom's mother wasn't having this match."

Mrs. Morgan was drawing a glare from across the table from the Baxters, prominent donors to the hospital, but she didn't seem to care. And why should she? She had more money than all of us combined. Especially since her husband, George, had died in a *mountaineering accident*, which was code for tumbling off the balcony of the Negresco hotel in Nice after drinking ten martinis with a young Miss So-and-So who most likely robbed him, then pushed him off, "but we'll never know, will we," the papers mused. Morgan money had silenced any further speculation.

I was happy for the distraction. Tom's words, at least the ones directed my way, had rattled me. And I was already plenty rattled.

Mrs. Morgan kept speaking through Tom's standing ovation, and then through the voice of Tom's successor at the podium, the hospital's leading heart surgeon. The Baxters kept glaring, and I tried to focus on words other than "my loving wife, Katharina."

Not "my brilliant wife, Katharina." Or "my gorgeous wife, Katharina." He used to say both quite often. Instead, he emphasized how much I loved *him*. He did not say how much he loved me. He did not say "thank you" or "I love you." He'd said I was a loving wife.

When we'd first become entangled—and if Tom's mother, Amelia, thought that Charlotte van Asletson came from a questionable family, then she certainly thought of me as a tramp that darling Tom had picked up at the bus depot—Tom had enjoyed what most men enjoy, trying to remove my clothing. But when we came up for air, it was clearly not just that he was after. It was also the complete opposite of Amelia Edgeworth.

"I don't want someone from my world," he'd said. "The last thing I need is someone who wants to become Amelia Edgeworth, who believes that if one doesn't have at least seven figures in the bank then happiness is just unattainable. I want someone who loves books more than bank accounts, people more than properties. Who will love me, our family. A hands-on woman, and not just in that way," he added, laughing at my raised eyebrows. "Someone intelligent, someone beautiful, and someone who puts being a devoted wife and mother above all else. Amelia Edgeworth did not, and I will not let my children relive my youth."

I was intoxicated by Tom, and with his vision of me as different from the women he'd known, and desirable precisely because I was different. *Above all else* did suggest that being a devoted wife and mother came first for Tom, but there were still many fascinating things—like working, socializing with friends, exploring the greatest city on earth—that would come in a close second, third, and fourth.

"I have two wild brothers. Twins. They made my childhood wonderful. I want a house full of cooing children," I said. But I was the youngest child by six years. I didn't know then that the cooing would be screaming and that "above all else" meant that the future Katharina Edgeworth would have to bury herself. That the only interpreting I would do was trying to learn my sons' different cries.

"Good," Tom had whispered into my neck, pulling down my cashmere dress. "Let's practice making all these wild boys."

And we had practiced, upside down, backward, in French, German, Italian, English, and animal.

Tom and I first met at a party thrown by the French consul general in the early spring of 1948. Marianne and I had befriended his social secretary, and we were squeezed onto lists for events that needed sparkly young women.

"Please tell me you speak English," Tom said as he sat next to me on a leather couch. "I just spent thirty minutes saying, '*Oui, merci, non, merci.*'"

"You're technically in France, you should be speaking French," I said, taking in all six feet three inches of him and the perfectly tailored gray suit that showed off his muscular form.

"Aha! You do speak English," he said, grinning at me, and what a grin it was.

"Only when pressed," I replied coolly.

"Then let me take it upon myself to do the pressing," said Tom, handing me one of the martinis he was holding.

We were engaged six months after we met. He proposed with a Band-Aid, wrapping it around my finger with care.

"I was going to buy you a ring, but then I decided that it would be far more fun to do that together, because I've learned over these few months that everything is far more amusing with you at my side. And I want you to have something you really love. So here," he said,

opening a box of Band-Aids, "is my other promise." He undid the
Band-Aid and wrapped it around my ring finger. "Katharina West, I
promise to always take care of you, to heal you of all that ails you, and
to stick to you like a—"

"Like a Band-Aid?"

"Exactly," he said, making sure it was wrapped perfectly. He leaned
over and kissed my hand. A week later, the Band-Aid was replaced
with a tasteful diamond ring from Cartier. He slipped it on my finger
in his bachelor's apartment on Lexington and we were married four
months later. As soon as we said I do, it was time to become more
than two.

CHAPTER 6

My vision for my life had been that of an international woman of something. Perhaps a translator like my aunt Hanna. Maybe something that allowed me to keep one foot in New York and one foot in Europe. A diplomat, if I really shot straight for the stars and didn't miss. When I was at the United Nations, that goal felt far more possible than it had at City Hall. On my desk, on day one, I found a headset, a typewriter, language dictionaries, a heavy black telephone, and piles of documents. One of them was the United Nations Charter. On that humid day, I sat down in my dark red Traina-Norell dress, took off my pristine white gloves—an ensemble bought at Macy's with half of my last City Hall paycheck—and read dozens of pages. The section that stuck with me then, and that I reread almost every week that I worked there, was Article 8: "The United Nations shall place no restrictions on the eligibility of men and women to participate in any capacity and under conditions of equality in its principal and subsidiary organs."

I wanted to work in New York, I always knew it was where my heart beat the fastest, but with my family in Europe, my vision was changing, and the UN seemed to make it possible. During my childhood, my mother, who spoke to me in different languages at breakfast, lunch, and dinner, said with frequency, "A woman with many languages can always find many jobs." It was an incantation in the thirties, when people were desperate for work, but for me, it finally came true in the forties.

Marriage and children did not fall into my grand plan. At Vassar for my bachelor of arts and Columbia for graduate school, I was focused on bettering my mind. At City Hall, I was focused on exploring my freedom. And at the United Nations, I was focused on experiencing the world, which often meant dating—or simply sleeping with—men from all over the globe: Argentina, Luxembourg, Mexico, Haiti, and even one visiting Greek official whom Marianne was bored with by lunch, so I became his dinner plans instead. I was well aware that I was supposed to want to get married, but it really did seem a waste when one worked at the United Nations. My mother had married right after university in Zurich and she'd always counseled me to wait until I was older. "I don't regret it, because I love your father," she'd explained. "But remove him from the equation and I would have done things very differently."

"Will you ever get married?" I asked Marianne one June afternoon, after she told me about the new delegate from India who had offered her a ride on his elephant for her birthday.

"And I think what he meant by elephant was—"

"Yes, thank you, I do get the reference."

"Well then, the answer is no. I will not. Nothing makes women more boring than marriage and children. And you? Please just shake your head in agreement."

I nodded my head yes, then shook my head no. "I think if I fell in love, and I mean, drunk in love, I would. Why not? My parents are still married. They've always seemed happy."

"Your father is an art historian. He's clearly a romantic. You are not a romantic, Rina. And thank God for that. Romantics make tiresome drinking companions."

"But I'm still a woman in 1946," I said, sitting on my desk.

She leaned in closer to me and jabbed at the UN Charter document. "How about you be your *own* woman in 1946?"

"How about it?" I said, laughing.

That evening, I grabbed her hand as soon as the clock struck five and said, "The champagne and caviar is on me."

"Liar," she said, pulling off her cardigan. "All we can afford are beer and chicken eggs."

"Well, that sounds pretty good, too."

The next day, it was like the goddesses of the world had been listening to us. Bloated from too much beer and chicken eggs, Marianne and I were both at the General Assembly in Queens for the meeting of the UN Commission on the Status of Women. Bodil Begtrup from the Danish delegation, and chairwoman of the new commission, stood up, smoothed her skirt, surveyed the very male-dominated room, and said, "I'll ask you, of all the rights you have, which do you think are too many for women? What is too much?"

Marianne and I looked at each other for a second, grinned, and then, sitting elbow to elbow in our shared booth, I translated it into French. That night, we did have champagne and caviar, splitting the bill between us, two working women who, in that moment, were quite sure they could conquer the world.

But two years later, it happened. Love.

"Oh, if I'd only known you'd fall head over heels for that tall, handsome, rich man, I would have had the consul general throw him right out with the garbage," Marianne said when I'd confided in her that I was utterly gaga for Tom.

"Do you think the consul general takes out his own garbage?" I said, lighting a cigarette.

"If you ask nicely."

I thought nothing would change after I got married. I was breathtakingly naïve for a woman who had experienced a lot more of the world than the average American. I forgot that—particularly at my advanced age of thirty-two—what was supposed to follow immediately after marriage, was children.

Tom Edgeworth loved children. Wanted an army of them. But my body had other plans. A gritting of teeth occurred. Months of "It will happen for us. It must. I'm going to be a pediatric surgeon." And then, "How can it not happen for us? I *am* a pediatric surgeon." The children he interacted with every day, none of them his, became a source of anguish. "How sad for Tom," his mother would say. "Nature isn't fair. Tom would be the best father." We went to doctors, we stopped going to doctors. We went to a Chinese herbalist, a voodoo practitioner, then back to the doctors.

After nine unsuccessful months, I overheard Amelia tell Tom, "She's thirty-two years old, after all. It's like trying to make a mummy a mummy."

Tom had not answered.

After that unfortunate night, Tom and I sat with the windows open, enjoying the smell of fall in the air. He'd put his drink gently on the table and suggested I quit my job at the United Nations. As a married couple we had new priorities. And soon, it would be a new year: 1950.

"I just translated as the Russian delegate stormed out of the Human Rights Commission meeting. And then there's everything that's happening in Korea. The situation is becoming dire. But you don't want me to help interpret all that. You want me to stay home and knit," I'd said, finishing my drink and promptly picking up his.

After we'd married, I had told Tom that I worried about losing all of my goals for my career, my general ambition. I had always worked for two reasons: for my own fulfillment, and to put food on my table. But one of those reasons had evaporated when I married Tom. I was very afraid the other one would, too.

"Ambitions change, Rina," he had said. "I think you'll see that when you're a wife and mother. You'll have other priorities, other things that inspire you, and nourish your soul. But if you're still devoted to peace, love, and—"

"Peace and security."

"Fine, peace and security. If you still need that, then I'm sure we can find a way to make it happen. Being an Edgeworth might not hurt your ambitions. It could actually help you."

The man did have a point.

"Besides," said Tom, "I did not say knit, I said relax. Stop taking the train for two hours a day. Your paycheck isn't needed anymore. Perhaps you can just go back when the children are older."

"It is still needed to me," I'd said, standing abruptly, my hand shaking the ice in the drink. I'd felt so flush with my UN salary compared with what I was making at City Hall. Suddenly, it had been reduced to silly girl money.

"Just think about it," he'd said. I'd thought about it for about thirty seconds, and the next day I gave Tom a firm no. "When I get pregnant," I'd promised. "Then they'll make me leave anyway. Despite all their talk of equality, I've never seen a woman bouncing a baby on her knee in the General Assembly."

Tom had agreed to my compromise, and finally, he made a far better suggestion.

"It's been a year of this trying, this baby obsession" he said, defeat in his voice. We were fanning around a New Year's Eve party at the Waldorf Astoria in the waning hours of 1949. "You've seen every doctor worth his salt, and plenty not worth a grain, so let's just stop trying with so much intensity for a while. I think we'd both be happier."

I let my head fall on his chest, and whispered "thank you." Then I picked up the nearest glass of champagne. "I'll drink to that." For once Tom didn't say, "Not too much. Champagne may be a false friend to fertility." Instead, he said, "To us. We're only two, but a good two. And one of us has enough personality for three."

"Which one?" I asked, winking.

Our marriage got so much better after that. We were still trying, of course. Tom wasn't about to give up sex with purpose. He was still deeply involved in the comings and goings of my menstrual cycle, but he was deeply involved in other things, too. He even took up cooking.

"My father didn't even know where the kitchen was. I want to cook for you when I can," he'd said when I saw him brandishing our best cutting knife.

"But what if you burn your hands?" I asked seriously.

"What if I do? Shall I cover them in mineral wool? Wear glass jars on them instead of mittens?"

"I mean, perhaps?"

He wasn't half bad in the kitchen, but going out together was even more fun. We explored our city like we had when we were dating. The theater, drinks with friends, sometimes his, sometimes mine, though rarely mixing them together. I still went out with Marianne, and while I could not accept offers of Eiffel Towers in pants, I no longer wanted to. When Tom let himself have fun, he was one of the best people to have by your side. We got a box at the opera for the season. We went to see Jackie Robinson play for the Brooklyn Dodgers, even bringing William and Amelia with us. "Are you sure you'd like to come?" I'd asked in utter shock, to which she'd answered, "I'm an elitist, Rina. Not a racist." And I'd smiled from ear to ear as she'd cheered Robinson on as the Dodgers trounced the Cincinnati Reds five to one.

"Now, that Jackie is the elite. And those Midwesterners are still quite awful at everything, I see," Amelia had said as their driver came to pick us up.

After baseball, Tom suggested golf. That year we went to see Louise Suggs win the New York Weathervane and Skip Alexander win the Empire State Open. We met people who had nothing to do with Lenox Hill and did the ultimate in leisure, alternating drinking and golfing at Saint Andrew's. We even took an extended vacation, Tom's first in two years. We went to see elephants in Kenya and Tom didn't work for two full weeks, though he did cap off the trip with four days performing surgeries in a rural hospital.

"These children need me more than the children in New York," he'd said as he returned to our villa with tired, bloodshot eyes.

"Shall we stay?" I'd asked, fully believing that we could be happy there. We could be happy anywhere, as long as we were together.

"New York calls," he'd said. "She always does."

And she did.

But it was a wonderful New York. We had separate careers, separate friends, but we mixed so well together in the second year of marriage. Perhaps not his sperm and my eggs, but us. And I'd gotten married for us, not for babies. If I had to be completely honest, having children didn't interest me past the fact that biologically, it did seem to be the correct thing to do, and it was the world's constant refrain for women, especially as we crept into the 1950s. *I'll like my own baby*, I told myself. All women did. And wasn't I like all women?

"You're not," Marianne reminded me one night at Café Lafayette. "You're better. Be better. You know, I read a fascinating piece in the *Times* about divorce. It's about as easy as sneezing these days they say."

"Did someone say divorce?" the bartender had shouted over, and I waved him off, unable to hide my grin. Married did not mean invisible, I had been happy to discover.

I looked up at the chandelier. It was still shining brightly. The city didn't have the same verve of the forties, but it was still swinging, having settled nicely from postwar platinum into a lovely rose gold.

Things changed again as year three of being a barren woman approached. The first glitch in our lovely coupling was that Tom started singing about me leaving my job again. This time, it had nothing to do with babies. On November 22, 1950, one LIRR train slammed into another, killing seventy-nine people. Two hundred doctors had to come to the scene—one of them a colleague of Tom's who had happened to be in Queens. "This could have been you," said Tom, putting the paper on the kitchen table of our two-bedroom apartment on Park Avenue. His hands were shaking as he pointed to the ink. "Look, the passengers in that last car. Every single one of them dead. You love to ride in the last car. Look out the back window. 'Packed like sardines in their own blood,' the reporter says. That's what happened to them. One poor girl who survived said, 'All I could see was parts of bodies, arms and legs protruding from the windows.' Katharina, I will not have that be your fate. I will not. You are an eccentric, but you are not a sardine."

"It's so awful," I said. It was all anyone had spoken about at work.

"And this just nine months after that other LIRR crash that killed, what, fifty?"

"Thirty-one," I muttered.

"Maybe you should take a taxi. It would be costly, but it's worth it."

"How about I sit in the middle car?"

"How about I have a drink?" He stood up, scared, angry that I was so stubborn and defeated. He knew I wouldn't relent until I was pregnant.

By 1951, things had changed again. Tom may not have been making new life at home, but he was saving lives at the hospital. He was no longer just a surgeon, he was chief of pediatric surgery.

That was when I started to see him less. But I was so proud of him, he was so proud of him, our whole world was so proud of him. I didn't want to take any of that away from Tom, so I never complained. He'd been dealing with my two-hour commutes since we'd met, what was a ten o'clock dinner once or twice a week? But six months into his new position, once or twice a week became every night.

"I love what I do," he'd said plainly, "but the hospital is near financial ruin. I think I can change that."

"Could you also cure heart malformations?"

"Who knows?" he said, shrugging, and I could tell a small part of him meant it. It was a difficult year, especially considering the wonderful previous year we'd had.

"How about Paris?" he'd said to me one night when I was crying, sick of being constantly short one husband.

"Yes, to Paris. Always yes to Paris," I'd said, drying my eyes.

In Paris, nature finally said yes to me. I became pregnant with Gerrit when I was thirty-four and with Peter a mere five months after Gerrit came into the world.

Two healthy, chubby boys. What a blessing for Tom. But after the talk of blessings and thanking God were over, the murmurs of "It's too bad Tom couldn't be a younger father. Have more years with his boys. Have time to add in a little girl. Oh, he'd be such a good father to a girl" began. Perhaps that Charlotte van Asletson and her sizeable hips would have made him a father before forty.

Now, five years into our marriage, and three years into Tom's stint as chief of pediatric surgery, I was no longer Rina the career girl. I was Dr. Edgeworth's loving wife.

I thought of Jilly with Gerrit and Peter. Jilly came to help about once every two months. She came so seldom because Tom thought it irresponsible for a mother to leave her children in someone else's care if she had the means to stay with them. As in, if her husband had the means. He had not learned this through his medical schooling, but from his own experience. "Children need their mother. I needed my mother, and she was never there. I had twelve different nannies. They changed so often I stopped learning their names. I just called them Nanny." It was a hard sentiment to argue.

The room erupted into applause and I looked up to see yet another man at the podium.

"And that's that," said Mrs. Morgan, patting my arm again.

I'd missed every word she'd said, but I put my hand on her arm in return. "Indeed it is."

She smiled at me and turned to the Baxters.

"Why, Jezebel Baxter," she said, leaning in, her red silk dress almost in her dessert. "You've been awfully quiet this evening."

The woman froze, her hair seeming to turn a shade lighter, even though that seemed impossible in the color wheel. Her hair was already the color that Tom's mother called "brothel blonde."

"It's Guinevere," the woman said through a forced smile. "Guinevere Baxter."

"Oh, so sorry about that, pet," said Mrs. Morgan, pulling her napkin from her lap and wiping the corners of her mouth, even though she'd eaten nothing but the stuffed olive from a martini. "It's just that dear Alistair here has had so many wives it's hard to keep up. At least Guinevere and Jezebel are close. His last wife was named Christine, and I called her Jezebel, too."

Guinevere Baxter stood up without saying a word and left the table.

Alistair looked at Mrs. Morgan and shook his head. "We've been quiet because it was the speeches. One is supposed to be quiet during speeches. And please, do have another drink, Auntie. I don't think you've had quite enough."

He stormed off, and I looked at Mrs. Morgan, who was shaking with laughter behind her napkin.

"Is he really your nephew?" I asked. "I had no idea."

"He is. And I paid for his ticket. His and that Jezebel's."

"Guinev—"

"Darling, I know," she said, waving her hand at me. "It's just that I don't like her, so I enjoy poking at her a bit."

"Why don't you like her?" I asked, even though I didn't like her much, either.

She eyed me as if I'd asked why birds fly south in winter.

"Katharina, she's stupid. It's like conversing with a guinea pig."

"Well," I said, trying not to smile. Mrs. Morgan really was very good at noticing when someone needed to smile. "Some people can't help that."

"They should try."

"Perhaps."

"You're not a guinea pig now, are you, dear?"

"No. I'm a loving wife," I said, fiddling with my napkin.

"Pish." She took a glass of wine from the table—mine, since hers was empty—and drank half. "You're more than that. Didn't you used to work for the mayor?"

"Yes. And the United Nations."

"Even better," she whispered and started clapping. Mr. John R.R. Rawlins, another tablemate, eyed her like she had slipped a rung or two, clapping for a speaker who was not there, but she was clapping for me.

Mrs. Morgan cupped my chin in her hand and thanked me for being such enjoyable company.

"Must run. I see other relatives I'm due to torment," she said with a wink, hopping up with the gusto of a much younger woman.

From my chair I watched as Tom made his way back to his seat. The noise around us had picked up, as the final speech of the night wasn't for another hour. He had almost reached our table, second from the front, when a flying mass of peach damask hit him like artillery. When it settled, I saw that somewhere in the folds of that voluminous dress was a woman I did not know. Tom didn't seem to know her, either.

"Doctor Edgeworth, you brilliant man," she sputtered, even as tears started to flow, marring her thick makeup. "I had to come tonight. I had to see you, to say thank you." She took Tom's hand and shook it, moving it up and down rhythmically as if he were a water pump. "You saved my son's life. His *life*." She smothered him in another embrace. "He is with me tonight," she said. "The son you saved." A young boy in a tuxedo appeared, as if produced from the folds of her dress. He had a noticeable limp, but smiled when Tom shook his hand.

"He was nearly gone," his mother said, clutching his shoulders. "I could see the spirits there, ready to carry him away." She pushed the boy closer to Tom. "And then you came. Misdiagnosis, you said. No one had been able to pinpoint his true ailment—Guillain-Barré syndrome—except the great Dr. Edgeworth."

"People sure do like that man," I heard a voice say behind me. I turned to see a waiter with a tray of martinis held firmly between his hands.

"He's an excellent doctor," I replied, plucking two drinks from the tray and downing them in succession. "And a very loving husband."

CHAPTER 7

"Oh, dear God," I said into the air when I woke up. My head was pounding, my eyes were pounding, even my teeth were pounding.

Tom was standing by the bed, dressed in a gray flannel suit. I sat up slowly, trying to get a better look at him, but feeling as if I might be about to have a heart attack.

"Who poured all that gin down my throat?" I croaked, putting my hand against my forehead as if some mysterious fever was to blame for the way it was hammering. It was actually quite tough to get a tropical disease at the Plaza.

"Did you have quite a lot to drink? Perhaps you were drinking for both of us. I barely had time for one glass of wine," said Tom, adjusting the sleeve of his white shirt.

I nodded and looked up at him, so handsome in his suit against the dove gray paint of our bedroom. No rooms in our apartment were white. "Too hospital-like," Tom had told the decorators.

"You were quite popular last night. As it should be," I rasped.

"It was a lot of small talk, but if it helped raise money for the hospital, then so be it." He turned around, looked in the mirror above my dresser, and undid the top button of his shirt.

"Are you going somewhere before our family day starts?" I asked after a moment. "I'd been thinking we might take the boys to the Museum of Natural History this morning."

Before he could respond, a wave of heat hit me and I felt dizzy. I lay down again and turned on my side, trying to hide my expression from Tom. I put my face into a pillow and heaved into it, then faked a cough. I wasn't eager to show him just how intoxicated I had been at his event.

"Not feeling well?" he asked.

"The alcohol has not quite released me from its grip, unfortunately," I said, my voice muffled by the pillow. "I think fresh air might help. Maybe we could walk across the park for a bit before hopping in a taxi."

"Katharina. I think that trek would knock you flat in your state," said Tom, opening his top drawer and pulling out a pair of monogrammed cufflinks. He went about changing the mother-of-pearl ones he had already put in. "I saw you speaking to Mrs. Morgan for most of the night. She's always good for a drink or seven. I assume that's what happened."

"Mrs. Morgan is good company. Too good sometimes. And the drinks were complimentary."

"So is the hangover."

"That's why I have you," I murmured. "Dr. Edgeworth. To pick me up again with his spells and potions."

"Yes, about that," he said, deciding to button his collar after all. "Unfortunately, I have to go in for a few hours. To the hospital. Maybe three or four. Or five. I just received a call."

I sat upright again, strengthened by my disappointment. "No, Tom! You promised."

That explained the suit. I thought he was just in the mood for overdressing. Tom's upbringing had been so formal I wouldn't have batted an eye if he said he was going to throw on a smoking jacket to take out the garbage, not that he ever took out the garbage.

"I know. I feel terrible about it," he said, reaching for his watch on the dresser. "I really do. I know how much the boys were looking forward to our family outing. But Mark Epstein is out with the flu and—"

"Who gets the flu in April?" I asked, utterly irked.

"People who spend their day with extremely sick children. They get the flu."

"Yes," I mumbled. "I suppose." Nothing makes a person feel worse about their own petty problems than someone bringing up "the extremely sick children."

I finished watching Tom dress and didn't say a thing when he kissed my head and walked out of the bedroom. My eyes were still fixed to the top of his dresser, a sleek thing carved in Denmark. There was a silver-framed picture of me in my wedding dress, a picture of the boys from when Peter was a newborn, Gerrit holding him on his lap, and a clock that was once on a ship that sailed the Pacific captained by a distant Edgeworth relative. The old timepiece informed me it had just gone seven. I lay back down, desperate to settle my stomach before the boys woke, but as soon as my head hit the pillow, Peter started wailing.

I hurried down the hall, kissed his fat cheeks, pulled him out of his crib, and slipped off my nightgown to breastfeed. When I'd first started nursing, Tom had tried to limit me to one glass of wine, "for Gerrit's health," but when I threatened to stop, he'd changed it to "whatever gets you through." I finished feeding the baby, then comforted Gerrit when he woke up screaming. I made breakfast. Gerrit put a bowl of eggs on his head. The bowl broke. The baby took off his diaper and peed on my foot. I cleaned it. I cleaned Gerrit. I cleaned myself. I tried not to vomit in the shower. Peter swallowed soap. I breastfed him again to calm him down. I vomited in the sink instead. Three hours later, I had us all in Central Park. Outside, April suddenly felt like June.

"Bird," Gerrit said, pointing as we walked, the boys' coats shoved into the bottom of the stroller. "Signor Montazelli." "Small dog." His words were starting to come fast, and it always fascinated me to see which ones lodged in his mind the quickest. Signor Montazelli was the New York Symphony conductor who lived on the first floor of our building. I looked down at Gerrit's "bird," a city pigeon that had found a discarded hot dog bun. I let him inspect the scene and pushed the stroller past it. When I looked up again, Gerrit had taken off.

"No, Gerrit!" I shouted, sprinting after him, stroller and all. I managed to grab him before he was run over by a bicyclist, but not before he fell into a large gray puddle.

I whisked him to a bench and pinned him to it as he flailed. I reached into my bag and took out dry shoes and clothes for him. I had taken to practically carrying a suitcase when I was out with the boys, an act I had regretted the day of the hail. At least this time, I had the stroller.

"Clean baby Gerrit," he cooed when I'd changed him.

"That's right, darling," I said as he sat on my lap. I kissed his mass of dark hair and plopped him next to me as Peter started to fuss in his stroller. I pulled him out. It seemed he wasn't fussing because he wanted to move; he was fussing because he was covered in white, thick vomit. I put Gerrit in the stroller, strapping him down as he protested, and began changing Peter into his spare outfit.

"Too much milk," I said to him sweetly as I stripped him, keenly aware of the glances from passersby. One child kicking the stroller and crying, the other naked.

Doing my best to ignore the looks, I managed to get both boys clean and started walking them toward Central Park West, automatically heading toward Tavern on the Green. Before I'd had children, when Tom and I were in our "trying years," a double entendre he adored, we would eat at Tavern on the Green most weekends, often meeting his parents there. I of course preferred when it was just the two of us, or even just me alone, *The New York Times* keeping me company, or some women's magazine that I pawed through to disguise that I was really watching the diners around me. My favorite was an older woman, a regular with faded strawberry blonde hair, who had spent years passing off her pet rabbit as a cat.

"Just pretend it wandered out of the kitchen and found its way onto my lap," she'd suggested on the day she was finally caught. "You do have rabbit on the menu, after all."

"We don't usually pluck them live from a briar patch, madam. They come to us already prepared. As in deceased," the manager had countered.

"Don't listen, Pickles," she'd protested, then gave the maître d' what appeared to be hundreds of dollars, sat down at the best table, and ordered the quail.

As we neared the restaurant, I paused the stroller and grabbed Gerrit's hand, looking at the polished women having breakfast, the men in their weekend trousers and sport coats, the young couples in hopeful spring colors under the red and green umbrellas on the terrace.

Pickles and his keeper did not appear to be present, but there was one pretty woman sitting alone, her dark hair freshly curled, the newspaper folded in front of her, a glass of wine on her table, though it wasn't quite ten. She moved languidly. I took a deep breath, wondering if I'd looked like that before I'd gotten married, before I became a mother. Unworried, unhurried. But this woman, in a dress the color of cherry blossoms, looked more than that. She looked shiny. Full of vitality, fully alive.

Gerrit pulled on my arm, reminding me that my past was very much past.

"Dinosaur!" he demanded, his insistent tone turning my stomach again. The fresh air was helping my hangover, but dealing with a fractious toddler certainly was not.

"It was you who chose this," my Swiss mother told me the first time she saw me hungover, my junior year in high school. We'd moved to Tudor City by then, on the far east side of Manhattan, and I had accidentally walked into Haddon Hall instead of Hardwicke Hall, where I lived, and had made myself comfortable on a stranger's couch. The next day, I remembered nothing, but my dehydrated body served as reminder enough. That, along with my mother's anger. Parental disappointment really does hit harder when voiced in German.

"I don't think the dinosaurs are awake today," I told Gerrit, even though we were on the Upper West Side and not too far from the Museum of Natural History. My head was pounding again. Tom was right, I might not make it out alive if I went inside the museum.

Keeping a tight hold on Gerrit, we moved on past the Tavern. Just eight streets north was the San Remo, where Tom's parents still lived. They could have helped with the boys, but the only day they they'd ever taken Gerrit was when I was in labor with Peter. At this hour on a Saturday, they were most likely getting ready for their weekend engagements. I imagined Amelia reading off the day's agenda to William while he ignored her and perused the paper, maybe flipping to the social pages with their photographs of the rich, pretty young women he cultivated. "Lunch with the Wilders," Amelia would say, "leaving time for a vigorous walk through the park, or billiards for you men. Then cocktails at "21" and dinner at Harry Constantine's." Later, someone would want to drag them to a little nightclub show at the Stork Club and Amelia would protest, saying, "A woman of my age and position really can't be seen at such a place," but no one would listen because everyone knew she really wanted to go. Then she'd start drinking Campari and telling the waitstaff she'd "just recovered from throat cancer and these really do help quite a bit, so please keep them coming," though her throat cancer was nothing but a bout of strep throat last December and even that was dubious, we'd been told. Her husband was convinced she'd just eaten a few cocktail peanuts with the shell on because she was too many drinks in to remember how to open them.

My own parents would have helped me with the boys, or I liked to think they would, but they were in Switzerland, having moved to Geneva for my father's job right after the war. My two older brothers and their wives had followed suit. Now all I saw of them was their handwriting.

"Zoo!" Gerrit shouted. I took the boys there once a week since we lived so close, but if I had to put my nose in that stink today I would be sick all over the children.

"Not the zoo, darling."

"Dinosaur!" Gerrit shouted again, trying to shake his hand free from mine. I crouched down, looked into his big brown eyes, and smiled. Around us, families strolled, tourists took photographs, and couples walked arm in arm as close as politeness allowed. Gerrit quieted a bit. I kissed his angry little face, enjoying the soft sponginess of his cheek, and said, "I'm sorry, darling, but let's do it tomorrow. Mommy isn't feeling very well this morning." He looked straight at me, the muscles in his face relaxing. I smiled again, he smiled, and then he got an odd look on his face and started sucking in his cheeks. His little rosebud lips opened, he moved his tongue to the roof of his mouth, moved it back down and spat onto my face. A wad of saliva hit just under my left eye, paused, as if as stunned as I was, then slid down my cheek.

I bit the inside of my mouth to keep it closed, kept my body still, and for a brief second, considered what it would feel like to slap my child. My desire to do so was overwhelming, and terrifying. I closed my eyes and let the thought die, gripping the stroller harder. I wiped off the spit, dried my hand on my dress and put my hands behind my back.

"Did you just spit on me?" I asked Gerrit, truly the stupidest question in the world, under the circumstances. "Why did you do that?" I tried again.

"Dinosaur!" he repeated mechanically.

"Fine!" I shouted into the air. Instead of hitting my child, I would give in to his demands.

I grabbed him much too forcefully and dragged him toward Central Park West. Before I could hail a cab, I had to pull the baby out of his stroller and set about folding it. "It's like a Rolls-Royce for mothers," Tom had said proudly when he'd brought it home. I'd wanted to mention that one sat in a Rolls-Royce, one didn't have to push it, but instead I'd just marveled at the contraption as if it were a spaceship and thanked him.

As I bent down to give the thing a kick, Peter tucked on my hip, I felt an ominously familiar sensation on my hand. Peter's diaper had just failed him, and the result was all over me.

"Goddammit," I said into the air. "God damn this awful, awful day."

An older woman looked at me, stunned, and then stepped into a taxi, as if to get away from my children and me as quickly as possible.

I didn't blame her.

I held Peter out at arm's length while trying to keep Gerrit from running into the road and looked down at my lavender dress, the one I'd bought at Henri Bendel in February because it had looked like spring to me. It was covered in soupy yellow bowel movement.

Where could I go? There was a restroom in Tavern on the Green, but I would not be let into the restaurant looking as I did.

I had to find a public one. I wrangled a cloth out of the bag while holding a toddler's hand and a baby, patted my dress, and wiped down the baby and the stroller. Then I dragged us all to a bench and tried to get my bearings.

Gerrit was howling to the point of getting me arrested, so I reached into my bag and took out a jar of crackers, hoping food would quiet him. I needed to figure out how to get us clean, and quickly. I loosened the lid, but stopped when I felt something hit my head. I touched my hair. A passing bird had emptied its bowels on my head.

I stared at my hand and the tear that had just landed on the cracker jar. I touched it, too dazed to realize it was mine.

"This is ridiculous," I said to no one, wiping my eyes with my sleeve.

I kept wiping, but the tears didn't want to stop.

"Let's just go home. Right now," I said, looking at the boys. "Who cares if we're a spectacle." We were still on the West Side, but no more than a mile from our apartment. I could make it that far.

I stood up, still crying, and pulled Gerrit off the bench. I placed him on the ground, but he was like a man who'd just seen sunshine after ten years in prison. He squirmed loose and took off like a shot.

"Gerrit!" I screamed. I shoved Peter into the stroller, clipping his leg slightly. I ignored his cries and ran after Gerrit.

"Gerrit, please stop, *please*!" I shouted, trying to control the giant stroller as I navigated the lunchtime crowd.

"Stop taking up the whole goddamn path, lady," a man bellowed at me as I wheeled Peter around him. I didn't even turn to look, eyes fixed on Gerrit.

He was at least fifty feet in front of me now, and the gap was widening. I sped up, then stopped just as suddenly as I'd started. Gerrit had fallen. He'd tripped over something, or just stumbled, and was lying facedown on the ground.

He was crying, I could tell, even though I was too far away to hear him. His body seemed to shudder with sobs. Suddenly, two women stopped to help him, one of them standing him up, the other looking around for his mother. For me.

I was supposed to run to him. To grab him from these women, hold him in my arms, wipe his tears, kiss his cheeks, and profusely thank his guardian angels. I remembered the woman from the gala fawning over Tom. The words "You saved my child's life!" would probably be required.

I did none of that. I just stood there, staring. Gerrit wasn't alone, he was safe, and I was not ready to admit that I was his mother. The one who had let him run off and fall on his face. I needed a few seconds before I fell victim to more judgment. To the comments along the lines of, "Thank goodness we were here. He could have been run over! Killed!" or the glances at my ruined dress and matted hair.

I closed my eyes again, unable to pull myself together. But just as I felt brave enough to walk into the fire, I heard someone yell my name. And not just anyone. Tom. He was rushing toward me, clutching Gerrit and howling my name. I was confused and utterly terrified. As they got closer, I saw that Gerrit's pant leg was pulled up and his leg was covered in blood.

I held on to the stroller even tighter, wishing I could sink into the ground.

"Katharina!" Tom called out again. "What are you doing? Why are you all the way over here? Didn't you see Gerrit? What's going on?"

"Dada!" I heard Peter squeal delightedly from his stroller. Tom had changed out of his suit. He was now in a light gray sweater, the sleeves pushed up to show his muscular forearms. His hands. "These hands are worth millions," one thankful father had said as he shook Tom's hand at last year's hospital gala. Sometimes I felt the same way. But today Tom's heroics, his life-saving hands, and his ability to swoop in to save his son when he wasn't even supposed to be in the vicinity just scared me.

"What the hell is this, Rina?" he said when he reached me. He tried to straighten Gerrit's leg, but the child refused, pulling his knee to his chest as he wailed. I reached for him, but Tom swatted my arm away. Tom almost never called me Rina. Only while naked or fighting.

"Didn't you hear our son scream? What's wrong with you?" he said, stepping closer to me. Intimidatingly close. "How long was he lying on the ground bleeding? How long?"

"How did you know we were here?" I asked, instantly regretting it.

"What the hell kind of question is that?" he said, grabbing the stroller with his other free hand and moving us over to the grass so we weren't blocking the path. Tom could of course handle everything at once.

"How did you know we were here?" I repeated, despite myself.

"Sam told me you'd gone to the park," he said, bending down and putting his free hand on Peter's cheek. "I left the hospital earlier than expected. I thought I'd come try and find you. Spend the day with my boys. You always seem to wander toward Tavern on the Green when you're here, so I went that way. But before I could get there, I saw my son lying on the ground, screaming in pain, being tended to by strangers."

"I was going to run to him," I mumbled, reaching again for Gerrit. Tom again refused. "I saw that he had fallen but I also saw that he was all right."

"He's bleeding and was surrounded by strangers!" he shouted. "How about you take care of your own children! The children we worked so goddamn hard for!"

We worked so hard for? All he'd had to do was sleep with me and pray that his sperm and my egg would do more than shake hands.

I looked at Gerrit's fingers gripping his father's neck. At his bleeding knee. Blood was the only bodily fluid I had not touched in the past four hours. I had dealt with vomit, urine, spit, and feces, both human and avian. But it was not worth explaining all that to Tom. "Do you know what I touch on a daily basis?" he would say. "How much blood and excrement? And the nurses? In a children's ward? Imagine what they are up to their elbows in." He would be right, of course. He always was.

"It was an unusually difficult day," I said, reaching for Gerrit's hand, grabbing it this time. Tom turned him away from me, and Gerrit's little fingers slipped out of mine. "I'm sorry," I said. "I don't know what happened."

"Your head was in the clouds again, as it always is. Just like that time when Gerrit was almost run over by the crosstown bus. Is it really so hard to keep two small boys alive? Is it?" He leaned down, took some sort of cloth from the bag, and wrapped it around Gerrit's knee. "Answer me, Rina."

I took a step away from him. From them.

"Sometimes it is," I said, my heart starting to pound. "Today it is."

"You want to leave?" said Tom, watching me back away. "Good. Just go. In this state, you're not helping."

"I know," I said, taking another step back, the tears starting to fall.

"Great idea. That's what we need right now. More tears." Tom broke his gaze and cooed over Gerrit, applying pressure to his knee.

I looked at Peter, still reaching up for his father, so desperate for him, so in love. Suddenly, my desire to be away from them, all of them, was overwhelming. My body, without my thinking about how to move it, moved for me. I turned on my heel and started to run.

CHAPTER 8

In a soiled dress, I sprinted. I flew down Fifth Avenue with my eyes fixed straight ahead. I would run until I collapsed. When was the last time I had left my children with my husband? Had it ever happened? Had he ever had them without me longer than the time it took for me to bathe? I couldn't remember an instance. But I couldn't remember much of anything. The only parts of me that had memory were my native New York muscles.

I reached West Fifty-ninth Street, the edge of the park, and my lungs begged me to slow down, but my legs wouldn't listen. If I sat, if I rested, my thoughts would catch me.

I kept moving. Past a row of wrought-iron benches with wooden backs, past a group of children I refused to look at, past the thick imposing form of the New York Athletic Club.

I hadn't run like this since college, when I was at Vassar sprinting up the frozen hills with my friends, knowing even then that we were experiencing something rare and fleeting. We had no idea that our adulthood would be marked by the explosion of a world war, but we understood that the freedom we had in college would be gone as soon as we gripped our diplomas.

I stopped for a few seconds, catching my breath. I leaned against a bench and looked up at the few clouds in the sky, moving quickly, running from the sun. I found the very last of my energy and kept running until I had to grab the fence at the entrance of the Fifty-seventh Street subway station. Before I collapsed on the ground, I hailed a taxi and limped in.

"Where to?"

I paused a moment, then whispered, "Chinatown."

I had only gone there in happy times. To eat noodles, thick and comforting, with my friends after a workday at City Hall. To drink cheap beer, the bitter cold of the alcohol knocking about the spiciness in the lo mein in the most enjoyable way. Back then, it was a part of the city that still felt like a lovely, wild place, even when the war forbade us to go anywhere but the corners of our own country.

I let myself sink into the taxi seat and rolled down my window, everything aching from my run, my hangover, my life.

I'd had to share my body during pregnancy, and had to keep sharing it while breastfeeding. The rest of me, while not growing or sustaining life, had become a playground for my children. I hated the feeling of being constantly touched. I was desperate for my body. My self. My air.

"Canal Street good?" the driver asked without turning around.

"Canal Street," I echoed, reaching into my dress pocket for money and then exiting the taxi in a daze.

I spotted the edge of a park from Mulberry Street and headed toward it. Why had I not run to Gerrit when he'd fallen? When he'd started to cry? Clearly, I could run, and quickly, at that. What kind of monster had I become?

I walked through the short black iron gates of Columbus Park, sat down on a bench, and put my hands in my lap. They were dry and thick, the knuckles covered in a layer of fat that hadn't been there before I'd had the boys. They looked nothing like my youthful hands, or the hands I'd had as a graduate student. The hands that used to put pen to paper for hours at Columbia University, turning French and

Italian rhythms into something beautiful for American ears. They also didn't look like the hands that had positioned the microphone and put on earphones at the UN. Neither my hands nor my self-regard reflected that woman anymore. I had not become a monster; I'd become a stranger.

I glanced up at the people in the park. All of them, except for me, were Chinese. Some little girls were running in circles on the grass. Some of their pants were a bit too short, but they seemed delighted to be playing on a sunny Saturday while their parents watched nearby. I had come to this part of Chinatown during my UN days, too. When Marianne and I would eat with the secretaries from the Chinese delegation and they would order for us, laughing at me when I told them I used to only order lo mein. "Didn't they pay you at City Hall? That's the cheapest food you can find," they'd tease and then order the salt-and-pepper crab. I'd always loved how no matter what language one spoke, laughter sounded the same the world over.

To the right of the girls, on squat wooden stools, was a group of men playing a game that I recognized as mahjong. In a grassy area closer to my bench, a young woman—a mother—and her children were busying themselves kicking rocks. She had twin boys, who looked about three years old, with impish smiles and straight black hair that appeared to have been cut into shape with the aid of a soup bowl. A little girl of perhaps four was holding the woman's hand. Secured to the woman's back with a winding strip of blue cloth was a sleeping baby. Four children, and the woman looked thirty at most.

She said something to the older children and they formed a circle and started kicking one of the larger rocks back and forth like a ball. She pointed to the door of the public restroom, and then they all tried to kick it inside—a goal without a goalie. When her daughter sent the rock flying through the door, the mother was chided by an old woman on a bench not far from mine. The mother just waved at her, smiling, and shook her head. She said something in Chinese that seemed to appease the onlooker.

I couldn't tear my eyes away from them. They all looked so happy. Jubilant, even. Especially the mother. How could a woman, alone in a public park with four children, be that radiant?

Her daughter had the rock again, and a clear shot of the bathroom door, but she kicked it instead to one of her brothers, who punted it right through. As they all celebrated, the baby woke up and began to howl. I heard a phrase shouted in Chinese. It was the older woman on the bench. She took the baby from the young woman's back, folding the tiny bundle into her body as if she were its grandmother, although I could tell by the polite way the mother had interacted with her that she was not. I thought of myself earlier in the park and the older woman who had seen me struggling and cursing. She certainly hadn't offered to help.

Without the baby tied to her, the woman looked even younger. The mother. The beautiful, happy mother, laughing with her children. It was true. One really did look prettier when one laughed.

Then suddenly, she stopped laughing. Her mouth compressed to a line.

She was now staring directly at me.

And she looked scared.

I felt the hairs on my arms bristle. Before I could turn around, a hand touched my shoulder. Gripped it.

"Sit with me, would you?"

CHAPTER 9

I'm sorry, but I was just going," I said, my heart beginning to race as I pulled away from the man's grip.

"Could I walk with you, then?" he asked. I could feel the mother watching me, and was grateful. Who would bludgeon a woman in broad daylight with a mother and children close by?

"You're Katharina Edgeworth. I'm Lee Coldwell. And I want to talk to you about an old acquaintance of yours," he said, his voice low but deliberate. "Jacob Gornev."

I stopped walking.

There had been a time when the name Jacob Gornev would have put a very big smile on my face. But I had not seen Jacob in over a decade. Hearing his name shocked me into stillness.

I studied the man in front of me. He was too clean-cut, too all-American to be a friend of Jacob's. He had the kind of blond hair that had surely been nearly white as a child but had dulled in adulthood, and eyes that didn't quite match, dark orbs in a serious face. His brown cap-toe shoes needed a good shine, but his tailored beige suit was presentable.

"Could we sit?" the man asked. "My apologies if I frightened you."

"You terrified me," I said. "How do you know who I am, how did you find me, and how do you know that I was acquainted with Jacob Gornev?" I meant to ask only one question at a time but three tumbled out.

"I'll explain," he said, gesturing back to the benches. They were the same as the one I had shared with Carrie in Central Park, only these looked like they'd endured many more storms.

"Nice day," he said as we sat down.

"Quite," I replied. I was perched on the edge of the bench, ready to leap up if necessary.

"Do me a favor," he said as he leaned back, as relaxed as I was jumpy. "Smile and laugh so that woman over there stops staring as if I were about to put a gun to your temple."

"Are you sure you're not?"

"Absolutely," he replied. In response, I smiled, though still warily.

"Thank you," he said. He fingered his hat, then removed it and put it in his lap.

"You and Jacob Gornev were at Columbia together, yes? During the war. Between 1939 and 1941."

"Yes," I replied, my mind racing. "I graduated in forty-two; Jacob the year before."

Lee Coldwell nodded. Then he reached into his suit pocket and took out a pack of Lucky Strike cigarettes. He tapped one out and offered it to me. I declined with a shake of the head.

He reached into his pocket again and removed a small box of matches. He lit one, lit his cigarette, then blew out the match. He then placed the used match back in his pocket.

My body went rigid. The way his hat brim had been turned down when I first looked at him. The business with the match. This was not the first time I'd seen Lee Coldwell.

"You were outside my apartment building. The man smoking in the rain," I said, now truly shocked. "Were you there because of me?"

"Sounds a bit like a movie title, doesn't it," he said calmly, looking at his cigarette. "*The Man Smoking in the Rain*. Bet it would be a hit."

"I need you to explain, immediately, why you're following me, or I'm going right now to find the police," I said, my fear multiplying with every word.

"Good luck with that in Chinatown," he said evenly. "The police may be just across the park, but they don't come around here much."

I glanced at the woman, who had resumed playing rock soccer with her children, her momentary concern for me dispelled.

"Look, let's start again," he said, sitting up a bit. "I've been doing this for ten years, and somehow it's still rough. Mrs. Edgeworth," he said, holding out his hand. He kept the cigarette between his teeth. "Mrs. Edgeworth, I'm Lee Coldwell, and I'm with the FBI. I followed you here, from Central Park, on your jog—you're surprisingly fast— then in a taxi and again on foot, to this park, because I would very much like to talk to you about Jacob Gornev."

"What do you mean, you're with the FBI?" I asked. Why would an FBI agent have any reason to stand below some housewife's window in the dead of night?

"Well," he said. "I'm trying to find someone whom Jacob Gornev might like to see again after all these years. Someone he might like to talk to."

"Why? Did he do something?" I said, thinking back to a man I'd once been so fond of.

Coldwell looked at me hard as he continued to puff on his cigarette. His stare made me even more uncomfortable than I already was.

"I was wondering if you knew," he said after a moment, "but you don't."

"What don't I know?"

"Jacob Gornev is an intelligence operative for the Soviet Union. We think he reports directly to a very senior member of the KGB."

"Jacob Gornev?" I repeated, deeply skeptical. The Jacob Gornev I had known did Indian yoga. He could hold a cigar with his toes and smoke it. He was so beloved at the Dominican lunch counter near campus that they roasted a whole pig on a spit for his birthday. This same man worked for the KGB? A sworn enemy to this country? It was unfathomable.

"Gornev is a Soviet spy. He was even when you were at Columbia. He's moved up their chain of command since then. He interested us less when he was near the bottom. He interests us enormously now."

I nodded to mask my utter confusion. I knew Jacob was born in the Ukraine and had some leftist leanings, but many students at Columbia did. Some even attended Communist Party meetings. But Jacob was different. He'd never mentioned the Communist Party. Seemed in love with his life in New York. I'd assumed his political activity was quite mainstream. I would never have been involved with him if I'd thought otherwise.

And I had been. Involved.

"I see," I said, more memories emerging from the folds of my mind. "Mr. Coldwell . . . I wish you luck with your endeavors, but I'm afraid you're mistaken in thinking I can help you. There are many reasons why I'd be of no assistance, the first being that I haven't seen Jacob Gornev since he graduated in 1941." I pulled down the hem of my dress and crossed my legs away from Lee Coldwell. "Unless you'd like to know more about his university days?"

"We know plenty about his university days," Coldwell said, lighting another cigarette, going through his same ritual with the match. "We know as much as we can know about him from the outside. He works for a shipping company, United States Shipping Incorporated, which despite its deeply patriotic name, is a KGB front. And he dabbles in the restaurant business. Again, owned by the KGB. That's enough to arrest him, but we want more before we do. So, what we need is someone—someone he likes and trusts—to have a conversation with him. A few conversations, if possible."

"A conversation."

"Yes," he replied smoothly. "I was supposed to arrange a chance meeting with you, spend a few weeks getting to know you, and then, once you trusted me, ask you to help. That's the usual protocol. But

I'm telling you now, long before I should, that I think you're the perfect person for the job."

The perfect person. The words rang false given the day's events.

"I can think of many reasons why I'm not," I replied quietly. "Perfect, that is."

"The truth is," said Coldwell, putting his hat back on. "We had a list of other people to approach. And you were not at the top of it. But after I watched you for a few days—apologies about that—you moved to the top."

I stared at Lee Coldwell, but the man I was thinking of was my husband. Even if I were interested in doing such a thing, Tom would never approve. Then again, after today, there could very well be divorce papers waiting, freshly inked, when I returned home.

"As I said, I haven't spoken to Jacob in over a decade. I don't think it would be easy for me to have a simple conversation."

"It might be easier than you think," said Coldwell.

"You seem to have a lot of things quite figured out," I said, "which is lovely to know about American intelligence, but I still don't think I can contribute. I'm sure there are dozens of people far more capable that you could approach—perhaps less abruptly than you did today." I exhaled slowly. "I'm not sure that a housewife can do anything the FBI cannot."

Coldwell shook his head. "We've tried to get undercover agents near Gornev. For about a year we've tried, and no one has stuck. He's involved with something new now and seems to have informants all over Washington, one of whom we know is working for the federal government. I'm sure there are others. We need someone to help us fish out the traitors."

This sounded like much more than a simple conversation. "And you think he'll just, what, knock back a bit of vodka and tell me everything because we went on a few dates together?"

Coldwell looked away from me. "Excuse my frankness, but it was more intimate than a few dates," he said. "Or so I was told."

My embarrassment lit up my face.

"Come," he said, standing. "I'll tell you more, but let's take a walk. I don't want to stay in one place longer than we already have. If you're okay with it, take my arm and walk with me out of this park."

I hadn't held a man's arm in a long time, and it felt good, perhaps because I already felt indebted to him. He had taken my mind off the morning and my many failures.

Jacob Gornev. We were indeed at Columbia together during the war. I was studying for my master's degree in Italian, the only Swiss language I wasn't yet fluent in. Jacob was studying for his degree in German. He was good-looking, with thick dark wavy hair and dark eyes, and enough charm to get many of the polyglots he carried on with into his bed. He liked to practice his German with me, since I was as comfortable in it as I was in English and French, and I liked to practice my Russian with him. Columbia required language students to choose a second one to study, and I had selected Russian, as I was already conversational. Mrs. Kuznetsov upstairs had loved to teach me, providing me with vocabulary and meals heavy on cabbage, all for free—before her tragic mishap with the ham, anyway.

"I noticed the match," I told Coldwell as we walked down Mosco Street. Around us, stores with their wares extended onto the sidewalk— toys, vegetables, cleaning supplies, dumplings and fish—many of them selling all those products at once.

"That night in the rain," I added. "You did the same thing with the match."

Coldwell nodded. "My father worked for the National Park Service. It rubbed off a bit," he said. "I can barely throw anything away. I even eat orange rinds."

"Do you really?" I said, pausing on the sidewalk.

"No. But I feel guilty that I don't."

"How long have you been watching me?" I asked. I should have been asking about Jacob, but it suddenly dawned on me all the things this man could have seen. All the terrible incidents.

"About a week," he said quietly.

I pulled my arm away from his and we fell silent again. Since becoming a mother, I had felt the world's eyes on me, those judging stares. Now I realized that one of those sets of eyes belonged to this man. Lee Coldwell. Another person not helping.

"Rough day today," Coldwell said finally.

"Wasn't my best," I replied, my gaze fixed on the sidewalk. "Why did you choose today, of all days, to speak to me, then?"

"Today you're alone," Coldwell said plainly. "And you are a woman who is seldom alone. Or so it seems."

"To say the least."

"Besides," he added. "I figured your day was already ruined. My approaching you could hardly make it much worse."

"I imagine an FBI agent might have seen much harder days," I countered. I wasn't looking for pity.

Coldwell paused. "I've never been shat on by a child or a bird while on the job," he said. "Pardon my language."

"There's really no other way to say it," I replied.

He stopped in front of a small teahouse and gestured for us to go inside. It was loud; the intonations of a language I didn't know always hit my ears differently than one I did. Without ceremony, we were seated at a plain Formica-topped table. Coldwell pointed to the table across from us and said, "That," to our waiter, who nodded, and a few minutes later brought us plates of dumplings. I hadn't had food like it, salty and comforting, since before I'd had children.

Coldwell ate his dumplings quickly, then pushed the plate away, while I savored them, realizing that I hadn't eaten a thing since breakfast.

"So," said Coldwell, picking up his ceramic cup of tea. "We've had our eyes on Gornev for a while, from a distance, but I see an opportunity right now that I want to seize."

"What kind of opportunity?" I asked, a wave of nausea rising.

"Recently, he's had a woman, an American, traveling to Washington for him. We think she's been a courier of sorts."

"What is she couriering?"

"I'll get into that later," Coldwell replied. "First I'll give you the big picture."

I nodded and tried to concentrate on not inhaling my last four dumplings.

"This woman, she's been rubbing elbows—and who knows what else—with government moles, but she's been tasked with something else by Gornev. And it's something which, frankly, looks like it could end rather badly for her."

"Why?"

"Because it involves going to Moscow, which is never a good idea. But her expanded role also means that Gornev will have to replace her while she's away. Probably with another woman."

"Why?" I asked, pushing my plate across the table. Coldwell signaled to the waiter to take it away.

"Because he likes working with women. Probably thinks it's less conspicuous. And his Washington people are now used to dealing with a woman."

"But why would Gornev ever pick me to replace this woman?" I asked, seeing where Coldwell's logic was going. "I'm not a communist. I'm in fact married to a man whose father is a king of capitalism."

"I'm not saying he needs to pick you for anything," he said, refilling my teacup. "I'm just asking, for now, if you would mind speaking to him. If it goes well, maybe he'll want to speak to you a few more times. Maybe things will build from there."

"I'm not a communist," I said again.

"I'm aware."

"Then isn't this fruitless?"

Coldwell said nothing for a moment, taking a sip of his tea and tracing the pattern in the tabletop with his finger.

"We heard he was in love with you." Coldwell looked up at me and stopped moving his finger on the table.

"Heard from whom?" I asked, before I could stop myself.

"We heard, is all."

"I'd say he was fond of me," I replied, choosing my words carefully. "That would be a fair statement."

"How is your Russian?"

"It's rusty. To say the least. Corroded. But it used to be quite good."

"You studied it for three years at Columbia, right?" His tone said that he already knew the answer.

"I did, but I was already conversational when I arrived. I studied it as an undergraduate, and my upstairs neighbor when I was little, Mrs.—"

"Mrs. Kuznetsov."

"Right, Mrs. Kuznetsov. I don't even want to ask what else you know about my life," I said.

"Then I won't tell you."

"She loved teaching me Russian," I explained. "She was lonely, so she would often spend time with me when my mother worked. My mother was a translator. Just at home, but a very good one. She was useful during the war."

"I bet." He reached for his teacup but put it down when he realized it was empty. "And your aunt Hanna was also a translator," he said. "An interpreter. During the Nuremberg trials."

"That's right," I said after a long pause.

"If you were to help," said Coldwell slowly, "if you see the threat against democracy, against America and the West the same way we do, then we'd put you in Jacob's path. Not to approach him directly, but to have him run into you. Something that feels natural. Unlike what I did today."

Since 1950, and the start of the Korean War, the threat against our way of life by the Reds had dominated the papers and evening news. D-Day was barely behind us, and already there was a communist campaign to take over the world, with the Soviets leading the way, China right behind them. Did I see it as a threat to democracy? Of course. But it was complicated. I knew that much from nearly six years at the United Nations.

"I would just, what then? Walk down the street and wait until he bumped into me?"

"Not exactly. For one, you wouldn't be alone when you ran into him," he said. "We'd want you to be with someone, one of our men, someone who is undercover right now, and whom Gornev knows. He has no doubt that our agent is a communist. Passionate about the cause and all that. He would surely stop if he saw him. So, even if he didn't recognize you right away, he'd recognize this man. But," he said, pausing. "I think he'll notice you first. You haven't changed much in ten years."

When I'd looked in the mirror that morning, I saw nothing of the woman I was at Columbia. My hair was shorter, I was twenty pounds heavier, I looked and felt frazzled. I shook my head no. "I don't—" I stopped, resting my hands on the Formica table. I had forgotten how comforting cheap, sturdy materials could be. They reminded me of my childhood, of my practical, dependable mother. "Thank you," I replied instead. "So, what, Jacob sees me with a known communist, we talk, and then he invites me to spy on my country? But instead, I start spying on him?" I said.

"There are probably a thousand more steps in the middle," said Coldwell, "but we can set up your background to make you far more of a match than you look like right now."

"And how will you do that? By plucking me completely out of my life?"

"No," he said. "There would be no disruption to your life, I hope. No true disruption."

I looked down at my dress, where spots of sauce had fallen. No amount of laundering could bring it back now.

"But as you have observed, Mr. Coldwell," I said, moving my napkin to cover the stains. "I am a woman who is never alone." I thought of Tom's face if I told him Jilly would have to come over because the government needed me to do a spot of spy work.

"Perhaps you could find a way to be alone, just a few times?"

I shook my head.

"No," I said. "That would be the hardest part. Harder even than Jacob believing I'm a communist."

"All that is down the line."

I stood up. "I still don't understand why you've asked me," I said, suddenly overwhelmed with the need to leave. "Surely Jacob was in love with other women over the past decade."

"He was," Coldwell replied. "And I looked into a few. But none of them were staring out their windows at three o'clock in the morning, observing the world from a gilded cage, desperate to escape."

"Most people wouldn't call 820 Fifth Avenue a cage."

"I think *you* would."

Coldwell put his hand in his jacket pocket, found a receipt, and wrote a phone number on it. He did not add his name. He pushed it across the table to me.

"Call me when you decide," he said. He reached into his wallet and put money on the table. It seemed like too much for what we'd eaten.

"I'll think about it," I said, folding the receipt in half.

"Think about it quickly."

CHAPTER 10

"Welcome home, Mrs. Edgeworth." Sam's voice slid through the air as he opened the taxi door for me.

"Thank you, Sam," I said. During my long cab ride home, the sun had begun to set. I had left my children in the park at noon, and I was coming home to them at eight p.m.

When I passed Carrie's floor in the elevator, I felt an urge to jump out and hide in her apartment instead of returning to my own. But no. I had created the day; I would see it to its end.

The doors opened. The apartment felt more cavernous than usual, and it was dead quiet.

Tom was in our bedroom, sitting on the large bed, papers in front of him, his horn-rimmed glasses on. He looked up at me as I stopped in the doorway.

"Is Gerrit all right?" I asked, my voice already catching.

"He needed stitches," he said flatly. "In his knee. Five stitches. He fell on a piece of broken glass." His tone was worse than flat. It was emotionless. Dead.

"Did he?" I said. I leaned against the door frame. What glass? Tom hadn't said anything about glass when he'd come to me holding Gerrit. "Did you take him to the hospital?"

"No," said Tom, whipping off his glasses and throwing them on the bed. "I sewed him up right here with dental floss."

I bit my lip. I would not cry in front of Tom again.

"Did you take the baby with you to the hospital?" I asked, my voice so quiet I wasn't sure if he could hear me.

Tom sighed and moved to the edge of the bed.

"No. Jilly came," he said. "So that I didn't have to. She's still here. She's in bed with him. I think they're both sleeping now. Gerrit's been asleep for an hour."

"Jilly doesn't have to spend the night," I said. "I need to feed the baby. I'll go replace her now. Which room—"

"You will do nothing of the sort," Tom suddenly roared. He stood and walked toward me, looming.

I froze.

"I told myself that we would speak rationally about all this, but it's not an option right now. I'm irate, Katharina!" he said, bringing his face even closer to mine. "What in God's name possessed you? How could you stand there at a distance while your son cried and not go to him? Is there something wrong with you? Something I'm not seeing?"

I shook my head no, silent tears escaping. "I thought it was just a scrape, Tom. If I had known he'd fallen on glass, I would have gone to him quicker. I didn't know he would need stitches." I needed to convince Tom, but I didn't know if I could convince myself. All I knew, then and now, was that I'd felt completely unable to move.

"That's preposterous," said Tom, practically laughing despite his anger. "Glass or not, you should have run to him when he fell. The moment he fell. And he should never have been that far away from you. He's *two years old*. What are you going to have him do next? Jump on the subway? Ride over to Queens?"

He spat out Gerrit's age as if I didn't know it. As if it were not me who had given birth to him, then spent months recovering from a traumatic labor. As if I hadn't been the one who'd planned his first birthday party while pregnant, hired the caterers, plus the lady with the guitar from Westchester who sang "The Farmer in the Dell" in the original German.

"I don't know what happened, Tom," I said, trying to pull my words together. "I'd had a very difficult day with them, and by the time Gerrit fell, I felt paralyzed."

"It wasn't even a day! It was what, a few hours?" he yelled.

"Even a few hours can paralyze you."

"With what?" he said, taking a step back, finally giving me room to breathe again.

I looked at him blankly.

"What paralyzed you?"

"I don't know," I said, my hands covering my ears to block his words. "With motherhood, I suppose."

He pulled my arms down. "Last I checked, motherhood was not a disease."

But it was. It could be. I wanted to shout that he had no idea. He knew nothing of the hard side of parenting. It was like what Mrs. Morgan had said about Charlotte van Asletson and her eyes—she could only see misery from her right side. Tom Edgeworth could see only one side of motherhood.

It was not something I could explain to him. Not now, perhaps not ever.

"You do know I've had children die as I was operating on them? I've touched them as they breathed their last breath. But I tried as hard as I could to save them. I have *never* been paralyzed."

"We are not cut from the same cloth, Tom," I said quietly. "I am a translator, not a surgeon."

"You're not a translator anymore. You're a *mother*," he said, shouting out the last word. He sat back down on the bed and put his head in his hands. "When I brought Gerrit to you, you just stared at him as if he were a stranger's child. As if you weren't his mother at all. It was a sickening look, Katharina."

I felt like I might faint, my body unable to handle my frustration.

"I am his mother!" I shouted. "And I love him desperately." I started to cry, really cry, no longer caring if I did. "I just don't have an explanation for what happened," I said, lowering my voice slightly. "I didn't have an explanation for you this morning, and I certainly don't have one now." Tom gave me his "please don't embarrass us" expression. It was because Jilly was in the next room. I had no doubt he cared more about her opinion of him than mine in that moment.

"I provide you with what you need, don't I?" he asked, quietly. "You're happy, aren't you?"

I nodded.

"All I ask is that you love me and love our boys. Is that too much of a request?"

I did love them. And Tom. The person I had stopped loving was me. If I were at a party, I wouldn't glance at me. I wouldn't want to speak to me. I'd become a woman who faded into the background.

Except this afternoon, when I was worthy of being followed.

"Was this enough, then? This little pause of yours today?" Tom asked. "Your fleeing the scene? Do you feel better now that you've had your brush with irresponsibility?"

"I don't know, Tom," I whispered.

He was quiet. The entire city felt quiet, as if Fifth Avenue wasn't thrumming with its usual energy right below our windows.

"But I do know that I want to see my boys." I started to walk back toward the bedrooms.

"You will not wake them, Katharina," he said, standing up. He moved quickly and reached for my arm, holding me back. "You will leave them be," he said, gripping my biceps now. "Especially Gerrit. He's finally asleep."

"I will see them," I said, ripping away from Tom. "I'm their mother. Even when I'm a bad one."

He didn't reply. But he didn't reach for me again, either. A few moments later, I heard the elevator ding and close. He was leaving the building.

The boys' rooms were close to ours, but I turned and walked into the hall, where I collapsed on the window seat. I dried the remaining dampness from my face. I looked at my hands for any traces of makeup, but there were none. Had I even put on lipstick and rouge that morning? I had. I always did. My ridiculous attempts at presentability. If I'd known what the day would bring, I might have worn a helmet instead.

I pressed my face against the cool glass of the window and looked down. There were still a few people walking past the zoo entrance. None of them were Lee Coldwell.

I crept to Gerrit's room first. He was fast asleep, his leg uncovered and propped on pillows, his knee wrapped in gauze. I woke up Jilly, thanked her, and watched her leave.

I got into Gerrit's bed and put my arms around him gingerly. I didn't want to wake him, but I had to touch him. I remembered how I'd screamed. How I'd imagined my hand hitting his face. Tom was right. I didn't deserve my children.

"I'm so sorry, darling," I whispered into his ear. "I don't know what's wrong with me."

CHAPTER 11

om and I barely spoke for two weeks. Two weeks in which I tended to Gerrit and Peter's every need as if they were newborns. I held Gerrit in my arms more than I did Peter, even toddling around the city with all thirty pounds of him attached to my hip.

As the teens of April turned into the twenties, I watched Tom walk into the elevator one Thursday morning. He looked straight ahead, straight through me: through my straining arms holding the baby, through the white Lise Charmel nightgown, hand-sewn in Lyon, which I'd picked because he'd admired it one weekend in a shop window. The doors closed and whisked him off to his important world as I stood there, a ghost in the home that he provided for me.

I turned the volume on the TV up. The Army-McCarthy hearings had begun broadcasting on the twenty-second. The Geneva Convention was going to start in three days. Lee Coldwell certainly was not the only one who saw communism as a great threat to democracy. I looked at Senator McCarthy, his hair slicked back as he talked to his counsel, Roy Cohn. Was I one of them? Automatically on McCarthy's side because the FBI thought I was the perfect person to spy on Jacob Gornev? I turned the volume down. It made no difference. I was at home, back in the role of the imperfect housewife, the flawed mother.

I checked on Gerrit in his high chair, took off the white nightgown, pulled the baby to my chest, sat on a dining chair, and thought about when everything had changed. Had it really been so long ago that I'd been pulling Tom toward me instead of a baby?

When we'd first started dating, Tom lived in a small one-bedroom apartment in a respectable but not very chic building at the corner of Lexington and Seventy-second. Though I would have gone home with him the night we met, it didn't happen for a few weeks more. Weeks when I learned that Tom couldn't speak French but could do practically everything else.

"You're a surgeon?" I asked on our first date at Le Pavillon across from the St. Regis, without argument the best French restaurant in town. "As in, you cut people apart and sew them back together?"

"A bit better than how I found them."

"And you're good at this little side hobby?" I asked, glopping béarnaise sauce onto my steak.

"I get by," he replied. "Haven't had a patient complain yet. But that's—"

"Hard to do from six feet under?"

"Exactly," he said, smiling and gesturing to the waiter to please bring us another round of drinks.

Tom, I realized quickly, was a man who always said please. He introduced himself to waiters, asked for their names, and chatted with them about where they were from. He reeked of wealth, from his cuff links, which were clearly platinum, to the way he carried himself, as if the sidewalks were raised just a few inches higher for him. Easy. Easy walking. Easy smile. Easy life. But it was also obvious that all that ease hadn't expunged his soul.

"Actually, I specialize in children's surgery," he admitted.

I leaned over and pressed my fingers into his arm.

"Ouch?"

"Just making sure you're real."

Three weeks later, we were in bed, and Tom very much proved that he was real. I'd had good sex before. Great sex. All those war years, feeling like the man you were bedding might be called to duty at any moment, so you better have a hell of a good time and give them something to remember as they slipped from this earth. There had been over twenty if I counted correctly, including Jacob Gornev, who was wild and wonderful, but Tom was the most generous lover I'd ever had. If I hadn't had two orgasms before noon, he would look at himself in the mirror and declare, "Well, I've accomplished nothing." Then we'd laugh and try to make sure he accomplished something.

One afternoon, when I had convinced Tom to have German food at my favorite little restaurant near Washington Square, a dingy place that hadn't upgraded a thing since the Great War, I thought about everything we'd done in the three months that we'd been dating. We'd seen *Aida* at the Center Theatre, *Macbeth* at the National Theatre, had soft drinks in Times Square, hard drinks at the Ritz on Madison, ten-cent cotton candy on Coney Island, kissed and kissed some more below the flags at Rockefeller Plaza, hid from the rain under the tracks of the Third Avenue El, and tumbled into bed, and kept on tumbling.

"Do you have a diaphragm?" he'd asked the first time we'd had sex. "If not, a prophylactic is just fine. But of course, I am a doctor, so if you need a diaphragm . . . ?"

"I have it all," I'd told Tom. I was thirty-one years old and had inherited the European view of sex as just another form of conversation.

In that German restaurant, I looked at Tom as he wiped his brow and rolled up the sleeves of his oxford shirt.

"Besides the sex, why do you like me?" I asked after a bite of New York's best roulade.

"I can't answer that," said Tom, sweating. It was the end of June and the restaurant didn't have air-conditioning, or more than two working windows. "This is like eating the nectar of the gods in the seventh circle of hell. Is there a river of boiling blood and fire in the back?" he asked, opening one more button on his shirt.

"There is, but that's just to make the *blutwurst*. Shall we order a plate?"

"If I faint, just throw water in my face and stomp on me until I come to, okay?" he croaked out.

"You're the doctor."

"Katharina West, why do I like you," he said, sitting back, trying to take a deep breath. "I like you because you're nothing like Daisy and Rose and Violet and all the other women my mother has tried to set me up with who were named after flowers yet have no roots, just petals that will wilt fast. Your petals are going to last, I can see that already, because you're smart and quick and you make me laugh. I like you because you care about people, people who look like you, people who don't look like you. Like me, you know that inside these gorgeous bodies," he said, moving his hand from his head to waist and winking, "we are all just blood and guts."

"Who is the gorgeous one?"

"*You*, of course, you. And staying on that subject, my favorite one, let me tell you more about your charms."

"I'm all ears."

"Lucky for me, you have a lot more than ears. You're worldly, yet caring. You don't just want to steam down to Argentina to tell everyone you took a trip, you want to explore, meet, greet, and repeat. And in the country's native language." He watched as a bead of sweat hit the table and wiped it with his napkin.

"Just shake out like a dog," I said, grinning, and to my surprise, he did.

"Think they're going to kick us out soon?" I asked.

"You kidding? There are four patrons in this restaurant." He took an ice cube out of his glass and dropped it down the back of his shirt.

"I'll tell you this," he said when I was done laughing. "My mother, who one day you will meet, though you should drink heavily first, has a long list of not-so-insignificant flaws. But she's funny. She'll make you laugh till your whole body hurts from it. And she's smart. A lovely kind of smart. An intelligence that just seeps out of her, though she never tries to prove it to you. Somehow, I ignore all her flaws because of those two things. So I suppose I want a woman who is nothing like my mother in most ways, but who *is* funny and lovely smart. Does that make sense?"

"It does."

"Also," he said, placing his hands back on mine. "I don't just like you. I happen to love you. Lovely smart love you."

Everyone at the UN was thrilled about my relationship with Tom, by my engagement ring, except Marianne.

"Are you sure you can still lift your hand with that flawless diamond on it?" Caroline asked me when I first came to work wearing it. Caroline was Belgian, from Spa, and certainly knew her way around a diamond. "Of course, who even cares if you can't, you'll have servants to lift your hand for you. You lucky thing. I can't believe I didn't go to that party at the consulate with you both. You meet heirs to tycoons of industry, and I meet waiters at the Divan Parisien who slip me free Camembert and think it's enough for me to go to bed with them. Now if I got that rock instead, I'd be in bed with all of them. Remind me to always go out with you, Rina."

"Your parents must be thrilled," said Abena, one of the Ethiopian secretaries whom I'd grown close to.

"They're not sad," I said, hugging her. "Considering my advanced age and all."

"It is a bit of a miracle," said Caroline, who was only twenty-four. "But with your beautiful face, it's only a *bit* of a miracle."

"But what about all our fun?" Marianne asked me when our office had cleared out. "What about eating, drinking, loving, laughing, breathing, crying, and repeat?"

"We can still have fun," I said, taking my eyes off my ring to look at her. "We can still laugh, breath, cry, repeat. Also, why are we crying?"

"Because we are only young once."

"Are we still young?"

"Young enough," she said, patting her cheeks.

"Then let's just keep on with this wild youth of ours. The city hasn't shut its doors to us just because I have a diamond on my finger."

"We cannot keep on." She dropped the files in her hand on her desk. "Our fun revolves around us working here and then going out, drinking too much and hinting at the possibility of sex with our tinkling laughs, shiny hair, and French verbs."

"What if I just hint at the sex and don't actually follow through on it?"

"You joke now. Trust me, it will be the working here part that will get tougher. Eventually, I'll walk down the hall alone, ready to interpret for the Commission on Human Rights, for John Humphrey or René Cassin or Eleanor Roosevelt herself, and I'll say, 'There went another perfectly good mind.'"

"Only perfectly good?"

"I'd say 'brilliant,' but I'm mad at you, so I've downgraded you to good. And once you leave here, it will shrink anyway, so there."

I did not want my mind to shrink. I wanted to translate what would become the Universal Declaration on Human Rights. I wanted to travel to Paris in December of '48 for the General Assembly meeting. But I also very much wanted to marry Tom Edgeworth.

When I turned thirty, my parents had given up on me ever getting married. I told them I wanted to experience the world, not marriage. That maybe I'd just become a man's mistress or second wife. That for now, I was wedded to my work. But then Tom Edgeworth and his long legs and good heart swung in. And suddenly, I wanted to be a wife. *His* wife. Not because he had platinum cuff links or didn't mind eating blood sausage while sitting in a pool of his own sweat, but because I loved him and I felt deeply that he'd always let me be, in his words, "Rina with her little languages."

I hadn't been wrong. What I had been wrong about was who I was allowed to speak them to, once I became a mother. No longer was I speaking French to Paul-Henri Spaak, president of the UN General

Assembly, or even to my multilingual friends. Instead, I was speaking them to babies who could not answer back. My mind no longer fizzed with intellectual rigor; it bubbled with boredom in French, Italian, German, and English.

I missed having my mind hurt from overuse by Friday evening. Tom had been quite wrong: nothing about my world had been little, especially not the languages.

CHAPTER 12

On the last Friday in April, just as New York comfortably settled into spring, Tom did the most un-Tom-like thing he'd ever done.

After I had put the boys to bed, done the dishes, and scrubbed down the kitchen, he gestured for me to have a drink with him in the sitting room. I took off my gingham apron, smoothed my hair, and smiled at him like the loving wife I was.

"I think you might need a break," he said before I'd even sat down.

"A break?" I said, too surprised to sit.

He gestured to the chair. "You look just like you did when you found out you were pregnant again."

"I feel a bit like that," I said. I sank down in the chair he'd pointed to. Tom handed me his Manhattan.

"Have that. Or take a moment and make yourself one."

I paused. I knew Tom was tired from his day at the hospital, but I seemed to recall that he'd once been perfectly capable of making me a drink after a long day at work. Not suggest that I do it myself.

"I'll just have yours," I said pleasantly.

He gripped the arms of the Noguchi chair he was sitting in, as if he were steeling himself. "I know that before Gerrit was born we decided it would be best for you to spend as much time with the children as possible," he said.

"Yes," I said, remembering that conversation as well as my wedding vows. It was another kind of vow, one so many women around the world made when their stomachs started to swell.

"Which is what nature intended," Tom continued.

"Yes," I replied, the drink suddenly tasting sour. I wondered if nature also intended for mothers to suffer from nervous breakdowns or start brushing their teeth with gin to take the edge off.

"I know some of your friends, like Carrie, have employed help," he continued, still gripping the chair, as if to stop himself being ejected from it.

"Carrie does have a nanny," I said, desperate for the alcohol to start working its magic.

"Right," said Tom, frowning. Memories of his own dozen childhood nannies were flooding back like a phalanx of buttoned-up ghosts, I was sure. "As you know, I certainly don't think that way of life is for us, but I have spoken to my mother, and to Jilly, and we've decided that you might benefit from a vacation."

"A vacation," I repeated.

"What's that face?" said Tom, taking in my reaction.

"I think I'm just in shock, is all."

"Well, that isn't all, so pull yourself together, Mrs. Edgeworth."

He stood up, then helped me to my feet. I watched as he went to the sideboard and opened the top drawer. He took out some papers and came back.

"I bought you a plane ticket to Los Angeles," he said, placing it in my hand. "I thought you might go for a few days. Five, to be exact. Stay with my sister and Kip. She's excited to see you."

"I'm sorry," I said looking up from the ticket. "My vacation is to stay with Arabella and Kip? In Los Angeles? For five days?"

"That's right," said Tom, looking proud of himself.

I thought by "vacation" he might have meant somewhere like

Geneva, to see my family. Or Paris, where they might meet me. Was Los Angeles with his sister's family a vacation? I glanced again at Tom, so pleased with his surprise, and told myself that perhaps it was. I had never been away from the children for five days. Fifteen months ago, pregnant with Peter, I had come down with such bad food poisoning they thought I would have to stay at Lenox Hill overnight. I was really looking forward to it. A night spent vomiting in a hospital sounded like a vacation, but in the end, it was decided that since Dr. Tom Edgeworth was my husband, I could recover at home. And that way I wouldn't have to leave baby Gerrit. Wasn't that terrific?

But now I was headed to Los Angeles. Alone. For five days without my children.

"That sounds wonderful," I said genuinely.

"Good. Life should be wonderful," he said, smiling. I smiled back.

He looked at my empty glass.

"Go on," he said. "Fix yourself another."

CHAPTER 13

Ten thousand feet, the pilot had said when he came over the speaker. We had been soaring through clouds as we left the East Coast, but now that we were closer to the west, the weather had changed for the better. The Dutch really should have built New York in a place with more sunshine.

I looked down at the mountains below, the tiny airplane window affording me a giant, scrolling panorama. A river the color of dark mustard cut through earth. There were patterns forged by human activity that nature could wipe away in seconds. I had forgotten how big the world was. Even America seemed dauntingly enormous. The closest thing I'd seen to this landscape in a long time had been the peaks and valleys in a bowl of meringue I was mixing.

The man next to me was older, near my father's age, but I couldn't stop glancing at him. I never sat next to men anymore who weren't my husband, or on increasingly rare occasions, my husband's friends. Mine had become a world of women. Women's bodies and women's conversations. Except for that day in the park with Lee Coldwell. His phone number was in my dress pocket, just as it had been every day since I'd met him. I had no intention of calling it, but I liked to touch the piece of paper, to recall the interaction. I would probably keep transferring it from dress pocket to dress pocket until it was illegible, the paper worn too thin to read. It would eventually disintegrate, and the day where I was declared *the perfect woman for the job* would vanish with it.

With my forehead against the window, I thought about the night before. I had been awake again, roaming our hallway, going to the window seat, looking out at that slice of the island directly in front of our building. I had forgotten about states like Colorado and Nevada. I had forgotten that the world extended past New York.

I'd forgotten that freedom was the most glamorous thing anyone could possess.

I'd spent summers in Switzerland as a child and then one summer in Florence while still in school, Mussolini's Italy of 1936, simultaneously electrified by its charm and horrified by its descent into fascism. Then the war had closed us Americans inside our own country—except for the men who'd fought for us. Tom hadn't been one of them. Money and medical school had kept him off the battlefield and on Park Avenue.

I settled back in the wide airplane seat and briefly shut my eyes. I wondered what my boys were doing without me. Were they happy with Jilly? Were they crying? I fell asleep thinking about their faces, imagining them contorted with grief because I'd left them. I didn't wake up until the plane started to descend through the clouds into Los Angeles.

After we'd landed, I clacked down the metal stairs, bathed in the dry Californian heat. Inside the airport, I immediately heard someone call "Yoo-hoo!" an aristocratic yodel that without a doubt belonged to Arabella Edgeworth Rowe. Tall and athletic, Arabella was older than Tom by two years, but even in her mid-forties, she was the picture of health. She had ruddy cheeks; thick brown hair that just brushed her shoulders, styled, but not too styled; a perpetual tan that never turned to wrinkles; brownish eyes with a dash of green; and straight broad shoulders built up by all the swimming she'd done over the years. Her mother loved to tell stories about Arabella in her youth and how concerned the Edgeworths had been that she spent all her time in the swimming pool as a teenager instead of at parties meeting boys from good families.

"I always said," her mother would crow, "who will you meet in the swimming pool? A lobster? Do you really want to be Mrs. Arabella Lobster?"

I always wanted to remind Amelia that the swimming pools in Manhattan, especially the private ones where Arabella was swimming, were crustacean-free, but Tom would shoot me a look when Amelia reached that part of the story.

Amelia's worries changed when Arabella turned seventeen and had never dated or shown interest in boys. Amelia's concern was no longer about lobsters, it was that her daughter was going to become Mrs. Arabella Lesbian.

"She was so . . . sporty," she'd whisper. "So uninterested in the things a girl her age should be interested in. Sports and jazz music and God knows what else, that's all she liked. 'Is she taking drugs?' I asked myself. I thought no, because of all that swimming. Can one even swim while high on cocaine? Or is that why she's so good?"

That was usually where Tom would pause the story and say, "Arabella was ingesting neither cocaine nor a woman's labia," and his mother would let out a scream. Then he'd pipe up about how all the medical research had shown that one could not catch homosexuality in a swimming pool.

His mother would wave him off, muttering, "Such a crude son, spouting nonsense," and keep on all the heart palpitations her daughter's athletic abilities had caused her.

Arabella went to Stanford for college, spurning her mother's alma mater, Bryn Mawr, with a cool, "It's not for me, mother," and William Edgeworth paid the bill because they were actually quite thrilled she was going to college and not indulging in other illicit activities too awful to name.

At Stanford, Arabella remained a fish, but it turned out there were men who liked that about her, even men from the right families. She met her husband, Kip Rowe, in the swimming pool. He was on Stanford's men's team and nearly made the Olympic roster for the Berlin Games. At their wedding in Santa Monica, they served lobster as the main course.

"In the end, it was for the best that he missed those Olympics," Arabella always said about her husband's near star status. "Hitler and all. Really put a damper on sport."

"Yes," I'd said many times, nodding agreeably. "Nazis and swimming just don't mix."

"Quite right," she'd say, either not noticing my sarcasm or choosing to ignore it.

As the people around me pulled at their suitcases and peeled off their sweaters, I gave Arabella a long hug. She was wearing wide-legged white pants and a light blue blouse tucked into the high waist, a perfect style for her tall frame.

"Look at you without a child hanging on you like a howler monkey," she said, pushing my shoulders back and examining me in my gray traveling suit and sensible black shoes.

"Indeed," I said, smiling. Arabella and Kip had four children, all swimmers, their daughter Bettina the strongest of them. Even if it had been a few years, Arabella knew something about how easily small children could morph into howler monkeys. Bettina, I remembered her saying, had been an especially difficult baby. But now she was the pride of the family.

"If she doesn't make it to the Olympics and experience the glory her father missed, I'll stab her," Arabella had lamented to me once over bottles of champagne in New York. Three very expensive ones, if I remembered correctly.

"But I thought it was for the best? Kip missing out on the Olympics. Hitler and all that," I'd said.

"Of course, it was for the best, but he's still shaken up about it. He cried once when we went to watch Bettina in the high school national championship down in Florida. Tears on his face. And in public," she'd whispered. "So, like I said, I'll stab my daughter if she's not draped in the American flag in Melbourne in 1956."

After that conversation, I'd written to Bettina, encouraging her to double down on her swim practices. I was very fond of the girl and didn't want to see her cut apart with gardening shears or whatever else Arabella could find.

"Shall we drive off then?" asked Arabella when I had collected my suitcase. We both knew she was far more capable of carrying it than I was.

"I have to take care of women's things first, I'm afraid," I said, trying to sound nonchalant. Arabella was not one for beating around the bush or being embarrassed about bodily functions.

"Oh, lord, are you still doing that?" she said, looking down at my breasts, which after a six-hour plane ride were enormous.

"For now," I said. "Tom thought it best that I keep up with it while in California. I went eighteen months with Gerrit. And it's only been twelve with Peter."

"I went about twelve minutes with Bettina and look at how well she's turned out." She pulled my suitcase toward her. "Go on then. I'll wait. How long does it take with that travel contraption?"

"Thirty minutes or so. Forty if I really want to do a thorough job."

"Please don't bother," she said, and I headed to the bathroom to fight with the glass and latex breast pump that Tom had shown me how to use before I'd left.

"I feel like a cow. And not a prize one," I'd said miserably as he'd pushed it on my left breast, prodding and poking at me.

"Yes, but all the studies show that—"

"I know about the studies," I'd said, trying not to let my emotion escalate. Ever since I had abandoned the injured Gerrit, I'd tried to be the epitome of maternal diligence and patience.

The contraption took me forty-five minutes to use in the airport restroom, and when I found Arabella half asleep on a plastic chair, she looked at my chest again and said, "Well, that's surprising. I thought after all that time you wouldn't even have breasts left."

We began walking to her car, picking up a porter along the way to carry my suitcase. When she handed it to him, she shook out her arm. "Rina, we have cement in California. You did not have to import your own."

"It's just clothes and gifts and odds and ends," I said, embarrassed. "I haven't had many occasions to wear nice things these past couple years. I'm looking forward to it."

"There is actually quite the soiree tonight," she said, jumping behind the wheel of her silver Jaguar. "Some Hollywood people. A friend of ours in the industry invited us. I'm in no mood for that kind of thing, but Kip will take you. He pretends not to care about celebrities, but he's dying to get a look at Ingrid Bergman, who's rumored to be attending."

"Is she?" I said excitedly. "I'd love to go." I smiled as the airport disappeared behind us. The only hint of glamour I'd experienced these past few years was at medical galas and staid cocktail parties with the *right* people.

Arabella and Kip's Spanish-style house in Venice Beach had a sweeping view of the water and was just a few feet from the boardwalk.

"I've been told that we should live somewhere more fashionable, the Hollywood Hills or Beverly Hills, but you know me, Mrs. Lobster, I just have to be near the water. And Mr. Lobster quite likes it, too. So much life in this part of town."

"Did someone say my name?" A smiling Kip greeted us from the doorway.

"Rina, you're here and looking so well," he said, giving me a kiss on the cheek. He had to lean over to do so. Everyone in the Edgeworth universe was exceedingly tall except for me. "I'm so glad you could come for a visit," he said warmly, ushering me inside. I followed, his sun-bleached hair and tan legs leading the way. Kip Rowe always looked as if he had just returned from a vacation.

"How was your swim, darling?" Arabella asked, catching up to him.

"Current tried to pull me under today. Strong as a neat tequila. But I fought back," he said.

"Please do keep me company after Kip drowns," said Arabella, turning to me. "Instead of swimming far out where he should, he chooses to breaststroke just where the waves crash."

"I like to feel the power of the ocean. Better for your muscles," he said, flexing his toned left biceps.

"I'll be sure to have them write that into your eulogy," said Arabella, though she reached out and touched his arm with approval.

As Arabella and Kip took my things upstairs, I took in their home. The ocean aside, it couldn't have been more different from 820 Fifth Avenue. The floors were a beautiful light oak and the rooms were exploding with light up through the vaulted ceilings. On the shelves near the Steinway piano were framed pictures of their children. There was one of Bettina in a cobalt blue bathing suit with a medal around her neck, her hair wet and slicked back, hitting just above her shoulders. She looked like everything that was good about America—youth and sunshine and athleticism and grace, all wrapped up in one pretty package.

"Max Greco, a photographer out here for the *Los Angeles Times*, snapped that of Bettina after she won athlete of the year at the L.A. swim club," said Arabella as she came back downstairs.

"She looks wonderful," I said admiringly.

"The man who wrote the piece that accompanied the photo called her the next Ann Curtis, but I hope she can do one better and win the gold in the hundred freestyle."

"The U.S. national team doesn't know what they're missing by not hiring Arabella Rowe to coach their women," Kip added. "She wouldn't let them out of the pool until they were eating world records for lunch. Though it would be nice if she just let Betty be a teenager for a while, too."

"He says that, but he's secretly the proudest father in the world and just happy that I'm the one doing the pushing so he doesn't have to," said Arabella. She leaned her head on his shoulder and batted her long eyelashes.

"I'm left to take care of the boys," he said to me with a wink. "They have potential, too, not quite like Bettina, but Scottie might get there."

"Scottie is built like a sea turtle, I'm afraid," said Arabella, descending the stairs. "Lots of midsection, not enough limbs. But stranger things have happened." She walked over to the piano and patted the picture of Scottie on the shelf. He was not photographed in a bathing suit, clearly not having earned that honor. "But tonight it's not about the boys, or any boys at all, it's all about Ingrid Bergman," she purred, rolling her R's. "Don't you think that's how Rossellini says it?"

"Oh, is she married?" said Kip, winking at me.

"Rina is going with you tonight so she can make sure that you are still married in the morning," Arabella said, doing an exaggerated version of her husband's wink.

"Good," said Kip. "Everyone who comes to Los Angeles for . . . the first time?"

"Third," I said.

"For the third time needs to visit the Beverly Hills Hotel."

I looked out at the water, at the waves crashing on the beach. They sounded crisp, as if the water were closer than it really was. It was because there were no sounds in the house.

After a long, brisk walk on the beach with Arabella, whose stride was as fast as my jog, she sat me in the kitchen to feast on a bowl of unidentifiable "but abundantly healthy" grains, which she claimed were second to none at absorbing champagne, and then helped me get dressed for the evening. I had worried I was going to spend the whole day thinking about the boys, about guilt and motherhood and whether I should have even gone to Los Angeles in the first place, but keeping up with Arabella had me thinking about little else besides my inferior build. One really did seem more productive with an extra six inches of leg.

In the guest room, Arabella watched me open my large suitcase, remove a few dresses, and then decide on a black dress with a high neckline. I undressed and put it on over my silk slip.

I took a look at myself in the long mirror, turning in a slow circle. I wasn't going to make the cover of *Vogue*, but I looked far better than I had in years. The smile on my face helped.

Arabella eyed me in silence then stood up. She pulled at the fabric around my neck. "What is that?" she asked, fingering it. "Is this wool or burlap?"

"A silk wool blend," I said defensively. "Good for travel. Doesn't wrinkle easily."

"Rina," she said, singing out my name. "You're going to the Beverly Hills Hotel in April. Even the walls there are the color of bubblegum."

"I'm afraid I didn't think pink while packing," I said, looking down at the clothes I'd selected.

"Still," she said, frowning at me. "This is California. Didn't you bring anything a bit more colorful? You look like you're about to bury a monarch."

"I didn't," I said, sifting through my dresses, all of them dark colors. "A lot of my old clothes just don't fit. My breasts . . ." I said, my voice trailing off.

"Right, that. Well, yes, I do understand the predicament. They are the size of spring melons. But I think we need to simply embrace them. We'll stuff your bra with handkerchiefs to prevent an embarrassing situation and find you something else to wear. You're going to Beverly Hills; there's nothing people love more in Beverly Hills than breasts. Breasts and an MGM contract, but you've only got the former on offer. Come. Let's look in my closet."

"But you're so much taller . . ." I protested as she dragged me to her bedroom.

"Rina, even a pup tent would be an improvement," she said as she flung open the door to her enormous closet.

Two hours later, I was sitting next to Kip in one of Arabella's dresses—light blue chiffon, revealing and too long—as he wound his car down Sunset Boulevard to the palm tree–lined driveway of the hotel that had "more glamour than a pound of caviar," according to Arabella. She didn't have time for such Hollywood theatrics, she'd repeated when Kip had pressed her to come, saying she planned to wake up early to swim in the ocean before "the sharks start moving."

"Arabella finds all this stuff rather silly," said Kip, slowing the car as we reached the valet line.

"So would Tom," I replied.

"I'll admit to you that I love it," he said. "I can't wait to see Ingrid Bergman. Don't let me throw myself at her and start weeping."

"I'll do my best," I said, grinning.

I looked out at the commotion in front of us, the people pushing their way through the door. I didn't recognize a soul, but everyone looked like a movie star.

When we reached the front of the line, we were helped out of the car by valet attendants in vanilla-colored dinner jackets. One quickly whisked away Kip's Jaguar, a flashier blue version of Arabella's, and we prepared to walk inside.

Ahead of us were men in tuxedos and women in colorful dresses, all silk and gauze, materials that were appropriate for eighty degrees. No practical wool blends in sight.

We wandered into the famous Polo Lounge. I was too nervous to even blink, feeling completely out of my element. But this was my vacation, my reward from Tom for being tethered to children for two and a half years. And I had once been a girl who kissed bartenders in dark corners and was eager to swing from chandeliers. A small trace of that woman had to be in me somewhere. "Do you know anyone—" I started to ask Kip when a voice interrupted me.

"Is that Kip Rowe? asked a man behind us.

"Mic Archdeacon!" Kip said with delight as he whirled around. "I didn't realize you'd grace a place like this with your presence."

"Well," said the man, who was just as tall and blond as Kip, "when

Ingrid calls you up personally and invites you, you certainly don't decline the lady."

"Oh, did she call you?" said Kip. "She just rolled over in bed and asked me."

Both men laughed heartily while I stood there with an awkward smile, holding up my dress with one hand. When their abdominals were done contracting, Kip introduced me, then quickly turned back to his acquaintance, blocking me out of the conversation. I listened as they exchanged gibes about each other's looks, barbs about women, and sexual innuendos about actresses neither of them had ever met. I took a step back, reluctant to leave the only person I knew at the party, but too repelled by the conversation to stay. I still heard snippets of it as I backed farther away—"upside down . . . lubrication . . . try the sautéed shrimp . . ."

"Psst," I heard someone hiss. I glanced around and saw an attractive woman in a white strapless dress waving me over.

I looked back at Kip and his friend, who was making a spanking motion with his hands, and walked quickly over to the hissing woman. "Sorry, was that directed at me?" I asked.

"Yes, I was watching you," she said, pushing her hair off her shoulder. "You were considering whether to edge back into that conversation, and I wanted to save you before you did. That man you were hanging about with, he's not your husband, is he?"

"My brother-in-law," I told her. She was about my height, but was wearing bright gold high heels and had the same air of command that statuesque Arabella had when she entered a room. She also had hair the color of a redwood. Altogether, she was as glamorous as a pound of caviar.

"Oh, good," she replied. "If he were your husband, I would have told you to start filing for divorce. Actually, I'm a lawyer. I could have started the paperwork for you."

"Are you?" I asked. "How fascinating. Are there many female lawyers in California?"

"Of course not," she said, shrugging her bare shoulders. "But I'm one of them."

"And you work on divorces?" I asked politely. I needed to keep the conversation going, not wanting to be alone again.

"Often," she said, swirling her drink around. "Divorces and other sorts of jams."

"Is there a worse jam than divorce?" I asked, feeling like an idiot the second I said it.

"In this town?" she said, laughing. "We have several flavors of jam. Many of them more terrifying than a little divorce. Faye Buckley Swan," she said, extending her hand. "I'm sorry I hissed, but I couldn't stand to watch you insert yourself into a conversation where you clearly weren't wanted, especially when you could just start your own. There are an awful lot of interesting people about—why not try someone else?"

"That's good advice," I said. "I used to be rather good at this, but recently, my ability to mingle has atrophied. Or died, actually. I think it threw itself off a bridge a few years back."

"And why is that? The bridge and all?" she asked.

"Just out of practice, I suppose," I replied, which was the honest answer.

"Well," she said, looking around the room, now even more packed, "this is a good place to dive back in the deep end."

"Bit of an intimidating room," I said, eyeing the perfect humans swanning around the beige, half-moon-shaped leather banquettes and leaning against wallpaper printed with enormous banana leaves.

"Nonsense." She pointed to a group of particularly striking young women in pastel colors. "Get closer, they all have fangs. So, tell me, whoever you are. Were you ill? Or perhaps in prison? What caused the bridge-jumping thoughts?"

"No," I said after a pause. "I wasn't ill. I just had children. Two of them in quick succession. I haven't been able to leave the house much these past couple of years, and my social skills withered."

"That sounds a lot like prison to me." She put her empty glass on a waiter's tray and reached into her bag. "If you need me to spring you from it, give me a jingle," she said, handing me her card. Then, as I was reaching for a drink, she winked and walked away. "I'm Katharina Edgeworth," I said into the air, but she didn't hear me. Alone again, I downed half the drink at once and looked at the thick white card I'd been handed. Faye Buckley Swan was indeed a lawyer.

I looked for Kip, but he had disappeared. I finished my drink in two more swallows, not the least bit at ease alone. What I'd said to Faye Buckley Swan was no exaggeration. I truly did not know how to mingle anymore. At the medical gala, Mrs. Morgan had taken pity on me. But no woman here looked a day over forty.

For an hour I wandered in and out of various rooms, all buzzing with excitement because Ingrid Bergman was rumored to be on her way. I tried to figure out what the party was for, besides to gawk at Bergman, but was told by a waiter only that it was a "studio party." I tried to speak to another woman who was on her own, but she walked away as soon as I smiled at her, having sized me up as not remotely famous.

Two hours later, I saw Faye again. I rushed over to her, dress in hand, this time fueled by six or seven cocktails. I grabbed another as I homed in.

"Hello, lawyer," I said, trying to place my hand on her shoulder. I missed and nearly put it down her dress instead.

"Hello," she said, looking me up and down. "How did you get so drunk in such a short amount of time?"

I opened my mouth to answer and she held up her hand. "Never mind, don't answer. I forgot what it's like to come to a party—especially one like this—and not know a soul. You have to settle for the company of Jack Daniel's."

"I'm a gin drinker," I said. My whole face buzzed. Even my eyes were tingling.

"Old Tom, then," she said, looking at my glass.

"I'm married to an old Tom," I remarked. "I mean, my husband's name is Tom. I suppose he's not that old, though he acts rather old sometimes. Then again, so do I. But I'm not really that old, am I? How old am I?"

"I don't know how old you are, but I do think you're quite amusing. And you seem happier than when you walked in."

"I'm Katharina Edgeworth. Rina to people who don't like four-syllable names."

"It is a bit long," Faye said, considering it. "Parents might as well have named you Rachmaninoff."

"That's my brother's name," I said, raising my glass.

"It isn't!" Faye exclaimed.

"No, it isn't."

"Ah. Well, Rina, you're an amusing drunk. Tell me, do you live here? Or are you just in Los Angeles to visit that ghastly man you were with and his wife?"

"His sister," I replied. "No, not his sister. He didn't marry his sister. She's Old Tom's sister. And Old Tom thinks I may be in the throes of a nervous breakdown, so he sent me here."

"Are you?" she asked, her face lighting up.

"I don't believe so," I said, looking at my hand holding the drink, as if for confirmation one way or the other. "Not at this precise moment, anyway."

"And why does he think you are?" she asked.

"Because I'm a mother. And sometimes I'm not very good at it."

"What were you before you were a not so good mother?" she asked.

"I worked for the United Nations."

"But no nervous breakdown there?"

"None at all."

"Only stimulated nerve endings, I hope," she said with a wink. "Wait!" she exclaimed. Look! There she is. Ingrid Bergman. She's really here!"

I turned to look where Faye was gesturing. Just fifteen feet away was the actress of the hour, beautiful, room-commanding, effervescent Ingrid Bergman. She was wearing a dress the color of snowflakes, and she floated through the room, flanked by two young men, parting the crowd with her electric smile.

"She's here!" I squeaked. I was not a woman who squeaked. But seeing a Hollywood star made me squeak. Or perhaps squawk. I'd had so many drinks, I'd lost control of my mouth.

"Come, let's get closer," said Faye. She started walking slowly toward Bergman, and I followed, until I found myself just steps away from her. She was like gravity, and I couldn't fight the pull. Suddenly, I was right in front of her. I smiled, feeling the heat of her fame radiating off her. I took one step closer and then somehow tripped over the hem of my very long dress. As I fell, what was left of my drink flew into the air.

"Ingrid!" I heard someone scream. "Are you all right?" I tried to pick myself up, but suddenly there were hands all over me, pulling me away.

"Get her out at once!" I heard a man's voice say.

"Please! Let her go. I'll take her home. Leave her be!" It was Faye. She put her arm around me and walked me out of the room. I closed my eyes, not wanting to comprehend what had happened, which, if my sloppy mind was functioning at all, was that I'd spilled a gin and soda on Ingrid Bergman.

When I opened my eyes, Faye was pushing me into a car. We took off with a screech of tires. "Are we going to the jail?" I asked.

"Pacific Avenue in Venice," she replied. "That's where you just told me to go. Is there a jail there?"

"Yes," I replied.

That was the last word I remembered saying.

When I woke up the next morning, the hangover I'd had the day I'd left Gerrit bleeding in Central Park felt like child's play. I crawled to the guest bathroom, blinded by the California sun, and forced myself to throw up. I took a shower, then after standing in the hallway for five minutes, terrified, I walked downstairs with utter dread.

"Look! It's John Wilkes Booth," Kip exclaimed as I walked into the kitchen. I was holding the wrapped presents I had brought for the Rowes. It was a ridiculous thing to do, to choose that moment to give them the gifts, but I had no other idea of how to proceed.

"I did not shoot Ingrid Bergman," I said quietly, placing the boxes on the counter. "I tripped on Arabella's dress."

"You might as well have shot her," said Kip, watching me climb onto a high-backed wooden chair. "At least that takes precision. Falling down drunk just takes stupidity."

"Are you all right, Rina?" Arabella said coldly, her voice sounding just like her mother's. Her hair was wet, and her cheeks were pink. She'd clearly been busy swimming while I'd been busy retching.

"I'm extremely embarrassed," I replied. "Mortified. I don't know what happened. One minute I was walking, a bit excited perhaps, and the next minute—"

"Look," said Arabella, interrupting me. "You're a disaster, Rina. That's quite obvious. I didn't want to believe my brother when he said you were acting irresponsibly. You know I've always liked you. Even when my mother wanted to have a hit man bump you off when Tom proposed, I stood up for you."

I didn't say anything, unsure whether Arabella was kidding.

"But you're exhibiting extremely manic behavior, just as Tom said. When you were here in the afternoon you were meek little Rina, scared of her own shadow. And then at night, you're a wild drunk, the life of the party, until you spill your drink on an Oscar-winning actress and then all hell breaks loose."

"That's completely untrue. I was—"

"Kip told me everything," she interrupted again. "And it's classic manic behavior. I was a psychology major at Stanford, I know all about it. What you exhibited last night was excessive involvement in pleasurable behavior."

"Kip didn't even see me," I said quietly, in the voice Arabella had just called meek. "He left me by myself. He was busy speaking to some utter—"

"I did nothing of the sort," said Kip, scoffing. "I was with you until you were too intoxicated to be around and not lose face. That's when I left you."

"I know I drank too much, and I'm sorry," I said, ignoring the bald-faced lie. "I'm just not very good at being alone at parti—"

"Just stop, Rina," said Arabella. "I don't want to hear any more. Have you always been this way? A manic alcoholic? Were we just not seeing it? And how exactly did you work at the United Nations with so many highs and lows? Isn't it all about being peaceful over there?"

"Peacekeeping," Kip interjected.

"Same idea," said Arabella, waving him off.

I looked at them both. Tall and proud, having grown up in a world molded around their desires. Arabella Rowe hadn't worked a day in her life except in the swimming pool. The rest of the world called that kind of effort leisure.

I took a deep breath and swallowed the bile back down. I pressed my fingers into the bruises on my hips and stared at the Rowes.

"I was very good at my job," I said loudly.

"You have a new one now," Arabella snapped back, as if her brother were feeding her lines via sibling ESP. "How about you try to be good at that one?"

"Let's just hope it doesn't make the papers," said Kip, picking up the glass milk bottle and pouring a drop in his coffee. "And if it does, let's pray that for Tom's sake they use your maiden name."

"Why on earth would they use that when they could use Edge-worth?" Arabella said.

"I'm going to pack," I muttered, heading upstairs. "I'm sorry that I caused such a commotion. It was not done on purpose. I'm sorry I embarrassed you and Tom."

When I got back to the guest room, I closed the door behind me and imagined myself sprinkling gin on a Hollywood darling. So what if I had? The world was still turning. I wanted to get away from a society where a few drops of gin on a starlet's dress were akin to the

Hindenburg disaster. I looked at the beautiful room, the ocean view. No one ever took chances in the Edgeworth family. Arabella's biggest rebellion had been swimming. It was all so conventional, so safe. So she'd chosen backstroke over necking with boys from Collegiate. What a revolutionary.

I filled my suitcase and walked out the front door without saying goodbye. When I got to the airport, I went straight to a pay phone and inserted dozens of quarters. I didn't need to look at the paper in my pocket for the number. I spoke to the operator, and she patched me through. The phone rang six times and then a man's voice answered.

"Lee Coldwell?"

"Yes," he said, his tone hinting of recognition.

"This is Katharina Edgeworth. I'd like to help you."

CHAPTER 14

The deli was on the corner of Amsterdam Avenue and West Eighty-seventh. I was to wait outside. There would be a pyramid of canned herring in one window, a display of smoked fish in the other, and a drawing of six sturgeon on the storefront. If there were no sturgeon, it was the wrong deli. At noon sharp, Lee Coldwell would pull up in a blue Pontiac with a small dent in the passenger door. I was to smile and wave, as if I were greeting my husband, quickly open the door, and get inside. We would start driving, and then he would tell me "what was what."

It had all sounded so simple when I'd called from Los Angeles, despite the distance and my jitters. I had hung up the heavy receiver of the pay phone feeling less like the failure that all the Edgeworths thought I was, and more like someone dependable. Even a bit important.

I spent the flight back to New York marveling that I hadn't let the piece of paper with Lee Coldwell's phone number on it disintegrate completely and had even summoned up enough of my old courage to use it in time. When the stewardess straightened her blue hat and came down the aisle to inform us that we were approaching Idlewild, I finally forced myself to reflect on my time in California. I thought about the disaster at the Beverly Hills Hotel. And about facing my husband in the aftermath.

I was ready to see my boys again. I hadn't missed them desperately, as Tom was so sure I would, but I did want to be with them again, to hold them again. They, at least, would still love me despite the Bergman fiasco.

I knew the look Tom would give me as soon as I walked into the apartment: exhausted disappointment, his expression du jour. Without having to utter a word, his face would say, "You, Katharina Edgeworth, are a woman who behaved like the town drunk in front of the who's who of Hollywood only a few weeks after nearly letting her son get run over in Central Park, then fleeing the scene like a bank robber. You should be stripped of the Edgeworth name and all benefits that come with it—the Iberian ham at Christmas, the twice-yearly invitation to the Vanderbilts' in Old Westbury, and certainly that flawless Cartier diamond on your left hand."

As the plane bounced across air pockets, my stomach turned sour, the sound of the ice cubes clinking in my glass of Coca-Cola making me feel sicker. But when I saw the lights of the sprawling metropolis below me, of incomparable Manhattan, I felt a rush of excitement. Perhaps my meeting with Coldwell would amount to nothing. FBI men like him probably asked ordinary citizens for small favors all the time. Informants, that's what we were called. In fact, I knew they did with at least some regularity because there was a big fuss in the papers a few months back about an informant in the Labor Youth League. He had reported to the FBI for nine straight years. And Joseph McCarthy, the man of the hour, had last year paraded FBI witnesses in Congress who were informing on communist cells in General Electric plants. The *Times* made these men out to be heroes. And who would say no when asked? Two wars within a decade had injected us all with a shot of patriotism. Even though the horrors were behind us now, I certainly still felt that charge of love for my country. Becoming acquainted with the workings of other governments at the UN had not changed that. But it wasn't why I'd said yes to Lee. He surely thought that was the case, and I would let him think it. He wouldn't understand that what I wanted was a day with a "to do" on my calendar. Something besides wiping children's bottoms with a gentle but effective touch or reading *Pat the Bunny* so many times I was ready to shoot said bunny.

When I got home, Tom hadn't expressed exhausted disappointment as I'd predicted. Instead, he'd been livid. The Ingrid Bergman disaster had not only made the California papers, but in *Daily Variety* they'd run a photo along with a surprisingly long article, stating that Bergman had "feared for her life as a woman lunged at her." Toward the bottom they'd speculated that I was most likely a "deranged fan." The only plus, Tom had said, recounting Arabella's distraught phone call, was that in the photo you couldn't see my face because it was pressed into the floor. They'd also repeatedly called me "the drunk guest," instead of Mrs. Tom Edgeworth. *The* drunk guest. As if I'd been the sole alcohol-fueled reveler surrounded by good Christians sipping chamomile tea. What was the solution? Tom had shouted. What were we to do? When had I become an irresponsible alcoholic— not just a negligent mother, but a public embarrassment? He could see it in my face, he'd said. The traces of my behavior. I looked puffy, my expression vacant. Where was the love of his life?

"I'll see a doctor," I'd replied, crying, holding the boys to me, relishing their toddler smells and laughs, even their cries. At that moment I forgot that Gerrit seemed to be vying for the title of America's worst-behaved toddler.

As I'd kissed them, Gerrit had hugged me, his little arms soft and comforting around my neck. He'd kissed my cheek, and then said, "Mama 'bandoned baby Gerrit."

I'd looked up at Tom, horrified. "I'm gone for seventy-two hours and he learns the word abandoned? Where did he hear that?"

"I don't know!" Tom had snapped, his shirt creased and in need of a wash. "It's most likely instinctual."

"Oh, of course it is," I'd said, hugging Gerrit with all the love I had left in me. I had done many things, but I had not abandoned my children. I'd practically been wearing them like a straitjacket since they were born.

Tom just stood there, watching me as if I were a chemistry experiment that might turn green, froth over, and explode.

"I'll get help," I declared, standing up. And I meant it. I knew I did need help. I wasn't a deserter and I wasn't an alcoholic, I just found that gin on the rocks was good company when the boys were asleep. I also knew what I needed didn't involve a doctor, or even a plan to dry out. The first step to my rehabilitation was following through on my promise to meet with Lee Coldwell. A medical appointment was just a good excuse to be alone.

"The doctor can see me at noon tomorrow," I'd told Tom the next morning. "Could Jilly watch the boys?"

She could, Tom had replied without bothering to call his mother. She could stay a few hours if need be. Yes, I'd said. The appointment would include not just a physical examination, a poking about at my puffiness, but a thoroughgoing mental assessment as well.

Tom had recommended a doctor with Lenox Hill hospital rights, but I'd found one on my own, I told him. A woman. I would be more comfortable with a woman, I'd said, my voice cracking. He hadn't pressed.

The day of the meeting, hours after Tom had left for work, and after I'd finished polishing silverware for guests that would never come, I'd taken off my apron and rubber gloves, climbed into Gerrit's bed as he napped, and held him to me, laying him on my chest just as I did the morning he'd been born. I'd put my face and nose against his neck and kissed his soft, chubby cheeks. My breathing was slow, my pulse lowered. Then I did the same with a sleeping baby Peter. In that moment, they felt like everything to me again, because in a few hours, they wouldn't be.

· · ·

Six sturgeon. I counted them again on the sign as my watch read 11:56. At noon precisely, I saw a blue car emerge from behind a green and white city bus and change lanes. It was a Pontiac Chieftain with whitewall tires, and in the passenger side door, there was a dent the size of a fist. When the car was fifteen feet from me, I plastered a smile onto my face and started to walk toward it with an air of confidence. When it stopped, I reached out and opened the door. It creaked slightly at the hinge, heavier than I expected. In one swift motion, I stepped in, gathering the skirt of my Balmain dress and pulling the door shut behind me. Relieved, I glanced at Coldwell and let my body sink into the padded upholstery. I looked in the rearview mirror to see if my hair was still all right, and then stopped abruptly. We were not alone. A light-skinned Negro man was sitting in the backseat. Somehow, I hadn't spotted him from the curb, too focused on the passenger door and its dent. He did not acknowledge me.

"You made it," Coldwell finally said, after we'd turned left on West Eighty-seventh, his eyes on the street. The city outside was loud with midday traffic, but inside the car the only sound was my pounding heart.

"I'm glad you decided to come," Coldwell added flatly as he turned right on Riverside, picking up speed.

The man in the backseat was looking out the window at the gray water of the Hudson, not at me. He had a stocky frame, good posture, and was wearing a navy-blue suit with a knit tie and a white dress shirt, nicely cut and fitted. I should have been paying attention to where Coldwell was heading, asked him questions, but I kept staring. Finally, the man turned his head away from the river and glanced at my reflection in the mirror. A chill raced up my spine.

"Good afternoon, Mrs. Edgeworth," he said quietly. His voice was low, with a distinctive rasp.

"Oh, right," said Coldwell, swerving to miss a large pothole on Riverside. "Excuse my manners. They seem to have departed a few years ago." He cleared his throat. "Mrs. Edgeworth, meet Turner Wells. Turner, you know all about Mrs. Edgeworth."

"Hello," I said quietly.

Turner Wells. I repeated the name in my head a few times. It felt like one that had been carefully inscribed on birth certificates for generations. But "all about Mrs. Edgeworth"? The way Coldwell said it made me feel laid bare, like a little girl playing spy or assassin with her brothers who is then assigned the job of making cold-cut sandwiches and iced tea for the boys.

"Turner here is embedded with the Civil Rights Congress—a heavily Negro organization. They're communists shrouded as some civil rights legal aid group. They defended and funded CPUSA during the Smith Act trials in 'forty-nine. Heard of them before? Mostly Negro and Jewish lawyers, though they've even gotten a damn Vanderbilt involved. Frederick *Vanderbilt* Field. Poor fool. Those Reds allegedly don't care about money, but I'm sure they're happy to strip him of his gold coins. That ring any bells?"

"A few," I said, raising my eyebrows at his description. I had read about the CRC in the papers over the years. I knew they were a legal defense group with chiefly lawyers among the top ranks, both Negro and white. And that they defended both Negroes and whites too, particularly Negroes on trial for controversial or most likely bogus charges, or white and Negro communists who had been caught, well, being communists. I remembered the Smith Act trials most clearly.

"They've got a big presence in Harlem. That's where Turner spends most of his time. But he's agreed to help us today."

"I see," I said, though I didn't yet understand what any of this had to do with Jacob.

"None of this is to be repeated," he said, not even glancing my way. "But you don't seem like a person who needs to be reminded."

"None of this will be repeated," I replied. I didn't have the courage to ask for further explanation.

Coldwell rolled down his window. "Nice day," he said as we slid into standstill traffic around 110th Street.

"Might be nicer if we made Mrs. Edgeworth less nervous," said Wells from the backseat.

I met his gaze in the mirror.

"Oh," said Coldwell, sounding surprised. He glanced over at me. "Are you nervous?"

"A bit," I lied.

"So, Turner here, he's agreed to help us. And the woman I mentioned before, the one who is running classified government documents up from Washington to New York for Gornev every few weeks—remember?"

"I do," I said evenly. He might as well have asked me if I remembered my own name.

"As I said, we've been watching her, and we're almost sure that she's about to sail to Russia this summer. From what we've been able to put together, she's going in July and is preparing for that trip now, staying in New York, and going to Washington less. So, in a perfect world, I'd like Gornev to take one look at you, confirm that you're in the party, and take you on for that work. He runs her, so he's the one to replace her. She's an attractive woman, you're an attractive woman. In my head it all makes sense, but I recognize that the odds are bad. Nearly impossible."

I let his words sink in, too anxious to be flattered by his compliment. "I thought the point of today was for Jacob and I to have a conversation. To get reacquainted. Isn't it a bit ambitious to start scheming about the nearly impossible?" My body thrummed with nerves. I felt like Coldwell was either making up his plan on the fly, or he was offering me a crumb when he really wanted me to eat an entire cake.

"I dream big," he replied, his eyes on the road. "But also, I had an idea. Not a terrible one, but we will see."

Coldwell reached down for his Lucky Strikes and tried to light one while maneuvering the Pontiac. When he'd succeeded in lighting the cigarette, he blew out the match and held it until it was cool. Then he put it in his pocket. I couldn't help but enjoy watching his ritual.

"Here's the thing," Coldwell said, his dark eyes focused in front of him. "The odds of this whole thing working out are extremely slim. Razor-blade slim. But that's how we operate. So, if this first conversation you're to have with Gornev goes well, and maybe your friendship with him reignites quickly, I'd like the next phase to happen fast. But like you said, you're not a communist, you have no history of communist activity—besides unknowingly sleeping with one in college— and you've married into a family of green-chasing capitalists. Some of these things are easily managed. We can give you a history in the party. Have our people on the inside pretend they've known you for years. Have you attend a few meetings. But your marriage, not so much."

"Marriages are a hard thing to manipulate," I replied.

"So I've heard." He sped up as soon as traffic started moving and cut in front of an old Buick. "Though it's convenient that your husband is a doctor. Big heart, all equal under the Hippocratic oath and all that."

"And all that," I repeated, letting my eyes flick back up to the rear-view.

"Mrs. Edgeworth," Coldwell said, letting his hand that held the cigarette dangle out the window. "After our telephone call, I couldn't sleep. You're not the only one in Manhattan who has trouble with that," he added, glancing at me. "And I thought: What if you were already doing the thing that he needs doing? What if you were—or Jacob believed you were—moving sensitive documents from Washington to New York for a communist group?" He paused as he passed a slower car. "Which brought me to Turner here. American Reds. And not just any group, but the CRC. Like I said, they claim to simply fight for equality in the courtroom, and that the Russians just happen to be supportive of them, but aren't actually involved. But they *are* involved. When they gave the CRC money to support the legal fund during the Smith Act trials, Jacob was involved, we're certain. Then they awarded Paul Robeson the Stalin Peace Prize like he was some martyr in Leningrad. Had W. E. B. Du Bois present it to him, of all people. And I'm sure you remember the We Charge Genocide disaster at the UN in New York and Paris?"

"I do," I said, surprised that the memory hadn't come to me before. "The CRC wanted to hold the United States accountable for genocide against Negroes, correct? The General Assembly was in Paris, and I'd very much wanted to go, but I was extremely pregnant and my boss preferred that I resign instead of running off to Idlewild."

"That's right. December 'fifty-one. Petition went to the Commission on Human Rights. Claimed that the American Negro is suffering from genocide because of our government policies, that we have 'deliberate intent to destroy them.' The U.S. press did a good job ignoring it, except for idiots at the *Chicago Tribune*, but it caused a damn big stink in Europe. Still, besides publicity tricks like those funded by both the Soviets and rich white donors like that Vanderclown, the Soviets aren't all that clued in to what the CRC is up to. That's what Turner says, anyway."

I waited for confirmation from the backseat, but Turner Wells remained quiet.

"'Course, the only documents that would be of interest to the CRC are papers about them specifically. Records outing men like Turner, they'd love to get their hands on something like that. They also want to know if their names are on any lists. There's been a big push in the American Communist Party to join the CRC, to help give it leadership, help keep it alive. So, they all want to know if the FBI is on to them. Also, whether any of their big-name members are due to get blacklisted like Paul Robeson. That's what the CRC wants, right, Turner?"

"I'm sure they wouldn't mind all of that," he said.

"Here's what I think," Coldwell continued. "You and Turner are seen together by Gornev today. You're talking, you're happy, maybe it looks more than friendly. You're speaking in a way that could inspire some assumptions. You make it look like you're accustomed to working closely together. Who knows what else?"

I looked at the floor, not letting my eyes go anywhere near the rearview.

"Gornev, he'll be damned surprised to see you, Mrs. Edgeworth, but there will be an extra layer to his shock, considering whom you're walking with. Then, if all goes right, he'll invite you for a drink—perhaps a meal—and the two of you will speak. Afterward he'll make contact with Turner—someone he knows already—and ask about you. Check you out."

Wells was looking out the window again, his expression distant.

"Turner will mention that not only are you in the party, you're also very sympathetic to the cause of the American Negro and you've been helping him for over a year. But in the last few months, now that your children are bit older, you've gone back and forth to Washington a few times. The FBI has been trying to shut the CRC down for years, saying they're a communist front organization, and they know that Hoover has his foot on the gas now. Turner can tell Gornev that he's afraid there are informants among their ranks, which of course there are, and that the Subversive Activities Control Board is inching in."

Coldwell fell silent, and I realized that we had driven all the way to Washington Heights, the trees growing denser as we moved farther north into Hudson Heights.

I, like everyone else reading *The New York Times* every morning in 1954, saw the word Red on practically every page. Russian Reds, Red China this and that, control of Red unions, warnings about Red teachers. The Subversive Activities Control Board was formed by our government to find and stomp out the Red threat in America, from schoolrooms to boardrooms. Russia was tightening their fists around us by the day, our president kept repeating. And if we women liked our dishwashers and our television sets, we better fight against the threats to our freedoms.

"From whom am I supposedly getting these documents from?" I asked finally, trying to absorb Coldwell's logic.

"We'll say that a Negro man, a janitor in the FBI building, is bringing out papers for Turner."

"And the story is that I've been the one carrying them from Washington to New York?"

"That's it, Mrs. Edgeworth," said Coldwell, as if he were speaking to a child who had finally put the round peg in the correct hole. "That's the story."

"Okay," I said quietly. "But why would I take such a risk? That's not just a small risk, right? That's a very big risk."

"Because of how much you care about the injustices against the Negro people. You worked at the United Nations. Cavorted with people of all colors. You grew up in a liberal household, your parents loved Roosevelt. They're even Europeans. It fits with your profile, it's convincing. Lots of liberal white people have been helping the CRC stay alive since it was founded."

"The Vanderclown?"

"Not just the Vanderclown. You ever read *The Maltese Falcon*?"

"Once, in high school."

"The damn fool who wrote it, Dashiell Hammett, Dashiell *Hammer and Sickle* to us, was running their bail fund for years. We got him thrown in a West Virginian prison and it's now ruined his career."

"So because the author of *The Maltese Falcon* is a member of the CRC, supports them, it is believable that I would be, too?"

"There's tons of these idiots. Hammett's woman, that playwright, Lillian Hellman, the one that penned the play about the lesbians—"

"*The Children's Hour*?"

"Yes, that one. She's involved too. Her idiocy has also cost her her career."

"So you want me to be one of these idiots."

"Exactly," said Coldwell. "What the CRC needs more than anything is money to bail people out. You've got money, you're a card-carrying Democrat, and you had an affair with a member of the United Nations Haitian delegation. That's more than half of your story right there, and we didn't even need to fabricate it."

"What does that have to do with anything?" I asked, feeling even more laid bare, blushing as I tried to do a mental check of every man I'd ever shared a bed or a backseat with.

"I'm not saying anything to embarrass you, Mrs. Edgeworth. What I'm saying is that your profile fits our needs. And if you're willing to take some risks in life, then you might also be willing to carry papers on national security matters to Jacob Gornev—and let me reiterate, that's the goal."

Suddenly, it all seemed enormous. The men in the car, how much they already knew about me. Even the trees around us. The city. What I had been asked to do. The lies I had told Tom to even get this far. Everything except for my courage.

I closed my eyes, willing the enormity away. I felt terrified, and too insignificant to be tasked with such a thing. This wasn't just a conversation. It was pretending to be sexually involved with a stranger, then slyly convincing someone—someone who I actually *had* been sexually involved with—that I was couriering government documents for a communist front group, and while I was at it, might he want me to carry a few up from Washington for the Russians? Not to mention convincing a communist that I, a woman who lived in one of the most expensive buildings in Manhattan, was a hero of the civil rights movement, fighting not just for equality, but mass democracy.

I thought about all the things I'd wished I could change this year. How I was not at the UN to translate the Convention on the Political Rights of Women, which I had been following so closely in the papers since 1952. How I couldn't be the interpreter for discussions on the continued fighting in Vietnam. How I had no money of my own to put in the New York Stock Exchange, which was humming along nicely. My lonely existence on Fifth Avenue. The day it had hailed. Feeling inadequate next to Carrie's gentle but effective mothering. The afternoon Gerrit fell. His warm saliva hitting my cheek. In just a few years I'd gone from a modestly important cog in international diplomacy to a toddler's spittoon.

No longer. I did, in fact, care about the injustices against the Negro people. And I cared about injustices against America, too. Why shouldn't I take part in stopping them? Why should I be reduced to serving boys their sandwiches, boys both big and little? Why should I be reduced to being a simple housewife? What if I really were the perfect person for the job?

"When will we be running into Jacob?" I asked.

"Let's see now," said Coldwell, turning the blue car onto an exit in sleepy Hudson Heights as he checked his watch. "In about an hour. Best to just get on with these things, I think, especially considering your restrictive schedule."

"Right. That little problem," I responded dryly.

I looked out the window, at the picture-perfect day. I had imagined these rendezvous took place only when the sun was low in the sky and the gloom effect was high, like the night I'd seen Coldwell outside my window, before I knew who he was.

"Maybe Mrs. Edgeworth and I should have a conversation first," Wells said suddenly. "Alone. Before we go off and try to convince Jacob Gornev that we are closely acquainted. Might be good if she didn't forget my name in the process. Know a little about me."

Coldwell rapped his fingers against the steering wheel.

"That's a fair point, Turner," he said. "But not in this neighborhood." I looked out at the sidewalk and saw a well-dressed white woman walking her groomed poodle.

Coldwell turned the Pontiac back to the Henry Hudson Parkway and drove fast down the island, not slowing until we neared the exit for 135th Street in West Harlem.

"This all right?" he said.

"It should do," said Wells.

Near City College, Wells pointed to a silver-fronted drugstore, green neon lights a bit farther on.

"I'll buy Mrs. Edgeworth a cup of coffee," he said. "If she's okay with that."

I nodded.

"Right," said Coldwell, pulling over. "Coffee, then. Don't be long.

Like I said, we see him in an hour, as long as he doesn't linger at lunch. Or it was an hour. Now it's less."

Wells got out of the car and opened the door for me. Coldwell got out, too, leaned against the car door and lit another cigarette.

Turner Wells was about five foot nine, built like a wrestler, and walked with his toes slightly pointed out. He gestured to the drugstore and together we went inside. He nodded at the young Negro waitress who greeted us by the door, and she took us to a booth in the back, away from the other patrons, at Wells's request. All of the staff, and all the other patrons, were Negroes.

"Coffee?" Wells asked. He took two of the paper menus that were resting between the salt and pepper shakers and handed me one. "And maybe something to settle your stomach."

"That sounds fine," I replied. "My stomach could use settling."

Wells looked down at his menu. "The first meeting I ever attended with the CRC was not easy. My stomach needed a lot more than just a sandwich."

"But you succeeded."

"After a lot of reflection, I did."

The waitress brought us two glasses of ice water, then wiped her hands on the striped apron covering the pressed blue skirt of her uniform and said she'd give us some time to look the menu over.

"I've only met Lee twice before," Wells continued, holding the well-worn menu up. "And both times he told me he was bad with women. I didn't really believe him. Thought it was just small talk. But he is terrible with women."

"He's a bit rough around the edges," I said diplomatically.

"Sandpaper."

He hid a smile. "I have interacted with Jacob quite a bit. Like Lee alluded to, he was helping the CRC with Benjamin Davis, a Negro communist, during the Smith Act trials in 1949. Extremely behind the scenes, of course. I wasn't there yet, but he came back to us last year to offer funding and to meet with William Patterson after the CIA and FBI started really pushing to shut us down. On those occasions, Patterson let me in the room. And I often left the room with Jacob, my friend."

"Your friend."

"Of course."

"But Lee approached you about this."

"Let's say we've been talking. Jacob told me that his woman, the courier, is heading to Russia. He wondered if I had any ideas about a replacement. I passed that question on to Lee."

The waitress checked on us, and we ordered coffee and cold ham and cheese sandwiches.

She came back with our coffee and Wells gestured to the pot of cream in front of me. I poured in a drop and watched it snake through the liquid. I took a sip, even though I knew it would be too hot. It burned my tongue, but as with the bruises on my hips, the pain came with a rush of relief, reminding me I was alive.

"I think Lee is even more nervous than usual. I suppose we all are these days. The Russians are crawling around everywhere. At the FBI, we're all scared they'll flip our country, public opinion, our agents. But even without the paranoia that comes with the job, Lee is gruff stuff."

"I take it Mr. Coldwell is not married," I said, after another swallow of the coffee.

"He isn't. He's married to the bureau."

"Are you?" I asked quietly, barely looking up.

Wells nodded.

"Married? Yes, I am. With five children."

"Five?" I said, my voice rising in shock. "No, you don't. That can't be."

"I do," he said, grinning. "Four boys and a girl."

"And you still have time to do this?" I said, gesturing into the air.

"Someone has to feed us all." He reached for his sandwich, which had just been placed on the table.

"Five children," I repeated, imagining four more Gerrits. How was it humanly possible to take care of that many children and live to see the age of forty, which is roughly how old I took him for?

"I don't have a favorite," he continued. "Unless you count Jane, then I suppose she's my favorite."

"Of course," I said, smiling wider.

Turner Wells was not bad with women.

"I suppose I should tell you more about me, about the CRC. But, like Lee said, it goes without saying that this is to stay between us."

His expression was serious, but not intimidating.

"Okay," I replied quietly. "Yes. As I stated in the car, I hope I'm a person who can be trusted."

"I'm sure you are."

He took a sip of coffee and kept his hands around the white ceramic cup.

"For the last three years, I've been a loyal member of the Civil Rights Congress. A leader, I suppose. I helped William Patterson with the United Nations appeal that you remember. I've also traveled south to work with our chapter in Louisiana. I protested the execution of the Martinsville Seven. And a lot more. It's been four years, and somehow my cover hasn't been blown. But it could be any day. We've got an informant in Western Pennsylvania, a former coal miner, who I'm worried about."

"The whole time you've been with the FBI, you've been with the CRC?"

He nodded. "To be clear, it's not exactly a communist front group, it's just that the FBI is convinced that it is."

"It's not?" Lee had seemed certain of that fact.

"It's complicated. Many members of the CRC also belong to the Communist Party. That's true. But much of what they do is good, necessary work. I wouldn't say that out loud to Lee Coldwell, but I'll say it to you. It's legal work that no one else is doing, especially down south."

I took a sip of coffee, the heat in my throat feeling stronger than usual.

"Now, if they were just defending Negroes in the South, taking on legal battles, providing representation, giving money, making noise, the FBI wouldn't be that interested. But since they also defend communists, we're very interested."

"Is it hard? Pretending to be one of them?"

"I'm doing my job," he said when he'd swallowed his bite of sandwich. "This is what Negroes in the FBI do. For the most part, we're sent to report on our own."

"Is this all right then?" I asked.

"This?" he said, looking around us.

"If someone saw you here. With me. Would this be all right?"

"What? Me eating a sandwich with a white woman?" he asked, his eyebrows raised.

"Yes," I said, suddenly feeling it was a very stupid question.

"It's all right by me if it's all right by you."

"It is. Yes. Of course."

"On the very slim chance that someone in this drugstore knows about me and the CRC, which they don't, I would just say you're involved. Coldwell is right that white people are involved. Everyone he named and dozens more. A white woman lawyer, Bella Abzug, she worked for us in the forties. Civil rights is not just a Negro issue, Mrs. Edgeworth."

"Yes, I know. I mean, yes, I agree," I stumbled.

He took another bite of his sandwich.

He smiled and said quietly, "I know you know. I know you agree. I read your file."

"Katharina," I said instinctively.

"What was that?"

"My name. Let's stop with the Mrs. Edgeworth. Actually, Rina. I prefer it when people call me Rina."

"Okay, Rina then," he said, finishing his sandwich. "Is that what I should call you in front of Jacob?"

"Yes. At Columbia everyone called me Rina, except for Jacob."

"I'd rather join everybody else than Jacob."

"It's still a tough thing for me to grasp. Jacob Gornev, a member of the Communist Party." It was, in truth, one of the things that made me the most nervous. I wondered if I'd soften too much when I saw him, if I would think of him as a Columbia student instead of an enemy. As a man I had once done a lot more than practice my Russian with.

"He's more than just a member," said Wells.

"If you're going to this much effort, he must be. But it's still jarring. He was such a delightful person at Columbia." I placed my empty coffee cup on the edge of the Formica table. "That's the strange part."

"People aren't simple. I'm sure he was delightful," said Wells. "And I'm sure some Nazis were a real belly laugh as well."

"Good point." I smiled. "I suppose that was an idiotic thing to say."

"No. It wasn't. Sometimes good people make terrible decisions."

"To say the least."

Wells left money on the table and gestured toward the door.

"Thank you for the coffee and sandwich. It helped, but I'm still terribly nervous," I admitted as we walked out. "All I've done for the past two years is be a mother. I don't know if I can even do this convincingly. I'm afraid I'll hurt you all rather than help you. A simple conversation feels not so simple to me, even with someone I know—or knew—so well."

Wells stayed quiet for a minute as the glass door shut behind us. "From what I've observed," he said, "mothers are pretty good at most things."

"Maybe your wife."

"Definitely my wife. Probably you, too."

"Do you enjoy it? I mean, what you do? Is this what you wanted to do as a child and all that?"

"Are you asking how they let a colored man into the FBI? And as a special agent?" he said, trying to hide a smile.

"No, I didn't mean it like that. I—"

"Don't worry, Mrs. Edgeworth. Rina. I'm still wondering about it myself. I'm only the tenth Negro they ever let play the game. So, let's go, you and me, and play the game while we've got the chance."

He opened the passenger-side door of Coldwell's car and I climbed in.

"Jesus Christ, there you are. I was about to drag you two out but didn't think it would look right. Did you all have a three-course meal? A digestif? We're tight on time now," said Coldwell. As soon as the doors were closed, he started driving fast and talking faster.

"Jacob just sat down to lunch. Eating with the delivery girl who's being restructured. Her name is Anne Palermo, but he calls her Ava Newman. All these comrades like to pop on some other identity when they pledge their souls to Russia."

"What does that mean? Restructured?" I asked.

"Nothing good for her, even if she thinks it's going to mean something good for her."

Coldwell parked the car hastily on West End Avenue and got out. He slipped into the phone booth on the corner, placed a quick call, and hung up without saying a word. A few seconds later, the phone rang.

I watched him speak into the receiver, his head bent. Then I looked in the rearview. Wells was watching him, too.

"Gornev's just finishing up at Vesuvius on Eighty-sixth. Some cheap Italian place," Coldwell said when he got back in the car. "I'll drop you at Eighty-fourth and you'll start walking up Amsterdam. Quickly. You want to run into him outside the restaurant. That bastard sure doesn't linger over linguini."

We took off in the car and raced down eleven blocks.

"Get out. Good luck," said Coldwell as he came to a stop. I looked at him, hesitating. He nodded at me in a way that was meant to be reassuring but fell far short. He took off as soon as I'd closed the door.

"It's just a simple conversation," said Wells as we stepped onto the sidewalk, our pace in sync.

"So I've heard."

Wells coughed. I looked at him but he wasn't looking at me. Ahead of us, I saw the sign for Vesuvius, illustrated with a very angry volcano.

"We should start talking again."

"Okay." I couldn't think of anything else to say.

"Maybe I'll talk, and you'll listen. But be sure to laugh a little, even if I'm not being funny."

I smiled.

"Better."

I tried to think of something to say, but Wells didn't let up.

"He is a very charismatic man."

"Jacob? Yes, he is."

"Are you angry that he lied to you?"

"I don't know," I said honestly, keeping my eyes on the restaurant. "I haven't thought about it that much. I suppose it doesn't feel like he was lying to me if he was lying to everyone. That was just his real life. A lie."

Wells slowed. "It was. But the tables have turned. Because now it's your turn to lie."

I followed his gaze. Coming out of the restaurant were a man, still easy to recognize as Jacob Gornev, and a beautiful blonde woman who had to be Anne Palermo.

She was wearing a dress the color of a tangerine. Some people would have looked ridiculous in such a bright shade, especially before the heat of summer, but it looked perfect on her. It was a sheath of light wool, tight on her curves, with a thin belt made to match and a hem that touched right below her knees. Her beige heels were low but fashionable, her hair waved, framing her delicate face.

"Speed up. A little. Laugh loudly. A lot," said Wells. "When's the hardest you ever laughed?"

"College, I think," I said, my steps quickening.

"Why?"

I smiled and shook my head no.

"Why?" he said again, now smiling with me.

"I can't tell you," I said, starting to laugh.

"Why not?"

"Because it's inappropriate. Banned-books levels of inappropriate."

"You're about to approach a communist spy on false pretenses. One you had a romantic relationship with. You think whatever it is you're remembering is the inappropriate part?"

"This whole day is inappropriate," I said. "But right now, I don't really mind."

Wells nodded and smiled.

"Keep laughing," he said. "He's about to notice us."

"Okay." I let out another laugh, but this time it felt forced, so I just tried to hold a pleasant expression on my face. I approached Jacob Gornev as if he were still a young man in his twenties, smelling of coffee and borrowed aftershave, standing in front of Butler Library waiting for me so we could go drink cheap wine in the student bars.

I could sense the exact moment he saw me. I pretended not to notice. But then he said my name, the words bursting out of him, practically singing in his Ukrainian accent.

"Katharina?" he said. "Katharina West?"

I felt genuinely jolted. It was so seldom that my maiden name was used now. Even my childhood friends knew me as an Edgeworth, knew that everyone wanted to be an Edgeworth over a West. But Jacob had no idea I'd married.

With surprise battling pleasure on his face, he came toward me. My heart pumped, exhilaration winning out over my nerves. Even though my memories of him had become far more complicated, I was happy to see Jacob. It was like time traveling to my days at Columbia—a time when the world was in turmoil, but I was perfectly at peace.

"Jacob Gornev!" I exclaimed. "I can't believe it. Is that really you? What a surprise. What an absolutely wonderful surprise."

He had the same lanky frame, the same dark eyes and hair, cut a bit too long. He wore a beige wool cable-knit sweater with leather elbow patches and a pair of respectable enough navy-blue trousers, which fell a bit too short over his brown loafers. He still had the air of a university student, even though he was pushing forty. His nose was pointier than I remembered and his two dimples, one on each cheek, were as enchanting as ever. On such a sunny day, his eyes looked brighter, full of life. He always had that way about him. As if he were uniquely able to take in more of the world than others could.

"Katharina," he said again, grasping my shoulders and kissing both of my cheeks. His smell was familiar, as was his grip—too familiar for me to feel any panic. But Jacob Gornev had been more than a friend. I could tell already that I would be too soft on him. This man did not seem like the enemy.

"Katharina West," he said again. "I can't believe it's you. I have not seen you for ten years. Is that right? Can it really have been a decade?"

"More than ten years," I corrected him.

"Wait," he said, suddenly looking at Wells. "What is this! I know this man you're with." His smile widened as he looked at Wells. He put out his hand and shook Wells's with gusto. "I was so focused on you, Katharina, that I did not see that you were with Mr. Turner Wells. What a small island it is. Katharina West with Turner Wells."

"How are you, Jacob?" Wells said politely.

"I'm very well. In shock, complete shock, but well. I used to be good friends with this woman," he said, looking at me with more surprise than pleasure now.

Wells nodded at Jacob's companion.

Jacob turned to her and grinned, seeming to have forgotten she was standing there.

"Yes, of course. I am rude. Ava Newman, you know Turner Wells, and this is Katharina West. They're a recent friend and an old friend."

"It's Katharina Edgeworth now," I said, smiling at Ava and extending my hand to her.

"Ahh, married," said Jacob, shaking his head. "*Eine Tragödie.* But how nice it must be for you. And your husband." He put his hands on my shoulders again and looked at me as if I had just returned from a very long absence, which I suppose I had.

"You look the same, Katharina West. You do. Happy and beautiful and intelligent. I assume you're still more intelligent than I am. I'd be disappointed if you were not."

"In that case, of course I am."

"Of course you are," he said, laughing.

Happy, beautiful, and intelligent. Those were certainly not the words that came to mind when I considered myself these days. Manic, as Arabella had said. Drunk, as the Los Angeles papers had claimed. Unreliable, as my husband constantly repeated. Jacob was seeing a former version of me, but I didn't mind. I missed her terribly.

"I was just headed home," said Wells pleasantly. Easily. As if he were floating through Manhattan on the back of a breeze. "Rina, thank you for lunch." I smiled at him. Of course he had remembered to call me Rina.

"It was lovely," I replied earnestly. Nerve-wracking, but lovely.

"Jacob, good to run into you. And Ava, nice to see you again, too," he said, bowing his head slightly toward her as he backed away slowly.

"I'll telephone you, Turner," said Jacob. "We can have a drink, yes?"

"Yes," said Wells, smiling. "I'd like that." He walked off. I watched him go but turned back to Jacob before he'd rounded the corner.

"Lucky me, alone with two beautiful women." He looked from Ava to me.

"A drink, then? While we're on the topic?"

"Not for me. I have to be off, I'm afraid," said Ava, her voice full of New England money. Up close she looked as if she'd grown up on a regimen of country club crab bisque and tennis matches. "Thank you for lunch, Jacob," she said. "And lovely to meet you, Mrs. Edgeworth. I hope to see you again soon."

She smiled and walked away, looking absolutely nothing like a communist. But maybe that was the point. Jacob was far too smart to send a woman in a gray, functional sack with a hammer and sickle in her purse on the morning train to Washington.

Jacob didn't watch Ava go, but I did. It was hard not to look at a woman with that much presence.

"Katharina West," he repeated. He eyed me up and down and back again. I'd worn a low-cut dress with a flouncy skirt in dependable navy blue that emphasized the good and hid the bad. It seemed to be doing its job. "I still can't believe it," he said, taking a step back as if I were an abstract painting that required decoding. "Have you been in New York all these years, Katharina? Was the island so cruel as to keep us from each other? Or did you run off back to Germany? Or Switzerland, was it?"

"Switzerland—Fribourg—but no. I've been in New York all this time. As tempting as the world is, New York always convinces me she's better."

"That's because she is."

Jacob took a step closer to me. One more, and his body would be nearly touching mine.

"Then what happened? Why did we lose touch? Things didn't end badly between us, did they? I seem to have only good memories." He gestured for us to start walking. "I'm going downtown. Can we walk together for a while?"

"I was just heading home."

"Where is home?"

"A few blocks south and east. Fifth Avenue and Sixty-third. Near the Central Park Zoo."

"Ah, I see," he said, grinning, showing off the slight gap between his straight front teeth. "You live in the zoo. That makes perfect sense to me. You spoke every other language, so you had to learn to speak hippopotamus."

"I think I live in another kind of zoo."

He nodded and said again, "Remind me, please. Why did we lose track of each other, Katharina?"

"I'm not sure. I think perhaps life just happened. I married after Columbia, and I suppose that changed things."

"Ah, marriage. Of course it did. That's why it's not for me." Jacob stopped suddenly in front of an Automat. "Katharina. I have a better idea than you going home. You'll disappear into the zoo, the domestic zoo, and I might never see you again. You have just had lunch with Turner, and I have had a late lunch as well, but please say yes to a drink? I know a simple but very good place in the East Village. Do you have time? Do say yes."

"I do say yes."

"Good. Come, then. Let's find a taxi, and you can tell me all about this thing they call marriage."

"I can tell you all about that and more."

After Jacob flagged down a cab, we sat in silence for a few blocks, until we crossed the park. "I have a restaurant," he said as we turned on Sixty-fifth heading to the FDR Drive. "Truthfully, it's my uncle's restaurant, but I tell the girls it's mine. Do you remember it? Did I ever take you? It's on Second Avenue."

"No, you never took me," I replied, trying not to let my deep nostalgia for those college years pull me under. "You did cook for me, though. Sausage that tasted like a slice of heaven. And cabbage the color of eggplants. All sprinkled with vinegar."

"That's still what I cook. Everyone likes sausage and cabbage. Everyone."

"Does your uncle serve it in the restaurant?"

"Of course he does. And the cook makes it even better than I do."

"Then that's what I'll have."

Jacob laughed, reached for my arm and wrapped it around his. "Good, Katharina. Good."

I rolled down the window, thinking my nerves needed some air, but as soon as it was on my face, I realized they didn't. It was my elation that needed to be brought down. I had checked the first box. I was alone with Jacob Gornev. And being alone with Jacob had always held the smell of excitement. We'd first crossed paths in the spring of 1940, when America was not yet in the war and New York still had its glow about it. And like Coldwell had said, he'd been in love with me, and though I'd tried to fight it, wanting to be attached to no one during those years, that love had been reciprocated.

The cab raced down the FDR and we got out on the corner of Second Avenue and Ninth Street. Together, we walked into a charmless office building, my heels clicking on the lobby's cheap linoleum flooring. Paintings of small blue flowers in various stages of bloom hung on the wall of a long, narrow hallway. When I thought we were going to run into a dead end, Jacob opened a nearly hidden entry, and we descended a few stairs to a small foyer in front of a glass door.

"I have definitely never been here," I remarked. "I would remember nearly walking through a wall."

"That's my mistake. But I was lazy back then," he said, maneuvering around me in the small space. "Morningside Heights to the East Village felt like New York to Moscow. I preferred to stay in the neighborhood and eat Spanish chicken. Do you remember how much I liked that Spanish chicken? The food in that restaurant was so fresh there were clucks coming from the kitchen."

"That is not at all true. The only clucking came from drunk coeds."

"You remember it your way, I'll remember it mine. But I do know—and you can't argue with this—the spiciness gave me the strength of a hundred men. Or at least one and a half."

I rolled my eyes, and Jacob grinned as he opened the glass door. Before us was an unexpectedly large restaurant, given that we'd had to practically crawl through the air ducts to reach it. There were red leather banquettes on either side of the room, tables between. The floors were light-colored wood, the boards narrow and uneven. The middle tables were covered in starched pink tablecloths under glass toppers, each with a milk glass vase holding pink carnations. Wooden chandeliers with electric candles hung from the low ceiling, and decorative plates lined the beams.

"It's a Ukrainian restaurant," said Jacob, dropping my arm when the door clanged shut. "In case you were not sure."

"It's called Vladimir's."

"Could be Russian."

"I do remember where you were born."

"What else do you remember?" he asked, his dark eyes looking right into my darker ones.

"A lot," I said honestly. "I think back to that time, to being a student at Columbia, quite a bit."

"Those untroubled days. Intoothant."

"Insouciant," I said, happiness lifting the corners of my mouth. "But I remember. That's how you used to say it at Columbia."

"Intoothant." He started laughing, throwing his head back with delight. "I said many things incorrectly back then, and you never seemed to mind."

"Of course not. Languages are meant to be reinterpreted."

Jacob caught the eye of a waitress, a petite blonde with hair like a pretty, flaxen helmet, and pointed to the back of the restaurant. She nodded, and Jacob gestured for me to follow him. It was a day for the back corners of restaurants, it seemed.

"Let's sit here," he said, pointing to a booth by a large mirror, the bottom corner slightly cracked. "Then we can check if we have food in our teeth."

"I thought we were just drinking," I said as I slid into the comfortable booth and looked around. The other patrons varied from a few fashionable women to what looked like casually dressed students. Most were speaking Ukrainian or Russian.

"Yes, but this is your first time at our restaurant. We can't drink without eating a little something. The sausage and cabbage you've been yearning for? Or roast pork? Fish in bouncy yet delicious gelatin? Borscht? Potato pancakes?"

"Maybe just dessert."

"Just dessert," he said, eyeing me curiously. He leaned back in the red booth. "All right, then."

The waitress came back with menus and glasses of water and he ordered two vodkas, mine on the rocks, and three desserts.

"Sochniki," I said, smiling after Jacob had squeezed it in the middle of his orders for nalysnyky and hombovtsi. "I don't think I've eaten that since I had it with you in that little Ukrainian place in Queens. Remember, we went there for breakfast a few times?"

"Katharina," he said, letting his hands drop on the table. "It sounds like your life has gotten dramatically worse since college. Plus one husband and minus sochniki. How are you still with us?"

I lifted my glass of water and murmured dryly, "I ask myself that question daily."

He laughed. He might not have had he known how much truth there was in my answer.

The maître d' came to deliver us our vodka, Jacob introducing me as "Not Russian, or Ukrainian, but able to speak Russian like a native."

"More like a curious visitor," I said in Russian, happy to still be able to converse in the language.

Our waitress came back with the desserts, touching Jacob's shoulder affectionately after she placed the three dishes on the table.

"They treat you as if you own the place," I said, digging into the sochniki, the golden dough and sweet cheese yielding easily to my fork.

"Only because I'm better-looking than my uncle," he said, shaking his head when I pushed the plate his way.

"This is delicious," I said, reaching for more.

With the sweet taste of the sochniki in my mouth, I felt like a completely different woman from the one I had been that morning. Was it because Jacob was just as amusing as he'd always been, or was it because I was not just eating dessert, but inhaling the sweet taste of freedom along with it?

"I'm thinner than him, too," Jacob said, patting his stomach. "For now."

I laughed with a mouth full of cake.

"I'm not declaring myself a motion picture heartthrob, Katharina," he said, watching me. He was pleased that I was pleased. "It's just that my uncle is quite fat."

"You can declare yourself anything you'd like. Our waitress thinks you're a heartthrob."

"Well, if she only has my uncle or me to choose from, then yes. I win every time," he said, putting an entire piece of hombovtsi on my plate. "It's like a rigged game of poker. Plus, I jog in the park." He put his fork down and mimed a runner's arm movements.

"Must be nice. But not as nice as living at the zoo."

"Of course it's not." Jacob put his fork down and picked up his drink instead. "We should spend days together doing nothing but remembering. Remembering how we met because you fell down the steps of Low Library."

"Butler Library."

"Was it?"

"It was. And fell seems like a significant exaggeration. I think I just dropped a book. Maybe two. Maybe my dignity. Okay," I said, laughing. "I fell."

Jacob laughed, too, then reached out and put his hands on my shoulders.

"Katharina West. Katharina, Katharina. I'm so glad I saved you that day."

"I don't remember being a girl that needed much saving."

"Oh, you weren't. You had it all figured out. Especially New York. You were my world-class tour guide. Uptown, downtown, upside-downtown . . ."

There's something about being in a room in very close proximity to someone you've already had sex with. Great sex with. You know your bodies work together and that knowledge is hard to ignore.

I looked down at my hands and reminded myself that the FBI was not interested in flashbacks; it wanted the here and now.

Jacob leaned back again. "But we both know all about the past, don't we? Instead, let's talk about *this* Katharina Edgeworth. What did you do after you abandoned me in 'forty-one?"

"Abandoned you? I believe you have that reversed. You were the one who graduated in 'forty-one. You said you were going to Moscow."

"Did I? Well, my apologies. For abandoning you, that is."

"Accepted," I said, keeping my body close to the table, ready for Jacob to reach out to me again.

"What did you do after Columbia?" he asked after finishing his bite. "Tell me how you've spent these lost years. And you can end with how you became acquainted with Turner Wells. Seeing you with him was quite a surprise."

How did I become acquainted with Turner Wells? It was a legitimate and disastrous question, one which neither Coldwell nor Turner himself had prepared me for. I managed to nod and started chewing very slowly, to buy time. After swallowing, I reached for my water, downing half of it. "Delicious, but quite sweet."

"That's the thing about dessert," said Jacob, his voice calm. The joy that had radiated from him since we'd spotted each other had disappeared. "It's predictable. It's always going to be sweet."

"Nice. That continuity."

"Sometimes. But you. You were never predictable."

"Me, well, I suppose we should pick up where we left off," I said brightly, still having no idea how my story would end. "After Columbia I became a secretary, then a translator." I was tempted to start from the day of my birth, so I could build my fake narrative, but my gut told me that was pushing it.

"Italian translation, yes?" said Jacob, pulling the plate away from me and plunging his fork in as if we were old friends breaking bread together, which I supposed we were. Though now I was an extremely nervous friend.

"A little Italian. A lot of French. But mostly German. It was the middle of the war."

"For the government, then," he remarked. "The American government."

"For the local government, actually. City Hall. At first, anyway. But then for the United Nations. Only French for them. I started there in 'forty-six, soon after it was founded. Needless to say, no German was required."

"Do you work for the United Nations now?" he asked, his voice even. Too even.

"No. I left when I was pregnant," I said.

"Ah," he said, a little less evenly. "That is what it's like in this country. America does not approve of mothers holding on to employment."

My boss at the United Nations had in fact asked me to resign at the end of '51 when I'd gone from showing to looking like I might give birth in the hallway. He'd asked me why I hadn't resigned already. He'd called my appearance "distracting." I could have told him that I was planning on it, but instead I said, "I will leave, but only so I no longer have to work with you."

The waitress walked to our corner with a coffee for me. I hadn't had any of my vodka, and she must have noticed.

"I really don't remember that your uncle owned a restaurant," I said, trying my best to steer the conversation elsewhere. I thanked the waitress but didn't touch the coffee. The nerves I thought I'd left uptown were back, and caffeine was the last thing they needed. I glanced around. "But I like it very much." I wondered if Jacob even had an uncle in New York, or if that was just his longtime story, his front.

"I'm glad. So, you no longer work. Pity, for someone like you. Tell me about your husband, then. Who is the man you married? He can't be as charming as me. Or Turner Wells."

He was certainly not dropping the thread to Wells.

"Depends on the kind of charm one finds charming," I said, reaching for another bite of dessert. I put an enormous piece of hombovtsi in my mouth to stall.

"There is only one kind, Katharina," Jacob said, finishing his vodka. He put his hands in the center of the table and leaned toward me, exchanging my coffee for the vodka. His hands looked dry and worn, the hands of a man who did more than push papers in a shipping office for a living. "You're either charming or you're not. Like you're either pregnant or not, dead or alive. There is no in-between with charm."

I nodded, hoping that I looked thoughtful instead of panicked. "My husband . . . well, he is charming, then. Tom Edgeworth. He's a doctor, a surgeon for children at Lenox Hill Hospital."

"A noble job," he said, leaning back again and gesturing to the waitress. "Not charming, but noble."

"What is a charming job?" I asked as the waitress filled his glass with more ice-cold vodka. She'd certainly applied more red lipstick between trips to our table. "Working in your uncle's restaurant? Running your uncle's restaurant?"

"Running? Yes, I keep it busy for him. I have another job, a serious man's job in international shipping, but this one is far more charming. Of course. No business needs charm more than this one. If your hosts aren't charming, the food won't taste as good and you won't want to return. Then your business fails. Simple as that. Charm runs the world."

"I thought it was money."

"Maybe a little of both, unfortunately," he said after he'd had a swallow of vodka. "You're very droll, Katharina. Very funny. Were you this funny at Columbia?"

"I think I was funnier," I said honestly.

"You're funny now. Still funny. And!"

"A little charming?"

"Very charming," he countered.

I picked up the vodka. I knew I shouldn't have any, that it was just about the worst idea, especially when I was supposed to be at a doctor's

office discussing my drinking habits, but I also didn't want to look as
if I were purposely trying to keep my wits about me.

I finished the vodka in a few thirsty gulps and put the empty glass
on the table. It was quickly refilled. My hand twitched, longing to pick
it up. I placed it on the coffee cup instead.

"Köstlich," I said, smiling. Delicious. "Do you find ways to use your
German? In international shipping?"

"Natürlich," he said, only half-smiling. "Now, tell me," he continued, leaning back comfortably. "How do you know Turner Wells?"
Christ. He'd come back around.

How had no one prepared me for such an obvious question?

"We were introduced by a mutual friend," I said, finally, not exactly
a lie.

"Who?"

"Hmm?"

"Who? I know Turner. Perhaps I know the friend, too."

Lee Coldwell. An FBI agent. I doubt you know him, but he sure
knows you.

"I don't think you would," I said finally. "It's a she, and she's Negro. I met her at work. At the United Nations," I added in a rush, my
conversation from the early afternoon winding into my mind like a
tributary I'd overlooked. Though I had not been in Paris for the petition, Turner was already undercover with the group in '51, and I was
still at the UN. It felt like an entirely plausible story. Perhaps the only
plausible way we would ever meet, besides being thrown together by
the FBI.

"Do Negroes work at the United Nations? American Negroes?" Jacob asked. I could see his mental wheels turning, and they were track-
ing only too well.

"Not many. Our mutual friend worked in the mailroom. But I'm
afraid she met the same fate I did. Jane Eyre . . . ickson."

What in all that was holy was wrong with me? I was awful at simple conversations. The only woman's name I could come up with was

Jane Eyre and then I turned her Swedish. An American Negro named Jane Erickson. I should be beheaded by Hoover himself.

"Janie Erickson. Married name," I added. "She's a lovely woman, but I don't believe you'd know her." My mind was spinning as I tried to remember the UN mailroom and if any of the workers there were Negro women.

"You don't think I associate with Negroes?" said Jacob.

"I didn't say that," I said, reaching for my vodka and taking a long sip. "One thing I always liked about you is that you associated with all different kinds of people. Even me."

"Even you," he replied, finally smiling. "You're right, I don't have the privilege of knowing Mrs. Erickson," he said, steady again. "But I remember Turner being quite passionate about certain causes when I first met him. Ones that reached all the way to the United Nations."

"He still is," I said quietly, my mouth warm from the vodka. "Passionate about important causes. As am I," I added, my voice quieter still.

"Here's to the unexpected," Jacob said after a long pause, lifting his glass.

"To the unexpected."

"Well."

Lee Coldwell's voice was as flat as ever, as if he were unacquainted with question marks.

"Mr. Coldwell, this is Mrs. Edgeworth," I pronounced. I had just left Jacob, declining his invitation for dessert to move backward into dinner.

"Yes, I assumed as much. How did it go."

"Well, very well," I said, my whole body warm from the vodka and adrenaline.

"He liked you? He wants to see you again? Gornev?"

"He does," I said confidently, though I had no idea if it was true. "No set plans, but he now has my telephone number and address."

"Good."

"So we wait?"

"We do not. We push things along. Can you call me again? Perhaps tonight? I'll have some ideas by then."

"The later the better," I said, buzzing with excitement, alcohol, and worry.

"Ten?"

"Two."

"In the morning? Fine. Speak then. And thank you, Mrs. Edgeworth."

"Thank you," I replied firmly. It was the most genuine thank-you I'd uttered in months.

I stood in the phone booth after I hung up and thought about Coldwell's words. "We push things along." What did that look like? Was it one more drink with Jacob or straight to cocktails at the Soviet Embassy? I didn't know, but I also knew I hadn't felt this alive in months. Years. Whatever Coldwell asked me to do next, I would say yes. The alternative felt too bleak. It felt like agreeing to spend life facedown on the floor, unidentifiable, uninteresting, except for my expensive dress and my riveting failings.

Before stepping out of the booth, I leafed through the phonebook. When I found a promising option, I dialed the number.

"Park Avenue Florists," said a pleasant female voice.

"Hello? Yes. I'd like to send flowers to California. Is that possible? Good . . . that's right, Los Angeles. They are for Miss Faye Buckley Swan at O'Melveny & Myers. It's a law firm. A large bouquet. The color? I don't know. Something not too feminine. They're flowers, right, you do have a point. No, no, not a cactus. How about something blue? Fine. Grape hyacinth, that will do. Wonderful." I paused. "Actually, one more order for California. This time, for Mrs. Arabella Rowe at 2700 Pacific Avenue. Let me see, for her . . . what was that about a cactus? No. She'd send a firing squad. Let's just do roses. White. And when I say white, I mean white as snow. Not a brown spot to be seen."

I hung up the phone and stood a bit taller. I was a woman who did things, a woman with tasks—and not ones that involved staring wistfully at Tavern on the Green and attempting to keep two children alive for one more day. Feeling lighter than I had since my return from California, I headed northwest to the Gramercy Park Hotel, sat in the lobby, and asked for a carafe of water. I drank as much as I could, closing my eyes and thinking about the many times I'd been there before, consuming all types of things that weren't water.

Before leaving, I went to the powder room, rinsed my mouth out with soap, which nearly made me vomit, and reapplied my lipstick and rouge. The last person I needed smelling alcohol on my breath was Jilly. As wonderful as she was, she'd still rush back to the West Side to tell Tom's mother, and the news of my relapse would reach her son mere seconds later. Everyone in Tom's world seemed to possess a tin can telephone that stretched directly to him. The only one who didn't was me.

CHAPTER 15

Where Mama?" I heard Gerrit's voice as soon as I was in the foyer. "No baby Peter. Want Mama. Mama. Mama."

"Darling! Gerrit!" I called out as the elevator doors closed behind me. "Here I am. Mama's here. I had to go to the doctor today. I'm sorry."

"I want Mama!" he said, running to me. Jilly had the baby in her arms. He was trying to squirm out to reach me, too. She placed him gently on the floor and he crawled over to me.

"Did everything go smoothly, Jilly?" I asked, Peter warm in my arms and Gerrit hugging my legs as I tried to squat down to his level.

"It went just fine, Mrs. Edgeworth," she said, heading swiftly for the entrance hall and taking her coat from the closet. If she were on fire she could hardly have moved faster. "Did everything go all right with you?" she asked cheerfully.

Tom's mother had clearly not only informed her of my plans for the day, after being filled in by her son, but also asked her to report on my condition when I returned.

"It all went very well," I said smoothly. "I'm feeling much better. These women doctors are just wonderful. Terribly insightful. And quite modern. I should have consulted with one earlier."

"I imagine so," said Jilly. "I go to the Edgeworths' doctor. Dr. Schulman. Have done so since I started working for them twenty years ago. I've never had a lady doctor."

"I recommend it," I said, praying I looked like a woman with so much spring in her step she could touch the moon. "I feel not only cured in the heart, but in the head. And Jilly," I added, smiling sweetly.

"Yes, Mrs. Edgeworth?"

"I appreciate your checking on my health, I really do."

She nodded politely and clapped her hat hastily on her dark, pulled-back hair. "I'll be off then, Mrs. Edgeworth."

"Thank you for everything, Jilly." I looked down and reached into my purse for my wallet.

"Oh, no, Mrs. Edgeworth," she said, pushing the button for the elevator. She pressed it twice more for good measure. "Thank you, but Mrs. Edgeworth, the other Mrs. Edgeworth, already took care of it."

Of course she did.

"Jilly?"

"Yes, Mrs. Edgeworth?" she said as Ronald held the door open.

"Thank you for watching my boys. When they are with you, I don't worry. And it takes a lot for me not to worry."

I was well aware that when a woman left her children in another woman's care, it meant that the caretaker had to leave her own children, her own life. A woman was only allowed freedom if a poorer woman was employed to help her.

"They're good boys," said Jilly.

"Not always, but I hope the good outweighed the bad today."

"Of course it did."

She was most likely lying, because the bad outweighed the good for me on most days, too, but she was too kind to say so.

"How are your boys, Jilly? Is Mel still at Queens College?"

"He is," she said with a tired smile. "He's happy there."

"Good," I nodded. "I don't mean to keep you. But thank you for your help. Goodbye, Jilly," I said as the elevator doors began to close.

I dreamed of working again, salivated over the prospect of heading to an office, but I knew I was extremely lucky to have had the kind of work that I did. I wouldn't still dream of returning to work had I been Amelia Edgeworth's housekeeper or watching someone else's disobedient children.

"Mama, I hungry, Mama," said Gerrit, reaching for my hand and pulling me to the kitchen.

"What would you like, darling?" I said, opening the refrigerator. I looked at the clock in the kitchen. It was almost eight p.m.

"Ice cream," said Gerrit, reaching up for the freezer.

"No, darling. We can't eat ice cream now," I said, pulling him a few steps back.

"I want ice cream cone!" he wailed. "I want it!"

"Mama can make you spaghetti?" I suggested. He shook his head. "Or a sandwich? A delicious ham and cheese sandwich?"

"Chicken à la king?" said Gerrit.

"What?" I said. "How do you even know how to say that?"

He dissolved into laughter. "Ice cream cone. Chicken à la king. Ice cream cone. Chicken à la king!" I stared at him, a possessed toddler with the vocabulary of a chef at Le Cordon Bleu.

"What did you eat with Jilly, darling? Was it wonderfully fun to spend time with her? Did she teach you to say chicken à la king? Did she take you to the park? It was a very nice day outside. Did you push the boats on the little lake? Were you kind to baby Peter?"

"Don't want baby Peter, want Mama!" Gerrit screamed.

"Mama is here now, darling. *Je suis là.*"

He threw himself on the floor and drummed his legs. Then he flapped his arms around, his little hands smacking the floor with impressive force. It always surprised me how much strength a two-year-old had.

"Mama, Mama, Mama!" he screamed.

Though still clutching the baby, I felt my pulse quicken, the anger start to rise. Tom was gone for at least twelve hours a day, every single day, and the children were never like this with him when he returned. It was desperately unfair.

I closed my eyes and willed my temper to hold. After the success of the day, I would not scream back at Gerrit. I might never have another day like today. I would not let it end this way.

I walked out of the kitchen and put the baby in his wooden playpen, which Jilly had set up in the living room, and picked up Gerrit, holding him to me tightly, rocking him until my biceps hurt.

"Who is my baby?" I whispered once he'd stopped howling.

"Gerrit baby," he whispered back.

"Who does Mama love?"

"Gerrit baby."

I kissed him, letting my lips linger on his cheek. Then I pressed my cheek to his, his skin soft and bouncy and damp from my kiss. His smell was almost as sweet as when he was a baby. In these moments, he felt exactly that. My baby. My first baby. Terribly unruly, but with bursts of goodness that made me keep going, thinking there was a rainbow instead of a monsoon on the other side.

"Do you love Mama?" I asked quietly. If his answer was no, I knew I would surrender to the monsoon.

"Love Mama," he whispered. "Fire truck. Ambulance. Mama."

All the things he loved.

"I love you too, Gerrit," I said, my voice cracking.

After Gerrit was appeased enough to be put down, I picked up Peter, who wasn't crying but deserved as much love. He clung to me, pawing at my dress, and I reminded him that those awful days were over for good. My breasts were finally starting to understand their reprieve, as was Peter. I just hadn't told Tom yet. He was sure to be far less amenable than my breasts. Maybe I would add it to the growing list of things I wasn't going to tell Tom yet. Or ever.

"Gerrit?" I said when there were no more tears, no more pawing. "Let's walk and get ice cream. Why not?"

"Ice cream!" he shouted joyfully. It felt like a good stand-in for champagne to cap off the day.

When I had put the boys down, their sticky faces made clean and soft, I walked to my bathroom. I heard the elevator ding and Tom call out my name. Instantly unnerved, I hastily applied some lipstick and rouge, brushed out my hair, and swallowed some toothpaste.

When I entered the living room, I prayed that I looked the very image of a happy, hale, sober wife.

"There you are!" Tom exclaimed, flashing a smile. "I was hoping I'd make it home before you fell asleep. How was the consultation?" He had taken his suit jacket off and was fixing himself a drink, still in his white shirt and beige trousers but with his silk tie loosened.

"Frankly, it was terrifying," I said, deciding some things I said should be truthful. And the start of the day had been terrifying.

"Terrifying," Tom repeated, fishing an olive out of the jar and plopping it into his martini.

"But I got through it," I said brightly.

"I'm glad you did. But you don't have to face this alone, Katharina. We're going to get through it together," he said, walking over and kissing me gently on the lips. "We just have to remember that all this, even California and the embarrassment, they're just small obstacles."

"Sometimes they don't feel small," I said honestly.

"Well, they are," said Tom, stepping back from me and taking a sip of his drink. "Remember, Katharina, perspective. Today, for instance, there was a family whose child has been diagnosed with brain cancer and—"

"Tom?" I said, interrupting.

He gave me a tired smile. "Let me guess. You're sorry to hear it, but let's talk of something else?"

"Please."

"Okay," he said agreeably. "I'm glad it all went well. Did the doctor tell you to stop drinking?" He took another swallow of his martini.

"Reduce," I replied, watching him.

"And physically?"

"She said I was in quite good health. Could stand to lose a few pounds but society tends to rush mothers on that front and at my age, it's even more difficult." The latter part of that sentence I had stolen from an article in *Redbook* that I'd cut out a week before. I had to remember to burn it in the morning.

Tom nodded thoughtfully.

"I think you look wonderful," he said, and I could tell he meant it. Tom's views on motherhood were extremely rigid, but he was never anything but complimentary about my looks, even though I was heavier than when we met. "Perhaps you can just take longer walks with the children."

I stared at him, burning to suggest the same to him. I was sure his miracle-working surgeon hands had never touched our ever-so-modern Rolls-Royce of a stroller. Of course, his walks would have to take place between the hours of midnight and five a.m., which could lead to his arrest on grounds of kidnapping or insanity.

"Perhaps I can," I replied. "Though I very much enjoyed walking alone today. Even just to the doctor's office. It was liberating to be alone."

Tom eyed me as if I might be going mad, which perhaps I was.

"Where is she located?" he asked, changing the subject. "Your female doctor." He looked toward our Persian blue couch and, beyond it, to the living-room windows.

"Near your parents."

He nodded.

"Did you talk to her about the bruising on your hips?"

"The bruising?" I asked, my grip on my glass of water precarious.

"Did she ask if I did it?" he said, his tone suddenly grave. "Did she ask if I hit you? If I hurt you?"

"No," I said. The thought had never even occurred to me before. "I told her the truth. I told her I did it."

It was the first time Tom had ever acknowledged my bruises. And they had been there, in varying sizes, and stages of blue, green, and yellow, since Peter was born.

"And she said she can help?" he asked.

"She did."

"I'm glad. Please let me know if I can. Help, that is." He walked over to the windows and looked down. "I love spring in Manhattan. Life returns to the sidewalk. Even at this hour. I suppose no one knows that better than you."

"But I watch it from inside."

"You're outside with the boys all the time, aren't you?"

"I am. Of course. But I don't have time to enjoy the life on the sidewalk then. I'm too busy watching them, constantly worrying."

"It will get easier. Peter's nearly fourteen months now. We're almost through the weeds."

He turned around and walked back to the bar, depositing his empty drink on it. The kitchen was just ten feet farther, but it would never occur to Tom Edgeworth to put his glass in the sink. "It's time to start a new chapter, Katharina. As I said, let me know if I can help."

"I think, in this case, only I can help," I said truthfully.

Tom walked back over to me, his leg brushing against the other sofa, and kissed me again, harder this time.

"I suppose there are things that we must do alone. That's our nature." He touched my face gently and kissed me, this time slipping his tongue into my mouth. "But you're a rock, Katharina Edgeworth. You'll sort it all out." He kissed my neck and moved back up to my lips. "Let's go to bed."

"You go," I said, stepping away from him. "I'll stay up a bit."

"The Katharina hour," he said, without anger or judgment.

"Hours, usually."

"All right. Good night, then," he said, then kissed me lightly on the cheek and walked off.

The bruises. It was idiotic of me, considering Tom was not only my husband but also a doctor, to think he hadn't noticed them. But he saw me naked so seldom after Peter was born, as he was never home and I was constantly exhausted. I was also embarrassed, and afraid for him to see them, so I'd taken great pains to cover them. Now they were uncovered. It felt strangely liberating to have spoken about it. We hadn't addressed the why, but at least we'd discussed the what. Though, not surprisingly, Tom had wrapped up the subject quickly.

I walked to the guest bathroom on the other side of the apartment and took off all my clothes. I turned on the light above the mirror to make the small room even brighter and studied my reflection. My body was padded in places it never had been. My hips. My stomach, which in the unforgiving light, also had visible dimples. I stepped on the scale that Tom had bought me after I'd had Gerrit. A hundred and forty pounds. It didn't sound so bad, but the mirror told me that it wasn't just the weight, it was the alterations made by motherhood. The two bundles of joy had wreaked havoc on my frame. Some of the bruises on my hips were fading, others dark and fresh, but the general effect was of the markings of a madwoman. I turned off the overhead light. In the dim light, they looked better. Almost beautiful, like the dots of a Seurat painting. My body was not that of a hurting, unhappy mother. I was a piece of art.

I went to the guest room and lay down on the bed. Before the kids were born, Tom and I had spent so much of our free time in bed. Making love, humming along to the phonograph, eating croissants that fell apart and then cursing ourselves for the thousands of crumbs that we could never rid from the sheets. After we'd gotten engaged, our bedroom life was even more heated with the promise that it would be just us, forever.

When we first moved into 820 Fifth, I thought I would never go into the guest room. Now I spent much of the night there. It was where I hid, where I fought insomnia, where I cried, even where I had orgasms. Since I'd gotten pregnant, it had been that way. While I was pregnant, my hormones were on fire, my sexual appetite huge, my body even orgasming as I slept. I had almost no other outlet since Tom seldom wanted sex anymore. Now, on a night when he seemed to desire me, all I wanted was solitude.

The reality was that we still slept together, a few times a month, but it had changed. It was no longer what drove him. Since he had had children, what pushed him was trying to keep every other child in New York City alive. How could I argue with that? How could he let down all of those mothers?

When I was eight months pregnant with Gerrit, I finally left my job at the United Nations. But it hadn't just been because of my boss's snide comments. I left because for the first time in our marriage, Tom needed me quite desperately.

No one cared more about Lenox Hill Hospital or the outcome of his patients more than Tom Edgeworth. Maybe he cared too much. Perhaps the best doctors were bulletproof. Tom, I found out, was not.

In January of 1952, in the span of two weeks, three children died under Tom's knife, all girls under the age of ten. It had shattered Tom, and had almost ruined his career. Not because doctors were not allowed to lose patients, but because it was different with Tom. Had he, colleagues started to wonder, been given his position because he had also helped increase donations to the hospital by 200 percent?

We were living in 820 by then, having bought our apartment three months before, and the UN had finally moved all their operations to the gleaming Secretariat Building on the East River. We were out of our Park Avenue apartment, with its tiny balcony, barely big enough for one person and a plant, but we were still surrounded by too much coffee, too many piles of newspapers, and an old guitar hanging from the wall, which we both played badly. No designers had come in yet to make it look "worthy of an Edgeworth."

Tom was full of joy then, so happy to see me plodding around with my stomach leading the way. He still cooked, still sang "Take the A Train" as I got ready for work, "Hurry, get on now, it's coming. Listen to those rails a-thrumming!" a vestige from my LIRR days, since I was taking a taxi to Forty-second Street in my current state. Then came the deaths by three. I was at work when a nurse from the hospital called. Tom had told me about the first one himself, an extracardiac procedure where the child had died in the first hour. Now his nurse told me about two more.

"I don't think he's doing okay, Katharina. And people are starting to talk. The mother of the first girl, she's extremely unwell herself. She wants Dr. Edgeworth investigated even though it was a very risky, last-chance type of surgery. Will you come to the hospital? I think he needs you."

When I arrived, Tom was shocked to see me, and when he immediately left with me, I was the shocked one.

In a taxi for the five-minute ride home, he started to cry as soon as the doors were closed. I had never seen Tom cry before, and I never imagined that it would be with another person present when I did. I had the driver stop at Seventy-fourth. Tom took a moment to collect himself as best he could, and we walked to the Conservatory Water, where dozens were skating on the pond.

"You took me to a place with children, Katharina?" he said, starting to laugh through the tears, which had quickly returned.

"Shall we head to a bar instead?" I said, my eyes welling with tears, too, my heart aching for my husband.

"No, let's stay here."

I put my hands on his, my gloves gripping his cold fingers.

"These heartbroken mothers," he said after we sat in silence for a while. "They think I'm incompetent and I don't blame them. I don't. Of course they think that."

"You are the most competent person I've ever met. But you are not God," I said as we watched the children in knit hats skate in endless circles. "These were extremely risky surgeries, right?"

"They were all more than a stitch or two."

"Sometimes, Tom," I said, putting my head on his shoulder, "God decides, not you."

"But three times in two weeks, Katharina? Three girls? And now all the questioning. Part of me wants to never walk through those hospital doors again."

"But they need you," I said, looking out at the children skating on the pond. "The hospital needs you, the children need you, I need you, and our baby is going to need you. And love you. That's what you have to remember. For every angry mother, there are so many who are thankful. Who love you for saving their child."

"I never want to lose another one," he said, wiping the tears from his face.

"You will."

"Not before the baby is born."

"Okay, not before the baby is born," I said, holding him tight in my arms. We repeated the same line together night after night like a prayer, and I repeated to Tom that whatever happened in our marriage, or in his professional life, he could always depend on me.

"I know I can," Tom had whispered. "I know."

The hospital had Tom stay home for a week as they investigated the deaths. He was finally cleared of any wrongdoing, but his brain didn't seem to believe it. He spoke to colleagues, superiors tried to help him, his mentor, Jack Armstrong, took him out for a stiff drink and shared his own hard-earned wisdom. But eventually, it was Amelia Edgeworth who helped Tom find his purpose again.

One Saturday morning she came into our apartment holding a large, rolled-up piece of paper like she was an architect.

"Hello, Amelia," I said as she rushed right past me.

"Where is my depressed child?" she asked, looking under the dining room table as if Tom had morphed into a dachshund. "Where is that boy?"

"He's in the library. May I ask what you're holding?" I asked, waddling after her.

"It's a letter."

"Large letter."

"Large problem," she replied without turning to look at me.

The letter was from a little girl who had been Tom's first surgery patient at Lenox Hill. She was a year old at the time, but now was starting to write, and Amelia had gotten her to write Tom an enormous letter, which included a drawing of Tom cutting a child into sixteen pieces and sewing her back together good as new. It was somewhat macabre, but very effective.

"See, Tom," said Amelia, pointing to the drawing. "You saved this girl, and now she is clearly going to be the next Hieronymus Bosch. You have saved countless lives. Including this one. Look at what this child can do now! There's real talent there. Or at least imagination. Is she still taking drugs? For her affliction? Don't answer that. The point is, feeling sorry for yourself will do nothing but make the world a worse place. So change out of your pajamas, take a shower, and return to work."

"Tomorrow," said Tom, staring at the drawing.

"Today," said Amelia. "My car is downstairs, I'll take you there myself."

"You're driving?" said Tom, looking up at her, love and appreciation in his bloodshot eyes. "Just take me straight to the ER then, when I go into cardiac arrest."

In the two weeks leading up to Gerrit's birth, Tom found himself again, but after he became a father, his worry about something happening to his son seemed to reach an abnormally high level, even for a doctor. His anxiety emerged in strange ways, one of them his conviction that the baby should never leave my side. In fact, if I could just shove him back into my body, that would be ideal. "There is no one better equipped to take care of a child, to love a child, than their mother." I was to breastfeed Gerrit "on demand." I was to be attached to him, even when Tom was home to relieve me. "Reread Dr. Spock's book," Tom would say. "Revolutionary," he declared. But the person who needed to reread it was Tom. After the death of those girls, he set out to prove to every person at Lenox Hill—patients, administrators, drunks in the ER—that he was as talented as a mortal could be, and that his ascendancy at the hospital had nothing to do with his parents' donations.

"Enough with the money, Mother," he'd even said. "I'll wring it out of other people."

He set about working, and wringing, and I started my life with my child, Gerrit and Mama, joined together in our snow globe that was that winter in New York.

I propped myself up to look out the window. How many times had Gerrit and I pawed at our windows during the first few months of his life? "You can't go outside," Tom had said. "It's too cold, and the Chinese recommend against it. They're very smart about these things." The guest room window also had a view of the park. If we ever had any guests, I'm sure they would have appreciated it. My parents and brothers had visited when Peter was born, but that was over a year ago now. We'd had no one else since. Large apartments were civilized. They gave you space, room to think, Tom had said when we'd bought the place, and I didn't know any better, never having lived in one. I'd agreed, excited for the life laid out before me. But now I knew better: large apartments were lonely apartments.

CHAPTER 16

I woke with a start. It was 1:15 in the morning. How had I let myself fall asleep?

I tiptoed into the hallway, to my favorite window seat. The black and white striped cushion conjured up beach chairs in Nice or Deauville or some other grand place, and I pulled my legs up, letting my dress drop down so that it barely covered my upper thighs. Most nights when I sat by the window, I contemplated all the things I used to do that I could not do anymore, the throbbing world below that I no longer felt a part of. It was a world of girls fetching sandwiches and sodas, the laughter of friends around them and the jingle of lipsticks and subway tokens in their purses. A world of men who went after money during the day and looked for women to spend it on at night.

But tonight I wasn't mourning that life. Tonight I was thinking about guilt, the feeling that had been eating at me like a parasite, since well before I met Lee Coldwell. Guilt that I wasn't grateful enough for the existence I had, that I wasn't well adjusted enough to being a wife and mother. Guilt about my difficulty raising two perfectly healthy children. Tom felt no such guilt, even when he saw me crying because Katharina West was so long gone she seemed never to have existed. I needed to feel less guilt.

It had gone well with Jacob, I knew it had. So well that I hoped Coldwell would want me to see Jacob again. Or maybe Coldwell would have decided he needed nothing more from me. Either way, I'd had today.

Outside, a group of young people were walking down the sidewalk together, like a small parade. One girl wore a light blue duster coat that was swinging around her, reflecting her joy. A young man to her right, in a camel blazer, was singing loudly and another behind them was drinking out of a champagne bottle. I heard someone curse at them. The boys laughed louder, and they stumbled on, the drunkest of them taking a minute to get his feet under him. When the group had made it across Sixty-third Street, the sidewalk below me looked lonely again, with only one man left standing.

He had on a gray felt hat and a navy-blue overcoat. He was looking down at the concrete, his hands in his pockets. Who stopped to contemplate the sidewalk of Fifth Avenue in the middle of the night? But when he slowly lifted his head and looked at the building—at my building—I sucked in my breath, and held it.

Turner Wells was outside my window at nearly two o'clock in the morning, watching me.

I peered down at him, finally exhaling, shock and curiosity getting the better of me. Our eyes met. The nerves in my hands woke up, alerted my arms, my shoulders, my breasts, my legs. I gripped the windowsill, stopping short of pressing my face to the glass. After a moment, he touched the rim of his hat. I was sure I saw a faint smile before he turned and walked on, uptown.

When he was out of sight, I tiptoed into the hallway, my heart racing. How long had Turner Wells been lingering outside my building? Had he been there when Tom looked out at the park from the living-room window? Unlikely. That had been three hours before.

I thought of Turner Wells's gaze on me earlier. In the blue Pontiac. While we walked down Amsterdam Avenue. I thought of Jacob's eyes on me. The way he had lit up like a paper lantern when he'd spotted me outside the restaurant. How he had looked in his uncle's restaurant when I'd said "dessert." I had not felt seen by men since before my pregnancies. The change was electrifying, like taking a long, hot bath after years of lukewarm showers. I put my hand on my heart, relishing how hard it was beating.

At 1:45, I gathered my purse from the living room. The elevator would ding if I called it. Instead, I crept down six flights of the service stairs. In the lobby, Eduardo, the night doorman, looked up at me and nodded discreetly as I slipped out the front door.

It was a cold night and I could have used a coat, but I blended in better in only my dress. I looked as if I'd been out to a party, like the inebriated coeds, and was just heading home. Instead, I went to the phone booth on the corner of Sixty-third and Madison. I folded the glass door open, picked up the receiver and dropped coins into the telephone. I hadn't placed a call at two a.m. from a phone booth since my UN years.

The phone rang once. "Coldwell."

"It's Katharina Edgeworth."

"I know."

I didn't respond.

"I have a proposition for you."

"All right."

"I'd like you to attend a party meeting. One with a few CRC members. Today is May twelfth. The meeting is this Saturday. It's in a real hole of an apartment on 102nd and Third Avenue. Turner Wells attends that meeting. They change location every week, to keep, well, us, off their trail, but he moves with the same group. Some CRC members stay away from formal meetings, since they're still trying to fight that communist label, but not all of them. Including Turner. He'll bring you."

"But I can't get away on Saturday."

"Impossible?"

"Difficult."

"In my world, anything that isn't impossible is possible."

"Not in mine."

I heard what I thought was the sound of a match being lit.

"Mrs. Edgeworth, tomorrow I'll have a box of books delivered to your apartment, but they'll come disguised as a shopping parcel. Something nice. I'll be sure they arrive while your husband is at the hospital. The books, I'm sure you have assumed, will be communist literature. Things you would have already read if you were in the party."

"That sounds fine," I said, as if it were normal for Lenin's collected works to be delivered via a Bendel's bundle.

"Read them and then get rid of them," he suggested.

"All right."

"For the meeting, what if you brought your children?"

"Mr. Coldwell," I said slowly. "There is no faster route to Tom Edgeworth beheading me than bringing his children to a Communist Party meeting."

"I'll leave it to you, then," he said, his voice sounding tired.

"Just like you left it to me today," I said, not able to let that electric shock from the afternoon go. "I had to come up with my link to Turner Wells in two minutes since you all didn't provide me with one."

I explained how I had improvised and Coldwell didn't respond. "Fuck," he said finally.

"Is that FBI speak for 'sorry about the oversight'?"

"It is. And it won't happen again. Make the meeting if you can. Call me on Friday to let me know if it's resolved. If I don't answer, try this number directly," he said reading off a phone number. "It's for Turner Wells."

I reached into my purse and scrawled it down with a green crayon.

"And if Gornev contacts you before that, of course let us—"

"Mr. Coldwell?" I interrupted.

"Yes."

"I need a doctor's bill to be sent to my house."

"A what?"

"A doctor's bill from a female doctor's medical office. A reputable one with rich patients. And she has to be on the Upper West Side. That's where I said I was today. Could you have that done?"

"I could have that done," he said. I couldn't tell from his tone whether he was amused or irritated.

"Thank you. And thank you for sending Mr. Wells to check on me from the sidewalk. It wasn't necessary."

"I didn't send Mr. Wells to check on you," he said.

"I see." If Coldwell hadn't sent him, I didn't know why he'd come, but I knew immediately what I wanted the answer to be. That he'd come just to see me, as Coldwell had that day in the park. In a city of millions, me.

We both sat on the line in silence as I spun my wedding band nervously on my finger.

"Mrs. Edgeworth?" Coldwell's voice said, snapping me out of my surprise.

"Mr. Coldwell."

"Perhaps simple housewives are not so simple after all."

"Perhaps none of us are."

CHAPTER 17

Before I fell asleep that night, I put my rings on the dish resting on my dresser and picked up the picture of me in my Christian Dior wedding dress so cinched at the waist that there was barely enough room to drink a glass of champagne. I would not even be able to put the sleeves over my arms now, having weighed twenty-five pounds fewer that day. I looked decent enough in my current state, but lately the picture inspired more sadness than joy. It reminded me that I was a different woman now. Even with a few personal concerns about our future, I had been a very happy bride on my wedding day, surrounded by love and marrying my favorite human being at the Plaza Hotel. The venue didn't much matter to me, but it had been incredibly fun.

Despite Amelia Edgeworth being quite convinced that I was about to bring ruin on the family, our wedding plans had started off very well. News of our engagement had been given a quarter page in *The New York Times*, much to Amelia's great relief, and that seemed to set us on a lucky path.

"If it had been only a sixth or an eighth she would have just buried herself alive," Arabella, in town for the Red Cross benefit, had joked afterward.

"Luckily, Rina went to all those good schools and we could gloss over her family background," said Amelia, carefully cutting out the announcement. "And thankfully they didn't mention her early years attending PS 666 or wherever it was, Rina."

"That's the one," I said, smiling. "I had my horns sawed off right before I met Tom. Really got in the way of wearing hats. Devil worship is not a milliner's dream."

Kip and Arabella laughed, and Amelia said, "What a humorous bunch you all think you are," and took her clipping to one of the apartment's twelve other rooms to tuck it away.

"Where are you two getting married?" Arabella asked, pouring us all drinks.

"We're not quite sure yet," I said, accepting the gin and tonic with thanks. "Honestly, I was thinking we'd just do City Hall since I have such fond memories there. With your family connections, and my history, I thought we could even get the mayor to marry us in his chambers. I'd love that," I said, smiling at Tom.

"Rina," said Arabella, practically spitting gin on the floor. "Can you stop being such a rebel for one minute? Mother is finally ready to embrace you, and you want to get married at the laundromat. Why don't you just wrap a bedsheet around yourself and hold some wilting dandelions while you're at it?"

"Arabella!" Tom shouted. "You're clearly drunk. Please stop speaking like this before you truly embarrass yourself. Though I think we're past that."

"I'll do one better and leave," she said, standing up. "Let's go to the Plaza, Kip. If Mother won't get her wish to have Tom married there, the least I can do is throw some money their way."

"I'm sorry," said Tom when we were alone again. "Money does not buy manners."

"She did hear me say City Hall, right? And of all the places that need money thrown at them right now, I think the Plaza is very low on the list."

"She has a good heart," said Tom. "But sometimes her mouth betrays her."

"I'll try to remember that," I said, finishing my drink in three gulps.

That Saturday morning, I slept in, not even hearing Tom leave for the hospital. When I finally got out of bed, I saw that there was a large package on my dresser. I opened it. It was perfectly crisp D. Porthault bedsheets in bridal white. On top of them, lying on a piece of tissue paper, were some quickly wilting dandelions. I looked at the note placed on top from Tom. "Voilà. Your wedding dress. When a bride is as beautiful as you, she can get away with anything." I laughed and told myself once and for all that I was marrying Tom, not his mother or his sister. And that getting married could really be fun if I just let go of what Arabella had called my rebellion. Of course, I saw a wedding at the Plaza as all too much. But if that too much made people happy, then maybe it would make me happy, too.

A week later, we were back at the Edgeworths' for Sunday breakfast. When Amelia sauntered out, she sat next to me and said, "Sorry about my daughter. I believe it was the gin talking."

"Indeed," said Arabella, sitting next to her mother. "City Hall sounds very adventurous. You'll have to advise me how to dress of course, but I think it's very modern of you. I'm sure it will be quite fun."

And because I was so shocked to receive an apology from both Amelia and Arabella, I responded, "You know, I've considered it and I really would like to get married at the Plaza after all. It sounds like a dream. It's so generous of your family to offer."

Amelia was on the telephone before I finished speaking. An hour later, a package from the hotel arrived with the menu options. Amelia ran toward me, waving it, and pulled me down onto the couch, pointing to the drink list first.

"We'll serve Dom Perignon as the main champagne and Pommery & Greno as the rosé. Though perhaps we should get some Veuve Cliquot Ponsardin for the drunks. Your international crowd must lap it up and I don't need them drinking down bottles at eighteen dollars each. Filet mignon for one of the mains, though is that just overdone at this point?" she asked, looking at Arabella, who shrugged and went back to her chess game. "Now, guinea hens," said Amelia pointing to the menu. "That would be surprising . . ."

"One does not need surprises at a wedding," Arabella piped up.

"Fair point, darling. What about Philadelphia capon . . . truffled, that's good . . . Blue Point oysters, filet of herring, hearts of artichoke with vinaigrette, canapé of caviar à la Russe, aiguillette of bass . . ."

Amelia took a pen from the side table and starting marking the menu as I watched. After being beaten in chess by his sister, Tom came over and plucked the menu from his mother's hands.

"Mother, you've circled every item on the menu, including mushrooms on toast."

"Tom!" she protested, trying to take it back from him. "Don't discriminate against fungus. Rina is French, she likes that kind of thing."

"She's Swiss," said Tom, rolling her eyes. "You've also circled nuts and raisins. Will a bird be in attendance?"

"Now there's an idea, Tom," she said, tapping her pen on the menu. "I wonder if the Plaza allows peacocks? Oh, let's be honest, for the right price they allow anything. Just ask your father."

"One of everything sounds perfect," I said, smiling. Suddenly I didn't care if Amelia thought I was Canadian, I was getting married to Tom. At the Plaza! And with surprising guinea hens! I was beginning to like the idea, even if it came with a side of Amelia Edgeworth.

"Now what about flowers, Rina?" she said, looking at me. "In a hotel of seventeen hundred chandeliers, you really don't need much. I'm envisioning something sophisticated, Carolina blues. We really can't do white or pink because of your advanced ages. It wouldn't strike the right note. Tom will be thirty-eight years old. There are men who are grandfathers at that age."

"This isn't Plymouth Rock for heaven's sake. Thirty-eight is a perfectly modern age. And a fine age for a groom . . . or a bride," he said, catching my eye.

"I'm a youthful thirty-one," I reminded them before Amelia changed all the flowers to wilting cacti.

I let Amelia plan everything, down to my dress. And when I let it all go, I did have a wonderful time. A bride—me!—in Dior. Christian himself sent me a note, in French, of course.

The dress was exquisite, but the best part of the actual wedding day was being surrounded by everyone I loved. My family came from Switzerland, including my aunt Hanna. Friends from Vassar and Columbia were there; Ruby and Patricia, who lived in Los Angeles and Washington, D.C., respectively, came into town; even my friends from the United Nations came—including Marianne Fontaine, who had threatened to boycott on principle, but finally gave in to the promise of endless champagne.

Tom and I were married in the Terrace Room under Charles Winston chandeliers, surrounded by orchids and bouvardia. The reverend from St. Thomas Church did the honor, and I carried a bouquet of white stephanotis, bright and virginal.

"Let me guess, that witch mother said they'd turn scarlet in your hands," Marianne had joked when I'd gone through the plans with her the week before the wedding.

"Actually no, but now that you say it, they just might."

"Oh, enough. Stop listening to those who want to force women to ignore the presence of their own vaginas."

I laughed and covered my ears.

"We did have fun, didn't we?" she said, pulling my hands back down. "How sad it has to end."

But as I got ready to marry Tom that day, a tiny slice of sadness managed to crawl inside the Plaza's best suite, where I was getting dressed.

"I brought you a gift," Marianne said, watching the hairdresser wave my hair just one more time. I had asked her to be my maid of honor, but she'd refused, and the role of bouquet holder in a very nice dress had instead gone to Arabella Rowe.

"You didn't have to," I said, catching her eye in the mirror.

"Don't be an idiot, Rina, of course I did. Don't worry, I brought you and Tom a boring gift. It's some sort of Swedish vase. All the rage right now. But I brought *you* a real gift. Would you like to open it now?"

"Of course," I said, grinning.

It was the French edition of Simone de Beauvoir's just released sensation *The Second Sex*, or *Le Deuxième Sexe*, and it was inscribed to me from the author.

"How on earth did you get this?" I asked, fighting back tears.

"A bit of United Nations string pulling. Did I pull the right string?" she asked, watching me.

I nodded a very genuine yes.

"I just want you to remember the incredible woman that you are. Just you. Not Mrs. anyone but you."

Another nod, and more pushing back of tears.

It had been the right string, but it wasn't the right string for the day.

I knew that after I married Tom Edgeworth, his family, his career would always take precedence over mine. I'd never be able to pick up and move to Geneva for a few years so that I could work at the United Nations office there and see my family every Sunday instead of his. And when I got pregnant, I would have to leave my pass, my key, my everything for some new interpreter to have. I would have to dial Fieldstone 7-1100 for the last time and say that Katharina West, now Edgeworth, was thankful for her time but had left the building.

I smiled at my reflection in the mirror, letting Marianne's face blur behind me. I reminded myself that I was living a dream, a fairy tale. This was the American woman's best bet. Marry a millionaire, a handsome and kind one at that. A doctor, for children. Just six months prior, my brother Timo had lost his job when the architecture firm he worked for closed their Geneva office. It was quite a mess for him and his three children, and his wife ended up taking a job in the evenings in a restaurant until he found something again. I had grown up during the Depression. Economic stability, and then some, was not lost on me as a big check in the plus column. I needed more than that, of course I did, but Tom knew about the more. He knew *me*. He was compassionate. We would find our way together.

I silenced my worries and gulped down a glass of champagne with Marianne and Arabella, who shockingly got along just fine. But when I was ready to make my way to the altar, holding my father's arm, that small itch of doubt returned. Just being near him made me want to jump on an airplane and go to Europe for a long, long spell.

My wonderful father, whom I now saw so seldom, was born in Lausanne, the son of a mid-level executive at a sugar refining plant in Brooklyn. He moved to New York when he was seven years old. But despite being born to pragmatists, Swiss ones at that, he was always a self-described dreamer. Unlike his father, he'd obtained a Ph.D. in art history from Harvard. "I skipped the sugar part, just held on to the refined," he'd joked, sticking his nose up into the air and laughing. In truth, there was nothing snobbish about Sebastian West. He just found the magic in life through paint on canvas, and up until the war, he taught others to do the same at Hunter College.

The dark-haired Wests had been the Westens until the authorities at Ellis Island hacked off the two last letters, taking the name from German to WASP. At the end of 1946, my family had gone to live in Geneva so that my father could teach art history at a very prestigious boarding school in Rolle that paid him twice what he'd been making at Hunter. My mother, desperate to go back, had spurred the move. "I'm becoming too American," she'd said. My twin brothers and their wives had gone with them, thrilled for a new adventure, to immerse themselves in Europe now that Europe was safe again. It had always seemed possible that I would join them. But now they knew I wouldn't. Who could ever ask Tom to abandon the hospital, the sick children? I was sacrificing my old family for my new family.

Seeing my parents and brothers, speaking to them, smelling them, I remembered my desire to not only be near them, but to travel the world like they did. To experience art and literature and life like they did. We were a family who used a pile of books as a coffee table and had puzzles with dozens of pieces missing. A family that didn't have cocktail hour, just cocktails. A family who spoke many languages and ate a shocking amount of beige food. Northern Europeans have really perfected the art of beige cuisine. Cheese fondue. Beige. Rösti. Beige. Bündner Nusstorte. Beige.

Was I really ready to start my own family? Would they even like beige food?

I had expressed that concern to my mother when she'd arrived in New York a week before the wedding, and she'd said, "Katharina, don't be scared to lose us by making your own family. I'll always be here for you, even if I can't be *here* for you." But in that moment, it didn't feel like enough. My stomach began to retaliate, the flight response growing. I told my father to stop for a moment, so that before the doors opened, before I saw people like Mayor O'Dwyer in the audience, I could look for Tom. I knew he didn't think of me as the second sex. He saw me as his equal. And that was enough to have confidence in our future. In my life as Mrs. Tom Edgeworth.

As I made my way down the aisle, I kept my gaze trained on his, and anxiety left me with every step. After we'd said our vows, Tom leaned over and whispered, "I lovely smart love you." With those five words, all the remaining doubt melted away. Who wouldn't want to marry that man?

At the end of the reception, as it was nearing two o'clock in the morning, Amelia pulled me aside and kissed me on the cheek. Shockingly, her lips were not ice-cold.

"What a party," she said, smiling.

"It's better than a party. It's an *event*."

"It is that." We looked at the crowd together and she waved to the mayor. "Oh, before you retire upstairs, be sure to take a picture with the peacock, will you, Rina?" she asked, winking at me.

"I will, of course," I said, grinning. "That will be the feather in the cap of a perfect day."

"You're welcome dear," she said, leaving me with my champagne and mushrooms on toast.

CHAPTER 18

Hello, dear. How are you? We haven't spoken since the incident, have we?" Amelia Edgeworth's voice seeped through the line somehow much more loudly than anyone else's ever did on our telephone.

"We haven't," I said, not knowing if she was referring to the incident in the park with Gerrit, the incident with the gin and Ingrid Bergman, or the incident the night before, when I told Jilly bald-faced lies.

"It could have been worse, I suppose," she said breezily. "You could have shot her."

So it was Bergman. I was sure Amelia had heard the story from Arabella multiple times, and by this point it was probably inflated to hot-air-balloon proportions.

"I wasn't carrying a gun," I replied, wishing I hadn't picked up the phone. But I had no choice; it could have been Jacob Gornev. "All I had with me was a handbag."

"And a drink."

"Yes, and a drink," I responded. Amelia loved a good verbal shot.

"Arabella and Kip, well, they've been practically upside down with shock since the incident, and Tom—"

"And Tom what?" I interrupted.

"And Tom is gravely disappointed, but not dramatically so," she said defensively. "But oh, what a mess, Katharina. It's a royal disaster. It really would be so funny if it didn't involve someone associated with *my* family. If it were one of those dreadful Kavanaughs on the ground floor of our building—the ones with beady yellow eyes and an abundance of stenches—well, then I'd be lapping this up like soft ice cream."

"Associated with" her family. As if I came in every week to iron their money and dust off Arabella's trophies. As if I wasn't a mother to two of her grandsons.

"As I told Arabella, I'm just as embarrassed as a person can be," I said. "And terribly sorry, too. I hope all of you will forgive me for my misstep, my stupidity, eventually."

"Well . . ." Amelia's voice had softened. She loved it when people groveled. It was probably why she let her husband sleep with half of New York City's chorus girls. A grovel and a bauble from William Edgeworth, and all was set right. "Will you be coming to the apartment for drinks on Sunday?"

"Did Tom say we would be available?"

"Of course. He would never turn down his mother."

"Then, I'll be there, yes. With pleasure."

"Bring the boys, will you? My little potatoes. Too bad they didn't get more of your color. You've got that lovely island tan."

That was how Amelia described anyone who wasn't the color of chewing gum, as if we had all paddled to Ellis Island via Cozumel.

"The potatoes will be in tow," I said. "Good afternoon, Amelia. Thanks for the lovely chat."

"Was it?" she said, before I could hang up. "A lovely chat? I'm ever so glad you feel that way. You know, I for one don't blame you for drinking," Amelia continued, like a good functioning society lady alcoholic. "If I'd had no help with Arabella and Tom, I would have pitched myself off the Singer Building when Arabella was two weeks old. Popped on my mink, then popped myself right off. I think this mandated pioneer woman way of raising your children, with your breasts exposed and your life of solitude—is excessive. But Tom's the doctor, not me," she said, sighing. "And you seem to be getting by, except for the Bergman situation. So he knows best, I suppose."

"I suppose," I repeated quietly.

"Chin up, dear. And lay off the gin. Try switching to wine. It has less bite. Till Sunday, then."

The line went dead. I glanced at the far right corner of the living room. Against the base of a Japanese lamp was a large Bonwit Teller bag. Ronald must have brought it up while I was on the telephone. Inside it was a parcel containing *The Communist Manifesto*, copies of *The Daily Worker*, and other party literature.

I picked up the receiver and called Amelia Edgeworth right back.

"Amelia. It's Katharina again," I said. "After I hung up, I realized something."

"And that is?"

"That I'm very much in need of your help."

I knew there was only one person who walked the earth whom Tom did not lord it over, and that person was his mother. William was no use. Now that he spent every other afternoon twisted around some lover at the Plaza, Tom saw him as a man who had lost his backbone, no longer someone to take seriously. But his mother, he adored. It was why her absence when he was young had stung so much, and kept on stinging into adulthood. "Plus, she's always been the brains," he maintained. And he was right. So it was to Amelia Edgeworth that I'd made my appeal. I told her that I was lonely. That I was terrified that I might snap and that even the great Tom Edgeworth wouldn't be able to put me back together. That I was desperate to get out of the house. That if I spent all my time with babies, my brain would turn into a head of cauliflower. And then I threatened divorce.

"I'll send Jilly over every few weeks."

"Every week."

"Very well."

"Shall we tell Tom or not?"

"Not. And Katharina?"

"Yes?"

"You knock over another celebrity with a trough of gin in your hand, and it will be you receiving the divorce papers."

"Noted. I'll be sure to only frequent parties with hobos and drunks from now on."

"You're not as amusing as you think you are," she said, and hung up the telephone.

When the phone rang in our apartment on Friday, Amelia was just calling to check in with her son. She wanted to make sure we were all still on for Sunday brunch, and would Tom mind also serving as her escort to a Red Cross dinner at Bemelmans on Saturday evening? It was extremely important, and William was "occupied." Because I was listening from the phone in the bedroom, I heard Tom hesitate before responding. "Of course I can, Mother. I'm sure Katharina won't mind."

This time, I certainly would not.

When Jilly came to the apartment at six p.m., Tom was already out of the house. I had read the literature that Coldwell had sent me, dumped it in a bin in Central Park when I was playing with the boys in the morning, and was now dressed in some old clothes that I used for housework, covered up by a roomy beige raincoat. I didn't wear a hat or gloves and looked a mess from head to toe, which Jilly would surely report back to Amelia. But I didn't even mind; let Amelia Edgeworth judge. I was finally free.

When I left the apartment at six o'clock, I could hear the boys screaming "Mama" until the elevator passed the fourth floor.

"I'm surprised we don't receive more noise complaints," I said to Ronald as the elevator headed to the lobby.

"I don't think Sam passes up every message."

"You all," I said as I exited the elevator, "are the best thing about 820."

As soon as I was on the sidewalk, I saw Carrie approaching the building, a bundle of flowers in one hand, Alice in the other.

"Rina!" she called out, waving the flowers. "There you are. I haven't seen you in ages." I went up to her and gave her a hug, then leaned down and hugged Alice, too.

When I stood again, I noticed she was eyeing me strangely and I remembered that I'd donned my best proletarian look—a plain white shirt, with buttons down the front, and a pair of blue jeans, a bit stained with bleach and rolled at the cuff, and old penny loafers from my Columbia days.

"Where are you off to? And where are the boys?" Her shock at seeing me alone was evident.

"I'm actually having Tom's parents' housekeeper watch them for a bit. Jilly. I—I haven't quite told Tom yet," I stammered. "I need to see if it works out before I do. But Carrie, I was just so desperate to get out of the house, even for a little while."

"I think that's wonderful, Rina. As much as we love our children, we must also love ourselves."

"Is it love ourselves? Or just not lose ourselves?"

"Whatever it is," she said breezily. "One needs to be alone occasionally." She whispered the last line, as if she feared she might burst into flames or traumatize Alice for life with her words. "You aren't angry about anything, are you? I called just yesterday and no one answered. I'm going to have to start shooting you notes via the mail drop."

"I'm so sorry," I said. "Ever since I returned from California, I've been a bit overwhelmed."

"I've been dying to hear about your trip." Carrie grabbed Alice's hand tighter as the child tried to escape into the building. "Matt would never let me travel alone. He'd attach Alice to me with Scotch tape."

I wanted to tell her that it took me nearly letting Gerrit bleed out in a public park to make it happen.

"Was it all very glamorous?"

"Aspects of it certainly were. You know Tom's sister, Arabella? She's quite distinguished, but not quite the wild type. Though I did go to the Beverly Hills Hotel with her husband, Kip, and I did see Ingrid Bergman rather close up."

"Did you really?" said Carrie, grinning. "Now I'm terribly jealous and quite mad that you didn't come pound on my door to tell me the second you came home."

"I don't think we're allowed to pound on doors at 820."

Alice pulled harder on her mother's hand and started whining.

"Please stop pulling Mommy, Alice," said Carrie gently. "Mommy is finishing her conversation."

Alice did not stop pulling. Carrie started walking toward the front door, letting her toddler win as we all did.

"Do call on me, Rina. I miss you. I'm lonely lately. Maybe I should have more children to keep me company." She smiled, and not as brightly as usual.

"I'll stop by soon, Carrie," I said as she went inside.

I turned away from the building, and though it was away from the subway stop, I crossed the street and stood exactly where Turner Wells had been very early Wednesday morning. I shifted my weight from my right foot to my left, and as I did, a gust of wind wafted warm air past me. I could still sense him there. He was the kind of man whose presence lingered.

CHAPTER 19

I started walking north, to catch the Lexington Avenue line at Sixty-eighth. Inside the station, I sat down on the worn wooden bench in the middle of the platform and opened a copy of the *Times* that had been left there. The entire paper seemed to be painted redder than usual. The Geneva Accords and the extraction of the French empire from Vietnam. A Korean War prisoner convicted of collaborating with communists. The Army-McCarthy dispute had entered week three. A Red teacher had resigned. I studied a beautiful drawing of a mink coat, but even that was misleading. "President of the Fur and Leather Workers Union convicted today of having falsely denied he was a Communist Party member; penalty up to five years in prison and a $10,000 fine," according to the article below. The head of the fur union was a communist? Who was next, Grace Kelly? I turned the page to an ad for exclusive twinkle coats at Bergdorf Goodman. Who was twinkling anymore? The threat of communism, and how scared we were all supposed to be of it, was quickly taking the twinkle out of our postwar joy. Maybe that's why what I was doing was important. Not just to get my own joy back, but to help get the collective joy back.

I closed the paper and opened a copy of *Harper's Bazaar*. The thick May issue, devoted to clothes for an air-conditioned climate, disguised what I was really reading, a pamphlet titled *The Communist Party, a Manual on Organization*. At dawn, the morning after I'd received all the books, I'd made a list with the most important ideological points from my reading. I'd stayed up nearly all night to do so, studying the letter from Coldwell on what to expect at the meeting and making a chart of the party hierarchy.

It had felt strange to use a ruler and draw straight lines, to organize my thoughts, to memorize. I was working, and on something that did not entail the upkeep of my apartment or survival of my boys. The last chart I'd made had been over two years ago when Tom insisted that I write down—and describe—all of newborn baby Gerrit's bowel movements. The first time I'd just written "disgusting" in the details column, but he hadn't found that very entertaining.

The train came, and I took a seat in the far corner by the window and opened the pamphlet again. It was tucked between a two-page advertisement—four svelte women showing off Catalina bathing suits. Poster girls for capitalism.

"The Communist Party is the organized vanguard of the working class, composed of the most class-conscious, the most courageous, the most self-sacrificing section of the proletariat." Since the pamphlet had appeared in my home, I'd been repeating that line quietly as I tended to the boys and my housework.

"The Communist Party of the USA leads the working class in the fight of the revolutionary overthrow of capitalism, for the establishment of the dictatorship of the proletariat, for the establishment of a Socialist Soviet Republic in the United States, for the complete abolishment of classes, for the establishment of socialism, the first stage of the classless Communist society."

The next section, circled by Coldwell, was about Negroes.

"The Party must mobilize the masses for the struggle for equal rights of the Negroes and for the right of self-determination for the Negroes in the Black Belt. It must ruthlessly combat any form of white chauvinism and Jim Crow practices. It must not only in words, but in deeds, overcome all obstacles to the drawing in of the best elements of the Negro proletariat, who in the recent years have shown themselves to be self-sacrificing fighters in the struggle against capital. In view of this, special attention must be given to the promotion of Negro proletarians to leading work in the Party organizations."

I didn't agree with a lot that the party literature preached pithily—when they'd come up with the abolition of private property, they'd surely never seen New York City—but the equality of the Negro, I did agree on. So if that was the primary reason I was supposed to be a member, I could play the part believably. Or so I hoped.

When I was very young, my mother had spoken candidly with me about her views on race. "Racism in America is a horrible thing. You must ensure that both your thoughts and your actions never contribute to that horror. Just treat everyone as if they were your brother. Because," she'd said, pointing to the Bible on the bookshelf, "they are."

When I'd punched Timo in the gut later that day, she'd changed her tune. "Maybe treat them as a first cousin, instead," she'd advised.

Words mattered, of course they did. I understood that my foreign-born parents preaching equality had helped shape me. My father said, "America is a country with open arms, but that's only true as long as the color of your arms is white. If they're not, then simply staying employed and alive in this country is a battle. Even in Manhattan. Don't ever forget it. Remember that every person is a work of art and should be treated as such." His ability to see beauty in everyone had impacted me, but New York's innate diversity had shaped me, too, from the public schools I attended to the freedom my parents gave me to fill my pockets with subway tokens and just explore the hell out of our city.

When I'd had the affair with the Haitian delegate that the entire FBI now seemed to be aware of, he'd spoken quite frankly. "In the United Nations buildings, we're fine. In bed, we're more than fine. Out there, we are not fine." I nodded, knowing he was right. The 1940s in New York were not the 1940s in Mississippi, but it was still America, and Manhattanites were not color-blind. "And neither are you," he'd said. "The only people who are color-blind are children."

The train came and I sat down and flipped to the end of the magazine where I'd slipped my diagram on the hierarchy of party units. There were two kinds, shop units—formed at a place of work—or street units. I would be going to a street unit meeting, since I didn't work. And because that's where Turner Wells went.

Each unit had members who were elected by their peers to lead. They were called the unit bureau. At the top of that group was the unit organizer, its political leader; then the agitprop director, the person in charge of its agitational and propaganda work; and the financial secretary. In the meeting I was attending, the unit organizer was also a member of the CRC.

I had done some things in my life that surprised me—fell in love with a millionaire, gave up my career for said millionaire; called Gerrit a "possessed demon put on this earth to snuff out my soul" when he peed in a heating vent—but never in my life did I think I would one day be attending a Communist Party meeting. I flipped the magazine open again. Behind the front cover was my forged application to join the party. It was backdated and had been signed for me by two undercover members, one of them a woman. "No one will ask for it," Coldwell had said, "but bring it anyway."

I would go by my aunt Hanna's name, Hanna Graf. The translator. My occupation was listed as housewife and my party dues were ten cents a week.

Jacob already knew my real name, but Coldwell had said it didn't pose a problem. That real communists, like Ava, often used aliases for party meetings, for if they were ever found out they could lose their jobs, their housing, go to prison, be fined thousands. If they were foreign, they could be swiftly deported. Just last month a bill outlawing the Communist Party in Texas had passed, allowing for twenty-year prison terms for anyone found to be a member. The governor had told the *Times* that he thought juries should be given the right to assess the death penalty for Reds.

After the doors closed at Seventy-seventh, I went to open the magazine again, but stopped when I felt eyes on me. As I looked up, a woman standing among the crowd slipped behind another passenger. I stood and offered my seat to an elderly, tired-looking Indian man who smiled gratefully. But I could not shake the feeling that a woman had been watching me. At Eighty-sixth Street I got off the train and waited for the next one.

The platform was full of people that had just missed my train. At the last possible moment, I leapt onto the next train, the doors nearly pinching my jeans as I did. Three cars down, I thought I saw a slim woman in a cloche hat do the same thing.

I clutched the silver railing and held my bag to my chest as the train sped to 103rd without stopping.

I hurried toward the nearest exit, and as soon as I reached the sidewalk, Turner Wells approached me. He smiled pleasantly as I breathed heavily. As he grew closer, my breathing remained labored, but I was matching his smile.

"Rina, it's nice to see you," he said. He was wearing light gray slacks with a short-sleeved, white, collared shirt tucked in. He looked neat and put together, as he had the day we met, but on his feet were a pair of the oldest-looking brown loafers I'd ever seen. They looked as if they'd be far more comfortable in a garbage can.

"Mr. Wells."

"Turner," he said.

I stopped walking a moment and let the sound of his voice fill the air.

"Turner," I said finally, "it's nice to see you again. I'm glad you're here. With me."

"In this instance," he said, gesturing for us to walk, "it's you here with me. This is my regular meeting, and you'll be my regular friend. Okay?"

"Okay. Are those your regular party shoes?"

"Party has taken on a whole new meaning," he said, laughing. "And yes. I actually ran them over with my car to get them to look like this."

"Effective."

We walked a minute, and I wondered if he would say anything about being outside my window. He didn't, but I could feel the moment in his silence. We had shared the best kind of silence from seven floors and one famous avenue apart.

"I don't know if this is relevant," I said finally.

"Everything that might be relevant is relevant," he said quietly.

"I felt like I was being followed on the subway. I felt watched."

Turner's smile dropped. "Could be Gornev having you followed. Could be nothing."

"Let's act like it's not nothing."

"We'll look into it," he said calmly as he gestured for us to walk away from the subway station. "And quickly," he added, his brown eyes shining under the street lamp. In that soft light, Turner could have been leading me anywhere, and I would have followed.

"We should talk about . . ." he said, his voice trailing off.

"The meeting?"

"That's right," he said, a faint smile on his face.

He nodded at me as we approached an alley. I took a few steps and looked back at him. He was glancing over his shoulder, too. There was no one behind us.

"Try not to be nervous, Rina," he said softly as we got to the half-way point. "I know that's stupid advice, but try anyway. Since I'm bringing you, no one will question your presence. Still, say as little as possible. If anyone asks, your story is the brilliant one you already gave Gornev. That you used to work at the United Nations, and while there, we were introduced and became friendly. I can vouch for your involvement with the CRC and eventually with the party. But you've only been a member for a year and you haven't been very active. You've been busy with your children. You owe dues. But you'd like to pay them and commit more time to the party now that your sons are older. Make sense?"

"It does."

"Good. Don't offer any of it up unless asked."

We left the alley and took a right on 103rd.

"This meeting is mostly white people, some involved with the CRC, some not. There are Negroes too, but many have stopped attending meetings lately. If they do, it's always this one."

"Why?"

"They've stopped because they're rightly starting to get scared of getting caught. But some will risk it for this one because the man who runs it raised $250,000 for the CRC last year. And they think he deserves a little loyalty."

"That's a lot of money," I said, thinking about Tom's four-million Lenox Hill fund-raising goal for the coming year.

"Gornev really never spoke of the party to you? Not a word?" Turner asked as we walked under another streetlight.

"No," I said, watching his face glow again. "I've thought about it quite a bit, tried to recall an instance, but I'm sure he didn't. Perhaps I was just too patriotic."

I had been careful about speaking German during the war. Even though I was Swiss, not German, it was a distinction many Americans were too agitated to make. After the United States entered the war, I switched to speaking French out with my mother and German only at home or at Columbia. I volunteered with the Red Cross, and donated enough blood in those three and a half years to keep a battalion alive.

"Jacob and I spoke about the war, of course, but it was often about how much Russia was helping the United States, not the opposite. Are you all quite sure he was such an active member in college?"

"Active is an understatement. He was agitprop director of the Columbia unit. The most effective they've ever had."

"I truly feel like an idiot," I said, picturing Jacob reading Chekhov while drinking a bottle of wine in his underwear. He wasn't exactly trading bonds, but he seemed like a very typical Columbia grad student. Smart, quick-witted, entertaining, sparsely clothed. "How could I have missed all that?"

"Simple. Because he made sure you did. Also, speaking of covering your cover, for people who know me as a member of the CRC, I was in the military, a soldier in Korea—that much is true—now I'm working as a bookkeeper in Harlem for a construction company, hoping to make my way up to management."

"I'll cross my fingers for you," I said, smiling.

Turner took a few more steps then nodded at a gray building that took up half the block. "That's where we're going."

We both looked up at it.

"Your windows are nicer," he whispered. This time our eyes met.

"Are you nervous?"

"Am I nervous . . ."

"To go to the meeting?" he added, grinning.

"You know, I'm not that nervous. In part, because I'm excited, but mostly, because you're here."

He nodded and gestured for me to follow him.

We trudged up five flights of stairs in silence before pausing on a landing. As I tried to catch my breath, I thought about Coldwell's suggestion that I bring the boys with me, present as their mother attended a Communist Party meeting under false pretenses. As she assumed the role of . . . what? What was I? A patriot, helping her country? But this felt very different from volunteering with the Red Cross or giving blood. Maybe I was nothing but a snitch. A stool pigeon. A rat. A mole. I knew that's the calculation that Turner had had to carefully consider, but here he was. And here I was.

"Do you need a bit more time?" Turner asked as I caught my breath.

The hallway was dark and dingy, with dust bunnies in every corner.

"No," I said, pushing myself off the wall. My heartbeat had not slowed, but it was being propelled by nerves, not exertion.

Turner knocked on the door. It was swiftly opened by a man, short in stature, with red hair and freckles dotting his pale skin. He was frowning, but as he opened the door wider and saw Turner, his expression turned sunny.

"Comrade Wells. I'm glad to see you."

"And I'm glad to be here," he said, stepping inside and gesturing to me. "This is Comrade Graf. Hanna Graf. She's been newly assigned to this unit."

The red-haired man nodded at me. "I'm Levine."

Jonathan Levine. He was the unit organizer. I could see his name on the chart still hidden in my magazine.

"Come, sit. You're the first ones here."

"As it should be," said Turner. "Thank you for hosting. This is a great space. It should seat all twenty-five of us comfortably. Oh, twenty-six with Hanna."

Twenty-three more people were going to come into this room? This studio apartment with one couch, two chairs, and a bed? It was impossible.

But I was wrong. As I sat silently in a chair in the corner by Levine's bed, twenty-three more people, seven of them Negro, piled into the room, sitting shoulder to shoulder on the floor, leaning against windowsills and sharing chairs. Everyone chatted happily as we waited for the twenty-sixth person to arrive. I thought Turner might act differently as he morphed into Turner Wells, CRC member, instead of Turner Wells, FBI Special Agent, but he didn't. He greeted everyone with kindness and a quiet enthusiasm that seemed present in any situation. When the last person arrived, Levine quieted the room and Turner introduced me, explaining that I had been at home with my newborn baby, but that I was ready to recommit myself to the party. That was greeted warmly, with a few of the other women congratulating me. The Negro woman next to me held my arm and said, "Toughest job there is. I'm so glad you're here with us now." *Enemies*, I reminded myself as I thanked her, and others, even shook people's hands. *Brainwashed America haters.*

After I'd been greeted like family, Levine launched into the meeting agenda. Then another member went over recommended reading for the week. Next, people took turns speaking about their individual work for the party, and their recruitment efforts. Finally, talk turned to the CRC, and cases they were working on. Turner stood and called for money and legal support for the group's executive secretary, William Patterson. He'd been sentenced to ninety days in jail for contempt of court after he refused to give CRC financial records to the IRS for inspection.

After an hour had gone by, there was a loud knock on the door. The room immediately fell silent. Levine moved swiftly to Turner and whispered something. Turner nodded, and Levine went to the door and opened it a crack. He said a few words, then opened it fully.

Even Turner could not conceal his surprise. Standing next to Levine was Ava Newman. Clearly, he had no idea she was coming.

"All of my excuses," Ava said as she made her way into the room. "I'm sure I scared all of you turning up unexpectedly like this. I couldn't leave my office until very late, as it was my last day of work. I'm terribly sorry." She took a breath and smiled. "I'm Ava Newman."

Anne, turned Ava, walked into the room, the Miss America of communism. She was not in her beautiful orange dress, but in navy blue slacks and a simple pink blouse tucked in, she was clearly not dressed for housework like I was.

I attempted not to faint against the woman next to me, as I was now sure that it was Ava who had followed me, who I had seen on the subway. Meanwhile, Ava explained that she had just left her job at the New York Public Library and that she wanted to join a street unit quickly. Her unit leader was supposed to have sent word to Levine. But she did not? Oh, she was terribly sorry. Incredibly embarrassed. But what luck. She knew someone in the group. What a small world, she said, looking directly at Turner with a million-dollar smile.

"It's *so* nice to see you again," she said.

"And you," he replied, barely able to conceal his shock.

"Why, it's only been a few days since we ran into each other with Comrade Gornev and our other friend," she said, nodding toward me.

"Yes," I replied, and a murmur of acknowledgment crept through the room. Some of the members were clearly familiar with the name, if not the man. And by connecting me with Gornev, Ava had vouched for me, too.

"Yes," said Turner. "You know Hanna Graf as well."

She smiled warmly at me and my new name.

"Let's continue with the meeting," Levine said as a young man eagerly offered Ava his chair.

After the finance secretary collected dues, we were invited to buy materials from the literature agent, a young Negro man who seemed equally devoted to Turner and *The Daily Worker*.

After my arms were filled with two copies of the paper and a book on materialism, I'd spoken to the kind woman who had congratulated me on surviving with a baby, and told her about how I knew Turner and had become involved with the CRC. Finally, Ava approached me, moving as elegantly in her trousers as she had in her tangerine dress.

"Katharina, I can't believe you're here." She gave me a hug and then sat on the floor, motioning for me to join her. She smelled like jasmine and oranges.

"Does Jacob know?" she asked quietly.

"Does Jacob know . . . oh," I said, looking away from her, at the people in the room, at Turner. He was having a conversation with two female members, but clearly trying to slip away to help me. He needed to slip much faster.

"I hadn't seen Jacob since college," I said, turning back to Ava. "He doesn't know anything about me other than what he knew of me at twenty-five, and what I told him when we ran into each other that day."

"So, Jacob doesn't know you're in the party?"

"I don't think so."

She nodded thoughtfully. "But maybe he assumed something because of Turner Wells?"

I thought of the way Wells had said "Rina" when we'd said good-bye. About how closely he'd walked next to me as we approached the drugstore, how closely he'd sat next to me tonight. The way his face looked when he'd slowly lifted his chin to look up at my window from the sidewalk on Fifth Avenue.

"Well, I'm sure Jacob assumed *something*," she continued, grinning. "Just maybe not this."

Before I could reply, Wells came to speak to us, his shoulder brushing mine just slightly.

"Comrade Newman, Ava," said Wells. "I'm sorry I did not know you were coming tonight."

"Oh, no, I'm the one who should apologize for being late. I know how disconcerting it is when there's an unplanned knock on the door. Moving meeting venues every week can only do so much to conceal us," she said, her voice dripping with sincerity. "And what an unexpected surprise to have you here, and Katharina. It's just such luck." She ran her left hand through her perfect hair, exposing a very thin gold watch that had been hidden by her sleeve.

Ava Newman was a baffling communist. She looked and sounded as if she should be saying, "Oh, no, *I'm* the fool that dropped the red dress in with the tennis whites / forgot to move the large pile of diamond bracelets on the card table / drank all of Grandfather's priceless champagne during the clambake." It was as if she'd wandered into the wrong building, the wrong life, all except for one thing. Her intensity. The rest of the evening's attendees were calm—engrossed and attentive, but calm. Ava Newman looked as if she had a ball of fire in each pants pocket and was ready to throw them at anyone who crossed her. In this case, anyone was the United States government.

It was no wonder she'd been tasked with going to Washington. What I needed to know was how Ava Newman, country club communist, had ended up at the same meeting as me? Did she follow me of her own accord—or had Jacob enlisted her help?

"Who is the unit organizer at the public library?" Wells asked her.

"Mary Krol. Dedicated woman."

"I'll ask Levine to connect with her, then," said Wells breezily. "I'm sorry you're no longer employed at the library—important work—but we are happy to welcome you here."

"I'm delighted to be here. A change of pace can really lift one's spirits. And can reaffirm even the firmest commitments."

"Yes, it can," Turner agreed. "But I don't remember you being involved in the CRC before. Is this a new interest?"

"Oh, no, not new, just stronger lately, what with Hoover closing in. Rumor is that he's trying to get the CRC and others to register as Communist front groups, so it feels like an important time to be involved. Long story short, Turner. I'd like to be *more* involved."

"You should speak to Rina about it," he said, shifting his eyes to me. "She's been spending the little free time she has traveling to D.C. on our behalf. Our being the CRC. We have a man there. It's complicated, but important. She can fill you in, right, Rina?"

"Of course," I said, my heart sounding like a timpani in my chest.

"Rina, shall we go to the little cafeteria around the corner and have a coffee together? A little chat?" Ava asked when Turner had left. "I feel like this is fate and the world wants us to get to know each other better, don't you think?"

I nodded helplessly.

Fate. Ava Newman and I at the same meeting was about as fateful as Caesar falling on Brutus's knife.

CHAPTER 20

I hope you don't mind me saying this, but you're quite different from the other women I've met in the party." I was speaking quietly, even though Ava had told me when we entered the McCord Cafeteria on Ninety-seventh and Third Avenue that I didn't have to. That after nine o'clock, the place was full of party members, men and women who stayed for hours carrying on the conversations they'd started in their meetings or dorms. Ava had struck me as an improbable communist when I'd met her with Jacob, but now that I'd been to a meeting and seen other party members in person, and hadn't only read about their red eyes and horns and fangs in the newspapers, the impression was confirmed. They certainly did not look like the monsters the press made them out to be, but they definitely did not look rich, or like leading ladies of the silver screen à la Ava Newman. Over coffee, against my better judgment, I said as much.

"How so?" she asked, looking surprised.

Did Ava Newman really not see that her pointy bra and big pink smile stood out in an old T-shirt-and-ChapStick crowd? "I suppose the other women I've met—"

Ava began to laugh, showing off her straight white teeth. Even her tongue seemed to be the perfect color. I wondered if she believed the masses were entitled to the kind of orthodontia she'd likely received.

"Stop, really, please." She held up her hand. "I didn't mean to tease you. Trust me, Katharina, I know I don't look like your average card-carrying party member. Is it the hair? Too blonde?" she asked, flicking it over her shoulder. "It's God-given. I have no control."

"Nope, it's the money," I retorted, finding my voice. "Not too blonde, too rich." Even dressed down, Ava had a whiff of generations-old bank accounts about her. "You sound rich, you look rich, and you speak like—"

"I've just eaten a truffle?" she joked, puffing out her cheeks.

"I know rich people. I married one," I continued. "So, if you're not rich, you're very good at giving the impression that you are."

"I'm not," she said, smiling. "My father is. House in Newport. *Mayflower* ancestors and all that. But he's also a union supporter and unbeknownst to most, a communist."

"Now this," I said, signaling to the waitress for more coffee, "is a story I'd love to hear."

"It's just your average Darien, Connecticut, Methodist-mining-executive-turns-communist story. Don't you know one or two of those?"

"Can't say that I do."

"You should get out more."

"That's the understatement of the century."

Ava eyed me curiously. "I can see why Jacob liked you so much."

"Did he like me? I suppose he did." I thought back to the nights— and days—we'd spent tangled in bed together. To the conversations that shifted seamlessly among English, Russian, and German, touching on food, history, the weather, the war, though never, I realized with a start, political ideology.

"Of course," she insisted. "That was quite apparent when he saw you. He was looking at a woman he'd loved." She was quiet a moment, moving her cup of coffee slowly around in a circle. "But it's funny, isn't it?"

"What is?"

She moved the cup a little faster. "That after all these years, both of you living in Manhattan, you never ran into each other. Not once."

I looked up, trying to hold the pleasant expression on my face and not let the shot of adrenaline I felt ruin my response.

"That's the worst part about college."

"What is?" Her voice, for the first time, revealed a slight edge.

"Leaving. When we were all living in Morningside Heights, practically shouting distance away, it felt like the classes, our conversations, our friendships, would carry on forever. But then you're handed a diploma, and everyone scatters, forced to put on the hat of adulthood. Especially during the war."

Ava stopped spinning her cup. "I suppose it is that way. I went to Mount Holyoke, and I only keep up with two or three girls. Sad, really, when we were all such good friends." The edge had disappeared. Her voice was cashmere again.

"Now we have new communities," I said lightly, feeling as if I'd managed to shut my window seconds before it rained.

"We do," she said, smiling.

"And while ours is a global one, it also feels tight-knit, that's what I appreciate," I said. "You, Turner, and I at the same meeting, I just love coincidences like that."

"Don't you though?" she said, revealing nothing.

"Do you know Turner well?" I asked, realizing I didn't know the answer to that question.

"Well, no," she said, glancing down at the table. "We've met, through Jacob, a handful of times over the years. I'd call us . . . comrades," she said, looking back up.

"When did you find out? About your father? If you don't mind me asking." She clearly was not going to divulge that she'd followed me on the subway or the source of her new passion for the CRC.

"Not until five years ago. When I was twenty-five." She pushed up the sleeves of her blouse, the verve returning. "I wasn't involved with the party at all before then. If anything, I was far on the other side. Too busy studying eligible men up and down the East Coast. I had a job at the NYU library, and I didn't think about much of anything except enjoying my very Manhattan life."

"You're not the first."

"And not the last. But I'm trying to change that. Not the enjoyment part, just the who-gets-to-have-it part."

"Which brings us to the why."

"My father is the why. But you have to look beyond that. Because before my father was the why, he was my everything."

"Is he alive today?"

"He is. Don't even ask that question. Feels like a curse." She shuddered convincingly.

"I'm sorry."

She waved off my apology. "He is alive, but my mother is not. She died when I was five, and it's just been my father, my older sisters, and me since then. Three girls and Papa."

"That can't be easy." I parented alone 90 percent of the time. I knew the loneliness of screaming out for help and receiving nothing but an echo, a reminder that all you have is two hands when you're desperate for four.

"It wasn't easy. But certain things helped."

"Like the party?"

"Like money," she said, grinning. Suddenly she grabbed the menu from the table. "I'm terribly hungry. But I always am. Are you? Shall we share something?"

"Anything." I would have eaten a bowlful of grasshoppers to keep Ava talking.

She signaled the waitress and ordered an egg salad sandwich with tomato.

"Anyway, the rest of the story," she continued. "The summer of

1948, my father was wrongly accused of stealing from his place of employment, Richard R. Myers Iron Holdings. They own several mines in Connecticut. Did you know there were mines in Connecticut?"

"Can't say I know very much about mining."

"Fascinating industry. Anyway, that summer, out of nowhere, Daddy was accused of cooking the books and stealing some ungodly sum of money. It's a big company, heaps of cash. Even worse, he was also accused of stealing away his boss's wife—taking her straight to a hotel room—repeatedly. He was swiftly fired, as you can imagine. Then he was deemed unhireable because said boss along with said wife slandered him from Maine to Manhattan. Even the sulfur mines wouldn't take him, and they'll take just about anybody with a nose that can handle the stink."

"But he was redeemed?" I asked, conjuring up a mental image of Ava's father as Cary Grant in a miner's hard hat.

"He was redeemed because of the miners themselves, the union. They had documents that proved it was a mucked-up accusation. They saved his hide, and he was made head of the whole company. But the best part is that his boss had to go work in . . . guess," she said, looking at me, her cool blue eyes shining.

"Sulfur?"

"That's right." She rapped her fingers happily on the table. "Now he comes home to his wife stinking like an egg salad sandwich gone wrong." She picked up her half and took a satisfied bite. "Now, let's be honest," she said after she'd swallowed. "The part about bedding the boss's wife was probably true. But my father's unattached. Why should he be punished?"

"And after the dust settled?"

"He felt indebted to the union, which led to him becoming a sympathizer, and a few months later, a card-carrying communist," she said proudly. "Not publicly, as you can imagine, but he's as devoted as they come. And now so am I."

"Because of your father?"

"Because of the men who supported my father. Because of seeing people motivated by something other than money. Trust me, where I grew up, the only true motivations are money and sex, and the two are usually laced together, tighter than a girdle."

"I don't think much changes past the Connecticut border."

"Oh, but it does. People in New York are motivated by delightful things. Like food, and art, an afternoon at the theater, a night on the town. And some, like Jacob and Turner, by the idea of a better life—for everyone." She took a last bite of her half of the sandwich and leaned back against the banquette. "Well, that's enough of Daddy and Connecticut. Let's talk more about Jacob, the reason we found each other in the first place. And more about Turner Wells," she said after a pause. "The other reason we found each other."

"Jacob," I said brightly. It was easier to start with Jacob, considering I had spent a grand total of twelve hours with Turner Wells.

"Let's start with Turner," she said just as brightly. "What is it that you're doing for the CRC exactly?"

It was probably the only question I was prepared to answer.

"They have a man," I said quietly. "A janitor at FBI headquarters. He's a good man, and he's become a friend to Turner. He's been able to pass along a few . . . insights."

"This man is at the FBI?" said Ava, looking truly shocked.

I nodded yes.

She sat back, looking at me like I could walk on water. "I must say I'm utterly amazed. And you're involved?"

"I'm helpful," I replied. "Or I'd like to think so. I go to Washington for Turner. I meet with the man, I head back up to New York. Our meetings are brief, but useful."

"Useful," she said, finally smiling. "I'm sure Turner finds them more than useful."

"I have a great amount of respect for Turner Wells," I said, finally uttering something that was not a lie.

"As do I," she said, spinning her watch around her thin wrist, her wheels clearly turning. "Do you think Jacob is aware that Turner has a man in the FBI?"

"I don't know."

"I'm sure he'd like to know. No, he'd be thrilled to know," she said. She tucked her watch back under her sleeve.

I nodded, very ready to change the subject.

"I can speak to Turner," she said. "But maybe it's better if you did. You've known him longer than I have."

"Since 'fifty-one. Our worlds overlapped that year," I said, thankful to finally have a story to rest on.

"Isn't that lucky," she said pleasantly. She signaled to the waitress for more coffee. "Lucky you, to have your life overlap with such interesting men. Like Jacob."

"Jacob," I said, grinning, thrilled to be moving on to someone I knew more about. "We had a drink together after you left that afternoon."

"Yes, he told me."

Of course he did.

"I didn't know what to expect, it had been so long, but he was just the same as he was at Columbia. Still full of life. In college, besides being very intelligent, Jacob always had things to say that curved slightly differently from what other people were saying. And what I liked best of all was that everything with him was big. Big thoughts, big dreams, big meals, big laughs."

"It is infectious, that kind of energy. I've always liked that about him, too," Ava said thoughtfully. "People like that are hard to find. Though that can be easy to forget, since they're so loud."

"He is still pretty loud," I said, smiling.

"I have the utmost respect for Jacob Gornev," Ava said, and I could tell she meant it. "I marvel at his commitment to the cause. I wish I were half as useful to the party as he is. But I'm trying."

"How did you meet?" I was starting to guess I wasn't the only one who'd been Jacob Gornev's lover.

"He recruited me," she said, her voice lower. "I met him through my father. You get a card-carrying communist as rich as my father and the whole party leadership shows up at his door. Jacob himself made that trip to Connecticut. After he noticed me lurking about, he asked me to help him with a specific task. I suppose I was rather good at it, so he asked me to do it again."

That task had to be Washington.

"That's how it works," she continued. "You know as well as I do. Your commitment to the party will be rewarded. Unlike in America's capitalist society, where your commitment leads to neither financial nor spiritual gain."

"Sometimes that's true," I said cautiously.

"Sometimes? Come on, Katharina. It's always true, especially for women. Jacob told me that you worked for the United Nations. Why did you leave?"

"Because I got pregnant."

"Well, isn't that just disappointing."

"It was exactly that."

"And now you're at home."

I nodded. *Yes, I'm at home. Almost all the time. But because of a stroke of good luck, I tell a few lies and poof! I'm let loose to spy on you.*

"But here we are now," she continued, smiling. "Comrades."

I nodded enthusiastically. Ava's suspicions of me seemed to have disappeared with my mention of the CRC's inside man. She was enjoying my company, perhaps even thinking of us as equals, two different women who had found themselves in very similar situations.

"Listen, Katharina," she said, leaning forward. "If you're up for it, there's someone in town I think it would be beneficial for you to meet. He's an important man. A representative of the international party movement. He's been abroad for quite some time but just arrived back in New York."

I nodded with interest, knowing that Coldwell would happily throw me off a cliff for such an opportunity.

"His name is Max. He works in transportation." Her voice neared a whisper. "To be specific, he buys airplanes for Cuban revolutionaries. What he's doing is extremely exciting. But he needs some assistance with the administrative elements. Would you like to meet him? See if you can be of any help? Not every woman in the party has your level of experience and speaks Russian. Jacob told me that you do," she clarified.

My level of experience. A month earlier, I couldn't imagine that I'd hear the words "Cuban revolutionaries" anywhere but on the television as they went on about Castro, or that I would be anyplace on a Saturday night but home with my boys, helping them grow while I shrank.

I was tired of observing the world via a television set. And I was very tired of shrinking.

CHAPTER 21

I walked Ava home to her building on Eighty-first and Broadway, then continued downtown six blocks at a pace just short of a jog until I found a pay phone. Coldwell answered on the third ring. After I told the story once, he had me recount it again.

"I don't know anything else except that his name is Max—although, I suppose that may not be his real name?—and that he supplies airplanes to Cuban revolutionaries. Finances them."

"You're sure?"

"Well, I'm sure of what Ava told me. Not sure of where the truth starts and ends regarding Max."

"No last name?"

"None. No blood type or college transcript, either."

Coldwell didn't laugh. "Where are you to meet him?"

"At a French restaurant on the Upper East Side. Tomorrow at eleven in the morning. Considering Tom is not scheduled to work, it's logistically impossible."

"We'll make it possible. Anything else I should know?"

"Ava Newman followed me to the meeting. Or at least to 103rd Street."

"Turner mentioned. You're sure it was her?"

"Yes. Of that, I'm sure."

"I don't know what is bothering me more about Ava," Coldwell said after a long stretch of silence. "The fact that she followed you, and then showed up at Turner's meeting an hour late, the fact that we missed that her father is a communist, or her request for you to meet this man. Regardless, you and I can't meet in public anymore. She'll definitely be following you now, if she wasn't already. Maybe because Gornev asked her to; maybe of her own accord, simply because she's curious about you, especially since she now believes you and Turner have a man at the FBI. That's a damn pot of gold, by the way. It's lucky as hell that she was at that meeting now that I think about it. You two were able to just hand her that story without even trying."

"There was a little trying," I said. A Communist Party meeting was not exactly dinner at the Colony Club.

"Right. Have I said thank you? Thank you."

I smiled and leaned against the glass wall.

"You and I will keep speaking on the telephone," said Coldwell, "but from now on, anytime you need to see someone in person, it has to be Turner. He is now your man on the ground. It's much safer that way."

"All right." I paused, my mind spinning in all the right directions. "What am I going to do with the boys, Mr. Coldwell? When I go meet Max?"

"Could you call that Negro woman?"

"Jilly." I'd never mentioned her, but clearly, Lee Coldwell had seen my whole life. "I can't call her again. She's with the boys tonight, and it's almost eleven. But that's not even the biggest problem. Like I said, my husband will be home."

"We'll get him out of the house. And we'll send someone. A Barnard student. She's the daughter of one of our agents. She's done this for us before, without knowing what she's doing, exactly."

A stranger with our children, and a student at that. Not a nurse or a doctor or Maria Montessori or someone the Edgeworth family had known for twenty years.

"She will do just fine."

"Good," said Coldwell. "And you are, too. Doing just fine."

Our elevator dinged at ten-thirty in the morning, just thirty minutes after Tom had been called to the hospital unexpectedly by a new employee. A young woman with pulled-back brown hair, wearing Bermuda shorts and loafers, the look that defined college girls in the spring, came in with a grin and extended her hand to me. "Good morning, Mrs. Edgeworth, I'm Sarah Beach. Are these your boys? Aren't they darlings."

The boys looked at her as if she were holding two pistols, one for each of their heads.

Gerrit took two steps toward her with the defiance that had marked him since birth and started stomping his bare feet. "No Sarah Beach."

She chuckled, then leaned down and picked him up. To my shock, he did not bite her, hit her, or put his fingers in her nose. "You're a firecracker, aren't you?" she said, flipping him upside down. He started laughing hysterically. "I bet you drive your mother crazy."

I watched her with awe as she swung him back and forth by his ankles like a macaque she'd just plucked from a tree.

"Anything I should know before you leave, Mrs. Edgeworth? Any foods to avoid? Are treats okay?"

"Avoid arsenic and whiskey," I said. She put Gerrit down and took the baby from me. "Otherwise, by all means, be my guest. You can give them sugar out of the bag if that's what it takes."

She laughed, and I leaned down and kissed Peter and Gerrit. "I love you very much," I said, each word ringing with truth. Tom was wrong about the boys having to be stuck to me and only me. Having them be around someone young, patient, and completely unattached to the Edgeworth family was not going to harm them forever. It might even help.

"I'm one of six," Sarah explained as I reached for my bag. "And my little brother was like this." She looked down at Gerrit, who was trying to get her to swing him again. "Still is."

I knew that the line "It gets better when they're older" was yet another lie to keep mothers from descending into the black hole of depression.

"But is he a functioning member of society? Did he grow a devil's tail when he hit puberty?"

"No. He's a freshman at Harvard. The unruly ones are always the smartest, aren't they?"

"That better be true. Thank you for your time, Sarah."

I left the apartment via the service stairs, took a left down the alley to Sixty-fourth Street, and jumped on the subway to meet Max at a restaurant near John Jay Park.

I didn't know how Coldwell had gotten Tom out of the house, or how long he could keep him out, but I knew it was supposed to be the least of my worries. I should be focused on making it seem like chatting about Cuban revolutionary activity was what I did best. Another Sunday, another communist fresh in from Moscow who wanted to meet me.

At a drugstore on East End Avenue, I studied my reflection in the window, and saw a nervous, scared woman. I remembered how being next to Turner as I'd approached Jacob had calmed me enormously. How I'd been smiling as I waited on the landing with him yesterday, not afraid to walk into that room with him next to me. His warm, competent presence had taken my mind off things. I reached into my purse, reapplied my lipstick, and thought of his shoulder accidentally brushing my arm as we sat in that tiny apartment. That alone had made the evening worth it.

Le Bain Marie was a little bistro with tables of dark wood topped by candles of varying heights. There were stuffed animal heads on the walls—two buffalo and three deer—and several cured ham legs hanging above the counters. It reminded me of the village restaurants in

Normandy, of driving on hilly roads between Switzerland and France during family holidays in Europe.

There was only one man sitting alone in the restaurant, in the very back corner. He stood when I entered.

I smiled and headed toward him.

"I am Max," he declared, taking my hand and shaking it with both of his, clearing any doubt that I had the right target. "You are Hanna Graf."

"I am," I said, trying to confidently wear the name.

"Good."

A waitress came and tried to give me a menu, but he declined it before it was in my hand. "I ordered with another woman already," he explained. "Venison for two."

I nodded and expressed my love of game meats. As he picked up his glass of water, I saw his hand was trembling.

Catching my eye, he mumbled something about low blood pressure and put the glass down, his hands under the table.

After ten minutes of polite conversation, the waitress set enormous slabs of venison in front of us. Max was a thin, jittery man, one who did not seem capable of tackling this cut of meat, never mind supplying Cuban revolutionaries with airplanes. Though what did the latter take but guts and money? Perhaps Max had both, though neither was evident. He was balding, sloppily dressed, and his eyes seemed to be twitching behind his glasses. I was not at ease.

"You speak Russian?" he asked after taking a bite of venison, which seemed to take about thirty chews to get down.

"I get by."

"You are a friend of Ava Newman's," he said in Russian.

I nodded. "I am. And I'm very fond of her," I replied in Russian.

"I like her too. But more importantly, I trust her. She said you're intelligent, an American who speaks Russian, and that you are very close to Jacob Gornev. Because of these things, I wanted to meet you."

I should have clarified about Jacob, that we had been close but weren't any longer. But my relationship to him seemed to matter tre-mendously. "We are very close friends," I repeated, echoing his use of the Russian present tense.

"Good. I trust Gornev, and I trust almost no one."

We ate in silence, chewing on our slabs of meat.

"A bit like eating a dinosaur," he said finally. I laughed, maybe be-cause he became more human in that instant, or because my rising fear needed a release.

"Come," he said, standing up. "You don't want to eat the rest, do you?"

I shook my head.

"Good. Let's go for a drive. I don't like to be trapped between four walls for too long. Makes my skin itch."

I followed him out of the restaurant like a loyal dog. It had started raining. On York Avenue, just before Seventy-fifth, he nodded at a white two-door Studebaker sedan. He went around to the driver's side and I opened my door. Just before I climbed inside, I looked behind me. There was no one. I closed the door thinking about how much I wanted to see Turner Wells.

Max pulled into traffic and we drove in silence for a while. When we turned on Second Avenue, he threw a series of questions at me in Russian that seemed to be testing my language skills more than my ability to do secretarial work for him.

He asked what I knew about the Cuban Revolution. I told him. Cuba was an original member of the United Nations. I pretended that I'd been following the revolution as if it were in my own backyard.

"Cuba is America's New Jersey," he said loudly.

That made absolutely no sense, but I nodded yes.

He asked if I'd ever been to Russia. I had not. Would I like to? Of course. Wasn't that the dream? Shouldn't be, he said, going as fast as traffic allowed toward the Queensboro Bridge. He was never going back.

"I would die there, Mrs. Graf. In a matter of months, I'd be dead." We rattled on to the bridge.

"No," I said, unsure how else to respond. "That's a terrible thing to say."

He turned and looked at me, his eyes off the road for far too long.

"Do you actually care about the situation in Cuba?" he asked as we moved toward the expressway. "You aren't saying yes because Jacob and Ava led you to me?"

"I wouldn't be here if I didn't," I said, still in Russian. That much was true. He just didn't ask which side I was on.

"And you also care about Ava?"

"Ava? Of course I do," I said, and it didn't feel like a lie. "She's one of my closest friends in the party." Also not a lie. I only had two.

He stayed quiet until we were on the expressway going toward Jackson Heights.

"Do not let her go to Russia," he said, speeding up again. "Do you hear me?"

"Ava?" I whispered.

"Do you hear me?" he yelled. "Do not let her leave the country!"

"Why?" I asked so quietly that I could barely hear myself.

He tried to pass a truck, speeding up before abruptly braking. He wove around three cars while coughing loudly, one hand on the steering wheel. Three fingers slipped off until he was driving with only his thumb and index finger.

"Here they want so much, but in Russia, they want everything. More information, more money. You take one bite of venison, then they ask you to eat the whole animal. They ask you to eat it alive. Ava will have to eat it all in one bite. And she cannot."

"I think she's very courageous. You all are. What you're—"

"Courage?" he said, laughing wildly, and going even faster. "What does that matter? You should know better, intelligent as you're supposed to be. It's not courage, it's what happens when you no longer care about yourself. I gave up caring for my own life long ago. That's how they peel you apart. Yes, my lungs are caving in, yes, my hands are shaking, but the Cubans need their airplanes, so I will get them their airplanes. They before me. The state before I. You see that devotion everywhere. Look at Gornev. Withering away, his heart beating too fast for a man his age. All that strength and they can still chisel away at him."

I thought of Jacob. Of his infectious laugh, his long, hungry looks. What had I missed?

"He is a patriot's patriot."

"We should be proud to put the state before us," I said confidently, thankful for my Communism 101 crash course.

"We should be proud if it didn't kill us. Gornev has ten years left, if he's lucky."

Ten years in the party, or ten years alive? I was too afraid to ask.

We hit a swath of wide-open road, the route to Queens completely clear. Max moved into the middle lane and sped up even more. As he did, the sky groaned, and it started to rain harder.

He swerved around the eighteen-wheeler that had appeared in front of us, bumping the wheel with his. The truck started beeping wildly.

"You have to help Ava. Do you hear me? She does not listen to me."

I looked at Max as if he had a scythe in his hand.

Suddenly, he accelerated sharply and I screamed, my eyes flying open. We zoomed down the expressway, the car rattling, groaning, begging us to slow, until a burst of traffic insisted that we do and Max stepped on the brakes, slowing the car to a stop. After a full minute of idling in silence, Max moved to the shoulder, exited, parked on the side of a neighborhood road, and cut the engine.

"Don't let her go, Hanna," he repeated. "If she goes to Russia, she'll be dead within hours."

"Okay," I whispered.

"Here," he said, reaching behind him in the car and handing me an envelope. "Give her this. Save her life."

I nodded yes.

"Don't forget to save yours, too," he said, pointing to the door.

CHAPTER 22

He nearly killed us!" I yelled into the pay phone on Lexington Avenue, the first one I'd found after getting off the Queens line subway at the first stop in Manhattan. "He clearly doesn't care if he dies, or who he takes along with him. In this case, me. He kept repeating, 'Don't let Ava go to Russia. Don't let her go.'"

I leaned back against the phone booth wall. I could not stop shaking. I felt as if I'd been electrocuted. I let my head hit the glass with a thud.

"What are you doing?" asked Coldwell.

"I'm speaking to you on the telephone."

"While . . ."

"While having a heart attack."

"Hang up the phone. Go get a drink."

"Max didn't want to speak to me about Cuban airplanes. He wanted to talk to me about Ava. But Ava had sent him to me to begin with. And then he hands me this envelope. 'Save her life,' he said. Her *life*."

"And all that's in the envelope is a piece of paper with an address on it."

"Yes, in Cuba. No name, no map, nothing but a street address."

"Read it to me again."

With an unsteady voice, I read the address in Havana for the third time.

"Listen, Mrs. Edgeworth," Coldwell finally said. "We owe you some remuneration for this kind of work. We pay our informants. That's what you are now. Forty dollars a week."

"That's your solution?"

"For now."

"Was no one following me? You've followed me while I stroll in the park with my children, you've watched me cry on park benches, but you don't have me followed when I'm going to meet a perfect stranger? Or does only the KGB do the following now?"

"It's not my place to comment on—"

"What in hell can you comment on, then? I love America, but no one loves it this much."

We both stayed silent, then I heard a very soft, very unfamiliar sound. A woman's voice. She said "Lee," and then the phone was silent again. Lee Coldwell was bad with women, but he had one in his house.

"Should we meet? Would that calm you down?" he asked.

"I thought you said—"

"I could have a woman pick you up. She would be very discreet. She could bring you—"

"No. I don't want to get in another car today. I don't want any discretion. I just want to be home with my boys." I hung up the phone and closed my eyes, until I was jolted by a knock and the face of an impatient man pointing at the telephone.

I started to open the door to leave, but stopped. "I'm sorry, I'm not quite finished," I muttered. I fished in my purse for more change. Coldwell answered after one ring.

"I would indeed like to be paid, Mr. Coldwell. That, I am sure, would make me feel better."

"We can do that today. We'll have the money delivered to you, and one of our men can look at that envelope from Max. Might calm you down."

"Who?"

"Turner Wells."

The air around me thickened. Coldwell knew I would accept. Of course it was yes.

"That sounds fine," I replied coolly. "I'll be on the West Side this evening. At the San Remo. Perhaps he can meet me outside. Seven or later."

"Consider it done."

I hung up the receiver and nodded at the waiting man, now wondering if he was waiting for the phone or waiting for me. "It's all yours," I muttered, not looking up at him.

I took a few hurried steps away from the phone booth and then stopped. I was letting other people decide my whole life. In my own home, my husband had decided my fate since the day I'd delivered Gerrit. And now that I'd worked my way free of Tom without him knowing, I was still being decided for. Lee Coldwell had decided I was his best bet as bait for Jacob. Ava Newman had decided that I was worth following, and handing over to Max, and Max had decided I was close enough to Ava that I was worth warning in his terrifying way.

I hailed the next cab.

It didn't matter that I'd much rather be in a subway car than in the backseat of a taxi. It was Sunday. I had to get Sarah Beach out of my house and pretend I had been in it all day. Then I had to spend an evening at the elder Edgeworths'. I croaked my address to the driver, slid to one side of the backseat, and closed my eyes. I didn't want to see where I was going or what lay in front of me. All I wanted to see, more than I'd ever wanted to, were my children. I wanted to hold them and not share them, happy for the first time in a long time that they were all mine.

"Eight-twenty Fifth Avenue, home to the stars," said the driver, winking at me.

"I think that's the Apthorp," I mumbled, handing him two quarters.

My feet touched the pavement in front of our apartment, ten feet back, and suddenly I stumbled backward until my body hit the cab.

Tom was walking inside, Sam already had the door open for him. I jumped forward and put my hand over my mouth. Sam saw me and I started shaking my head fast and hard. There was no time for subtlety. I pointed to my husband and shook my head again. I ran as fast as I could to the back of the building, reached for the door used for basement deliveries, and banged on it with both fists. It was opened by a stunned housekeeper.

I sprinted up seven flights of stairs, threw five dollars at Sarah Beach, and pushed her into the stairwell. I had beat Tom in.

When the elevator dinged, I was sitting on the couch with the boys, reading *Pat the Bunny*, and showing Peter how to lovingly touch the fur. I had been smacked in the face with the realization that whatever happened in my strange new universe, I did not want them to grow up without me. What would become of Gerrit if I weren't there? Reform school, then prison.

"That Sam can talk," Tom said, taking off his jacket, barely looking at me. "Can you get the boys ready, Katharina? We have to be at my parents' in less than an hour, and I'd like to walk."

Of course I could. And a walk, what a good idea. The only thing Tom enjoyed more than healing the sick was a brisk walk.

We had been at the Edgeworths' for an hour, and my nerves and nausea from the day were still paralyzing me, despite our walk through the park. I sat on the leather couch like a statue, afraid that any movement would release pent-up tears. In my purse on the ground next to me was the letter from Max. When Amelia Edgeworth finally joined us, she awakened a sleeping Gerrit. Amelia was a woman who could not move quietly. Her jewelry jingled, her heels clicked, she sang sentences, and she never, ever hid her discontent.

"Apologies, my darlings," she trilled as she swept into the living room and kissed the boys. "My little potatoes! How I've missed you."

I rose, and gave her a polite peck on the cheek as she took Gerrit in hand.

"I don't love that dress, Rina," Amelia said, eyeing me. "That shade of yellow, and the cut. Makes your hips look puffy."

I cleared my throat. If anything could get me talking, it was Amelia and her criticism.

"Funny you say that," I murmured. "Your son loves that word, too. Puffy."

"Well, darling," she said, taking me in from head to toe, "it's more polite than saying fat."

"She's not fat," said William from the opposite couch. "She's perfect. Your generation just thinks we're still in the twenties, that girls need to look like boys. Don't listen to her, Rina, your backside looks great."

"Is there a closet I can hide in?" I asked Jilly as she approached with a tray of cocktails.

"Several," she murmured as all the Edgeworths laughed.

"Still that sharp sense of humor," said William, winking at me and walking over to Jilly. "Glad motherhood hasn't softened that."

"What are these?" I heard Tom ask. He was looking at a stack of pictures on the buffet.

"Oh, those are from the hospital gala. Jack sent them over since we couldn't be there. He knows I love to see what everyone was wearing. There are a few of you two."

"Come look, Katharina," Tom called.

I walked over to Tom and propped myself against the buffet. "I look terrible in every one," I said, flipping through them.

Tom took them from me, studying the images. He didn't say a thing about my appearance, instead pointing to a woman in the background.

"Helen Fourtou looks very good. Slim."

"Sorry?"

"Helen." He paused, realizing his gaffe. Tom prided himself on being the opposite of his philandering father, and his comment was pure William. "It's just that I haven't seen her in a while. Not since she had the baby," he backtracked.

"She looks wonderful," I replied, because she did. She looked exactly as she had before the baby, as if she'd just grown it in a backpack and slipped the thing right off nine months later, incurring no damage to her dainty frame.

Tom set the pictures down and moved over to the boys, who were starting to fuss. He took Peter by the hands and tried to get him to walk.

I sat down in the nearest chair. It was only seven, but it felt like midnight.

"Did I tell you?" said William, looking at Tom. "Bettina lost her race in London. Arabella is crushed. She said Kip was almost in tears. That man has very active tear ducts. Is there not a medical procedure that can be done?"

"It's a product of being from California, darling," said Amelia from across the room. "The men are raised differently there. They're allowed to have hearts."

"She didn't lose," said Tom dryly. "I spoke to Arabella this morning. She came in second place. She had a medal around her neck, not a noose."

"Second, seventieth, you know that's all the same to them," said Amelia.

"The Olympics aren't for two more years. They need to let that girl breathe, or the pressure of it all could just crack her arms right off."

"Don't be so dramatic, Tom," William chided. "Bettina's an Edgeworth more than a Rowe. She's tough as steel. She thrives on pressure."

I thought of the way Max had looked in the car, of how he'd hit the truck tires with his own. There was pressure on him from someone, somewhere. His arms had definitely been about to crack right off. Maybe the same kind of pressure that was on Ava Newman, only she could handle it better. But what if she couldn't? I had to give her Max's letter.

"Are you better then, dear?" Amelia asked, coming to sit near me. "Is Jilly's help allowing you to rejoin the world a bit?"

"It is. I'm very grateful to both of you."

"It's really the least I can do. I didn't realize it was quite so bad for you. We've been so busy lately, what with the trip to the Orient and all the fund-raisers and social events that take place in May. Quite demanding to be an Edgeworth this time of year. Easier in the summer, isn't it, when the city finally closes its eyes."

"I imagine it's a rather punishing schedule."

I hadn't bought into the communists' teachings, but it wasn't difficult to see why they were so keen to take money away from people like Amelia Edgeworth to give to the destitute.

"Excuse me a moment," I said, getting up. I walked to the kitchen, took the bottom of someone's discarded martini, and threw it back. I did the same thing with another glass. I couldn't let the Edgeworths see me drink, but I wasn't going to get through the afternoon without something. Jilly came in and I put the glass down quickly and slipped out of the kitchen.

Jilly followed me into the living room with a tray of food, blinis smeared in cream and caviar. She placed the tray on the coffee table, and as soon as she stepped away, Gerrit ran over and stuffed three blinis in his mouth, chewing as fast as he could, as if we might grab them back otherwise. Then he started to choke, spitting everything out on the woven geometric rug.

"Not the Antonín Kybal!" Amelia shouted. "It just arrived from Prague!"

I rushed over to the carpet, picking up the food before I picked up my son, but Tom lifted him up and started performing some medical maneuver.

The baby fell on the rug, crying because he'd been abandoned by Tom, and everyone looked at me, their eyes imploring me to deal with the chaos so they could return to the quiet of their charmed lives.

"Let me help you, Mrs. Edgeworth," came a voice as I grabbed the baby and held spit out food in my hand. The voice belonged to Jilly.

"Come with me," Amelia said to a still-screaming Gerrit. She pulled him out of Tom's arms. "Let's find something to amuse you. You're like your grandfather. In need of constant entertainment. I will solve this problem in a snap."

When she came back five minutes later, Gerrit was not just quiet and smiling, but glowing. In his hand was a large antique pistol with a mother-of-pearl handle.

"Mother!" Tom shouted, rushing to them.

"It's not loaded, Tom. Stop panicking," she said, shooing him away. "He likes it. Look how happy he is. Elevates that cowboys and Indians game to new heights. I even found *you* a toy." She handed Tom a quill pen and then took it right back from him with a smile. She tucked it behind his ear. "Here, darling," she said, bending down to Gerrit's level. "Pretend to shoot your father."

"She's not boring, my wife," said William, laughing and moving close to me. He kissed the baby's head. "Little potato."

I was in urgent need of boredom. I was quickly learning that a brush with death was not best followed by cocktails and the eccentricities of the very rich.

I carried Peter into the library, trying to distract him by pointing out the windows, not wanting to hear Gerrit delighting in the staged murder of his father.

Peter hit the pane of glass and smiled.

"Mama," he said.

"Yes, my darling, that's right. Mama and her windows."

Had all this been easier with one baby? Perhaps it had. I didn't think the clouds of despair had fully descended until I'd had two.

I held Peter tighter and thought about Max accelerating on the highway. Would I have died if we'd crashed on the expressway? I pressed my face against Peter's and felt awful and reckless. Maybe women were supposed to stay cooped up in their towers so that we stayed alive for our children. Maybe oppression was just a protective measure. I looked around the apartment. No, it couldn't be. After all, it was so easy to just slip right out the window of a tower and fall. The outside world was much safer.

I leaned my forehead against the window, waiting for Turner. I let my eyes take in the sidewalk on the west side of Central Park. There he was standing across the street. Same hat, same stance, same quiver up my spine.

This time, he was not looking at the sidewalk. He was looking up, waiting for me.

In the other room, Gerrit was screaming again. In Tom's hand was the revolver. I looked from him to William, who had earmuffs on.

"Can't take the sound of your little man, Katharina. I love him, I do, but it helps if I can't hear him as well." William pointed to his earmuffs. "Used to do it when my children were small, too. Just ask Tom's old nanny. What was her name?"

"Which one? There were over a dozen," Tom said.

"That isn't true," said William, repositioning his earmuffs. "Your mother did everything for you. You should thank her."

"I do," said Tom, genuinely, because when it came to parenting, Amelia Edgeworth was Maria von Trapp compared to her husband.

"Picked these up in Gstaad," William droned on. "Actually, it's quite cruel that I've never bought you a pair, Rina."

"I'm all right," I said hurriedly. "Tom, why don't I take the boys out for some air?" I said. "Run around in the park for a bit."

"It's nearly dark outside," he said, walking over to the window. Gerrit followed, right on his heels, still sobbing and reaching for the gun.

"We can catch the tail end of the sun," I said, grabbing Gerrit and heading to the stroller.

"Let them go, Tom," I heard William say. "My ears are hot."

Before Tom could say no, I rushed out of the building with the boys. I was, as Tom had pointed out, losing daylight fast. Once on the sidewalk, I turned to check the fifth-floor row of windows that belonged to the Edgeworths, but I didn't see anyone staring out. Why would they bother? My life with the boys was about as interesting to them as Jilly mopping their floors.

We waited to cross the street, and I was so out of sorts I missed the crossing signal.

"Mama go. Green go," I heard Gerrit say from the stroller, bashing his little hands against the metal bar.

Turner was nowhere in sight, so I walked toward Tavern on the Green out of habit. Anyone who studied my movements knew it was my likely destination.

When I was about ten yards from the restaurant's front door, I saw Turner step out from the shadows. Every suppressed emotion from the day rose to the surface, begging for my attention.

"Mrs. Edgeworth," he said quietly as he came next to me. "Rina." The boys didn't even seem to notice him, as they were ahead of me in the stroller, and calm in the darkness. "You've had a hell of a day."

The evening was almost making up for it. "Turner," I said, my mind and body flooded with the relief of being near him. "It was the strangest thing. Max, or whoever he is, seemed a bit neurotic, but not to the point of nearly killing us. He ordered us venison. Who wants venison as a last meal?"

"Watch the hole there," said Turner, reaching for the stroller and pulling it over for me. For the briefest of moments, his hand touched the side of mine.

"Excuse me," he said, moving it away. "I'm of course here for the envelope, but outside of that, I wanted to speak to you," he continued, letting go of the stroller. "I wanted to see you."

I didn't respond, not trusting myself. My brain had words ready that I surely couldn't say.

I peered at the boys in the stroller. They were falling asleep.

"Let's sit a moment," I said, and we sat next to each other on the part of the winding bench closest to the streetlights. I looked at him and then slowly reached into my bag. I handed him the envelope that

Max had given me. He took it without touching my hand. Then he unfolded the sheet of paper, looked at it, and folded it again.

"I'm supposed to give it to Ava, and I'm supposed to forbid her from going to Russia."

"I wish I could tell you who Max is," Wells said after we sat together in silence a moment. "But I know Coldwell is looking into it."

He turned to me and placed the envelope between us. He laid his hand on it, and I laid my hand on the other half.

"What should I do with this?" I whispered.

"We talked about taking it for further examination, but Max can easily get a message to Ava. He doesn't need to encode anything for it to reach her."

He opened the envelope, looked at what was written. "I think it's just an address. Must be some address, though."

I watched his hands as he put the letter back in. "I still don't understand why he gave it to me."

"Maybe he wasn't going to until he met you. Maybe now it's not just for Ava, it's for you, too. A place to go, if you're ever desperate for one."

I nodded and he let the envelope go.

"I'm just fine right here," I said quietly.

He leaned back on the bench and put his legs out straight in front of him. He was no longer wearing his party shoes.

I said as much.

"Can't wear those when I'm not at a meeting," he said, laughing. "Hoover wants us to be 'models of the clean, manly life.' To get into the FBI you have to pass a firearms test, keep your weight in check."

"Even undercover?"

"I have a little more flexibility than most. But I'm a former military man. Dressing as a hobo all the time doesn't make sense. At a meeting, it makes some sense."

"Weight in check," I said, smiling. "It's a bit like prepping for Miss America."

"Except that Hoover doesn't let the misses past the secretarial pool. What you're doing is as close as he'll let women get. Especially when there isn't a war."

"I'm glad there's no longer a war."

"Only because we live in Manhattan. There's a war about to ignite down south."

"For good cause."

"I hope so."

The trees rustled from the slight breeze and we sat and listened to the peaceful quiet of the park after dark.

"Coldwell sent a girl named Sarah Beach to help me today, with my children," I commented, thinking of all the competent girls who would study until their brains hurt only to become housewives instead of FBI special agents. "She was a bit of a miracle."

"Joe Beach's daughter. He used to be a Franciscan monk."

"Did he? That explains it. I was pretty sure that she was hiding angel wings under her Brooks Brothers casualwear. She managed to tame my boys without threats, bribery, or handing over a bag of Domino sugar. Maybe she drugged them, but I'm not going to look into it."

"For a person who nearly met her maker today, you're pretty amusing," said Turner, looking at me.

"The last two years, I've been telling jokes to babies who can't respond. I've been saving them up."

"You're probably even more amusing when death does not knock on your door."

"Maybe."

"It's nice," he said, sitting back again. "Very. Not a lot of comics in the FBI."

"No? Hoover seems like a barrel of laughs. Rubber chickens in his back pocket. Pulling quarters out of the agents' ears."

"Not so much," Wells said, laughing, really laughing. It was the first time I'd ever seen him laugh like that and I immediately knew that I wanted to make him laugh like that again.

"Walk?" he said, standing up.

"Walk," I repeated. I checked on the boys, who were still sleeping, and started pushing the stroller beside Turner.

"So, I give the envelope to Ava."

"Definitely," said Turner. "And soon."

"But if she doesn't go to Russia, do they, do you need me?"

"We need you," he said quietly, keeping his eyes on the path in front of us.

We passed a man on a bench, playing the guitar and singing quietly. He was clearly playing for himself, not for money, as there were very few people out to give him a dime.

"'Thump, thump, thump, went his foot on the floor. He played a few chords then he sang some more,'" said Wells in his raspy voice.

"I like that," I said, smiling up at him.

"I didn't write it. Langston Hughes did. But I think it every time I pass a street musician. Or a park musician." He paused. "Do you have my telephone number memorized?"

"I do," I said.

He made me recite it back to him as we walked on, but there was no need. I would never forget anything about Turner Wells.

CHAPTER 23

J ust one minute," I said to the cabdriver as I put the baby on my hip and gripped Gerrit by the hand while trying to pay the driver the fifty-cent fare. I was sweating along my hairline, down my temples, and the back of my neck was drenched. I didn't know if it was because May in Manhattan had grown as humid as May in Mombasa, or because I was extremely nervous to hand Ava Max's letter. "It feels like an opportunity, a lifeline," Turner had said before I left the park. "If you can get it to her tomorrow, get it to her tomorrow."

And here I was, in a position to most certainly give it to her. Except I was afraid that I had no idea what I was doing. That she didn't know what she was doing, either. That none of us really did.

"Jump, baby!" said Gerrit, holding Peter's feet, trying to push his legs up. "Fly airplane, baby!" he said, pushing so hard that Peter started crying.

"Enough, baby!" I shouted as I tried to get them into Ava's building, a rectangular block with some art deco flourishes called the Eden. I hadn't much noticed its architecture when I walked her home in the middle of the night. Now I could see that the building was handsome but run-down, like a girl who was overlooked at a dance, but if you caught her profile in the right light, you'd wonder why.

I pushed the boys through the portico entrance, embarrassed to be showing up at her door that way. But what other way could I show up? With my one free hand I pushed Gerrit into the elevator, and we exited on four. Ava's door was painted dark green with gold numbers just like the others. There was no sign that America's most striking communist lived in apartment 4B. "I'm sorry to bother you like this, I should have called, I should have just asked Jacob for your telephone number." I had been rehearsing that line in the taxi.

"Definitely don't ask Jacob for her telephone number," Turner had said.

I ran my hand down the front of her door, brushing off a small flake of loose paint, and knocked again. After my fist hit the wood, both of Gerrit's did too. No one came to the door. I knocked again, Gerrit kicked the door, and the baby started crying again. Still nothing. Gerrit looked up at me. "No, Mama."

"You're right, darling. No one is home. Silly Mama." I crouched down, tried not to drop the baby, and slipped the envelope under her door. I hurried the boys back into the elevator and to the nearest pay phone.

"4B?" I asked Turner. "You're quite sure?"

"I'm positive."

"She wasn't home," I said, breathing heavily from the weight of carrying Peter. "I pushed the envelope under the door. Do you think that was . . ." The words "incredibly stupid" came to mind.

"I'll see if we can have someone tail her home. I'm sure she will receive it."

"I should have waited."

"I think waiting would have been a very bad idea."

"Thank you, Turner," I said, trying to hold on to the sound of his voice, to his affirmation. Though he didn't reply, I could almost hear him nodding. I imagined him in a kitchen, or perhaps a bedroom. I imagined him with a glass of water next to him, no alcohol or cigarettes in the house, the opposite of Lee Coldwell. I hung up the receiver, and then Gerrit pulled on my skirt so hard that it almost came off. A reminder that my pleasant imagining would always be cut short by my reality.

When the elevator opened into our apartment, I was shocked to see Tom standing in front of the couch looking very worried.

"Tom! You're home. What's the matter?" I asked, scooting the boys straight across our own Antonín Kybal carpet.

"Where were you?" he said, looking at me as Gerrit tried to escape. I let the boys out and Tom let Gerrit grab his legs. He tousled his hair without looking down at him as Gerrit screamed, "Dada!"

"On a walk, a brief walk. Very brief," I said, watching their interaction. Something was off about Tom. He usually at least bent at the waist to greet his children, but he was patting Gerrit as if he were a very vocal cat. "We had some errands to run," I said as he looked at my empty hands. "We dropped off the dry-cleaning."

"Something has come up," said Tom.

"Is everything okay?" I asked, wanting to sprint back to the elevator. He had caught on to one of my lies. Or he guessed something was different. There was no other reason he could be home.

I watched him finally reach for Gerrit, but his expression didn't change. He still looked stunned.

"Tom," I said, gathering my courage. "I can ex—"

"We'll be going out this evening," he said, interrupting me.

"What? What do you mean, 'we'?"

"Just you and me."

"Why?"

"We've been invited by the Maximillian Millses," he said, his voice almost at a whisper, hoarse from reverence. "The *Maximillian* Millses," he said again, in case I hadn't understood which Millses. "Jilly and my mother are coming to watch the boys."

"The Maximillian Millses," I repeated, utterly shocked and completely relieved. "Jilly and your mother? Why not just your mother?"

"Because I'd like them to be alive and with ten fingers—each, not between them—when we return," he said. "You know my mother can't watch the boys on her own. She'll forget to remove the bullets from one of those antique guns or just let Gerrit sail out the window to his death. It's not safe."

I nodded, basking in the pure relief that Tom hadn't figured out the lies I'd been singing. "Are we to go to a party with them? A fund-raiser of sorts?"

"My entire existence is a fund-raiser of sorts these days, but no." He took a step closer to me, and then in the same hoarse whisper said, "It's a dinner at their house." I took a step back and Tom nodded. "Now you understand my terror."

I did, and now mine was escalating quickly, soon to overtake his.

"You should start getting ready immediately," he said, giving me a once-over. "Please feel free to hire anyone you need to help you. Have them come to the house, please. I'm in no state to watch the boys without you near."

"I'll start making calls. I'll telephone Jean-Pierre. I'll telephone Bergdorf's."

"Good." He put down Gerrit, leaned over, and took the baby. "Katharina," he said, still staring at my dress. "I don't think it needs to be said, but your look needs to be conservative, staid. Sophisticated is the better word, but appealing. A woman with gravitas, but who is an agreeable conversationalist. Pleasant. But memorable. You should perhaps—"

"Tom, I understand," I replied, before kissing Peter. "I promise not to embarrass you."

Tom nodded. "All right. But most importantly, please, don't drink at all."

I paused and looked at Tom, clutching the baby, Gerrit gripping his leg again. I pulled Gerrit away from him.

"Won't that look odd, though? What shall I ask for, warm milk?"

"I think a drunk woman flapping about a six-story town house would look odder."

I walked back to the bedroom with Gerrit. If Tom wasn't instilling terror in me, this would have been something to look forward to. Now I was just scared that I'd come off like a nervous, unsophisticated housewife who couldn't handle a drink. I wish I could just tell Tom, *But I'm quite something else altogether, darling. I'm an FBI informant, don't you know? Why just this morning I was slipping a note under a beautiful communist's door in the hopes that she might go to Cuba to assist with some airplanes. What's a revolution without airplanes, I always say.* But no. Instead I would have to croon, *Every day I fall in love with Tom Edgeworth all over again. By the way, might you want to write Lenox Hill a big fat check? The sick children don't heal themselves, my dear.*

I opened my closet and tried to breathe. The Maximillian Millses. No family inspired more intrigue in New York than the Maximillian Millses. Not European royals or movie stars, or the women on the many best-dressed lists with money falling out of their ears. They were shrouded in mystery because they had gobs and gobs of money, but kept extremely low profiles, eschewing almost all social events and often dressing terribly when they did appear. "They're too posh to wash," a woman, and a Rockefeller at that, had once whispered to me at the medical gala when a lesser Mills had been in attendance. She'd been wearing a dress two sizes too big and wrinkled from bust to hem. She looked so odd that she might have inspired pity if anyone in the room didn't know who she was. But of course, everyone did. She was a Mills, and she could wear anything she wanted.

There were many Millses. There was Edward Mills and Chilton Mills and Humility Mills, whom everyone called Pretty Lity, but none of them were Maximillian. Never Max, certainly not Maxim, only Maximillian. He who broke off from the booming family business, frontier enterprises in Iowa, and started an asset management company in New York, giving the extremely rich family their first New York presence. The other Millses flitted in from the middle of the country for events in the spring and fall, but they didn't stay for more than a couple days.

Maximillian had dared to make New York home, bought the most expensive one on the market, and then proceeded to invite no one. We had never been, even Tom's parents had not entered. Now, for reasons unbeknownst to Tom, we were on our way.

When I hung up with the hair salon, Tom walked into my room. "Let me choose your dress, I'm too nervous to be useless."

"Bergdorf's is bringing five."

"Which five?"

"A fencing costume, a hula skirt, a pair of pajamas, a negli—"

"Enough. Just call for me when they arrive."

Tom chose a dark pink silk Jacques Fath evening dress with a cinched wasp waist that fell into architectural pleats rather than a full skirt.

"Sophisticated," Tom said as I joined him in the elevator.

"Crippling," I murmured as I tried to take a deep breath.

After two minutes in the taxi, Tom still looked like he'd seen a ghost. He was not ready to walk into that house.

"You look green in the face, Tom," I said, taking his hand. I had never seen a person so committed to raising money for a good cause. He was going to have to be hospitalized for how much he cared about that hospital.

"Do I? I have to shake it before we arrive."

"Shall I tickle you? Still got that quill pen your mother gave you?"

Tom laughed.

"I forgot how entertaining you can be."

"You've forgotten a lot about me," I said, stroking his hand.

When we arrived at Seventy-ninth Street, just a few minutes later, Tom was no longer the color of fungus. And when the doors were opened by a butler, he had turned back into sleek and sophisticated doctor and heir Tom Edgeworth.

"Right this way, Dr. Edgeworth, Mrs. Edgeworth," said the butler, who had a strong British accent. He walked us through a marble-floored foyer that had blue and gold coffered ceilings, at least thirty feet high, then through a pair of gold-plated wrought-iron doors, and deposited us into a cocktail room with intricate mahogany inlay tiles and a ceiling that closely resembled that of Paris's Sainte-Chapelle.

There were twenty people in the cocktail lounge, under the painted stars, and not one of them was a Mills, but there, in the center, was Mrs. Morgan. I had to plant my feet and reach for a glass of water to keep myself from running to her.

"I see Jim Mellon," said Tom, smiling. "At least they got the guest list right," he murmured before heading to him. He turned back to me, remembering that he probably shouldn't abandon his wife, but when he saw Mrs. Morgan approaching, he nodded.

"Oh thank God you're here, dear," she said, grabbing my hand. "Can you believe this house?" she said far too loudly. "In precisely two hours, I'm planning to pretend that I'm losing the plot, as in I'm utterly senile, just so I can wander about the place. Will you come with me? It's twenty thousand square feet, and there's even a saltwater swimming pool. These Iowans should host the next Olympic Games so that your niece doesn't have to paddle to Australia. The dining room alone seats fifty, and then of course there's the great room for dessert. They only have a dinner at their house once a year; the rest of the time they entertain at hotels and such, and that's very seldom. Can you imagine? Having a house like this and not entertaining? What do they have here instead, solitary Bible study?"

"Only once a year? I thought it was a bit more frequent than that," I said, trying to identify the other guests. "That's rather dreary, only one dinner party a year, not that I'm beating their track record."

"But here's the thing," Mrs. Morgan said, handing me her drink and putting my water glass down on a table with a bang. "If they hosted a dinner at home more than once a year, no one would call it *the* dinner."

"Is that what this is?" I said, grabbing her hand and nearly knocking her over. "This is *the* dinner?"

"Katharina? Are you quite all right? Of course this is *the* dinner. Didn't Tom tell you?"

"He just said a dinner, not *the* dinner."

"Perhaps he didn't want to make you nervous."

"Perhaps he doesn't know."

"Oh please, he knows. People like him are born knowing these things. I bet Tom's first words were 'Cocktails at five.'"

She was probably right. I could imagine Amelia instructing the nannies not to teach him the word mama.

"Anyway, isn't this place just delightfully gaudy?" she said, grinning. "One inch away from bad taste, but a very important inch. The architect worked on the restoration of Versailles. Can't you see it? The gilded sculptural decorations, the harmonious white and gold tones," she said, nodding toward the far wall, "an homage to farming, science, the arts. And that rotunda when you came in? Those are thirty-two-and-a-half-foot-tall ceilings. There are also eight bedchambers—not bedrooms, mind you—a private garage for four cars, a roof garden, and a studiolo. Note the 'olo,' very important."

"What did you do, pay off the architect for a blueprint?" I asked, sipping the rose water Mrs. Morgan had handed to me. I put it down when I realized it was mostly flowers and gin.

"And why not?" she said, winking. "I like to be educated."

"What I can't understand, though," I said, "is why they invited us."

"Easy," she replied, her voice finally lowered. "They're going to donate to the hospital. They wouldn't invite Tom if it wasn't the case."

"Are you quite sure?"

"Of course. Everyone knows Tom is the hospital's equivalent of the Salvation Army volunteer at Christmas. We might as well get him a bell and a red bucket."

"Is that a compliment or quite the opposite?"

"A compliment, of course! I mean, Rina, it's a miracle. That man of yours is a miracle. His father is an absolute dog—entertaining, but you'd think God had granted him double the genitals for the amount of philandering he does. And here comes Tom, the patron saint of sick children, with barely enough time to keep one woman happy."

She raised her eyebrows at me, and I raised mine right back.

"I don't see Maximillian," I said quietly, taking in the room again.

"Oh, no, dear, don't be silly. The Millses only join during the last five minutes of cocktails, then they walk guests over to dinner."

"Have you been to *the* dinner before?"

"Once, dear. They're strange, but not stupid. They know that old money makes new money look greener. But the ghastly Jezebel was in attendance, Jezebel One that is, not Jezebel Two, and I got too drunk to remember what the house looked like. Don't let me do that this time. And speaking of strange, there they are."

We looked at the door as Maximillian and Martina "Minkie" Mills entered wearing rather casual day clothes. They looked like they were going to a garden luncheon, not hosting *the* dinner.

Maximillian, a distinguished fifty, tall as all Midwesterners seemed to be, with graying brown hair and expressionless blue eyes, was wearing a boxy brown suit, winged-tip two-tone shoes, and had on a rather loud floral tie of pinks, greens, and oranges. I looked again and noticed that it matched Minkie's floral dress perfectly. Minkie, unlike her husband, was smiling. She walked her petite frame and unfashionably long blonde hair into the room and straight to Jim Mellon and Tom.

"Good lord, who made their outfits? Judith Garden?" Mrs. Morgan whispered through her grin. "But straight to Jim and Tom. At least she understands the old money hierarchy. You can't go to a female Morgan before a male Mellon."

"Which means she's coming here next?"

"Exactly."

"That's my cue to leave you," I said, winking at her and going to converse with a plant. Luckily, I was intercepted minutes later by Tom, who walked with me as the group went to the dining room.

While anyone else hosting a dinner known as *the* dinner might have had cherry blossoms from Japan flown in to decorate the table or Hawaiian orchids shaped by expert hands on the big island, the Millses had one very long rustic table with nothing but place settings and daffodils on it. Tom was seated on my right, and Lavinia Reede, whom I realized I had met a few years back, was on my left.

"Rina, it's Vivi Reede, aren't you looking well," she purred as we took our seats.

"And you look beautiful, as you did when we met. It was at the medical gala, wasn't it? Two years ago?"

"Indeed," she answered. She must have been forty by now, but she looked not an hour over thirty.

"I never see you around town. You never did join the Colony Club, did you? I remember us discussing it."

"Not yet," I said, smiling. "The club I'm currently a part of has much younger attendees. As in babies. It doesn't even require one to wear pants. It's not very chic."

"You should consider Colony. I do enjoy your company. That depressed woman's humor of yours is very droll," she said, waving her free hand in my direction as the other clutched her cocktail.

"I think I will when the boys are older," I lied.

"So no club, what do you get up to then? Are you just glued to the Army-McCarthy hearings like I am?"

"I've tuned in here and there," I replied, my heart starting to beat faster. I had been watching every night when the boys fell asleep, not sure how I felt about my own small role in what the liberal papers were calling McCarthy's Salem witch trials.

"Well, what do you make of it? You worked with Soviets at the United Nations, didn't you? And Red China?"

"I worked with people from all over," I said, desperate to steer the conversation to Norway or Iceland—somewhere cold and uncontentious.

Lavinia's husband, seated on the other side of her, joined the conversation. "I always liked McCarthy, but now I'm not so sure. I think he's making too much of a fuss. Communism. Very bad, of course. The devil's work. But the army run amuck with communists? He should really start with the universities. Columbia, or so I hear from our Charles, is just a mess. He's a sophomore there now. We said Princeton. Or even Brown. Bully for Brown. But no, he wanted to stay in the city. So Columbia it is. Very mixed school. Good families, but lots of rebels and bootstrappers, too. Not that there's a thing wrong with bootstrapping," he added quickly. "And how about you, do you think communism has infiltrated our lives? Are we being threatened?"

"Excuse me?" I said, blinking in terror.

"Communism. You know, the Reds. Do you think they've really painted the army crimson? Or at least magenta? That's how McCarthy seems to see it. I always thought he had some sense in him, that he was a traditionalist like me, but I don't like the way he's been going after these lawyers like they just picked up a law degree at the local five-and-dime."

"That Fred Fisher he keeps trying to burn down went to Bowdoin College and Harvard Law," said Lavinia, patting her husband's hand. "Does that really scream communist to you?"

"It does not. I don't know," I stumbled. "I've really only caught a bit of the hearings, what with the boys being so young; I don't want to expose them to too much."

"Well," said Lavinia, finishing her champagne, "it's our civic duty to stay informed."

I was not going to let Vivi Reede write me off as a complete idiot. "In truth," I said, finally finding my voice, "I've been more focused on the Geneva Conference. My family lives there, and what with my work at the UN . . ." And just like that, we'd moved on to Vietnam.

As the dinner wrapped, I still hadn't spoken to either Mills, and Tom had only spoken at length to Minkie, with just a one-word hello to her husband. Not surprisingly, he was again turning green. But when we went to yet another cavernous gilded room for dessert, where there was a bluegrass band from Iowa plucking banjos in front of a priceless painting of Louis the Beloved, Minkie Mills walked straight across the room and took my arm. I was so nervous that I looked down to make sure it was still attached.

"Mrs. Mills," I said, finding my tongue. "It's been such a lovely evening. I'm sorry that we've never met before this. I have great admiration for you and your family. Thank you for inviting Tom and me."

"Thank you, dear. I'm so glad you could come. Usually I dread these things a bit. We never intended to make them into such an event; it's just that Maximillian is a bit of a loner, so we settled on having just one dinner a year, that way he could look at it like a holiday. Like Christmas, but without Jesus. I mean, he's here, don't get me wrong." She stopped and looked at me. "Apologies, dear, I do tend to babble."

"You're not babbling," I said. "I like that approach to the dinner. Like a holiday."

"Thank you, dear," she said, genuinely flattered. "It was I who made the guest list this year," she added cheerfully, "that's why this is the best one yet."

"Good guests," I said honestly. "Mrs. Morgan is one of my favorite people in New York."

"Mine, too," she said, grabbing a breadstick from the cheese tray and waving it around, "though I did just find her sitting by the edge of our swimming pool with her feet in the water."

"But that's precisely why she's one of my favorite people in New York," I said, smiling.

She laughed and ate half the breadstick. "I let her stay, don't worry. Oh, and dear," she said, smiling at me. "Maximillian is going to give two or three million to the hospital, so tell Tom to stop sweating."

She didn't give me a chance to thank her, and I didn't tell Tom to stop sweating. I was rather enjoying watching him, one of the most suave men in New York, become a nervous wreck among society. But when I told him in the cab home, he rolled down the window, stuck his head out, and actually screamed with glee, like a very vocal cat.

When we got to our building, Sam brought me a bouquet of magenta roses. "Mrs. Edgeworth, from your hairdresser," he said. "I didn't bring them up, as I didn't want to interrupt your family. Shall I bring them up now?"

"They look really nice down here, Sam," I said as Tom practically skipped to the elevator. "Why don't you keep them? I'll just take the card."

I looked at the card before joining Tom. The card was indeed from Jean-Pierre. I turned it over. On the back it said "TW telephone 2."

"She got the envelope," Turner said as I stood in a glass telephone booth picking at a thread in my old blue jeans at precisely two in the morning.

"You're quite sure?"

"I'm positive. And Rina?"

"Yes?"

"I hope you enjoyed your night out. You looked beautiful."

I hung up the phone, grinning. Suddenly, that unforgiving torture chamber of a dress was my very favorite.

CHAPTER 24

I woke up just three hours after I'd spoken with Turner, went to the hallway, and sat by the window. I wanted to replay the telephone call. The sound of Turner's voice as he told me I looked beautiful. I wanted to sew the memory into my mind, so that it would always be there to return to. I let my forehead rest against the glass and looked down at the sidewalk on the other side of Fifth, tracing it with my finger, right to left, left to right, until I heard Tom's voice bellow from the bedroom. "The baby's awake!" he called out. I stood and rushed down the hall. But it was okay. The stitches of my memory were already in place.

I fell back asleep with Peter, and when we woke up Tom was gone. With the baby on my hip, we looked in on Gerrit, who was still dreaming, and started making breakfast. An hour later, I was eating with the boys when the telephone rang. Sam had a note for me. I opened the card that he brought up on a silver tray. Not surprisingly, Ava Newman was requesting my company.

I put the boys in front of the television and telephoned Turner.

"Good morning," he said. And something about the way he said it made me feel like we'd spent the night much closer to each other than we really had.

"Good morning," I said, smiling wider than I did most mornings. I told him about Ava's note.

"I'll go, of course, yes?"

"Of course," he repeated.

"Do I mention the envelope?"

"I think you have to."

"So then I just tell her the truth. Max asked me to give it to her."

"In this line of work, the truth is rarely recommended, but here, I think it's your best option. Try to get her talking, like you're a concerned friend. Why is Max so worried about her? Why does he not want her to leave the country? And then maybe she'll tell you more about what she's been doing in Washington."

"So that I can replace her?"

"Ideally. Sounds like her choices are Cuba or Russia. Either way, that leaves one seat on the D.C.-bound train open for you."

I looked at the boys. There was more food around Peter's chair than there was on his plate. Gerrit had jumped down from his seat and was eating it happily. How a woman like me was going to get to Washington, I had no idea, but first, I had to worry about getting downtown.

At noon, with the overpaid and extremely patient Sarah Beach at the house, I walked to the mailbox to drop off my note to Minkie Mills. As Sarah had kept Gerrit from Scotch-taping himself to my calf, I had scribbled out:

> Dear Minkie,
> With hosts as gracious as you and Maximillian, your dinner was in fact a holiday. Thank you for such a memorable evening. I enjoyed it tremendously, as did Tom. (As did Mrs. Morgan and her feet, but that goes without saying.)
> —Katharina Edgeworth

I made sure my letter was safely off, then took the subway to Fifty-third Street, practically spinning in circles to see if I was being followed by the FBI, the KGB, or both. I didn't see anyone, but just in case, I went north on foot when I should have been heading west, and then finally turned the right way when I was certain I was alone.

Ava was standing out front of the Rivoli Theatre in a yellow dress. It was casual, but it still felt as bright and promising as a sunrise.

"Rina," she said affectionately. She put her hand softly on my shoulder. "Thanks for coming. I had such a nice time with you after the meeting, I thought we could do it again, but before midnight."

"I'm so glad you sent a note. It's hard to get away, what with the boys," I said, smiling. "My husband doesn't like me to leave them too much. But sometimes I manage."

"I'm glad you managed today."

"I reminded him that I hadn't been to the cinema in nearly three years," I said, looking at the marquee.

The first part was a lie; the second part was true. I had not been to the cinema since before Gerrit was born.

"No cinema in three years? But they have the best air-conditioning! For that alone you have to get your husband to let you out more."

Were communists allowed to care so much about air-conditioning? I didn't ask.

At the ticket counter, I reached into my purse and insisted I pay the dollar forty for our admission fee.

"Thank you," she said as we waited for the cashier to make change. She opened her purse to show off a silver flask. "Ever see a movie drunk?"

"Not in a long while," I said, unable to suppress a grin.

"Ever steal anything on your way in?" she said as the man ahead of us dropped his wallet on the ground. She rushed over, picked it up, and tapped him on the shoulder. He seemed exceedingly thankful, both that his wallet had been returned and that a woman with Ava Newman's face was doing the honors.

"You know," she said as she joined me. "Not a car or anything. Something easy, like pickpocketing."

I pictured myself calling up Tom from prison. *Oh, hello, dear,* I'd say brightly. *Just doing a short stint at Sing Sing on some mucked-up charge. The police called it pickpocketing, I call it borrowing for an unspecified amount of time, like eternity.* It would not go well.

"I never have."

"Not even as a child?"

"No. But my mother is the kind of woman who can melt your confidence in a glance. I wouldn't have dared." I paused. "Why do you ask? The wallet?"

"The wallet," she agreed, waiting a beat too long. "I think it's a sign of a good . . . person," she said, eyeing the crowd around us. The word communist was on her lips, I could tell. "You never wanted more than you had."

"I wasn't exactly wanting."

"Still. My sisters and I weren't wanting, but we stole all the time."

"Well, I have brothers. Their preferred crime was fistfights."

We entered the theater and headed upstairs. "*Carnival Story.* Sounds a bit ridiculous, but who cares? All I've watched lately are the Army-McCarthy hearings, and as theatrical as they are—may that man burn," she whispered, "it does seem to raise my stress levels rather than lower them. Did you watch yesterday?"

"I tuned in," I said, which wasn't a lie. Ever since *the* dinner, I was determined to watch at least a few minutes every evening.

"That pig McCarthy daring the Eisenhower administration to indict him for receiving secret information? He doesn't know squat about secret information. He thinks the hotbed of communism is Fort Monmouth, New Jersey. An army base! It's laughable. He's laughable. And I would laugh, if he wasn't just evil walking."

"He is that," I said in agreement. I was no fan of communism, but I was also no fan of McCarthy. And neither, it seemed of late, were most Americans. If he had lost Vivi Reede and her husband, a couple who had written check after check for Eisenhower, then he was going to lose everybody.

"Jacob says I need to learn to relax, but I told him I'm not wired that way. I feed on . . ."

I could tell Ava was about to say danger. Even in the dimly lit theater I could see the D dangling on her lips.

"I feed on activity," she said finally. "I get a sense that you do, too, even if you haven't had much of it lately. That's why I sent you to meet dear old Max."

"Max," I repeated, louder than I expected to. "He certainly provided . . . activity."

"And he can provide more than that, if need be. Which is why I wanted you to meet him. In this world, it's good to have both a gas pedal and a brake." Ava leaned her weight on the armrest and inched closer to me. "It was you who dropped the envelope, yes? From Max?"

"It was. I was hoping to find you home, but you weren't and I had the boys with me. I'm sorry I had to slide it under your door. It probably wasn't the right thing to do. But it seemed important."

"Did you read it?" Ava asked. Despite the darkness, I could see the change in her face.

"I did," I admitted. "He was so upset, I wanted to make sure I wasn't going to give you anything that would upset you, too. But all I really gathered is that he wants you to travel to Cuba instead of Russia. I didn't know you were planning on going to Russia," I lied, trying to sound unconcerned.

"I am," she whispered excitedly. "It's been on the table for some time now. It was all Jacob's idea actually. He thinks I could make a real difference here in the U.S. party, but to do that, I need to learn from the Soviets first. He'll come over, too, when his health is better."

"Is he unwell? He seemed so vivacious when I saw him."

"Oh, you know Jacob," she said, sitting back. "He always seems vivacious. And he is, he still is actually quite vivacious, he's just a bit run-down at the edges. He works too much, as I'm sure you're aware. So that's where I come in. I want to help shoulder the responsibility."

"But Max does not want you to go."

"Yes, I know he doesn't. He's a dear," she said, smiling. "He worries about me. He doesn't think an American woman can handle being in Moscow on her own. That I'll be safer in a place like Cuba because it's so close to our own shores. And since he travels there quite frequently, he knows all the good hiding places. But he doesn't understand what I'm made of. I need to go to Moscow for Jacob, but also for me. I need to do something that lays the path for our future. You understand that, surely?"

I nodded, truthfully. "I do. But Cuba could help lay that path, no? Castro? 'History Will Absolve Me'?"

"Not in the right way. Max knows my heart is not in Cuba, but he's still convinced that it would be better for me. He's just too scared to tell Jacob."

"Why?"

"Because," she said, not able to hide her surprise, "Jacob is one of the only men in America who is allowed to give Moscow orders, instead of the other way around. That's why I know I'll be okay in Russia, because everyone associates me with him."

I thought back to the wild look in Max's eyes as we sped down the highway. What was waiting for Ava in Russia? She seemed quite sure that her association with Jacob would protect her, but I was starting to have serious doubts. "When will you leave?"

"Soon," she said, grinning. "But not too soon. We've only just met. We must have some fun first."

"Fun . . . three-letter word . . . I feel like I've heard it before."

"You're desperate for it, I know," she said, laughing. "Come on, why not start now?"

Ava Newman was effervescent as ever, but I was sure that there was more to Max's message than a simple coin toss between reporting to Moscow or hiding out in Havana.

We found two seats in the front row and watched the rest of the upper balcony fill up. As an attractive Negro man came in, Ava raised her eyebrows.

"For a moment, I thought that was Turner Wells. But Wells is even better-looking, isn't he?"

I smiled and said nothing.

"Really, don't you think Turner is one of the most handsome men you've ever seen?"

I thought she was going to add "for a Negro." Or "if that's to your taste." But she didn't. She just reached into her bag, removed the flask, took a swig, and gave it to me.

"He has a lot of presence," I said diplomatically. I pulled on the flask to keep myself from saying anything else.

"Oh, is that what we're calling it these days?" she murmured.

"That's what we're calling it," I replied, laughing.

The man who had almost lost his wallet came in, waved to Ava, and sat across the aisle from us.

"Think how many people we could feed if we stole that man's wallet."

"Ava—"

"Oh pish, Katharina. I'm kidding."

She clearly wasn't.

"My sister Ginger always got caught when she shoplifted. She had the dexterity of a panda. Then she'd start crying and look at me and I'd pretend that she wasn't quite right in the head and we'd get away with it. But she's gotten better in her old age. Steals from her husband all the time, though she claims she has no choice. Her priorities, of course, are rather Connecticut."

"But here you are. The Connecticut priorities long gone."

Ava started to laugh. "Do not get me wrong, Katharina Edgeworth, I can't shake Connecticut completely, try as I do. I love broiled salmon, I have an extremely accurate backhand, and I look exceedingly good in tennis whites—or so I've been told. But other than a meal at home with Dad and my sisters, that town, the lifestyle, and certainly the morals are dead to me."

"What about your sisters? Are they in the party, too?"

"Dear God, no. Not those two vanilla milkshakes. My father had enough common sense to only confide in me." She paused. "They will die clutching not their pearls, but their money. But I was always different. Or that's what Daddy says anyway. What do you think they do, my sisters?"

"They're housewives."

"Exactly. Overeducated housewives. My sister Tracy was first in her class at Bennington. An absolute science whiz. She was all set to study chemistry after graduation, was even admitted to Johns Hopkins, and then William Kennedy Thayer proposed. A man she simply couldn't say no to. So now she lives with him in Cos Cob; they have three children, two dogs, one shared drinking problem, and the only kind of chemistry she performs is in the kitchen, perfecting her mother-in-law's baked Alaska recipe, which, frankly, is and will always be inedible. Tastes like ice cream wrapped in a gym sock."

"And the other sister?"

"Ginger? Less drinking, more children. How does that saying go?" Ava said reflectively. "'Shall I buy a dog or have a baby? Depends, do you want to ruin your carpet or your life?'"

"Is that how the saying goes?"

"That's how it goes."

"Got one about pickpocketing?"

"Nope. I'm trying to be a good communist, remember? I owe it to the world, after being such a good capitalist in my youth."

She lay back in her seat and closed her eyes, showing off perfect winged eyeliner.

Ava clearly believed in all the party espoused, was even willing to risk her life going to Moscow, ignoring Max's somewhat tamer suggestion. Still, I couldn't help but feel as if communism had simply found her at the right time. I imagined that she'd grown terribly tired of the sweaty young men trying to paw at her, of another bowl of ham and pea soup at so-and-so's debutante ball, of facing a future of raising children who played tennis instead of kick the can, and who had homemade chocolate mousse instead of fire in their bellies.

Ava opened her eyes and looked out at the crowd, taking them in with the same enthusiasm as she did everything.

"We should pickpocket that one," she murmured as a stout woman with an alligator purse and large diamond earrings walked in.

It seemed like one day Ava had just started choking on entitlement. The unfairness of it all, but also the boredom that came with it. It was a great fight to acquire wealth. Something to wrap your life around, but once you had it, the only thing to focus on was living rich. And that, I had quickly learned, could be a surprisingly dreadful bore.

I'd been around the Edgeworths for less than a decade and about once a week I started to choke on their entitlement. I didn't fault them for being rich. Someone in that long line of Edgeworths had worked very hard to get there. What I couldn't stomach was how the future generations felt they deserved all their money, their lives of comfort. Admittedly, Tom was different—I would never have fallen in love with him if he weren't. But the rest of them—well educated, attractive, moneyed—were just so sure that they deserved everything about their good life. I understood how someone like Ava, who looked at the world defiantly, could get to a breaking point and say, "Now how about we go about this differently?"

As the lights dimmed to almost nothing, readying the room for the movie to start, Ava leaned my way and hissed.

"Yes?" I said, laughing.

"I just wanted to say, before we lose ourselves to the picture, that I have the utmost respect for you, taking care of those tiny human beings. I bet you're glad to be away from it for a few hours."

"I'm pretty sure this cinema is heaven."

"Honestly, I don't know how my father did it."

"Even without knowing him, I can tell you that there aren't many like him."

"How do you deal with the quirks of it all? Of motherhood?" she asked, lowering her voice even more. "Or parenting, I should say, to include my dear old dad."

"The quirks . . . that's a diplomatic way to put it. I suppose you just do, because the quirks you're dealing with have heartbeats. So late at night, when the world is asleep, you take a bath, have a martini, and continue."

"That really is the only advice mothers need, isn't it?" she said, pausing to light a cigarette. "'You take a bath, have a martini, and continue.'"

"It's served me better than anything else," I replied dryly.

"And the good parts? Holding a sleeping baby and all that?"

"It can be wonderful. It *is* wonderful. But . . ."

"There's an asterisk? No one tells you there's an asterisk. Certainly not my sisters."

"You know how every year there is some movie that is supposed to be the best picture ever made? As in so good that you'll watch it and never be the same again."

"*Citizen Kane. Casablanca.*"

"Right. Movies like that. Anyway, you go to the theater, and you're so excited to see it. You've been meaning to go for weeks, life has gotten in the way, but you're finally there and you're thrilled to experience what everyone has been talking about."

"And then?"

"And then it's wonderful, it is. But because you're supposed to love it so much, you feel like you don't love it enough. Because you've been told that Orson Welles hung the moon, you're a little disappointed by his performance. Maybe what he hung was more like a shooting star."

"You feel about holding your babies as you do about Orson Welles on-screen?"

"In a way. It's magical to hold a sleeping baby, but I don't think it's the most magical feeling I've ever had. I've experienced things that were just as good."

"Like—"

"The Communist Party?"

"I was going to say sex," Ava said. "Or falling in love. No, sex."

"Like all of that," I replied.

"Sometimes, and really only very occasionally," she said thoughtfully, "it makes me sad that I don't want to know that feeling. Like I'm simply wired wrong."

"You're not wired wrong," I countered. "Sometimes it makes me sad that I'll never *not* know that feeling."

"That, *and* you don't know what it's like to steal," she whispered.

"I imagine it's terrifying."

"Depends what you're stealing. Information, instead of things. Ideas. It's different, right?"

I nodded in agreement.

"And besides," she said, flashing her million-dollar smile, "it's rather thrilling to be terrified."

CHAPTER 25

My head was swimming with Ava Newman when I exited the Fifth Avenue subway station and rushed to the apartment. As I did, I saw Carrie coming out the door.

"Carrie," I called to her as she headed uptown. She didn't turn. "Carrie," I said again, louder this time.

I watched her pause and finally turn to look at me. She was not smiling.

I looked at her in her pretty red dress, her expensive beige alligator shoes. She was the picture of Upper East Side perfection.

"You don't have Alice," I said.

"I don't. I'm going to the hairdresser." She looked at me, up and down and back again. Not in the way that women lovingly appraise one another. Her expression was full of disdain. "And you don't have the boys."

"I don't. The Edgeworths' housekeeper, Jilly, is here. She came to watch them again so I could get some air."

"What kind of air?" she asked flatly.

"Fresh?" I said, laughing.

"Fresh. Clever," she replied. She looked down at her watch, but I could tell she wasn't registering the time. She was trying to make it look like she was in a hurry.

"Carrie, is something the matter?" I asked.

"With me?" she said, raising her right eyebrow. "No. Of course not. There's nothing wrong with me. But I must be going, Rina, I'll be late to the hairdresser."

Even though we were the only ones on the sidewalk, she pushed past me, clipping my shoulder with hers. I stood there stunned, before turning to follow her.

"Carrie, stop, please. What's eating you? You're clearly upset with me."

"I'm not upset. I'm late," she insisted.

"Then give me the short version."

"Fine. The short version is that my sister Grace is here visiting," she said coolly.

"How lovely," I replied uncertainly. "Where is she in from?"

"San Francisco," Carrie said, glaring at me. "I haven't seen her in many months. Her husband teaches at Stanford and they've had quite a packed schedule. So to catch up properly we decided to go to dinner together at Tavern on the Green and then have a nightcap with friends at the Beresford. We decided that on such a nice night, it would be a crime not to walk there."

I nodded innocently as a bead of sweat slipped down my back.

"Enough. Just stop the act, Rina. I saw you," she said, hissing my name like it was an insult. "I saw you with that man," she added angrily.

I opened my mouth to say something—anything that could calm her down. A lie. Another lie.

She kept going. "We could have just walked up Central Park West, but the sun hadn't quite set, so we stayed in the park, on the path. Our shoes were getting dirty and we were about to move to the sidewalk when I nearly fainted, Rina. Because there you were, practically sitting in a Negro man's lap."

I took a step toward her but stayed silent. Still unable to find the words.

"Save your lies, Rina," she said, stopping me. "Please don't say, 'He's an old friend,' or 'I know him from the United Nations.' Sex, lust, love, whatever you want to call it, what I saw wasn't friendship. So don't deny it, Rina. It won't work."

Carrie took a step toward me, so close that I could smell her rose-scented perfume.

"You're cheating on your husband with a Negro man, Rina? What in the hell is wrong with you?" she hissed.

"I'm not."

"Don't waste your breath. And please don't offend me by speaking to me like I'm Alice."

"I'm not having an affair with that man," I repeated.

"Rina, I saw you. I stood there. I watched you."

I didn't protest further. "Are you going to say anything to Tom?" I asked quietly instead.

"I haven't decided. I certainly should. What is for certain is that I'm done saying anything to you."

She turned away and hurried up Fifth. I watched her until her red hair and graceful form disappeared.

Never alone. I was still never alone. In a town of nearly eight million, there were still familiar eyes on me.

I sat on a bench, running my fingers across the slate. Carrie could judge me, threaten to tell my husband—hell, she could even tell Tom for all I cared in that moment. It might put me in a prison of Tom's making for the rest of my life, it might be what finally brought our divorce, but it wouldn't change what I'd felt that evening. Something so strong, so tangible, that it was even visible in the dark.

CHAPTER 26

I inhaled sharply and approached apartment 5C. The door was open. I peered in, expecting the apartment to be empty, but Jacob Gornev was right there, asleep on his couch. I looked down at my watch. It was the right time, I was sure of it. I knocked on the door, in an attempt to rouse him, but he didn't stir.

I stepped softly inside. The living room was sparsely decorated, anonymous. As if he'd just moved in and might be leaving soon.

Turner had called me two hours earlier. He'd met with Jacob the night before. Jacob had wanted to catch up, which was code for asking a hundred and one questions about me. "I think I did okay," said Turner, who had, of course. "But now he wants to see you. He asked me to be the messenger. I'll have Sarah Beach come, and you'll go to Jacob's. Yes?"

"Yes. Though I do hope Sarah Beach attends classes sometimes."

"I'll relay that message, too," he'd said. I'd hung up the phone, but my hand lingered on the receiver for a minute afterward, the closest I could get to the man Carrie was certain I was having an affair with.

I took another step inside the apartment. I looked down at Jacob's face. He was much paler than the last time I'd seen him. He was sweating around his hairline and his mouth was open, as if he was desperate for more air. Ava was right; he looked unwell.

"Jacob," I whispered. He didn't budge. Finally, I crouched down and touched his shoulder, then shook it. He jumped up and knocked me over.

"Katharina, it's you," he said.

"I'm so sorry to have woken you," I said as he took my hand and helped me to my feet. "I should have left when I saw you sleeping, but the door was open, so I thought you were expecting me."

"I'm always expecting you," he said. "Now that I've met you again, I keep looking for you on the street, when I come out of restaurants, but I hadn't seen you again, so I thought I'd send you, Katharina West Edgeworth, a message. Bit long, your name, isn't it?"

"This from a Ukrainian," I said, releasing his hand. "Your middle name is Vladislav."

He started to laugh. "How do you remember that?"

"I remember everything from the Columbia days," I said, my smile inching higher. I pointed to the half dozen books on his shelf. Three of them were in German. "The days of you translating Goethe, Bertolt Brecht." I grinned, seeing his worn copy of *Die Dreigroschenoper*.

He reached for my hand again. I thought he was going to pat it in his affectionate way, but he held on to it. I didn't pull it away.

"Anyway, I don't think fate is kind enough to keep bringing people together, so I'm glad you sent a message."

Despite his warm touch, Jacob seemed a very different man from the one he'd been three weeks ago. He was much thinner, his shoulder bones pressing against the fabric of his shirt. His face was white, and his eyes were rimmed with red. He looked sick, and not just with a common cold. Even his hand felt limper. Only his voice sounded the same.

He let my hand go. "I've found that people are more fearful of open doors than closed ones," he said.

"In this town, that's probably true."

"This town," he repeated, clearing his throat. It sounded like there was a bear trapped in his lungs. "It attracts the best and the brightest and the worst of the worst. The criminals, the saints, the beauties, and the gargoyles. And they all deserve it. They all deserve a slice of New York, don't you think?"

"I do," I said earnestly.

"I don't think I'm supposed to love New York so much," he said.

"Why not?"

"Wall Street," he said, shaking his head. "It's no good."

"The street or the activities?"

"All of it. They should just plow it down and make it a skating pond."

"Now, there's an idea."

"But there is so much in New York that is good," he said, his voice rising like a skyscraper. "There's so much energy here, I never just feel like walking, I want to be running, bouncing. Everyone deserves to live a life that they love so much that they want to bounce through it."

Jacob may have looked like the blood was draining out of him, but his brain, his nature, never stopped leaping.

"Which is why," he said, pausing, "I am an equalist. No, let's just say it as it is, shall we? I'm a communist."

"So I've heard," I replied.

"Turner Wells told you."

"He did."

"What else did he tell you?"

"What else did he tell *you*?"

Jacob raised his eyebrows and sat down. As he did, he winced. "I've been sick," he said, closing his eyes. "Which I'm sure is obvious. But I'm getting better now."

"I'm glad."

He looked at my face, put his hand on my cheek, let it slide slowly down my neck, my arm, then rested it on my knee.

"Are you sure you're married?"

"Very married."

I thought of Carrie's threat. Very married for now, anyway.

"Is that any fun, very married?" he asked. It seemed an honest question.

"It has its merits."

He laughed, which turned into a wheeze. "Timing is a strange thing, isn't it, Katharina? Beautiful Katharina."

"That is most certainly true. About timing. The rest of it, I don't know."

"I'm not lying about the beautiful part, Katharina. I never lie," he said, moving closer to me.

"*That* is certainly not true."

"Okay. It's not. But I only lie for a good cause."

He put his head back on the couch, as if it had just gotten too heavy to keep upright. "I should have told you when we were at Columbia. Maybe we could have gone through all this together."

"What is all this?"

He sat up again and smiled. "It's a lonely life sometimes, isn't it?"

"That's not the word I'd use to describe my days. Lonely sounds appealing."

"Maybe it would all have been simpler if you had married me." He put his hand back on my knee.

"Maybe," I said, smiling, thinking that though nothing about Jacob was ever simple, perhaps marriage would have been. "But instead you're married to . . . the KGB?"

"Maybe," he said, laughing heartily. I'd forgotten how few things in the world felt as good as a full, true laugh produced by Jacob Gornev. "Turner said you're as good as they come. I told him I knew that already. But you, with him, I have to say that came as a surprise," Jacob remarked.

"My love life," I said frankly, "has been a surprise."

"A letdown?" he suggested.

"No. A surprise."

He nodded thoughtfully.

"Even though it might not look that way, given all of Tom's money, I did marry for love."

"And is it enough?"

I shook my head no. "It was. Things have changed. Now it might not be."

"What's changed?"

"We had children. I became Katharina Edgeworth, mother. All those little languages of mine reduced to a mere parlor trick. 'Katharina can speak German! Katharina can speak French! Go ahead, darling, speak to the ambassador's wife.'"

"Does he call them little languages?"

"He does."

"Said like a true monolingual," Jacob said, sinking farther into the couch.

"He is that."

"But Turner Wells doesn't think that way."

"No."

"Because Turner Wells has that quality."

"Which quality?"

"Of seeing the light through the trees," Jacob said, smiling.

I raised my eyebrows.

"More than anyone else in America, the Negro will benefit from a classless, stateless society, one without color lines. Turner Wells sees that. Even if it takes time to get there, he knows it's an outcome worth fighting for."

"I know. It's why I was attracted to the party in the first place," I offered.

"No. You weren't at first. You were attracted to Turner Wells."

I looked right at Jacob and waited for him to continue. He didn't.

"I suppose that I was."

"I suppose that you're in love with him."

Married women like me were not allowed to fall in love with anyone else. We couldn't even look at another man. Our sexuality was supposed to die as soon as we heard our child's first cry. But that wasn't what had happened to me. I thought of myself in the guest bedroom at night. I was not thinking about my children. I was not thinking about Tom. I was lying on my back imagining Turner Wells.

"I could be," I said evenly. I looked at the ground but didn't let go of Jacob's hand. "But as I said: Marriage is a surprise. So is Turner Wells. So are you."

I almost added Ava Newman to that list, but I realized that Jacob might not know that we'd spent time together.

"Katharina," Jacob said softly, but his words turned to coughing. He smiled at me, the mood breaking.

"I don't know about your husband. But I like Turner Wells," he said once he'd regained his voice.

I thought about Carrie, how she could right now be in the process of ripping apart my marriage with her well-timed observations. Did I care? I did. But not enough to stop what I was doing.

Jacob leaned in, his mouth close to mine, and smiled. He placed his finger on my lips and sat back.

"Cards on the table, then. What did Turner Wells tell you about me?"

"He said that you're practically running the Communist Party in Manhattan. That there are people above you, but that on the ground, you do it all. And that everyone knows you and everyone likes you."

Jacob stood and went to close his front door.

"And?" he said, coming back to the couch.

"And that you have important ties to Moscow."

"What kind?"

"He didn't say." I had to get Jacob to trust me, but I also needed him to keep trusting Turner Wells.

"He didn't?" Jacob looked at me with a hungry, passionate expression that even time and illness could not alter. "He didn't tell you who I'm working with at the KGB?"

"He did not." Jacob started coughing, deeply. He cleared his throat and coughed again until he was blue in the face.

"Does he know that Ava is going to Moscow?"

"He mentioned that."

"Did he mention why?"

"No."

"Do you want to know why?" he asked between coughs.

"Only if you want to tell me."

"I know you like her," he said. "I know you've seen her. So I'll tell you why. I want her to go to Moscow because the FBI is tailing her. I've been under FBI surveillance for months now, but with her it's new. And she's American, so it's too risky. She'll be safer in Russia than anywhere else. I need her to get the hell out of New York. I think I have a month to do it, maybe two. If she's not gone by July . . ." He started coughing again and went to the kitchen for a glass of water. He sat next to me and drained it. "What's this stuff even good for?" He went back to the kitchen and came out with two drinks. Real drinks this time.

"Take this, Katharina," he said, handing me one. "We need to have a long conversation."

CHAPTER 27

I had been waiting for Ava to contact me, but on a day that loomed large in my mind, I realized how much I wanted her verve, and her guts, by my side.

For the past two years, on May 26, I had gone to Turtle Bay and stood in front of the United Nations buildings. It was the anniversary of my first day working at the UN, the day I walked off that bus at Lake Success, passed those flags, and said, "Hello. *Bonjour!*" to a brand-new life. A better life. I'd performed this ritual in 1952, '53, and was getting ready to do so again today. Only this time, I was finally considering signing up for a tour to enter the General Assembly Building, that beautiful piece of modernist architecture I never got to see. I was gone by '52 when it opened, so I had only ever known the General Assembly to meet in Queens.

Some people felt the Holy Spirit in churches; I felt it in front of iconic buildings. I nearly had my soul come out of my ears the first time I was in Bryant Park and saw the American Radiator Building up close. Those dramatic black bricks piled up with gold leaf molded by the hands of men. The same thing happened when I got to know the New York Public Library as an adult. The Waldorf Astoria. Rockefeller Center. And the Woolworth Building. I knew I'd have the same reaction when I went inside the General Assembly. That more than any other building in New York, it would feel like my church.

After asking Jilly if she wouldn't mind watching the boys for two hours, I picked up the phone again and called Ava Newman. She was home.

"Can I ask you a favor?" I said as she breathed hello into the phone.

"Of course. Need something stolen?"

"No, more like a shot of courage. There's something I want to do, have wanted to do for two years, but never felt like I could. Until now. With the right company, that is."

"Well! This sounds exciting. What should I wear? Or *not* wear?"

"Wear your most international outfit," I said. "Can you meet me outside of the United Nations headquarters on Forty-second Street?"

"Thirty minutes?" said Ava excitedly.

"I'll be there," I replied. "Wearing a beret."

"Should I ask why?" she said, laughing.

"If I can build up the courage to go inside the General Assembly Building, I'll explain everything."

"Listen, Rina, you've called the right person," she said, hanging up.

Ava was standing right outside the United Nations entrance in a powder blue dress embroidered like an Indian sari. Her look did not scream CPUSA.

"The UN was not created to take mankind to heaven, but to save humanity from hell!" Ava bellowed as I approached her.

"Dag Hammarskjöld. UN secretary-general," I said, smiling.

"Good speech," she said, turning to stare at the building.

"Good man," I replied.

"What an impressive pile of concrete," she said as we took in all 380 feet of the building, the shining Secretariat Building towering above it.

"Limestone."

"Just like the Great Pyramid. How international. Now, let's go in, and you can explain to me why you haven't set foot in here before. Nice beret, by the way."

I repositioned it on my head and held my breath until we were through the bas-relief doors and the security check. I felt like I could finally exhale when we walked past the building's row of fifty-foot-tall windows, had climbed the stairs, and were about to be led inside the General Assembly Hall.

"I thought maybe I'd just feel too much, that I wouldn't quite be able to take it because I loved my work so much. I liked the person I was at the UN so much. I knew that the me visiting this building that I never got to call my own wouldn't measure up to the me I'd been before. So I never came."

"But you're here now," she said as we walked through the double doors, at the back of our tour group of fifteen. "Do you finally think you measure up? I think you do."

I walked into the Hall and stopped. It was so much better than it looked in the papers, better even than on television, with its towering ceiling, the raised speaker's rostrum, and the green marble podium, positioned below wooden paneling and the beautiful UN seal.

"If my soul escapes, maybe you could catch it for me," I whispered.

"Sure thing," she said, looking up at the ceiling as we walked down the center aisle.

"Look," I said, nodding. "That's his desk. Dag Hammarskjöld's."

"Not bad, not bad at all," she said. She put her hand on my shoulder and squeezed it. Maybe Ava was more than the Miss America of communists. Maybe she was simply the best among them.

"You must have really felt like something, *someone* working here," she whispered as we sat down in two of the 1,800 chairs to listen to the tour guide. "I really mean that."

"I did." I nodded, trying not to choke on my own words. "I wasn't in Manhattan for most of it. This building wasn't finished until the fall of 'fifty-two. The Secretariat Building opened in January 'fifty-one, but we didn't leave Lake Success till May, so I only worked there about six months. All that time at the UN, and right when I could have walked to work instead of commuting an hour each way to and from Long Island, I had to leave."

"That's utter garbage, isn't it?"

"It is," I said, smiling, half listening to our guide, mostly noting the steadiness of my heart. I'd been right. This was the right year to finally walk inside.

"But look at you now. You're glowing. A heart in port."

"That's a good way to put it."

"I hope you find yourself back here one day," she said as they escorted us out of the grand room. "Working here, that is."

I looked back to see the secretary-general's desk one last time.

"Do you read the help wanted section of the papers?" Ava said as we followed the tour group toward the building's exit.

"The help wanted section? Not since I graduated from Columbia."

"You should. You know, if you ever need some motivation to keep going with work, our work in particular. Or if you ever decide to come back here."

"Why is that?"

"'Help wanted female. Receptionist. Under 30 desired. Help wanted female. Secretary. Age up to 28 years. Pleasant disposition. Help wanted male. Engineer. Help wanted male. Physician.' No age limit, no pleasant disposition needed, no shorthand required. When you read the help wanted section, you realize that to men we're human, smiling typewriters that conveniently double as a source of their perverse fantasies."

"Did you just say perverse fantasies?"

"I did."

"The thing is," I said as we walked across the plaza to admire the Secretariat Building, "it wasn't just the work. It was the life. The life I had in here, the life I had outside. The friendships. There was a girl who worked with me, and, I suppose, I'd just never had a friend like her. She left a gaping hole in my heart when I left that building forever."

"She was . . ."

"She was and is Marianne Fontaine. A French girl. An American

French girl. I adored her like you can only adore someone who is not related to you. Together, we inhaled everything about postwar New York. And then I had children and she dropped me like a bad habit."

I had tried to see Marianne many times. But she always had excuses, and after a few of them, her message came in loud and clear. A partner in crime meant a partner in *crime*. Not a partner in peekaboo, bath time, and nervous breakdowns.

"Being a woman is complicated. And I think it's especially complicated right now. More than it was during the war. Sometimes people—women—get angry when we don't make the same life decisions they do," Ava said thoughtfully, interrupting my thoughts. "They want us to, because they want us to enforce that they're doing the right thing. They want us to serve as confirmation for their decisions. In Marianne's case, that was not getting married, not having kids, and living an intellectual life, right?"

"That's exactly right. Plus a gallon of fun on top of all that intellectual rigor."

We sat on a nearby bench and turned our attention back to the General Assembly Building.

"You lived that way too, maybe you thought you always would," said Ava, "but then you changed your mind. Maybe she assumed that you'd want her to change her mind, too."

"But I didn't. What I wanted was her. For our friendship to continue like it was."

Ava raised her eyebrows.

"Except for the sex with all the wrong men," I said quietly. "I understood that that had to end. For me, anyway."

"Because now you're having sex with all the right men?" she asked, grinning. "Or at least one of them. The one who is not your husband."

"I plead the Fifth," I said, putting my face in my hands.

"It's okay," she whispered. "It's a woman's right to do what she wants with her mind and her body. Even the UN says so."

I understood why a woman like Ava was attracted to the Communist Party. Maybe she believed in certain tenets, like the importance of a society that was motivated by factors other than sex and money. But for a woman as smart and dynamic as Ava, I suspected it was mostly that the Russians let her play the game. There were no female special agents in the FBI, but there were certainly women in the KGB. Maybe they had to go to bed a bit to do it, but at least the door was open. In America, that door was bolted shut.

Perhaps the world's women were all just very sick of having doors bolted shut.

"Come on," said Ava, grabbing my arm and standing us up. "I don't want you to run into that French beast, or to get too caught up in the might-have-beens. You've got a good life now, and a purpose, too. Peace is lovely and it's nice to spend your days rowing in Eden, but what America needs is an uprising. That's what we're contributing to. For now, let's row to a bar instead, shall we?"

"Let's row," I said, smiling, letting her pull me back to blue skies, to the present day, to a new New York.

CHAPTER 28

"Turner, I need to see you in person," I said. I wanted to tell him all about Ava, about our two hours together, but I focused first on what the FBI had been waiting for. "Jacob asked me to go to Washington. For him. He finally asked."

"When can you meet?"

I looked at my watch. It was two o'clock in the morning, and I was standing in the phone booth at Sixty-third and Madison. "Sometime in the next two hours."

Peter had woken up a half hour earlier. I'd gotten him back to sleep and hoped he'd now make it until the morning. Tom had seemed so exhausted from a four-hour surgery that I imagined he would, too. Gerrit never woke at night anymore, needing his energy to continue terrorizing upper Manhattan during daylight hours.

"Where are you now?"

"Near my apartment."

"I'm home, as you know, but I have to be downtown in a few hours anyway. Long story. Shall we meet at—"

"City Hall?" I said instinctually.

"Good. Meet me outside the Municipal Building. Leave now. You'll beat me there, but I'm right behind you."

I reached the building in twenty minutes. I got out of the taxi and walked with my head down to one of the limestone arches. Just the sound of my heels on the ground made my heart twist with nostalgia.

I stopped and listened for footsteps belonging to Ruby and Patricia, for the swish of our skirts. But Patricia had moved to Seattle and had four children. We only kept up with each other through Christmas cards and the occasional postcard. "Rina, I've been meaning to write, but Teddy accidentally broke my nose with his very firm skull. Can you imagine it! But who can blame the darling. In short, four children is a circus, but I wouldn't trade it for a thing!" her last letter had said. She sounded nothing like the girl who'd screamed out bad poetry in Washington Square Park or mixed us drinks with 94 proof whiskey in our apartment while the heater rattled. "Enough of these, and that thing will sound as pleasant as a steel drum," she'd say, grinning.

Ruby had fought marital handcuffs longer, moving to Washington, D.C., to work for Margaret Chase Smith when she was elected to the Senate in 1948. But by the time Smith gave her famous anti-McCarthy speech in 1950, Ruby was already gone, busy having babies in Smith's native Maine. She didn't even bother to send Christmas cards anymore.

A few minutes later, I saw a man in the shadows of one of the arches. There was no one else around. I heard him open a door. Without hesitating, I went toward it and stepped inside. It was Turner. He flicked open his lighter, which provided more atmosphere than illumination.

"Be careful," he said quietly.

We walked down two flights of dark, dank stairs. Then he opened another door and I saw a familiar sign. We were in the City Hall subway station. It had been closed since the mid-forties, but it looked the same as it had when I exited there for work, with chandeliers and skylights, which let in sunshine during the day.

"Are you all right?" said Turner, coming close to me.

"Yes, I mean, I think so," I said, my body responding to his presence. "I think what I am is happy."

"Good, then tell me everything."

I could not tell Turner everything that was running through my mind, but I could tell him about Jacob.

"I spent three hours at Jacob's apartment," I said.

In the faint light, I saw him smile. "I wish I could say 'Give me the three-hour version,' but it will have to be the fifteen-minute version."

"He told me some things you all know. His work at United States Shipping Incorporated, which is indeed a KGB front. He reports directly to the KGB in Moscow. He is the main point of contact for Ava and their Washington source. Or sources. He arranges the meetings and then gets the papers to Moscow. But he told me some things you maybe don't know."

Turner raised his eyebrows. "Like . . ."

"Like he used to be Ava Newman's lover."

"How convenient. And his apartment still looks like a fire hazard? Wall-to-wall books, and a well-stocked bar?"

"No, it was nearly empty."

He flicked his lighter open and closed and glanced at me. "The papers from Washington. They go to Moscow. You're sure?"

"Yes. Via the consulate."

"Names?"

"None yet."

"He didn't say Nick Solomon?"

"No. Why?"

"That's who Ava Newman meets in Washington. He's the only man we know about. He works at Treasury. But it seems like he can't possibly be the biggest fish. She wouldn't be making all those trips just for someone from Treasury."

"Hopefully I'll be able to tell you about that soon. Jacob asked me to go back and forth to Washington in Ava's place."

"Because she's going to Moscow?"

"Yes, by July. Ask me why she's going to Moscow?"

"Why?"

"Because the FBI is tailing her, and he's worried about her. Very worried. Especially since she's American. He's convinced she'll be safer there."

Turner's expression turned thoughtful. "But Max isn't. He's convinced she'll be safer in Cuba."

"I don't think she's considering Cuba."

"What? Why the hell not?" said Turner angrily.

"I don't know," I said, lowering my voice. "I don't think she told Jacob about it, but she did tell him something else."

Turner looked at me.

"That the CRC has a man in the FBI. The janitor. I told Ava. Now Jacob asked me how he can have access to him."

"Of course he did," Turner said, smiling again. "I should have seen that coming."

"What will you do about it?"

"We can leak something small. Something that will prove it's true, but that's not very damaging."

"Okay."

"So, Ava will be gone by July."

"By July. Jacob says he plans to follow her, when his health is better."

"When will that be?"

"Considering he could barely rise to greet me, it won't be July."

"And when are you going to Washington?"

"Friday."

"Anything else?"

"Just that he knows Ava's being tailed by the FBI, and he knows he's being tailed by the FBI."

"Well, you know what?"

"What?"

"He's right," he said, smiling. "But he doesn't know that I'm also on his tail."

"No, he does not." I looked up at the chandelier and reached my hand up. "How did you know to come down here?"

"Sometimes this job requires you to hide with the rats."

"I did not feel like a rat when I worked at City Hall," I said. "I felt like a grown woman doing important things. I loved that feeling."

"That was the best thing about being in the military, too," he said. "I always felt like I was doing important things. Sometimes it was scary as hell, but it mattered, so you got over it." He lowered his head and looked at me.

"What you do now matters," I said.

"It does, but it's more complicated."

"Than the military?"

"Definitely. I never questioned what I was doing with the military. But now . . . The thing is, Rina, I like these men in the CRC. Paul Robeson is incredible. Talented and kind. His politics may be in the wrong place, but his heart is not. Same goes for Dashiell Hammett. He's a good man. Some of these people in the CRC, most of them, have made one wrong decision and ninety-nine right ones. Does that make them good or bad?"

"Depends what the bad decision was."

"Joining the Communist Party USA, joining CRC leadership, or giving the CRC money to defend, among others, communists."

"Then it's bad."

He flicked the lighter open and closed again. "After all these years, I can say with conviction that it's more stupid than bad."

"But you're still reporting on them. You're spying on them."

"I am, because I know they are doomed with or without me, and I'm searching for the light through the trees." I smiled, remembering Jacob using the same phrase. "Or in Manhattan, let's call it the streetlight through the alleys. I wake up and look out at this wonderful city and I want to move it ahead. Plenty of people where I live are going nowhere fast. These little boys—and girls," he said glancing at me.

"What does the future hold for Negro children? Dead-end jobs. Jobs, not careers. Never careers. Even with the *Brown versus Board* decision, that's not going to change the jobs these kids get. They're not all going to head to Harvard and Vassar in their letter sweaters after graduating from integrated schools. How many Negro girls were at Vassar with you?"

"Zero."

"Columbia?"

"A handful. A small handful. I remember three."

"Don't you want Negro girls to go to those schools, to aspire to something other than watching your children so that you can go to work?"

Both of us were well aware that Jilly was doing exactly that for me.

I nodded and we stayed quiet for a minute.

Finally, I smiled and said, "Shall I join the CRC, then?"

"I can say unequivocally," he said, grinning, "that we'd love to have you." He flicked his lighter closed. "All this aside, I do believe communism is dangerous. It's just another form of false hope. Of brainwashing. Of striking down independent thought. You can bet I sang that out when I met Hoover, and I meant it. And that conviction keeps me from letting lines in the Negro newspapers like 'If a Negro doesn't like communism, he should keep his mouth shut and not be a stooge for the FBI,' really get to me. I know that what I'm doing is opening doors. And that the Negroes who did it before me, those seven other men, helped me get this far. I know that quiet fights, the kind where you have to say a lot of 'yes, sir,' and take on a diminished role because of the color of your skin, are still good fights. Worthy fights. Besides, selfishly, I like this job. It's exciting, challenging." He paused. "And sometimes the company I keep is pretty good, too."

"Lee Coldwell and his two-tone voice?"

"No, I was thinking more of you."

Turner flicked the lighter open again and held it out to me.

I rested a finger on it. If I moved it one centimeter I could have gripped his hand. I closed my eyes, willing the moment to last. When I opened them, his half smile had been replaced by a very different expression. In that brief moment, something shifted.

I didn't move. Neither did he. We just stood there, two people brought together by outside forces who had surely been unaware of what could ignite. I looked up from his hand to his face, to the eyes I'd wanted on me since I'd first seen them in Coldwell's rearview mirror. Finally, I let go and he flicked the lighter shut.

"Good for you, Rina," he said softly.

I turned away and went home to my boys.

CHAPTER 29

I'm Hanna Graf."

I was standing behind the Lincoln Memorial, on marble stairs that descended to the Potomac River.

I hadn't been to Washington in years. I'd traveled there a few times as a child with my parents, usually because my father wanted to see an exhibition at the National Gallery of Art. An expert in the Pre-Raphaelites, he would spend hours rhapsodizing about their hair: *Flaming June*, *The Lady of Shalott*, the red tresses of *La Ghirlandata*.

On my last trip to Washington with my father, I finally saw *Ophelia*, John Everett Millais's magnum opus. It was the end of the twenties, I was twelve years old, and I had long black hair that hung down to my waist. *Straight as thread, thick as bread*, my father used to say. But after seeing Ophelia moments before she drowned, I felt as if my hair was pulling me under. That night, I took my mother's best sewing scissors and bobbed it, following a trend right before it went out of style.

My parents were aghast. My brothers called it modern. "None of the girls have had long hair for a decade, Dad," said Timo. My other brother, Anselm, agreed. "She looked as if she were about to leave in a wagon for the gold rush." I hadn't worn it long since.

"Nick Solomon," said the man who had just sat next to me.

Jacob had described him as built like a bull, but with the stamina of a distance runner. He was a stocky, handsome man, with dark curls, a graying mustache, and an air of intelligence about him. Coldwell and Turner already knew Nick was a communist, supplying Jacob—and by extension, the KGB—with classified information from the Treasury Department and other agencies. What they wanted to know was who else was working with Nick to supply these documents, and what agencies they were in. How close to the White House or the Pentagon they were situated.

In the bright sun, I squinted my eyes and said, "Glad to meet you." Nick had a British accent, which Jacob had described, but I was expecting a hint, not full Eton. He was born in Russia, educated abroad by the British, and had become a naturalized American. Despite the jeans he was wearing, his look was certainly more Oxford than Leningrad State, even though he'd gotten his Ph.D. in economics from Stanford. On the phone I'd asked Coldwell how Russians were being hired at Treasury and he'd shrugged. "They saw an American with a Ph.D. from Stanford who worked at Agriculture, and they didn't dig deeper."

Nick and I bantered about the weather, but he stopped short after I murmured some nonsense about a few crew boats gliding on the water.

"Listen, I'm just going to get to what's important, and I mean important," he said quietly. "We've got a man, Ron Farmer, Jacob knows him well. He's nervous. Dangerously nervous. During the war, he was outed as a communist. He almost had to resign until we were able to spin a case for his innocence. He's convinced it's going to happen again. Tell that to Jacob, okay? That's the first thing you tell him."

"Okay," I replied.

"Let's walk. There's an overpass if we walk down these stairs. To the right."

We walked on the thin sidewalk under the stone bridge. There, in the shadows, he handed me a bag. "Documents. Negatives. Anything else?"

"That's all Jacob asked for," I said quietly. "Though he did want to know if you were going to start developing film again," I said.

"Developing film? Come on now, Hanna," said Nick, walking out from under the bridge, to the sidewalk near the river. "Who the hell does Jacob think I am these days, Slim Aarons? I don't have time to run a photography studio out of my house. What am I going to tell my fancy Georgetown neighbors when they pop over for a drink? Just ignore the clothesline with close-up shots of classified documents? Do you know how close I, all of us, have been to being found out lately? Just last week Ron had to shove aircraft production figures in his pants. Do you know what would happen to him if he was discovered with aircraft production figures glued to his ass?"

"Nothing good."

"Yes, Hanna, that's right. Like a life sentence, nothing good."

I nodded uncomfortably.

"Hanna, have you ever hidden highly classified government documents in your pants? Do you know the risks we are taking? Do you get it?"

"No," I said evenly. "I have not."

"Sorry," he said, leaning forward, putting his arms on the white stone. "I know you're taking risks, too. I know you could get caught as well."

The biggest risk I was taking was with my husband, with my marriage, but the gamble was worth it. I had known that the moment I climbed into Lee Coldwell's car.

"I'm sorry I have to send it undeveloped," Nick continued, walking again. "I have a man at Treasury with me that develops film for us when he can. But right now, it's not possible. They can do it in New York. They prefer not to, but they can."

"That's fine," I said, very ready to run right back to Union Station. "They'd also like your party dues and an itemized list of what they might expect on each—"

"You know what these Russians can do with their itemized list?

They can take it and shove it up their—" He cut himself off and looked at me.

"I know you're new, but I don't think you get it. Let me explain how things have escalated. They're typing top secret documents in rainbow at Defense," Nick whispered. "Three, four different colors. The text is pink. You can't photograph any of it. That's what our people are dealing with."

They had someone at the Defense Department. Coldwell was going to lap that up with glee. Or as much glee as Coldwell was capable of showing.

Nick was still talking. "Look, I know I can be hot-tempered, but I'm fine. Don't tell Jacob I've cracked. But I really am worried about Ron. You need to tell Jacob to do something about it, about him, before I have to do something about him."

"I will."

"I think Jacob needs to get himself to Washington. He should speak to Ron. And if he can't make it, then Ava should come, one last time before she leaves. Ron loves Ava."

I wanted to ask when Ron met with Ava. How the FBI had missed someone undercover at Defense. But all I said was, "Who doesn't?"

"We're all happy for her. Being sent to Moscow. It's a big deal. But we'll miss her. I'm sure she'll return, though. Brave kid like her. They form you to their liking and then send you back. They don't keep you."

"You're not afraid for her?" I asked, before I could stop myself.

He ran his hand along the stone and stopped when a police boat passed us on the water. Both of us looked away from it quickly. "I've been afraid for many people. I'm afraid now for Ron. Ava Newman has never been one of them. I would follow that woman into a ring of fire."

I nodded. "I know how you feel."

"Jacob said you speak Russian," said Nick as we walked on, the spires of Georgetown University coming into a distant view.

The old me would have said, "I try" or "I get by." But instead I replied, "I do."

"That's good. I imagine that helps with Jacob. So make sure he gets it, about Ron, okay?" he said again. "Tell him Ron needs to be reminded why he's taking such risks. How important his being at the Pentagon is, how valuable it is for the cause."

We turned around and walked back toward the monuments. Defense at the Pentagon, not in some lesser office on the other side of the river. I was going to deliver Christmas morning to Lee Coldwell.

"Tell me about yourself, Hanna," Nick said as we approached the same set of stairs. "Besides your knowledge of Russian, how did you get here?"

I could have told Nick many things. That I had worked for the United Nations. That I cared about the brotherhood of man. That I was desperate to wake up each day with a purpose, or even just a task to carry out. That I hadn't disappeared yet. Instead I took a deep breath and said, "Jacob Gornev was my lover in college."

Once back in New York, all I wanted to do was get that information out of my bag, but before I could give it to Jacob, I had to give it to the FBI. I had to give it to Turner Wells.

Wells was sitting alone in a booth at the Eighth Avenue Coffee Shop in Penn Station. He was wearing the same navy-blue suit I had first seen him in. His stocky body looked even more solid, his short hair newly cut. He was reading a magazine, his head bent. Seconds after I spotted him, he looked up and saw me. He gave me a half smile. The best kind of smile.

"You're here," I said, unable to stop myself from grinning. Turner's presence emptied out the station. Suddenly, there was no one running to catch the LIRR to Lake Success or elsewhere. There was no one waiting for the seven p.m. train to Boston. There was just him.

"I'm here. I'll take that and be right back," he said, reaching for the bag. When he returned, I pressed my tongue against my bottom teeth to keep from smiling too widely.

"I'll be waiting for you here, in this coffee shop, every time you come back from Washington," Turner said when he returned. "I'll go to a van we have parked on Eighth Avenue, photograph what you have, then you leave and hand everything off, just as Jacob instructed. Easy, right?"

"So easy," I said, grinning. "Simple, even."

If Carrie were here now, there would be no questioning if she should tell Tom. She would have simply said, *Tom, Katharina is just not yours anymore.*

With unfinished coffee left on what I now considered the best table in town, I exited the station and called Jacob from the nearest phone booth. He instructed me to go to a store called Milton's Luggage on Sixth Avenue. I was to buy the Alexander Executive attaché case. In the bathroom of the Excelsior Hotel, I was to transfer the documents into the case. Then I was to head to the Rivoli Theatre—where Ava and I had gone.

"A man will sit next to you," he said. "He'll be carrying the exact same Alexander Executive attaché case. He'll switch the bags. Then you leave the theater and call me again."

I went to Milton's Luggage, the hotel, and then the Rivoli Theatre as if there were stars under my feet. Suddenly, I loved the feeling of being watched. I knew Turner was following me from a distance, as he'd told me he would. I looked for him once, couldn't see him, and smiled anyway, carrying myself a little more gracefully.

"Success?" Jacob said when I called just over an hour later from the pay phone near my apartment. His accent sounded stronger over the telephone.

"Success. It was exhilarating," I said honestly. "But Jacob, you have a problem in Washington." I should only have been telling Lee Coldwell, but I knew it was a detail that would make Jacob trust me. That would ensure a future with more Washington trips and time with Turner Wells, instead of one where I was trapped inside changing diapers and fighting back tears. I had come alive, and I was not going to bury myself again so quickly.

"What's my problem?"

"Ron Farmer. Nick says he's going to crack. No. He said he's going to shatter."

CHAPTER 30

"Hello, Katharina, it's your *Mutter* here!" my mother yelled into the telephone. "Can you hear me? These overseas connections still haven't improved, have they? Can you hear me, *schatzi*?"

I folded the note I was holding, which had arrived from Minkie Mills that morning:

> *I expect you to come over for lunch one of these days, since that would make me very happy. And you can tell Dr. Edgeworth to expect three million for Lenox Hill in a matter of days. An anonymous donation that will be made with great consideration.*

I opened a drawer and placed it carefully inside.

"*Ich kann dich hören, Mutti!*" I said loudly, switching to German. *I can hear you.* In fact, I could hear her surprisingly well given that she was across an ocean.

"How is my daughter? How are the babies?"

"They're well, we are all well. Peter is almost walking."

"Well, that's very exciting," she said through the static. "Don't rush him, though. Children walk at different ages. I'm sure your husband is in a panic over it, but remember, you didn't walk until fifteen months.

One day you just stood up and ran straight to the open window to terrorize an overweight pigeon who died from shock moments later."

My mother loved to tell this rather embellished story.

"But back to the present," she continued, "I meant to call when your father and brothers were here, but they've barely been home since the Geneva Conference started. Your papa even set up an easel outside the Palace of Nations. At first they thought he posed a security risk, but he moved fifty feet back and they let him stay. He did a wonderful painting of the secretary of state refusing to shake hands with Chou En-lai. And of course Hanna was hired on as an interpreter by the Vietnamese delegation. Having that affair in Saigon a few years back has been nothing but good for her."

"I wish I was there. Terribly," I said, trying not to let my voice crack. I longed to see my parents, my aunt Hanna, my father's paintings. I wanted to be part of history. I was happier than I'd been two months before, but I still did not feel the sense of purpose, of changing the world for the better, that I had under the employ of the United Nations.

Behind me I heard something crash. I turned around to see Gerrit holding one half of a porcelain plate. The rest of it was all over the ground.

"Smash, crash?" he said, looking at me.

"One moment, Mother," I said, hissing "no" at Gerrit. "Gerrit is having an argument with the Limoges china." I shoved both children in front of the television and went back to the phone.

"Is there anyone to help you?" she asked, her voice sounding farther away.

"The television."

"I wish you'd change that, Katharina. Women all over New York are in need of employment. God knows your husband has enough money."

"Yes, Mother," I murmured.

"When the twins were born, your father was an assistant professor at Hunter. He wasn't terribly busy and cut down to just teaching one class so that he could help me. That's rare, I know, but we put family ahead of his career at that time. Or perhaps we always did. And your *grand-mère* Arlette came in from Brooklyn to help. I couldn't have done it alone. We shouldn't have to. That attitude is very American. Don't let your husband impose that pioneer spirit on you too much. It's quite all right to ask for help."

"It's starting to change," I told her, and it was. It just had nothing to do with my husband. On the table in front of me was a bronze Dunhill lighter, just like the one Turner had used in the subway station. I'd taken the boys to buy it with me the very next morning and had been carrying it ever since.

"Did you hear me, Mother?" I said again, but our connection had been cut. I hung up the phone and heard another crash. Gerrit had jumped off the couch with his brother's pants as a parachute.

"Park!" I screamed and started the scramble to get out of the house. I used to be a woman who left the house with two dollars and keys. Now I needed a stroller, two humans, three changes of clothes, and enough food to nourish them through winter.

As I was leaving the building with the boys, I saw Carrie, and she didn't even glance at me. I pushed the fifty-pound stroller with fifty pounds of children in it as fast as I could until I caught up with her.

She turned on her heel, put her hand against my chest, and said, "I haven't told him yet, so stop chasing me like a plague. But I will tell him. Until then, I'll enjoy watching you beg me not to. There's at least some pleasure in you being so pathetic."

I had greatly underestimated how much people loved and revered Dr. Tom Edgeworth.

Before we could go to the park, I was to call Turner and tell him about my conversation with Jacob after I'd handed off the attaché case. I walked the boys to the closest phone booth on Fifth. As I did, I saw a man slip between two cars on Seventieth. I looked at the space between the two Buicks. I was sure I'd seen him. I told Turner as much when he picked up the phone.

"I'd be lying if I said I wasn't nervous," I whispered.

"Are you nervous about going to Washington again?" Turner asked.

"Only about the frequency. Jacob now wants me to go every ten days. It's impossible," I said, trying to hide the panic in my voice. "I'd like to do it. Of course. I want to help. For America," I added.

"For America . . ." Turner repeated. "Can we meet today?"

"I have the boys," I said reflexively, though I realized that was not an imposition for Turner Wells. "But yes, let's meet. Please. In front of the Museum of the City of New York? One hundred fourth," I added quickly. It was closer to Turner, and it was a place that always shined brightly for me, as I'd gone so many times with my father.

"I'll be there in thirty minutes." When the line went dead, I turned around and dropped the phone.

The boys were not in front of me.

"Gerrit!" I screamed, and pushed the glass door open.

"Peter!" I shouted, flinging myself onto the sidewalk. "Peter!" I screamed again. People were staring at me. A woman approached me, ready to ask me if I needed help. "I—I lost my—oh my God, what have I done?" I said feeling faint.

But then I saw it. Half a block down, in the middle of the sidewalk, dangerously close to the road, was the stroller.

I sprinted to it and threw my arms around both boys, still tucked into their seats. "Did you roll away?" I said through tears. "Did the stroller roll away?"

I studied the sidewalk. There was no incline.

I'd been telling myself that besides my encounter with Max, I wasn't in any mortal danger. But maybe I was wrong. And worse, perhaps it wasn't just me in danger. I gripped the stroller until my hands shook.

Turner was already standing in front of the museum when I arrived. I stopped and watched him for a moment before he saw me. No one looked better in a suit, or flicking a lighter, than Turner Wells.

He saw me and approached. I told him what had just happened with the boys and watched as the muscles in his neck tightened.

"You are undoubtedly being watched," he said.

I nodded. "I can survive that, as long as it doesn't affect my children." I waited for him to reassure me. He didn't. "Please tell me it's not going to affect my children."

"I don't want to make empty promises, but I can say that this, all this, has not negatively affected my children. It's put food on our table."

"All right then," I said, my twisted nerves starting to untwist. "But Washington every ten days, I don't see how I can do it. Leaving for a few hours is one thing. Having my in-laws' housekeeper cover for me every once in a while, fine. But with that schedule, I will get caught."

"By whom?"

"By my husband."

"What would make it better?" he asked as we sat on the stairs in front of the building, looking out at the northeastern corner of the park.

"I don't know." I closed my eyes.

"What if I take the train down with you?"

His voice had dropped. His breathy way of speaking was quieter, yet somehow more forceful.

"Then," I said, looking straight at him, "I'd find a way to go to Washington every day."

My next trip was five days later, June 1. I met Nick by the rowboats on the Tidal Basin. It was quick and unenlightening. I reported that I'd told Jacob about Ron. Nick was already aware, and he was thankful. But he said very little else.

Turner said that the next time I went, I needed to be more enlightened. To play my part convincingly, I had to have more awareness of what I was couriering—which meant I needed to look at the documents before I headed to the Rivoli Theatre.

Ten days later, in the train bathroom, I opened the bag Nick had handed to me. There were six rolls of film and a few negatives. The film was from the Department of the Treasury and the Bureau of Intelligence and Research. I held the first negative to the light. It looked like production figure charts of airplanes. Performance records.

When I received the bag back from Turner at the Eighth Avenue Coffee Shop and went to transfer it to the briefcase, I noticed there were no negatives. The airplane figures were missing. Some things, I realized, were just never going to make it into the hands of the KGB.

"Happiest you've ever been?" I asked Turner on the last day in June, after my fifth trip to Washington.

He paused and looked at me. "Flying to Korea. And then flying home from Korea. First it was the high of anticipation, then it was the high of relief. That I was still alive."

"I'm glad you came back."

"Me, too. And you?"

"I should say holding my babies for the first time."

"But . . ."

"But the truth is, my years at the United Nations, the first two in particular. The war had just ended. I was so excited to be young, alive, and swimming in intelligence."

"Your own."

"Sometimes my own," I said, reaching for the coffee he'd bought me. "Mostly the intelligence of others. And all working so hard for peace."

"It's the same thing you're doing now, you know? You're working for peace. Democracy."

"And what are you working so hard for?"

"The American people. My fellow Negroes. Women, children. You."

I drank slowly, covering my wide smile with the chipped cup. "I need to be getting to the theater. But I'll see you again. Soon." I couldn't keep the anticipation out of my voice.

"Every ten days."

"You know what I hate?"

"Tell me."

I leaned in close and whispered, "The other nine."

CHAPTER 31

Rina!" I turned around to see Ava Newman in a white linen dress and a straw hat, carrying a large bag, rushing up Fifth Avenue on one of the hottest days of July.

I was on my way to the park to let Gerrit jump in whatever puddle, fountain, or open fire hydrant we could find.

"So these are your boys," she said, rushing over breathlessly and kissing the baby right on the cheek. "Do you comb their hair over their horns, or how does it all work?"

"Martian baby!" Gerrit yelled.

"He thinks Peter is a Martian," I explained. "I don't know where he gets these things."

"They're very cute, especially since they're locked in that thing," she said, smiling and gesturing at the stroller. "What is it, exactly?"

"It's a hunk of junk that I will personally take a torch to when both boys are old enough to walk," I said, kicking the stroller. "Try not to be too jealous." Even with beads of sweat on her brow, and slightly frizzy hair, somehow Ava had never looked better.

"I have a gift for you," she said, holding out the bag.

"A gift! Why on earth?"

"Because even mothers—especially mothers—deserve gifts sometimes," she said as I took it. "Don't worry, it wasn't expensive." I looked inside. It was a large black Bell telephone.

"In case you ever need a lifeline," she said, watching me carefully.

I reached into the bag and pulled it out. "Ava!" I said as I ran my hands over the base. "But this is my telephone." I looked up at her in utter disbelief. "From the United Nations. It has a dent in the side from when Marianne Fontaine knocked it off my desk with one swift shake of her backside." I turned it over in my hands. "And right there on the cord is my red nail varnish. Chen Yu Opium Dream to be exact. What else can one do when working after hours, but anticipate the real after hours?" I said, smiling as I ran my hands over the receiver. "This is amazing. Thank you, Ava. Really." I looked at her. "Do I want to know how you got it? I don't, do I?"

"No," she said, laughing. "Let's just say I *don't* have the dexterity of a panda. And I slept with someone."

"No!"

"No."

"No?"

She started laughing. "How about you don't lose sleep over it, and I promise that whatever I did, it won't get either of us arrested."

I picked up the receiver and held it to my ear, thinking of all the conversations I'd had on it. Eleanor Roosevelt herself had even called me once when she couldn't find my boss. I put the receiver back in its cradle and smiled at Ava.

"Now, this is a present."

"Good," she said, leaning down and kissing Gerrit this time. "I've got to dash. Back to the Eden, which, with my air-conditioning going in and out, feels more *Inferno* than *Paradiso*."

I leaned forward and hugged her before she dashed. She still smelled like jasmine and oranges.

"Ava!" I called out when she was down the block.

She turned and looked back at me.

"You're a gem."

She tipped her hat and walked off.

America hater, I reminded myself as I watched her disappear. *Treasonous woman*. Still, I clutched the bag as if it held all of my youth and turned the stroller toward the park.

Two hours later, all of us looking like we'd lost a wrestling match with a fire hose, we walked back into 820.

"Mrs. Edgeworth," said Sam as we rolled in. "You have a telegram."

"Thank you," I said, taking it from him.

"Do you need any assistance, Mrs. Edgeworth?" he asked, looking at the shopping bag cutting into the crook of my elbow.

"I'm all right," I said, heading for the elevator. "But thank you for asking."

"Mrs. Edgeworth?"

"Yes, Sam?"

"I spoke to Mrs. Kirkland earlier. She asked if your husband was home."

"My husband? Not me?"

"Your husband," said Sam neutrally.

"Thank you, Sam. Maybe I will take that help after all."

When Sam left the apartment, I gave him three dollars, and it wasn't for his help carrying the shopping bag.

Inside the apartment, I stripped the boys and let Peter crawl naked over to the couch to pull himself up as Gerrit ran wild. I tore open the envelope, certain it was a message from Coldwell or Turner. It was not.

"I'll be in New York on July 10," it read. "Please meet me for a drink. 6 p.m. El Morocco. Only respond if you can't make it. But know that if you do, I'll ignore it.—Faye Buckley Swan."

If I had to fake my own death, I would be at El Morocco.

I hid my telephone on the top shelf of my closet and thought about the lies I could spin to arrange to meet Faye. If Carrie had already spoken to Tom, I wouldn't have a chance.

Asking Amelia if Jilly could watch the boys was the easiest solution, but I needed to save her for more important occasions. I could fake an emergency of sorts, but most emergencies were medical, and I cohabited with one of Manhattan's best doctors. I could stage my own kidnapping, could simply disappear—or perhaps I could try something novel with Tom. I could tell him the truth.

When I finally heard the elevator ding and the doors open, it was nearly midnight. Tom wandered into the living room a few moments later, his movements betraying his exhaustion. Still, he smiled when he saw me, glancing down at the book in my lap.

"You're home early," I said jokingly.

"At least I'm home the same day I left," he replied, taking off his suit jacket. "That's something."

"It is indeed." I didn't mention that these days, the hours Tom kept were a blessing.

He leaned over and kissed me on the cheek.

"It must be nice to read a book," he said, sitting beside me. "I miss having time to do such things."

I wanted to tell him that it was a prop. That I hadn't absorbed a word, because I was too exhausted from watching Gerrit run from the cyclists in the park like they were the bulls in Pamplona.

"*Le Deuxième Sexe,*" he said, looking at the cover. "Beauvoir. That women's book was a bit of a thing, when? The year we got married?"

A bit of a thing. And written in a little language. Surely the only big things that happened were in the company of men at Lenox Hill. I put the book down on the couch next to us. "I'd call it more of a sensation."

He didn't answer, pulling off his tie and draping it on the edge of the couch.

"I have a favor to ask you, Tom," I said after we'd chatted about his day and he'd relaxed a little, crossing his legs, right ankle over left knee. Carrie Kirkland clearly hadn't said a word.

"Okay . . ." he replied. I could hear the hesitation in his voice. He put his foot back on the floor.

"When I was in Los Angeles . . ."

At the sound of those two words, Tom's body shifted.

"When I was at the Beverly Hills Hotel," I amended as his spine straightened even more. "I met a woman, a lawyer, whose company I really enjoyed. She was intelligent, witty. She reminded me of the girls I used to be friends with in college, and at the United Nations. Punchy women, if that makes sense."

"Aren't you still friends with punchy women? Carrie is quite punchy," Tom offered.

"Carrie is far more placid than punchy. Not that I like her any less for it." That was a lie. I did like her less for it. Racism and veiled threats. She was actually far worse than placid. My only other friends with children had had them far earlier and didn't want to relive the baby phase. And as Marianne had made clear, the ones without children had no desire to experience mine.

"I suppose I'm not punchy," said Tom.

"You, Tom Edgeworth, are perfect, not punchy," I replied honestly, looking at his weary face, his hands that pumped life back into children. "You're too good to be punchy," I added, guilt creeping up my spine. I looked again at his hands. No bolt of electricity shot through me.

"I'll take that as a compliment," he said, his posture relaxing as he again crossed his ankle over his knee.

"I don't know how to put it, Tom," I said, pausing. "I suppose I just felt good talking to this woman. I felt alive. I haven't made a friend in a while—it's hard to when you have no job, or a university crowd to belong to—but Faye and I could become very good friends." Of course, I was already making another rather punchy friend, but now wasn't the time to mention my new communist confidante. Selling him on Faye was proving to be hard enough. "Which brings me to the favor," I said brightly. "She's in New York and would like to meet me for dinner at El Morocco tomorrow at six."

"Tomorrow?" Tom echoed.

"She lives in Los Angeles and is only here for a very short time,"

I lied. Faye could have taken up residence in New York for all I knew. "She sent a telegram to say as much. Do you think it would be all right if I went? Would you mind? Perhaps we could ring your mother and ask if she and Jilly could help like they did when we went to the Millses? Or we could hire a babysitter?"

"A babysitter? As in someone we don't know? To watch the boys in our home?"

Tom looked at me as if I'd suggested picking up the local heroin dealer and having him show Gerrit how to juggle needles.

I nodded, but stopped as his frown grew even deeper. If he knew that every ten days his sons were with a babysitter for twelve hours straight, he would simply drop dead on our overpriced Swedish sofa.

"Preferably Jilly and your mother, of course."

Tom stood up and massaged his temples. Deciding whether to let me out into the wild was very stressful.

"Tomorrow at six?" Tom clarified.

"That's right."

"And you feel this is something you . . ."

"Something that I'd like to do. Something that would make me very happy."

He walked over to the windows and opened the only one in the living room that wasn't already.

He turned around, leaned against it, and looked at me. "All right, then. You go. I don't want to disturb my mother's routine or poach Jilly from her yet again. It's a Saturday. I'll watch the boys."

"You? No, Tom," I said, standing and walking toward him. "I think, I mean, why not try Jilly? I'm sure she would enjoy spending time with the boys."

"Katharina," he said, his voice dropping. "Jilly is not just a woman for hire. She does more than clean and cook, she manages my parents' home. She's very busy," he concluded firmly, as if the Edgeworth residence were Standard Oil.

"Of course," I replied apologetically. "Jilly is phenomenal, like family, but a break from managing the home, your parents' lives, to spend time with children, it could—"

"I've been meaning to spend more time with the boys. Work has been all-encompassing, and I miss them. Peter still hasn't walked yet, has he?"

I shook my head.

"Concerning. Perhaps he will for his father." Tom looked out the window as the sounds of a car honking drifted up to the room. "I'll do it," he declared when it was quiet again. "We'll have a great time. And you'll be home by what, ten?"

"Ten? Faye is only in town for a few nights, so I'm sure she'll want to have a drink after dinner," I said, keeping my voice light. "But you'll be asleep by then anyway, no? And Peter, now that he's not—" I had almost said it. *Breastfeeding.* "Now that he's well over a year, he doesn't wake up until almost three if he wakes up at all. He sleeps through the night most of the time."

"Still. I'd be more comfortable if you were home around ten," Tom said firmly. "And please don't drink."

"Chocolate milk for me all night. Thank you, Tom. It's really very good of you."

Tom smiled, looking proud of himself. I watched him stand up, walk to the refrigerator, and examine the food I had made for him. He took out a beer instead, opened it, and walked off to the library to drink it alone. I watched him go, wondering where the man I married had gone, wondering if he felt the same about me. I'd become estranged from the women I'd been closest to, I'd lost the badge of honor that came with working at the United Nations, and I'd almost lost every shred of my independence.

But still, Faye wanted to see me again. Me.

I had been to El Morocco a few times with Tom after we were married and before we had children, but it had never been his speed. Full of society types, celebrities in dark corners, and good-looking people desperate to be photographed, a scene that Tom had seen too much of in his youth. Now he preferred serious people doing serious things. But I still enjoyed a dip in the fishbowl.

I sat back in the taxi and took in the city. It looked so different when I was alone, better. Despite the temperature, I rolled down the window and draped my arm on the door, remembering that even when the sun started to set, New York refused to go with it. The city didn't rest in the evening, it glowed with electric lights and candlelight in cafes and restaurants, with cigarettes burning and headlights, with vice and possibility. Even when the world was growing dark in your mind, New York refused to agree. She always kept a light on for you. And when the sun started to fade, when our minds welcomed the worst of our thoughts, she was there with her vigil, her open arms.

Tonight I felt like her open arms were ready to wave me forward, to guide me to something delightful.

The taxi shot down Fifth Avenue, the driver weaving through traffic, the moguls of New York. We glided past the side of the Plaza and the Pulitzer Fountain, and I imagined all the women who had perched prettily on its edge, holding on to someone's hand. I had done so, surely Ava had, too. I could picture her listening to the water as she looked away from the city's iconic hotel, when most of us looked right at it. New York was a town that lured beautiful women, but something about Ava made it feel like she'd lured New York. I didn't need to lure Manhattan, I just needed the freedom to fall in love with it again.

"Visiting?" the driver asked, catching my wistful expression in the rearview.

"No. This city is mine, from spark to dark."

"Poetic," he said as he stopped the car. "That'll be fifty cents, Emily Dickinson."

"Here's a dollar," I said, winking at him.

Invigorated by my ride alone, by the night ahead, I walked into the restaurant, tipped the doorman, and surveyed the fishbowl. The faces were new, but the desire was the same: to see and be seen, and hopefully get photographed while doing it. Everyone I passed was picture-perfect. Sitting at the center banquette against the wall, a position usually reserved for celebrities of Bergman's ilk, was the queen of the room, Faye Buckley Swan. Her pale shoulders were exposed, just as they'd been in Beverly Hills, her dress was ink black, and she looked so good that it seemed as if the restaurant had been built around her. That she was not only patron, but muse.

When the host and I were halfway across the room, she looked up, smiled, and gave me an approving once-over. "So, this is what you look like sober," she joked as she kissed me on the cheek after I'd greeted her.

"How do you know I'm sober?"

"Because I know what you look like drunk. The dress fits you better, too," she said, pointing to my knee-length red Chanel.

"Please, let's never talk about that dress," I said, sitting down across from her. "It proved to be a hangman's rope in disguise. I should have just worn a bedsheet."

Faye Buckley Swan was very pretty. Her redwood-colored hair looked darker in the nearly windowless El Morocco, and it gave her an air of mystery I hadn't noticed before. But more than that, she had presence. The kind of presence New York society girls, California society girls, even Cleveland society girls dream of having but that some women just have naturally—even lawyers.

"I'm so sorry about all that," I said as she leaned back in the blue zebra-striped banquette, her spine seeming to float against it instead of sinking. "I'm dreadfully embarrassed. You did get my flowers and the note of apology, I hope?"

"I did. They were beautiful. Thank you," she said, picking up her aperitif. "But really, no need. I loved that evening. All quite exciting. And then captured by the newspapers so we could have the memory forever. Here," she said, reaching across the table and opening her small handbag. "I brought you the clipping from *Daily Variety* in case you wanted to—"

"Oh, please, no!" I said, putting out my hand to stop her. "Please, I don't think I can look at it."

"Rina, don't be silly," she said, grinning at me and removing her hands from her purse. "Of course I didn't bring it. I'm not a monster. I'm kidding."

"Oh, thank God," I said, exhaling. "I want to see that picture of me about as much as I want to return to the Beverly Hills Hotel."

"What picture?" she said innocently, shrugging in her black cocktail dress. "Anyway, she should have laughed it off."

"Bergman?"

"Sure. Anyone with millions should laugh most things off. Especially if they were also gifted symmetrical features and doting admirers."

"Did she? Laugh? The only thing I could see was the waxed floor—and my life flashing by."

"No," said Faye, starting to laugh herself. "Not at all. Perhaps she would have if she'd married someone more amusing. Or maybe she shouldn't have married at all. In my line of work, I'm learning that's usually best for Hollywood types. Or legal types." She picked up her drink and looked around the room. "Half of these people look very ready to have me cut the ties that bind them. I should just sprinkle my business cards around the restaurant."

"I take it you're not married then? Just a wild guess."

"Actually, I was. I did the whole ring by spring thing. The ring was pretty, but the result wasn't. I'm divorced now. Have been for the last three years. It's been glorious. Conveniently, I served as my own counsel."

"And no children?"

"Certainly not. They're just obligatory accessories."

I burst out laughing. "How do you figure?"

"Well, after you're married, the pressure is on to have them. It's why my husband wanted a divorce. That, and my lover. Actually there were two of them. Three if you count the Italian count. Though that only lasted about thirty minutes." She waved her hand in the air. "A tale for another time. Anyway, these days, children are expected in a marriage. There's no more 'Oh, I simply can't bring a child into this war-torn world.' So even if you don't want them, there they are. Obligatory accessories. Canes, sunglasses, crutches, children."

"There's a certain amount of truth to that. But I do love mine, most of the time."

"And I'm sure those with a busted leg love their crutches. Come, let's get you a drink and discuss your marriage."

She raised her eyebrows at the waiter, who immediately stopped what he was doing and approached. I realized what it was about Faye that gave her such presence. It wasn't beauty, it was self-assurance. She knew she was lovely to look at, but more importantly, she knew her mind worked faster than most.

"It was something Tom, right? Your gin. Tom Thumb?" Faye asked.

"Tom Thumb?" I said, grinning. "What is that? Gin for babies?"

"Now, there's an idea."

"Just a coffee for me," I said to the waiter. "I'm trying to drink less, actually," I explained to Faye. "After the incident, I thought it would be best."

"It *would* be best. But not tonight. Any night but tonight. I need to laugh, and you don't seem ready to prostrate yourself in front of any starlets this evening, so we need another source of mirth."

"In that case, it was Old Tom," I said, unable to keep from smiling.

"Old Tom on the rocks," Faye said to the waiter. "And I'll switch to champagne. In fact, we both will. Old Tom and champagne, sounds like a very good night out. Though young Tom would be even better."

"My name is Tom," said the waiter, laughing.

"Well, there you go."

After he left, I looked at Faye quizzically. "Do you think his name is really Tom?"

"Absolutely not. I think it's something very long like—"

"Like Rachmaninoff?"

"Exactly."

When the champagne was poured and our meal ordered, she took a long sip of her drink and flipped her hair from her shoulders.

"Now that we don't have *le tout* Hollywood around us, tell me all about yourself. I know some, but not enough. What was it that landed you all the way in California? Trouble at home?"

"You could say that. It's a long story, but I suppose it can be summarized as I tried to murder my son and got a free vacation out of it."

"Did you!" she exclaimed, putting her glass down so firmly that a few drops splashed out. "How utterly fascinating." She spread her free hand out on the table like a fan. "Do go on."

My body tensed instinctively as I thought about that day. I realized that I hadn't told anyone what happened, my version of it. Though I was terribly short of female confidantes, I was now plus one UN telephone, thanks to Ava Newman. That was something rather delightful. And so was Faye. "My son fell in Central Park," I explained. "He was running, quite some distance from me, then he fell on some glass, and was bleeding quite a bit. And I didn't help him, I simply froze in place, like an ice sculpture with no heart. In the end he needed stitches, and my husband thought I needed a lobotomy."

"And then?" she asked.

"I suppose that's it, really," I said, the image of bleeding Gerrit flashing before my eyes. "Those are the important parts."

Faye raised her glass, and Young Tom the waiter came and refilled it.

"Let me try to understand something," she said after he'd slipped away.

"Please."

"You could not have prevented him from cutting his knee. You didn't see the glass."

"I suppose if I'd done a full sweep of Central Park before I let my kids play there, I could have."

"Right. But that's an insane person's behavior, yes?"

"Let's go with overly concerned mother."

"So, the only thing you're guilty of is not reacting fast enough."

"Not reacting at all."

"But you would have eventually. You wouldn't have let the sun set on your bleeding child."

"I'm not so sure."

"Of course you wouldn't," she said, putting her elbows on the table and leaning toward me. "You'd had a hell of a day, and your reaction time was slower because you were shaken and exhausted. Trust me, if this were a court, I could get you excused."

"I may take you up on that one day."

She laughed, thinking I was talking about motherhood. Which I was, and which I wasn't. The way things were unfolding with Jacob and Ava, Turner and Coldwell, I didn't know where I would end up. A courtroom felt entirely possible.

"You do know how much easier it is for women to get divorced these days? There are these new courts, just established. Family courts, they're called. They focus on divorces involving children. I've argued in one."

"You seem too young to have done all that you've done."

"I'm forty, but I look amazing for my age," she said, grinning. "But when I say it out loud, *forty*, people assume I'm practically deceased," said Faye, pointing to my gin, which was still untouched.

"Practically," I said, taking a long swig. "There should be a pasture for women who practice law at forty or who give birth after thirty. Just like for old mules. We could hang around and pluck one another's whiskers."

"You're very funny," said Faye, laughing. "And listen, Mrs. Tom Edgeworth. I've seen you very drunk and not at your best and my opinion is still that you're great-looking, even at your advanced, nearly dead age." She put down her fork and knife. "After we devour these steaks and things," she said, "let's go to some crummier place. I'm in the mood for trouble. Let's go somewhere with dirty floors, lurk in dark corners, and drink everything put in front of us. Or I can do all that and you can have a coffee." She knocked back the rest of her champagne and placed it on the table with a bang. "Thoughts?"

"I don't need any more trouble, but why stop now?" I said, cutting into my steak. I considered my activities over the last few months. Nearly crashing to my death in the rain, moving stolen classified documents up and down the Eastern Seaboard, lying to Jacob (and to the KGB by extension), stealing moments with a man who breathed life into me, and being threatened by Carrie because I'd been in the wrong place at the wrong time with said man. I was already in plenty of trouble—what was one more night?

We both ate quickly, paid the bill, and jumped into a taxi heading downtown.

"I went to a horrible little hole in the Village the last time I was here," said Faye, rolling down her window. "The drinks were awful, but the men were gorgeous. I know you're married and all, for now, but what do you think?"

My mind flashed to Turner, how he looked waiting for me at the Eighth Avenue Coffee Shop or standing outside my window on Fifth Avenue. Marriage was complicated. So was lust. "I think that sounds like the perfect scenario," I said to Faye.

"Good," she cooed.

"How did you get your job? As a lawyer," I asked as the cab made its way downtown.

"During the war, of course," said Faye. "That's when every woman who is currently in a top law firm edged her way in. With the men off at war, there was a shortage of lawyers. Even ones with ovaries would do to fill the vacuum. I was a legal secretary, and when I pointed out that I'd gone to Yale Law, they took me on as an associate. All but two women gave up their jobs when the men came back; I was one of them. They all said we'll always be associates working like sled dogs, pulling the men on their way to becoming partner. But I would rather be an associate sled dog than not be in a law firm at all. Be a nobody."

We were both quiet for a moment as her words sank in. She would rather be a sled dog than stay at home. Like me.

"That sounded awful," she said, reading my silence. "Trust me, it's everyone who is not a lawyer that has it figured out. As long as you're happy, then life's a tango rather than a square dance, right?"

"I wouldn't call myself happy. Though I'm better now than I was in California."

"You'll have to come back and give us a try. Maybe wear shorts next time. Nothing longer than the Bermuda variety. Come," she said as our taxi slowed. "Here's the miserable place."

We walked inside and the very college-aged crowd made room for us at the bar.

"At least they respect their elders," I mumbled, ordering a gin straight up.

"They're older," she said, nodding her head slightly to indicate a group of men in their thirties.

Seeing her gesture, one of them immediately came up and offered to buy her a drink. Faye was dressed to sashay between luxury hotels and the "21" Club; he was dressed to stomp between a poetry reading and a one-act play, done in the original Romanian.

"Buy you lovely ladies a drink?"

Faye looked at me and winked. He was dressed like a college student, but he was very easy on the eyes. "Tell you what . . ."

"James Harris."

"James," said Faye. "I'll buy a bottle of champagne or homemade whiskey or whatever they sell here and you have a glass. Then after I'm done speaking to my friend, I'll come find you and we can either have long conversations about great American writers, because based on what you're wearing, I'm assuming that's your life's purpose, or we can kiss passionately in the corner and decide if we want it to lead to more. See if our tongues get along and all that."

"What is your name?" he said, taking her hand in his.

"Faye Buckley Swan."

"Faye," he said, looking at her. "I think I love you."

He turned to me, took my hand, and kissed it. "I think I love you, too."

The bar did have champagne, and we sent James Harris on his way to ogle Faye from the corner.

"Did you attend some underground charm school or something? I think that man is ready to give you a kidney."

"More like his manhood. And no, I just happen to love men. Especially ones that look like that. It's a product of growing up in Los Angeles. Everyone thinks Californians are just tan idiots, but they're wrong. We were raised on the smart, snappy language of cinema and have to study hard to keep up. Not to mention all that very blonde competition. The bar is high in the Wild West."

"This bar feels high," I said, starting to slump a bit against it.

"Then we'll just get higher," she said, refilling my glass until it was spilling over the edge.

"I could use a few lessons," I said, observing her.

"Why?" she said, watching me knock back my entire glass of champagne, which to my drunk lips tasted like drinking just bubbles and air. "You're happily married." She raised her eyebrows at me.

"I think the problem is that I'm not happy. So I'm not happily married. Does that make sense?"

"It does," she replied. "But I think marriages can weather storms like depressive episodes, even affairs. As long as there's more love than hate."

"There's more love than hate," I said. "But I don't know that there's enough love. I care for old Tom deeply, of course I do. It's just that sometimes, perhaps often these days, I'm not too fond of this version of Tom and I'm not sure if there are any versions of him left. Maybe when he leaves medicine," I said looking down at my second glass, which was already empty. "But that could be never."

"'I care for him deeply' is the polite society way of saying 'I'm bored and fantasizing about another life.'"

"I don't know," I said, refusing to picture Turner. "All I know is I need something stronger," I said, tapping my glass.

"Cheers," she said. "To whatever is in this. May it bring a jolt of the good life."

Four hours later, at just past one in the morning, Faye, James Harris, and I piled into a taxi heading uptown.

"Are you sure you don't want your own taxi, Rina?" she said. "I'm way up on the West Side at the Lucerne."

"I don't want to be alone yet," I said. "And the taxi ride will sober me up."

"That's never happened," James muttered.

I closed my eyes in the taxi, my head hanging out the window like a golden retriever. I was too drunk to keep my eyes open, and too exhausted, but like a man who's lost his sight, my nose seemed to work on canine levels. As we rattled up Tenth Avenue, I smelled New York. The streets that needed to be washed, the sewers that were moving the night away, the bleary-eyed waiters serving whatever meal came between dinner and breakfast, the dry air and the moonlight, the intoxicating scent of chaos and potential.

"Please come see me again," I said as we stopped in front of the Lucerne. I lifted my head and kissed Faye on the cheek. I was so drunk that she was starting to sparkle. I had to walk, and get something terribly greasy and fattening to eat, before I went home to feel the wrath of old Tom. *It's not even ten p.m. in Waikiki* was the best excuse I'd come up with and it was probably not going to make Tom laugh.

"I promise," Faye said. "Until then, telephone this sled dog if you need counsel, or counseling, or simply a friend."

CHAPTER 32

By the time I had walked a ten-block loop, eaten a hot dog and french fries, had a strong cup of coffee, and reached Eightieth again, I felt able to walk in a straight line.

As I contemplated whether I could survive a crosstown taxi, I realized I was very near Ava Newman's apartment building. The Eden. Ava Newman, rowing in Eden. My friend, my comrade. She was leaving for Moscow soon, to save herself from people like Turner Wells and me. But she was still the Miss America of communists. And she'd broken into the United Nations for me. I couldn't let her go without saying goodbye.

I was in sight of the portico entrance when my nerves started prickling before my mind could catch up. There was a man approaching the door. He moved with familiarity. Before I could glimpse his face, his back was to me and he was opening the door. Even in my faded, drunken haze, I knew it was Jacob Gornev. The lanky frame, the languid gait, that inimitable air of confidence, even in ill health.

I was about to call out to him when I stopped myself. There was only one reason a man arrived at a woman's apartment at such an hour.

I watched the door close after him and looked up at the building.

When I saw a light turn on behind the white curtains of a fourth floor apartment, I turned and stuck out my limp arm for a taxi.

Tom was not waiting for me with an antique revolver in the living room. Nor was there a note saying to leave the Cartier ring and never return. The apartment was quiet. I tiptoed through it, let my dress tumble to the floor in the guest room, threw some water in the direction of my face, and fell asleep.

Most mornings, I was woken by the cries of a child, but after my night with Faye, it was by the loud, angry voice of Dr. Tom Edgeworth. I tried to keep from being sick as he listed my shortcomings. I was irresponsible, ungrateful, blotto, embarrassing, thoughtless, reckless, unreliable. The last was Tom's favorite; of course, it was how he'd ended his tirade.

"I'm sorry," I said, my head half under a pillow, trying to block the morning sun.

"You said ten o'clock."

"No, *you* said ten o'clock. I said that I needed a night out. Needed a friend. Needed some levity in my life."

"What about me? Do you think every day of my life is a parade? That I go to work for some *levity*?"

"You could go out on weekends. You used to. *We* used to."

"We have different responsibilities now. Our children. Peter was inconsolable without you. I couldn't get him to sleep until midnight. I can still hear him screaming."

"How terrible for you," I murmured. Then, just in time, I grabbed a trash can and heaved into it.

Tom watched me with utter disgust.

I wiped off my mouth and looked up to meet his angry gaze. Did Tom really have no idea how long it took me to get Peter to bed most nights? Or realize how many times he had been gone for twenty-four hours since the boys had been born? Calling to say he was just going to sleep at the hospital since he had surgery in the morning, even though we lived only a seven-minute taxi ride from Lenox Hill?

"Clearly, you've stopped breastfeeding," he said, looking at me in my bra, which was gaping on my much smaller chest.

"I stopped after California."

"After California?" he said, his face turning even grayer as he realized it had been three months. "And you didn't consult me about it? About what the implications will be for Peter? You breastfed Gerrit through your second pregnancy."

"And look at him," I said dryly.

"Yes, look at him," Tom shouted. "Energetic, daring, athletic, cunning, linguistically advanced, and very loving."

"It's true that Gerrit is all of those things, and many other things, but Peter is certainly not a lump of coal." My stomach was threatening me again and I moved back to the edge of the bed.

"I wish you had asked me."

"And I wish you had asked me if I wanted to do it in the first place."

"It's best for the boys. And you."

"That's where you're wrong," I said, my stomach churning.

"So, last night. Staying out until all hours, drinking with some woman, some terrible influence, to the point of vomiting—"

"That terrible influence went to Yale Law."

"Because the world has never had a crooked lawyer with a good degree?"

"I enjoyed myself," I said quietly, the night with Faye now feeling so far away, and so close to coming back up again. "And I deserve to enjoy myself on occasion."

He looked at me in my underwear, gripping the trash can, and shook his head. "Get yourself together, Katharina. You look like some coed who just tasted liquor for the first time. Clean up and take a shower. I'll take the boys to the park and you can join me in the next hour, looking—and smelling—nothing like you do now. And let me tell you what you're really going to enjoy: playing with your boys in the park while green in the face in ninety-five-degree weather."

I waited to hear the elevator ding and then finished being sick in the bathroom. I was in the shower when the phone rang, and I ran, soaking and soapy, to answer it.

"Rina. It's Turner."

"Turner," I inhaled sharply, immediately knowing something was wrong. No one from the FBI ever called the house on the weekend. If they had something to tell me, they did it far more covertly, like Turner had done with the flowers. "Turner," I said again, terrified.

"Ava Newman . . . Ava. She died last night, Katharina. I was told that she hung herself in her kitchen."

"What?" I whispered. "No. You must be mistaken . . . no, Turner," I said, starting to cry.

He let me cry, staying silent on the other line.

"I almost went there last night, to her," I said when I could speak again. "I was standing in front of her door."

"Why were you in front of her door?"

"It's a long story. I was drunk and I realized I was near her apartment. I wanted to see her before she left. I wanted to thank her for her friendship, as preposterous as that sounds. But I didn't go inside."

"Why?"

"Because I saw someone else go in," I whispered. "Jacob. Jacob Gornev went in her apartment building."

"What?" said Turner, much louder than I'd ever heard him. "Are you sure? When?"

"Last night," I croaked out and then started crying again. "In the middle of the night. I thought he was there to . . . I thought it was something else."

"Can you leave your apartment? Can you meet me?" he said, sounding nothing like his steady self.

"I don't know."

"Try. Get in a taxi and meet me near the fountain in the park. One hundred sixth and Fifth Avenue. You know it."

It wasn't a question. Turner was well aware that when it came to Central Park, I knew every corner.

I threw on a dress, pulled my hair back, and wrote Tom a two-word note. *I'm sorry.*

CHAPTER 33

I exited the taxi at Madison and 106th and ran west to the park. Standing by Untermyer Fountain was Turner. I kept running until my body hit his and I buried my face in his chest. He let me. He put his firm arms around me and listened as I said, "She didn't hang herself, Turner. She didn't."

"Let's walk," he said quietly. "Through the park, on the street, wherever you'd like."

I stood up straight, let my hand touch the water spraying from the bronze statues, from the three sculpted women in motion, and splashed it over my face.

"Let's go to the street," I said. "It's too pretty in here for such an ugly conversation." We walked to the sidewalk together, to the hiss of cars and busy sidewalks.

"Tell me again about last night," he said as we began walking uptown. He was calmer than he'd been on the phone, but he was not the unflappable Turner Wells I had grown accustomed to.

He moved closer to me as a couple passed us on the sidewalk, his body brushing against mine. He didn't pull away for another block.

As we walked, I told him every detail—about leaving Faye and realizing I was standing in front of Ava's building; about seeing a man that I knew in a flash was Jacob.

"You know the way he walks," I said as an ambulance drove past us. "He has that ever-so-slight hunch. On some people, it would look inelegant, would age them, but on Jacob it just adds to his personality. His flaws have always given him more appeal."

"He has many flaws and much appeal," said Turner, signaling for us to sit on a bench just inside the park at the corner of 110th.

"Who told you?" I asked. "Coldwell?"

"Yes. This morning. A friend in the police force tipped him off, so he was in front of her apartment building when they carried out her body."

"He saw her? He confirmed it was her?"

Turner nodded.

"But Turner, why would she want to die?" I said, grabbing his arm. "Did Ava Newman really seem like a woman who wanted to die? Ava was a woman with at least nine lives packed into one. Enough beauty for a dozen, enough brains for a dozen more. A trip to Moscow on the horizon that she was excited about. Another man begging her to go to Cuba. Revolutions to start, hearts to break; does all that point to a woman who is going to string herself up like Christmas lights? Who would make love to Jacob, then pour a few highballs and say, 'You know what? It seems like just the right time to kill myself'?"

"Did I say I didn't believe you?" said Turner.

"No." I fell silent.

"I don't think Ava wanted to die," he said. "In fact, I can almost say with certainty that she didn't."

I opened my mouth to respond.

"Almost," he repeated.

We sat in silence together as I tried to imagine the world without a good woman in a tangerine-colored dress who was led terribly, terribly astray.

"Can I ask you something, Turner?"

"Always," he said, looking at me, his expression unreadable.

"Why did Lee Coldwell choose me? To approach Jacob, to be an informant?"

"I'm glad you were chosen," said Turner quietly. "You're good at this."

"I don't think I was supposed to like Ava Newman as much as I did. I don't think I'm very good at this at all."

"Hard not to like Ava Newman."

I thought about the way Ava talked about Turner in the movie theater. It was also hard not to like Turner Wells.

"Did you choose me to do this?" I asked, looking at the edges of the park.

"A lot of people chose you," he said finally. "Just some of them didn't understand why they were choosing you. Months back, Jacob told me that Ava was probably going to Russia. He let me in on a few hazy details of what she was doing in Washington—though we already knew—and that he wanted someone very American to replace her. I told Coldwell and we started ripping apart Jacob's past, going deeper than we had before, and we found you. With your UN connection, Coldwell decided that you would be the easiest person to give a history to. We decided to tie you to me. And then we decided to present you to Jacob, to plant the idea of you in his head."

"Had you seen me before? Before the day we met in the car? Had you watched me before?"

"Once," he said. "You were leaving your house with your husband, you were on your way to the Plaza Hotel."

I nodded. "The ghastly medical gala."

"You had the devil in your eyes," he said, smiling. "You looked ready to go to war. You didn't have a lightness about you as most women do when they're going to a party. I thought that was a good thing."

"Do you still?"

"I think . . . I think my opinion has changed. Now I think you deserve some lightness. Some joy."

"I think that's easier to have when you're next to me," I said quietly.

"You don't need me."

"But I do," I insisted, without looking at him. "I do."

He stood, and held out his hand. I took it and we walked to the northern edge of the park.

Across 110th were brick buildings, far more run-down than those on Fifth, but stuck between them was a beautiful, colorful house. I looked closer and saw that it was a hotel. It was olive green with a multilayered portico in front painted muted tangerine and mustard. It seemed to be confused, Tuscan in character but displaced in Harlem. However, I had perfected my Italian in Morningside Heights, so maybe that was just the way of New York.

I was no longer crying, my hands were no longer shaking, and I was no longer in denial that Ava was dead. Instead, I was only thinking about Turner. Nothing was being said between us. But something had to be.

"How do you do this?" I whispered.

He didn't answer, looking at the same hotel I was.

"How do you live a lie? Every day, lie, lie. Even when terrible things happen. Even when people die. How do you keep lying? Pretending to be a person you're not."

"I think I can do it because I've surrendered myself," he said thoughtfully. "I am a very small dot in this world. My actions are of little significance. But put together with the actions of many, they could have great significance. I want to move the country in the right direction. Then when I'm terribly old and terribly unimportant, I can say that I walked the right path."

"You," I said, looking over at him, "are already a man of great significance. You don't need to work for the FBI to make that true. It will always be true. Turner . . ." I said, keeping my eyes on his. "The time I have spent with you has been extremely significant in my life."

He moved closer to me, his body only inches from mine.

The air grew thicker and fuller.

"Turner . . ." I closed my eyes, willing myself to find the courage I'd been lacking for the last two years. "I find you . . ."

He didn't have to say anything. It was obvious that I was speaking to a man who thought about me. Who saw me. That, I realized, was one of the reasons I couldn't stop thinking about him. With Turner Wells, I felt very seen.

"I find you very attractive," I finally whispered.

"Katharina." Just my name, nothing else, the silence sitting between us, extending the minutes, the quiet.

"What do you think was the last thing she saw before she died?" I asked.

"I think," said Turner, glancing again at the hotel. "When there is that much fear—either because you want to die or because someone else wants you to die—you stop seeing anything. All you see is that want."

He looked at me.

"Rina," he murmured, and then his mouth was on mine, his arms were around me, and nothing else was said.

I'd wanted to kiss many people in my life. I'd never wanted to kiss someone more than Turner Wells.

Then it was said. "We can't," he murmured. "We can't."

"We can't," I echoed.

But our hands and our lips wouldn't listen. They whispered, *We can.*

CHAPTER 34

This time, when I returned to the apartment, Tom was holding the equivalent of a gun. He was gripping the boys, both boys. When I walked inside he pulled them even closer, as if they belonged only to him. As if he were going to take them away from me.

"Mama!" Gerrit screamed, but Tom wouldn't let him go to me.

"Rina, just go to the bedroom. I'll put the boys in front of the TV." I watched him wheel in the playpen and place both boys inside, moving it closer to the television set.

When Tom came in the bedroom, I was standing by the door, leaning against my dresser. He gestured to the bed, for me to sit down. I shook my head no.

"Do as you please," he said, sitting down. "That seems to be your refrain lately anyway."

"I'm sorry about today. I wasn't ready to start this again. I needed more time."

"Isn't it nice to just make impulse decisions. To not evaluate right or wrong."

"I don't often make impulse decisions," I said thinking about what I'd done only a half hour before. I could still feel Turner on my lips, his body pressing against mine. But the sensation was quickly disappearing, reality pulling on my skirt again.

"Do you not like this life you have?" Tom asked, gesturing to the door. "Two healthy children, a husband who provides for you, who is loyal to you, is that not enough?"

Loyal. I thought of Turner, the shot of life that I felt as soon as his lips had touched mine. Tom was loyal, I had no doubt. I remembered taking a six-month-old Gerrit to the hospital to visit Tom at work. When we were leaving, a nurse pulled me aside and said that she'd never met a man as proper as Tom Edgeworth. Never a wandering eye, and certainly not a hand. She had told me how lucky I was, and I'd told her that I knew. But life had been different then.

I nodded. "I like many things about our life. My life."

"That's shocking to hear, frankly. Because the way you've been acting it seems like you're experiencing some severe buyer's remorse. About me, about the kids. That you wish you had never tied yourself to a soul or had any children. All you seem interested in right now is a drinking habit and the company of ridiculous women. Does that sound about right?"

I shook my head no.

"You're sure?"

"Of course I'm sure."

"Carrie Kirkland told me that you are having an affair," he said, standing up and looking at me straight on.

I looked at his handsome face and shook my head no, too exhausted to start crying.

"Are you having an affair?"

I shook my head again.

"Why does Carrie think you're having an affair?"

"I don't know. I've been different, I haven't been myself. She's probably reading into that."

"That's not what makes people think you're having an affair. That makes people think you're drinking too much. Seeing a man locked in an embrace with you, that's the telling sign."

I thought of Turner's lips. His hands. A kiss that made the wind sigh with approval. Hands touching exposed summer skin. But it had ended there. We had not reached for more. But if we'd dared go into the hotel across the street, if we'd been somewhere with fewer eyes, less judgment, less room for guilt, I would have reached.

"I am not," I whispered.

"Fine," he said, looking away from me. "Please put the boys to bed and sleep in the guest room. We really should just start calling it your room. And starting tomorrow, I'm going to have a psychologist come see you every day when the boys are napping. I'll stay out of your hair so you can properly bond with your children again, but that bonding will be done within these very pleasant walls. I don't want you to leave this house unless it's to take the boys to the park and once for ice cream on Friday. You need to remind them that you love them. They're feeling abandoned. And if *you* don't want to feel very abandoned, you better stop this rebellion. Affair or not, I've had enough with your bullshit, Katharina."

He walked to the living room and called his parents' apartment.

"She's back, Mother. Yes, I know. *I know.* I think she'll be able to handle it now. Plus, I'm here."

The man who had spent two waking hours a day with his children since they were born was their savior, and I was a madwoman.

I heard the receiver rattle.

"Katharina," Tom called out.

"Yes?"

"Peter took his first steps today. It was a real sight."

CHAPTER 35

Holding the phone to my cheek while the boys played at my feet, I listened to Coldwell's calm voice.

"It is surprising. Her suicide."

"Especially since it's not a suicide. Especially since Jacob Gornev killed her."

"Whatever it is," said Coldwell. "The police are all over it. They're trying to keep the press away, because when her picture goes out, pretty as she is, was, it's going to be a circus even if they don't manage to tie her to the Communist Party. But despite the failings of the New York Police Department, they should at least be able to do that."

"But no circus yet."

"Not yet. So far, she's just a woman who'd had enough."

"Jacob certainly thought she'd had enough."

"Listen, Mrs. Edgeworth. I think it's real swell that you and this woman bonded and all, but we can't look too interested in the case be-cause then the police will wonder why," Coldwell continued, ignoring my tirade. "I've got someone on the squad. And he reiterated that it really looks like a suicide. A simple suicide. What you saw was probably Gornev going in for something . . . quick. And then leaving. But you didn't stick around to see him leave."

"You know, what I remember about Jacob in the bedroom is very clear. And I assure you, after I had sex with him, all I wanted was a cigarette and a sidecar. I didn't want to string myself up with rope to meet my maker. So, forgive me, but I don't think—despite your *man on the squad*—that Ava slept with Jacob for one last thrill before offing herself. As the only other person in this mess who has gone to bed with Jacob Gornev, let me just go ahead and tell you that Ava's something quick was not followed by a quick little suicide."

Coldwell was silent, not even a smoker's exhale. "I think you're complicating things."

"I'm the one complicating things? 'A simple conversation. A simple suicide,'" I said, barely able to mask the disdain in my voice. "Sounds like everything is simple in your line of work. How about if Jacob pops over here wanting to *simply* kill me? Should I be fearing for my life, Mr. Coldwell?"

"Be vigilant, but not afraid, Mrs. Edgeworth."

"Sound advice. I'll have it embroidered on a pillow."

He didn't reply.

"I'm telling you, Mr. Coldwell, Jacob killed her. I dated that man, I was in love with that man. I know what he looks like even from the back. Are the police even considering him yet?"

"I doubt it."

"But you will."

"We want the sharks," said Coldwell. "If Jacob is the shark, we'll get him. But I think he's a frail man getting frailer by the day. And that even Ava Newman could have overpowered him."

"He may be a walking corpse, but he's still a goddamn shark," I said.

The line went dead.

An hour later, I finally had the boys down for a nap. I sat by the window and looked out at the sidewalk. Too many emotions were swelling in me and I only wanted to focus on one. Lust. Pure, complete, reckless, incredible, life-changing lust. I closed my eyes and leaned back, but no sooner had my spine uncurled than the phone rang. I lunged for it after half a ring. I knew exactly who it was.

"A Doctor Creighton is here to see you," said Sam's skeptical voice. I had given both him and Eduardo a very big tip and asked them not to share my comings and goings or the presence of Sarah Beach. I had never mentioned the man who'd just arrived. He was fully Tom's idea.

"Thank you, Sam," I said unenthusiastically. "Send him up."

The elevator dinged, and a man with a gray beard and a doctor's bag emerged, the prerequisites of any psychologist that Tom would hire for me.

"Mrs. Edgeworth," he said kindly, his voice monotone. "I'm Doctor Creighton. You husband asked if we might talk today."

"And every day this week."

"He's a little worried about you."

"That's an understatement." He was one step from shackling me to the couch.

"Shall we sit here?" he asked me, gesturing to the couch in the living room.

"No, let's move to the library where we can close the door. My children are sleeping."

It was the only time of day when I was not actively mothering and now I had to spend it doing psychoanalysis.

"May I sit here?" he asked, pointing to a leather sofa. I nodded and watched him take out a paper and pen.

"Would you like to sit as well?" he asked, confused that I was observing him when it was supposed to be the opposite.

"I'd rather stand by the window. If that's all right."

"Whatever makes you the most comfortable."

"I like the window," I said, looking down at Dr. Creighton's bag. It still looked quite full, probably packed with a straitjacket in exactly my size.

"Now, your husband said that you've had trouble with alcohol these past few years," he said, looking down at his paper.

"Probably no more than most."

"He said that a few months back you went to see a doctor about your drinking. A woman," he added with a very raised eyebrow. "And that lately you've been able to reduce."

"That's true. I have." I handed him the doctor's letter regarding my condition that the FBI had kindly provided back in May.

"But then, just two nights ago, you went out for dinner and did not return until two in the morning. The only explanation that you gave him was that you were having a nice time. That you needed a release, to explore the bonds of female friendship."

"That's about right."

"It took you until two in the morning to experience a release?"

"No. It just took me that long to come home."

The doctor scrawled something on his paper in sloping, small print.

"Your husband said you were very excited to see this woman."

"I was," I said, thinking about Faye. "She's fascinating. And humorous."

"She's unmarried?"

"Yes."

He wrote on the paper again, this time his handwriting was even smaller.

"Is your interest in this woman . . ." he said, looking up at me. "Does it go beyond appreciating her humor?"

"Are you asking me if I am having an affair with Faye Buckley Swan?" I almost started to laugh.

"I didn't say that," he said, scrawling again, probably the word *lesbian,* underlined and circled.

"Well, I'm not. All that interests me is occasionally keeping company with people that are neither my children nor my husband. They seem to see me differently."

"All right," he said, capping his pen. "Let's put others aside for a moment, and talk about how you see yourself, Mrs. Edgeworth. When you look in the mirror, for example, when you are brushing your teeth or applying lipstick in the morning, who do you see? What do you think of yourself?"

"Every morning I see a loving mother, a dutiful housewife, and a loyal spouse."

"Is that what your husband would like you to see," he asked, touching his beard, in a pantomime of thoughtful consideration, "or is it really what you see?"

"I just said it was."

"But that's a surprisingly happy take considering your recent emotional releases. Your husband said that you've been inflicting pain on yourself. Enough to cause severe bruising."

Tom had still never asked me why I did it. But he did find it important enough to discuss with a complete stranger.

"I've stopped," I said. And it was true.

"Why did you stop?"

Because I'd had coffee alone with Turner Wells. Because I had to run documents from Washington for Russian spies. Because after a long and horribly lonely two and a half years, I could leave my boys for more than fifteen minutes. Because finally, I felt my body was slowly becoming mine again.

I turned around and smiled at Dr. Creighton. "Husbands just know best sometimes."

"I don't think you believe that," he replied. "Let me ask a different question. Why did you start inflicting pain on yourself in the first place?"

"Maybe I was having a long bout of hysteria."

"Female hysteria?" he asked, uncapping his pen and writing again.

"Are there different kinds?"

"Very much so." He looked down at his notes. "Are you still affected by the events of the war, Mrs. Edgeworth? Is that a source of strain in your life?"

"The war?" I asked incredulously. "It was terrible, but it's no longer a source of strain. The men who fought may still feel the strain. I spent the war in Manhattan."

"How about the Red threat? Is that making you nervous?"

"Nervous?" I said, turning back to the window. "I'm a housewife, Doctor Creighton. I barely give it any thought."

"All right," he said, barely masking his frustration. "Then what do *you* think the problem is?"

I decided to try honesty.

"I think the problem is that since my boys were born, I don't recognize myself. I don't recognize the woman I see in the mirror. Neither when I brush my teeth nor when I apply lipstick."

"Who do you see?"

"A woman I don't know. Someone I'm not fond of. The woman I used to be is gone, and I miss her. I miss her so much that my bones hurt when I think about her."

He nodded. "There are two versions of you, then. Or do you feel that you've made an internal split?"

"No." I shook my head in frustration. "There is only one woman . . . it's that this new one has been deeply and terribly unhappy. Despite what my husband believes, I have felt better recently. I've felt more . . ." Attractive, intelligent, worthy of the perfect kiss, worth risking it all for. "More important."

"And why is it that you feel more important?"

"Because I'm leaving the house. Alone."

He put down his pen again and looked at me. "Mrs. Edgeworth, I think one of the problems is that you have too much time. An idle mind is the devil's playground and all that. Living as you do, I imagine your only job is to raise your children, which leaves ample amounts of time for your mind to wander, and especially with women, an idle mind can be a dangerous thing. Now, there have been many studies on occupational therapy for women suffering from similar episodes of identity confusion. I've seen other female patients find great joy in hobbies. Quilting. Ceramics. Macramé."

I leaned back, wringing my hands together. "Dr. Creighton," I said slowly. "I have no interest in sewing during the two hours a day when

I'm not watching my children. I have a master's degree from Columbia, and it is not in quilting."

He was quiet for a moment. "In that case," he said, staring at me, "I'll leave you a bottle of Thorazine."

I nodded. "That sounds like a good solution."

Tom thought everything could be fixed with the miracles of medicine, surgery, or psychiatry. But he was wrong. My problem was that I wanted out of this ivory tower.

"Your husband would like me to see you every day this week," Dr. Creighton's voice interrupted me. "Shall I come at the same time tomorrow?"

I put my hands in front of me and nodded. "Though I can't predict when the boys will fall asleep. And Peter is walking now. He's quite excited about it and doesn't want to nap." When Gerrit had first walked, Tom had not been home and we hadn't even had a thirty-second conversation about it. "Gerrit walked today? Did he? At ten months, that's early. Must be the Edgeworth blood. Could you please bring me a steak knife? And the béarnaise."

"Shall I come at the same time anyway?" Dr. Creighton asked.

"By all means. You can always wait here in the library. There's plenty to read. I personally recommend de Beauvoir."

After he left, I went to Gerrit's bedroom and laid down next to him. I looked at my sleeping boy, leaned over, and kissed him. I was proud to be his mother, but I was more than his mother. I walked to the bathroom and emptied the bottle of Thorazine into the toilet. Then I took out my tube of Mother's Friend, the cream Tom had bought me to prevent pregnancy marks on my stomach. It hadn't worked. I picked it up and let it fall into the garbage can. I took out a large bottle of Miles Nervine. I'd kept it on hand since Peter was born, as the women's magazines had instructed. *Be sure to have bromide on hand for your nerves.* I'd never tried it; I surely wasn't going to start now.

Still clutching the bottle in one hand, I picked up the telephone. Turner answered after one ring.

"Tom has me held captive in my home," I explained. "I can't go to Washington on Wednesday, I can't even go to Central Park." I paused. "But I will not stop thinking about Central Park," I said quietly.

"Me, too," said Turner. "Me, too."

I walked back to the bathroom and added the bromide to the pills already floating in the toilet and flushed them all down. I didn't need drugs. What I needed was to hold on to this new version of Rina Edgeworth, one kindly provided, with pay, by the United States government.

CHAPTER 36

After a week of good behavior, with only one episode when Tom witnessed me crying, he let me out of the house, under his supervision, like an orderly who takes their mental patient outside to watch grass grow. Tom assumed my tears were over the boys, as Gerrit had given his baby brother a bloody nose that afternoon. Instead, I was crying over Ava. I was crying because Turner was not outside my window, or on the other end of my telephone, or waiting for me in the Eighth Avenue Coffee Shop. I was crying because I had started to feel better, and now I felt myself shrinking back into my tiny, isolated world.

I had told Dr. Creighton that the Thorazine was like a wonder drug. How joyful I felt. How fulfilled. I even knotted up some dental floss in macramé knots and said I'd found real happiness in the act. "It's beautiful," I'd declared, "and handy when eating a salad."

He'd nodded seriously. "I'm glad," he'd said, despite my theory that therapists preferred when their patients didn't heal and continued to require their services. "Thorazine and a little perspective, some appreciation, and I think you'll be just fine."

"Perspective . . ."

"Yes," he'd added with his upper-crust diction. "Think of how many women would love to be in your position. Two healthy children. Both boys. A successful, committed husband. The key to happiness is being satisfied with what you have in life. And you, Mrs. Edgeworth, have a lot."

"I do," I'd replied, resisting the guilt he was pushing on me. "But sadness found me anyway. Even the rich aren't immune."

I got rid of Dr. Creighton after that. Riding the high of firing a therapist, and pleasantly surprised that my husband didn't wheel me off to Bellevue after I did, I imposed one vital and rather enormous change in my life. I invited Sarah Beach to the house one Sunday afternoon, when Tom was certain to be home, and declared her our new babysitter. After thirty minutes of interrogation—questions about her parents and her GPA at Barnard, as well as showing her how to perform chest compressions on a teddy bear—Tom agreed she was suitable company for the boys.

"She seems exuberant," he said, smiling.

"Sometimes even Americans can be exuberant," I responded.

A few days later, I was waiting for Sarah to arrive, as I was meant to finally see Turner again, when the phone rang, and I heard the voice I'd been terrified to hear.

"Katharina," Jacob said. "There you are."

"Jacob, it's been too long," I said, trying to keep my tone even.

"What are you doing this afternoon? Could we meet? I have a favor to ask you."

"Of course. Yes. We can meet." I put my hand over the phone. Peter was walking over to the bar and Gerrit had a crystal decanter in his hands, about to pour himself and his baby brother two whiskey highballs. "But not quite yet. In an hour?"

"Fine. Let's meet close to you. How about Tavern on the Green. Ever been there?"

"A few times," I replied. Now I wasn't just worried, I was panicked. "I'll be there by two."

His voice was hoarse, but he didn't reveal a thing about Ava Newman.

I hung up and called Turner.

"In an hour? I'll be there, too. You won't see me, but I'll be there. I promise."

"Of all the things you could have said, that's the best one," I whispered.

Jacob was already at Tavern on the Green when I arrived. He wasn't sitting at the restaurant, but standing out front. He had on wire-framed sunglasses, a pair of old jeans, and a Columbia University T-shirt. His body was even thinner than the last time I had seen him, and his shoulders were slightly sloped. With every step I took, I grew more certain that it was him I'd seen outside of Ava's apartment. He kissed me on the cheek. My body bristled. He smelled like sweat and a bottle of whiskey. He lifted his sunglasses. His eyes were half-closed, but noticeably bloodshot. He had killed her, and now he was one hell of a mess.

"Jacob, I'm so happy to see you, but you don't look well," I said, returning his kiss. He no longer tasted like memories; it was a taste much closer to death.

"I know. I've been sick."

"That's what you said last time."

"I'm still sick. I think it's the weather. I'll probably be sick until the fall. July is the ugliest month in Manhattan."

"Why not August?"

"Because the rich leave in August, and we can all breathe again."

"The fall," I said, matching his slow steps. "That's a terribly long time to be unwell."

"Some people spend their entire lives unwell. I won't complain. Come, Katharina, let's walk uptown. You can say something to make me laugh."

"To make you laugh . . ." I was too scared to not let him guide the conversation. "Did you hear about the two peanuts walking at night through Central Park?"

"No . . ."

"One was a salted."

"That is a very bad joke, Katharina," he said, laughing.

"It's bad, but it does the job. Sometimes, that's all you need—something, or someone, to do the job." I was a fool to bait him, but I hadn't come to be his entertainment.

"Still a very bad joke," he said pleasantly.

We walked together, two former paramours who had lied, schemed, and killed their way into a very complicated situation.

"Will you start going to Washington for me again, Katharina?" he said as we walked slowly north.

"As Turner told you, or I hope he did, it's been impossible," I said. "My husband has been very present. But I can try again."

"It's important that you do. Imperative, in fact. Nick says they need someone to go every week now. That their new material is extremely time sensitive. Can you go every week?"

"Every week?" I heard my voice falter. "Yes. I mean, I can try," I repeated. I should have just said yes, especially now that Tom knew about Sarah. Anything to keep me as Jacob's courier, to keep me in the game, especially with Ava gone for good. But I found myself too disgusted by him to just nod along in submission.

"You were correct about Ron," said Jacob. "He needed to be handled more delicately. He's a very smart man. Very committed. But he gets nervous."

"Not surprising, given where he works. Do you ever get nervous?" I asked.

"Of course not. I'm a New Yorker," he said, trying to lace a little Queens through his Ukrainian accent. "Do New Yorkers ever get nervous?"

"Extremely. We tend to be a very nervous people."

"Well, this one isn't. Probably because my fate is sealed."

"In what way?"

We approached a group of children and Jacob wandered through them like a ghost, forcing them to maneuver around him.

"They know who I am," he said. "The American government, that is. I'm just trying to do as much as I can until they force me to stop. They don't know all the particulars yet," he added, looking at my worried expression. "Otherwise I'd be finished. Their intelligence services are very slow."

"Should you still be in New York then? And should I be walking with you in Central Park?"

"Are you afraid to?"

"No." I was afraid for very different reasons.

"Good. You shouldn't be. We've been friends a long time. Or at least we were a long time ago. That's alibi enough."

So was being an FBI informant. "But you're still going to remain Nick Solomon's contact?"

"Of course. I don't trust anyone else to do it. There are very few people I trust. But I do trust you. And Turner Wells. You can tell him that. Though, he's busy with other things."

I didn't know if he meant the CRC or me. Right now, Turner Wells was busy with making sure Jacob didn't butcher me under a bridge.

"Did you go to Washington to speak to Ron?" I asked. Jacob had slowed considerably since we'd started to walk.

"No. I had him come here. The FBI would have been too delighted to see me go to Washington. They would have put ten men on me. Ten clean-cut, beady-eyed, Bible-salesmen types. You'd think they'd have been smart enough to hire at least some people who didn't look like Sunday-school teachers."

In fact, they were. "I don't think motorcycle gangs line up to apply to the FBI," I said instead.

"Regardless, Ron agreed to come to New York because he also wanted to see Ava," said Jacob. "He was very attached to her. But he'll be the same way with you soon."

I didn't reply, waiting for Jacob to say something more about Ava. To acknowledge her death. He didn't.

"Thank you for going to Washington," he said finally, pushing up his sunglasses. "It's been a difficult month."

"Anything to help you, Jacob."

"Even though I'm not nearly as handsome as Turner Wells?"

"You're Jacob Gornev," I replied. "You don't need to be."

CHAPTER 37

Sarah Beach arrived again on Thursday morning to watch the boys. I rushed out in a haze of kisses and goodbyes after Tom left for the hospital and settled into my train car just as the doors closed. The wheels creaked out of Penn Station and into the sunlight.

"Do you mind if I join you?" I heard a man ask ten minutes after we had rolled out of the station. Without looking up, I broke into a grin.

Turner Wells sat down next to me.

"Is there any news about Ava?" I asked as he crossed his ankle over his knee, his thigh brushing mine as he did.

"There isn't. I wish there was, but I haven't heard anything. Let's just talk about the weather instead," he said. "The weather was good that day in the park."

"It was very good," I said, grinning. "It was perhaps the best weather I've ever experienced."

"Now shall we talk about . . . sports?"

"I'd rather talk about you," I said, looking at him.

"First, let me say something and then you can ask me whatever you want."

"All right."

He leaned closer to me, very close.

"I, too," he whispered, "find you very attractive."

Every nerve I had stood on end.

"Now, you may ask me what you wish, but let me get in one question first."

I looked at him with feigned suspicion.

"The time when you laughed the hardest. You said you were in college, that it was 'banned-books levels of inappropriate.' Will you tell me what it was?"

"I will not," I said, laughing.

"Will you give me a hint?"

"Fine. A hint. It was indeed in college, in my friend's sitting room. She was dating a great-looking man who was also a modern dancer. And when they were in bed together, he . . . oh, God, I can't say it," I said, starting to laugh. "Let's just say there were some moves. Major moves."

"Some moves," he said, grinning.

"She showed us the moves. Like dance moves. But naked. To be clear, she was fully clothed when she told the story."

"But the moves themselves were naked?"

"Stop! I can't. Enough about the moves," I said, hitting his arm before I nearly fainted from embarrassment. "I want to talk about you, I really do. I want to know everything that I don't already know. I just want to know *you*."

"Starting with . . ."

"Would you say you have a happy marriage?"

Turner seemed unfazed even though my heart was pounding. "My wife is a saint, but the marriage is complicated."

"How complicated?"

"Perhaps as complicated as yours. But make it five children, thirteen years of marriage, and a job that depends on secrecy and lies."

"Have you ever strayed outside of your marriage?"

"I have not," he said quietly. "And until recently, I'd never wanted to."

I closed my eyes and felt his leg move closer to mine, our thighs touching as the train rumbled on.

By the time we reached Philadelphia, our car had emptied quite a bit. I was about to stand to go to the dining car when the conductor stopped by our seats.

"Ma'am," he said, smiling at me, his blue eyes focused on mine. "There are several open seats in front of you if you'd like to move. Have some more room." His eyes flicked over to Turner and then back to me.

"I'm just fine," I said, smiling confidently. "Maybe passengers boarding in Baltimore will want those seats. But I do appreciate the gesture."

He nodded, eyed Turner warily, and then moved down the aisle.

"I'm just fine, too," said Turner toward the conductor's receding form.

When we arrived at Union Station, we walked down Massachusetts Avenue for ten blocks together before I left Turner for Georgetown.

He pointed to a bus stop. "I have to leave you here."

I nodded, wanting to wander the city together, like two people without any cares in the world but each other. Instead, I watched him walk away. When he was almost out of view, he turned and winked at me.

I met Nick at a small restaurant called Martin's Tavern. The exchange was quick. He gave me the materials, film that needed to be developed. He seemed far more on edge than the last time I'd seen him. After we gulped down our drinks and walked out, he said, "Tell Jacob one thing, but don't write it down. I found out yesterday, and it's too delicate to be said over the telephone."

"All right."

His voice lowered. "Tell him that there's a door open in the governor's room."

I nodded without comment, then hailed a cab to Union Station. If anyone was watching me, rushing to a pay phone was not going to be in my best interest. I looked all over the train for Turner. He wasn't there. But I knew that somehow he'd be waiting at the coffee shop, looking up at me as I walked in the door.

I returned to my apartment at six p.m., empty attaché case in hand, lips still feeling the lingering kiss that we'd stolen in the darkest corner of Penn Station.

"Gerrit, darling!" I called out. "Sarah, I'm back." But it was silent. Tom was sitting on the couch, a tumbler of scotch in his hand. He was still in his suit, a light gray one with a window check. His tie was not even loosened.

He looked at me with utter disdain, the way he looked at his father when he drank far more than was necessary and skulked off to call some woman half his age.

"Who is Coldwell?" said Tom, his voice thick with anger.

"What?" I whispered, almost unable to get the word out.

"Sarah Beach said a man called and said 'Coldwell,' but then hung up the telephone."

"I don't know a Coldwell."

"You're lying."

"I'm not."

"Then the bigger question," he said, his eyes red and exhausted, "is how stupid do you think I am?"

CHAPTER 38

Tom and I slept apart that night. Or, Tom slept while I lay wide awake, staring at the ceiling. Sometime around three a.m., I heard banging on the stairwell door. I kicked off the sheet and sprinted toward it, certain that Jacob was on the other side.

I got there first, but Tom was right behind me. He yanked the door wide open. Standing there was not Jacob Gornev, but Matt Kirkland, Carrie's husband.

"It's Carrie," he said, out of breath. "She's bleeding. And she's pregnant. What should I do?"

"I'm coming down. I'll come right now," said Tom, flying down the stairs with Matt. "Katharina, bring me my bag," he called out, but his voice was almost gone, he was moving so fast.

I ran to the library and turned on the light. His medical bag was next to his desk like it always was.

With the bag on my arm, I too flew down the stairs and knocked on the door. Matt opened it, grabbed the bag, and slammed the door in my face, leaving me alone in the stairwell. Back in our apartment, Peter was howling.

When the boys and I woke up in the morning, all three of us in the master bedroom, Tom was still not home. At noon, he telephoned.

"Tom," I said, out of breath from rushing to the phone.

"She miscarried," he said. "Carrie. She was hemorrhaging, losing a lot of blood, especially for how early it was in the pregnancy. If they had stayed home any longer . . ."

"Tom—"

"The outcome would have been very different."

"Oh, how horrible. Poor Carrie. I didn't even know she was pregnant." She may have stabbed me straight in the back, but I did feel for her.

"She was five months along," said Tom flatly.

"Was she?" I said, thinking back to our outing in April. She probably didn't even know she was pregnant yet.

"When will she be home?"

"Could be several days. She's very weak."

"But she'll be all right?"

"I think so. Though having another baby may be more difficult."

"How awful. I know she wanted more. Poor, poor Carrie."

"Indeed. I'll see you at home."

Three days later, I walked into Carrie's room with two dozen roses and a new doll for Alice.

"Oh, Carrie," I said, leaning down and wrapping my arms gently around her shoulders. "I'm so sorry."

"Rina," she said, hugging me. "I'm sorry."

"You should be, you witch," I whispered as I kissed her cheek.

"I am a witch. It's none of my business. Your marriage, everything. It's none of my business."

"It's not. But let's put it behind us. Tom hasn't divorced me yet." I didn't add that I felt certain it was going to be on the table soon.

"I'm glad you're here. And thank God for Tom. Your incredible husband. I don't think a rocket ship could have gotten me to Lenox Hill faster."

"I'm so glad," I said, thinking about Tom, and the kind of man he was. A part of me had forgotten, which was very unfair.

"I'm so sorry I told Tom about—"

"Please. Let's forget it."

"I should know better than to meddle in a marriage. It's just, I was in shock." She leaned back and closed her eyes. "I was not well," she said. "I suppose I'm still not well."

"Who would be? After what you went through."

I would forgive Carrie because the world always forgave people like Carrie.

"My body is only the half of it," she said, pulling up the covers. "It felt like I was in labor again, and I just kept thinking, it's not ready to be born. Why is it being born? I'm murdering my own child. It's going to die."

"But that's not what happened," I said, sitting down on the edge of her bed. I reached for her hand, my weeks of anger shattered by her hours of anguish. "You didn't have any control over what happened. Sometimes our bodies win over our brains."

"I know. Tom spent the whole night after it happened sitting in my room with me, talking about it. Did he tell you?"

He hadn't.

"He explained that miscarriages often occur because the baby isn't healthy. That there's a problem with the chromosomes. That it was not because my body decided to fight against my baby."

"Of course not, Carrie."

"But I can't stop thinking about it that way," she said, her chin quivering. "I keep thinking about mothers as murderers. It's just in a terrible loop in my head. That word."

"Carrie, don't say such a thing. You just need some rest."

"No, Rina, think about it," she said, letting go of my hand and sitting up. "Even with our living children we are murderers. By making Alice, I didn't just create a being who will live, but one who will *die*. I gave her life and illness and suffering and eventually death. I gave her death. Isn't that awful to think about? That horrible thought has replaced the one about how we are always tethered to our children. I wish I could return to it."

"But you can. And you also need to start thinking about motherhood differently. It's very powerful, like you said. We make the dark and the light."

Carrie looked at me as if I had just placed an axe delicately against her neck.

"Where have you been, Rina?" she said, looking up at me with her beautiful blue eyes. "Actually, don't answer that."

"It's not what you think." It was so much better than anything Carrie Kirkland could imagine.

"I understand we are all human," said Carrie weakly, "but why would you ever jeopardize your family life? And Tom's happiness? He is one of the best there is, Rina."

I took Carrie's hands again.

"I don't know where I've been," I said truthfully. "I really don't. I suppose I've been a little lost. But I think I'm finding my way again."

In her sterile hospital room, those words rang true.

That night I made love to my husband. I told him he was an amazing man. And I meant what I said. Be appreciative of what you have, Dr. Creighton had advised. Tom Edgeworth was not a maker of life, he was better. He was the force that pushed death away. What an incredible thing to be.

CHAPTER 39

When I woke the next morning, in my marital bed for the first time in a long time, Tom was not next to me. I slipped out of the covers and walked around the apartment. It was only six a.m. Both boys were still asleep, but Tom was nowhere to be found. I moved quietly down the hall to the window seat. My admiration for Tom, my making love to him, had not diminished how I felt about Turner. It hadn't changed how magnetically pulled I was to him.

I admired my husband. But I was no longer the girl whose heart soared when he walked in the room. My knees did not go weak when he said, "I lovely smart love you." Besides, Tom no longer said things like that. We had grown into two very different people sharing one very large apartment, two children, and many fond memories that were growing more distant by the day.

I felt my stomach muscles quiver. I didn't know if it was guilt or sadness. I flicked on the radio and lowered the volume. Adlai Stevenson, who had been at the UN when I was there, was speaking about his presidential ambitions again, but this time, he was addressing women.

"In modern America, the home is not the boundary of a woman's life," he said crisply. "There are outside activities aplenty. But even more important is the fact, surely, that what you have learned and can learn will fit you for the primary task of making homes and whole human beings in whom the rational values of—" I flipped the radio off and glared at it. Even the most liberal male believed that women could do no more than cultivate the minds of our babies.

The phone rang, and I leapt on it before it woke the boys.

"Katharina Edgeworth," I said brightly, quite sure who was on the other end of the line.

"It's Coldwell."

I said nothing, afraid he would sense my disappointment.

"I don't want you to think that every time your phone rings someone else is dead, but someone else is dead."

"What?" I asked, gripping the desk, utterly panicked. There were very few people left whom we both knew. My body went cold. "Who?"

"Gornev."

I reached for a chair and sat down. For a few seconds, I feared he was going to say Turner. Now, conflicting emotions were flying through my mind, but relief was winning.

"He wasn't in good health, as you know. He died of a heart attack. He was found by his neighbor. He was in bed. Alone," he added.

"Ava is dead, and now Jacob is dead."

"It's strange, isn't it," said Coldwell in his flat voice. "They're two of the sharks we wanted, and we didn't even have to throw the harpoon. That said, now it's going to be a lot harder to get to Nick's group. We know some, but I want to know more. We'll have to really scrape to keep that going."

I knew what he meant—scrape to keep *me* going. For with Jacob and Ava dead, what purpose did I serve?

"It's strange news, I know. I hope you're fine," said Coldwell. "You'll hear from me soon."

The phone cut out. I rested my fingers on the buttons and dialed Turner. After two rings a woman picked up. I let the receiver fall back in its cradle.

I sat down and pressed my palms against my eyes and started to cry.

I cried because I wanted to hear Turner's voice. I cried because I heard his wife instead. I cried because Jacob was dead and I had loved him once. I cried because of the man he had turned into. I cried because with him gone, I was gone. The FBI couldn't use me much longer. Coldwell might be dancing around it now, but in his next phone call, he would say it.

I heard Peter stir and wiped my face with the sleeve of my robe. I fed the boys, played with the boys, fed the boys again, and collapsed with them in the afternoon, so emotionally spent that I was sure I'd fall asleep alongside them. But I couldn't quiet my mind. I ran my fingers through Gerrit's dark hair, taking in his peaceful face, listening to Peter's quiet breathing. They were so easy to love when they were asleep.

No Jacob meant no Nick. No Nick meant no meetings with Turner in Penn Station. No reason to see Turner at all. The KGB wasn't going to let Nick and the rest of their government sources just disappear into the starry night. They'd find him a new contact and fast. I needed to figure out who it was and ingratiate myself to them.

The only place I knew to look for information was Jacob's apartment. It was the last chance I had of proving my worth, and of keeping any remaining connection to Nick. I remembered that the space was spare, monastic even, but maybe something was hidden there. A phone number. An address. An alias. Anything.

Sarah came while the boys were still sleeping and I paid a cabdriver five dollars to speed like the taxi was on fire to Jacob's apartment by Chelsea Park.

Outside his building, I slammed the taxi door and sprinted to the fifth floor. Before I could second-guess myself, I reached for the doorknob. I'd barely turned it an inch when the door was yanked open and my body was slammed into the hallway.

I looked up to see Turner Wells.

He stared at me in shock, put his fingers to my lips, and then helped me inside the apartment, locking the door behind us.

He pointed to the bedroom.

"Rina!" he whispered. "Are you all right? I can't believe I just tried . . . I didn't know it was you. Are you all right?" he said, his hands cupping my face.

"I'm okay, I am," I said, catching my breath. We both sat on the ground in the empty room while I regained my wits.

"I don't understand," he said, still looking at me like I might crack in two. "What are you doing here?"

"What are you doing here?"

"I'm—"

"Never mind. I'll go first," I said, putting my hands on my knees as I leaned against the wall. "Turner, I don't want to become irrelevant. To you, to Lee Coldwell, to the FBI. I want to keep doing what I'm doing. I want to keep seeing you. All I did with Nick Solomon is go where Jacob directed me. But now I don't know where to go. So I came here. I thought maybe there would be something of Jacob's that would guide me to Nick, so I wouldn't lose my place in all this." I paused to catch my breath. "In other words, I'm desperately grasping at a dream that I would like to keep dreaming."

Turner moved next to me.

"It is obvious to me, and probably Lee, that your worth to the Bureau does not begin and end with Jacob Gornev. Also, we'll now watch Nick Solomon's every move. If Lee wants you to run into him, I'm sure he can arrange it. But to be frank, I don't know what Lee wants anymore."

"Oh," I said, feeling foolish and wholly out of my element. I looked down at the floor, remembering how I had sat there with a very alive Jacob just weeks before. "I can't believe he's dead," I said, looking around the empty room.

"You might be more surprised than he was," said Turner. "He knew he was dying, don't you think? From the way he spoke at the end?"

"I don't know. Maybe I just didn't want to see it." I put my hand next to Turner's on the floor. "Now you. Why are you here?"

"Because I'm an idiot who doesn't give a damn about his career it seems," he said, standing. "And because I wanted to assuage any doubt I had that Jacob killed Ava."

"Are your doubts assuaged?"

"Yes," he said, helping me to my feet. "But we shouldn't be here. The Soviets wiped this place already, but still, we shouldn't linger. Let's go."

Turner took a folded newspaper and a lighter off Jacob's nicked-up dining table. We hurried out of the apartment and walked toward the river. "The end of July," he said as we approached the piers, where a lone Cunard ship bobbed in the water. The commotion, the tearful goodbyes and elated hellos that took place there during the war days were gone. The piers were far less busy; everyone wanted to fly to Europe now. But they weren't completely abandoned. The Cunard ship still looked proud, and the passengers who were embarking appeared eager to leave behind the dog days of summer in New York.

"I always feel a certain sadness when August looms. A kind of urgency. If I haven't done all the things I wanted to do in a summer, I start to panic," said Turner as we gazed out on the boat.

"Things like what?"

"The iconic New York things that you just have to do in summer."

"A day at Coney Island, eating ice cream in Central Park, the fireworks, and all that?"

"And all that," he said, turning to look at me. "Rowing on the Hudson. Rowing in Eden."

I pushed off the railing and studied him. *You can anticipate someone's words,* my aunt Hanna had told me. I was not anticipating this. He stood straighter and looked away from me.

"You know who used to say that?" I said slowly.

"Who?"

"Ava Newman used to say that."

"I suppose she did," he said, staring back at me.

I felt my gut wrench.

"You know what I think?" I said quietly. "I think you knew Ava Newman far better than you have let on. I think you knew her very, *very* well."

"No, Rina," he said, taking a step toward me. "You're letting your mind go in the wrong direction."

"I'm letting it go straight where it seems to belong. 'Don't you think Turner is one of the most handsome men you've ever seen?' She asked me that, you know. Why would she ask me that?"

"Because she thought we were sleeping together."

"I'm going to need you to be decidedly less cryptic, Turner," I said, suddenly feeling faint in the heat.

"We're too close to the vacationers," said Turner, watching the passengers ascending the ramp. "Let's go sit over there," he said, pointing to the edge of an unused dock. "Bad seats, good view," he quipped as he walked and I followed, my heart feeling like it was going to abandon me for good.

"What's that state over there?" he said, pointing.

"New Jersey."

"Ah, then the rumors are true. There is a world outside Manhattan."

"Not for me," I whispered. "Not lately."

"Futile-the winds- / To a Heart in port- / Done with the Compass- / Done with the Chart! / Rowing in Eden- / Ah-the Sea," quoted Turner quietly. "It's a poem by Emily Dickinson. Part of a poem by Emily Dickinson. The first time I went to Ava's apartment with her, I recited it because the name of her apartment building is the Eden. She really liked it. I suppose she took to stealing a few lines."

A heart in port. Ava had used that phrase, too, had said that my heart in port was at the UN, but I knew that right now, my heart in port was wherever Turner's was. And suddenly, I wasn't convinced that Turner's heart was with me.

"Let me start at the beginning. Because if I don't, you might not believe me. And that's not even an option, okay?"

I nodded.

"Earlier this year, in February, I got the feeling that Ava was starting to second-guess what she was doing."

"Why?"

"It started as an instinct. The third time we met, seeing how I was fond of Jacob, and that he was supportive of me, of the CRC, she expressed her concerns about his health. She thought he'd had a heart attack that he'd hidden from her, and she was worried he'd have another. His superiors wouldn't let up on him and she didn't know what to do. She seemed scared and frustrated." He leaned forward, putting his elbows on his knees. "I've learned that when a person is scared and frustrated, it means a door is opening, even just the smallest bit."

"So you knew they were entangled."

"I knew they were something. But I was far more fixated on becoming someone she could trust. Someone she might confide in."

"What did you want her to say?" I asked, my anxiety starting to release its chokehold.

"*Turner, I've made a very big mistake.*"

"Did she ever?"

"Not in so many words. The thing is, I liked Ava, much as you liked Ava. I appreciated her energy and her loyalty, and I assumed she was just very misdirected. That she had been guided the wrong way out of love for Jacob. I didn't know about her father, but now I can see, she was misdirected by love for her father, too."

"You told her," I said, starting to understand. "You told her who you were."

He nodded. "I took an incredible gamble, one that would have gotten me fired on the spot, or worse, if Coldwell or anyone else knew. Still, I told her who I was. I told her that there's been talk of Hoover passing a witness immunity bill later this year. That all a person has to do is give evidence concerning the other members of the conspiracy. I wanted to help her find her way to do that. I told her that the

FBI would be able to make accommodations for her now. That she wouldn't have to wait until the bill was passed."

"Is that true? Could you have?"

"For a woman, and one like her? Yes. It had been done before, and I was confident it would be done again, especially if she really sang for her supper."

"But you never told Coldwell."

"No. I knew it was an incredibly stupid thing to have done, because she could have just turned on me. Told Jacob. Blown my cover with the CRC, with everyone. She could have easily laughed at me and betrayed me."

"But she didn't."

"No. She didn't," he said. "Nor did she jump at the chance I offered. I think she was scared of becoming a public figure, which is without a doubt what would have happened. A public trial for Nick Solomon and the rest of them, with Ava held up as an example of how even a smart, rich American woman could have her head turned by the evils of communism."

"So instead she just decided to keep going? Go to Russia, keep doing the Soviets' work?"

"It's more complicated than that," he said, squinting out at the water. "And the complications are why she's dead. Ava told me that in a moment of desperation she suggested to Jacob that they strike a deal with the FBI to save his life, but that he didn't react well."

"Why would she do that?" I said, incredulous.

"Old-fashioned love. Rumor has it it can move mountains. But not communist leaders, it seems."

"I wish I'd known. I know you couldn't have told me, but I wish I'd known so I could have just pulled her away and hidden her in a cave."

Turner leaned back, nearly closing his eyes. "Ava Newman would never have let you hide her in a cave. And after Jacob refused to save himself, she became fixated on the idea of going to Russia to prove herself, to convince him she'd just had a moment of weakness. From what she told me, Jacob said he was sending her to Moscow to save her from the FBI, but I never bought it. As soon as she told me how emphatic he was, I became emphatic, too, just in the other direction. I was planning on telling Coldwell that I thought we could extract her, but then she died."

"Because Jacob murdered her!"

"Someone murdered her. Maybe Jacob, maybe someone else was in the apartment already. Either way, Jacob definitely told Moscow that she was considering turning herself in. And that alone is as good as a bullet to the head, or a noose around the neck. Even if he didn't string up the rope himself, he killed her. He was loyal to Moscow till the end."

"Max tried to save her," I said, thinking back to that terrifying day.

"And Ava thought she would be saving you by handing you to Max. Or at least she wanted to open a door for you."

"Or give me a lifeline," I said, thinking of my UN telephone.

He turned his head away from the water, away from the sun reflecting off it. "The thing is, if she was reckless enough to suggest they try to broker a deal with the FBI, maybe she also mentioned me. The person who gave her that idea in the first place."

My breath felt shallow, the oxygen sprinting away from me. "Did she?" I whispered.

"I don't know. I never got the chance to ask. But Jacob's apartment used to be stuffed like an olive. Books everywhere, papers everywhere. Ava once told me he kept things in a safe, but that he wasn't very safe about the safe. But a few weeks ago, you told me that his place was monastic."

I nodded.

"And when you were at Columbia? Did he also live that way? Bare walls and all?"

"No. It was a mess. But in an appealing way. An intellectual's stuffed olive."

I pictured Jacob's Amsterdam Avenue apartment, a tiny efficiency with a fire escape as a balcony but no shortage of character. "There were always towers of books, piles of school papers, bottles of cheap wine, and bags of bread crumbs for the pigeons." Jacob had changed so little; why hadn't it occurred to me that there was something not right about half-full shelves?

Turner read my expression. "I never saw his last apartment in that state, which means it had to have been nearly cleaned out, even before he died. In this game, that's never a good sign. I started to worry about my cover, and whether Jacob had kept information about me in the apartment that is now sitting in Russian hands. And of course, as you saw today, if there was a safe, it's long gone. All that remained were some old clothes and some books—including this."

He opened the newspaper and handed me a green leather volume. *The Sorrows of Young Werther.*

"I saw this on his shelf when I was in his apartment with him," I said, turning it around in my hands. "I think I gave it to him."

"I think he's giving it back."

I ran my fingers against the gold lettering and Turner gestured for me to open it.

On the inside cover, it was inscribed from me to Jacob, dated January 1940. The inscription had been crossed out, one blue diagonal mark through it. Underneath it, in Jacob's small print, was written, *"Es tut mir Leid."*

"Do you know what this means?" I said to Turner.

"I don't."

"It's usually translated as 'I'm sorry.' But it's more than that. *Es tut mir Leid.* Word for word it means 'It hurts me.'"

"I'm sure it did hurt him to kill Ava," said Turner, looking at the carefully printed blue ink. "I'm sure he loved her, just not enough."

We sat in silence for a moment as I tried to push the image of Ava's shock, of her last moments, out of my mind.

"One last translation between polyglots," Turner said, closing the book and resting his hand on it.

"I think he meant it for you as much as he did for me," I noted quietly.

We both watched as a man and a woman tumbled up the ramp of the ship, the last passengers to board. They were laughing and out of breath and seemed just delighted to be leaving New York.

I looked out at the water that was murky and warm but always found a way to dazzle me, especially in summer.

"Turner," I said. A hundred yards ahead of us, the ship crew was pulling the walkway up to the deck, preparing to depart. "What if we just ran away?" I nodded toward the boat. "Just ran away from it all. Just got on a boat to France."

"Are you sure that boat's going to France? It could be going to someplace really crummy. But even then . . ." Turner's gravelly voice trailed off. "I won't pretend I haven't thought about it. Very often."

"Turner, I—"

"I'm moving to Washington on Friday," he said, interrupting me.

I waited for his eyes to meet mine, every nerve in my body screaming.

"You're what?" I whispered.

He finally looked at me.

"I'm moving. My whole family is moving. The Bureau has enough information to shut down the CRC for good, which means I've done my duty. And more than that, I told them enough of what I just told you to worry that my cover's been blown. Not just with the CRC, but with the KGB. That could mean . . . I don't know exactly. It definitely doesn't mean anything good."

"If it means nothing good, shouldn't you go a lot farther than Washington? Shouldn't you be going to Fiji?"

"Let's start with Washington. Then maybe one day, Fiji." He put his hand on top of mine. "Meet me there?" he asked, smiling.

I nodded yes, but I was crying. I would not be meeting Turner by Chelsea Piers or Central Park again. We would not be boarding a boat together to France or Fiji or any wonderful place. That's what he was telling me. That in all likelihood, I would never see him again.

I leaned back against the old boathouse, trying very hard not to show that my heart was breaking, the pieces multiplying with every breath.

"Honestly, Katharina . . ."

"Yes," I whispered, tears falling on my lips.

"I'm overwhelmed. You overwhelm me. And I'm going to miss you very much."

"Not as much as I will," I said, opening my eyes.

"I think you're wrong about that."

"No," I said, shaking my head. "Turner. You came into my life at a time when I desperately needed something." Something I still needed. "This is, this has been, one of the most important stories of my life."

"A story?"

"I can't think of a better word."

"You always have the right word. The right thing to say. It's something I've come to rely on. I like story."

"Then you are my favorite story."

"If I can't take you to Washington, do you think I can take that with me?" he said, nodding at the Empire State Building. "We really do have the best buildings."

I nodded. "Just look at it for a while and stitch it into your memory."

"Good advice," he said, holding my hand even tighter.

"Where was I before all this started, Turner? I don't even remember. Brushing my teeth with gin."

"Did you really brush your teeth with gin?" He turned away from the Empire State Building and back toward me.

"Only once. There was a water main outage."

Turner started laughing before leaning over to wipe my tears.

"Katharina Edgeworth, thank you for overlapping your world with mine for a little while. Whatever this story was, it added life to my life. And I loved it," he said quietly. "In my mind, there's now a separate map of New York. Rina's New York. And it will always stay apart from the rest."

I nodded, not yet trusting myself to speak again.

"You may not have the most exciting existence at present, Katharina, Rina, but that doesn't mean you can't be an exciting person. Don't let your circumstances extinguish you. Okay?"

"Okay," I repeated. "Okay."

An hour later, I walked away from Turner Wells, leaving my heart lying at the edge of the Hudson.

CHAPTER 40

"ello, Sam," I said into the phone the next morning. I was in the kitchen, before the boys were up, alternately crying and making breakfast. Tom was, of course, already at work.

"Announcing Amelia Edgeworth."

"You can't be serious," I said, nearly dropping the phone.

"I'm sorry. She's already in the elevator."

Right then, I heard a ding.

"Rina! I'm not waking you, am I?" said Amelia, walking into the apartment.

I went to meet her. "Hello, Amelia. You're not, clearly, but the boys are still asleep."

She ignored me and walked into the living room. I followed her like a little duck.

She sat, asked for a drink, then examined it and me as I handed her orange juice.

"Rina, you look a wreck."

"Allergies," I said flatly.

"What is one allergic to in summer? Joy?"

"Perhaps," I mumbled.

"Look, Katharina," she said, grimacing as she took a sip of juice. "I shan't beat around the bush. You look extremely bad. Is it all those late nights out with the hobos?"

"None of those lately," I said dryly.

She put her glass on the side table. "If you're wondering why I came here unannounced, which I know you are, it's because my son called me yesterday. He mentioned that you're drinking again. And that your behavior has been . . . hard to predict. That you've been crying. Sobbing, actually. That you're unhappy, thus he's unhappy. And I hate when Tom Edgeworth is unhappy. Families are like a pyramid. If the husband is unhappy, everyone is unhappy."

"He has not expressed this unhappiness to me," I lied. The truth was, I had paid very little attention to Tom in the last eighteen hours.

"Sure, he hasn't." She walked to the bar, took the vodka, and added a pour to her drink. She took a sip, smiling contentedly. "Rina," she said, turning back to me. "This little breakdown of yours. Tell me, are you trying to be more memorable?"

"I don't think I know what you mean," I said, smelling the alcohol from six feet away.

"Perhaps that's not the right word," she said, sitting back down. She flexed and pointed her thin, elegant feet. Everything was thin and elegant about the Edgeworths, even their toes.

"Let me try to explain. As you know, my husband thinks of himself as a great explorer of women. The Marco Polo of womanizers. This is boring behavior. But when it started, I thought that if I made myself more interesting, he might be more interested in me. So, I'm asking you, is that what you're doing now? Trying to take Tom's attention away not from other women, but the hospital? His patients?"

"It is not." Only Amelia Edgeworth could liken her husband's philandering to a thirteenth-century Venetian explorer.

"Fine. Then are you acting this way because you want a divorce?"

Turner Wells's face flashed in my mind like a neon sign in Times Square.

There were many things I could have expressed to Amelia. The truth. Confusion. Heartache. Lies.

I chose lies. "I do not."

"Should I believe you?"

"I hope you will."

"I'll choose to believe you, then," she said, reaching for her drink. "Divorces are messy affairs."

"But if we divorced, Tom could marry the right girl. The girl you wanted for him," I said, refusing to hold back the shot.

"You are now the mother of his children," she said, looking at me, her face still beautiful and regal at sixty-eight. Whatever pact she'd made with the devil was clearly going strong. "That means that you are the right girl now. Besides, I don't hate you, Rina." She finished her drink and handed me the glass. "I never did."

"I'm glad?"

"You should be. I do find you complicated. And as we all know, complicated is better than boring."

I didn't reply.

"So, it's this motherhood thing that is making you look so cadaverous," she said, giving me another once-over.

I shrugged.

"Small children are terrible, Katharina. Everyone knows it, but nobody says it out loud. It makes us look weak and cowardly. Unfeminine."

"But why can't we say it out loud?" I said, placing her glass on the bar. "Why can't we at least say it to one another? Women like you and me."

"I'm not supposed to tell you it's horrible, Rina! If I did, you would never have had them. And then what? No heirs to speak of. No little potatoes to give kisses to."

"Or pistols."

"Listen, he stopped crying, didn't he?"

"There are other ways."

"Katharina. Your parents are poor as alley cats—I suppose you are, too, without Tom's money—but at least you've got claws like one."

My parents lived in Geneva. My father was a professor of art history. From what I knew, they were not eating discarded fishtails for breakfast, lunch, and dinner. And until very recently, I had been making forty dollars a week.

Amelia lifted her hand and ran her nails across the table.

"So go ahead and sharpen your claws, Rina. Figure out what you have to do to survive and do it. And if it requires a check— to keep on that Sarah from Barnard or some other bushy-tailed babysitter—tell me. But don't tell me when the men are watching. It would be—"

"Unfeminine."

"No, dear. It would be stupid."

At that moment, the elevator dinged and Tom entered the room. Both Amelia and I looked at him like he was an intruder.

"I called the apartment after my morning meeting and Father said you were here. I was worried," he said, his gaze darting between us.

Clearly, the woman he was worried about was me.

"And I'm worried about your marriage," Amelia said. "Rina is suffering," she said. "Do you see how bad she looks? Of course you do. Everyone can see it."

"Excuse me?" I said, looking at her.

"Rina is suffering?" Tom echoed.

"That's what I said."

"There's suffering, and there's *suffering*, Mother," said Tom with exhaustion in his voice. Such talk always exhausted Tom.

"Being a mother is real suffering, Tom," said Amelia firmly. "And don't you ever say otherwise, or you will not be welcome in this house anymore."

"This is my apartment," said Tom.

"Not bought by that pittance of a doctor's salary."

I stared at Amelia, stunned.

"You men refuse to acknowledge it all. Giving birth? It's not exactly one long nude cocktail party with quite the favor at the end."

"Mother, you're drunk," said Tom. He went to the kitchen and fetched a glass of water.

"Why don't you follow suit, Tom? You could use a drink."

"I'm going back to work," he said, heading to the elevator. "You two can continue this discussion without me." As he walked out of the room, I heard a cry. Peter had woken up. A few seconds later, Gerrit followed suit.

"No, Tom, you will not," Amelia countered. "You two join your calloused hands together and go have breakfast. I'll take care of the babies."

"Mother, I don't have time—"

"Don't adopt that tone, Tom. Your excuses are lost on me. But do remember this. Just because I wasn't always there—though I was there plenty—doesn't mean Rina will be anything like me if you let her off the leash. She's made of stronger stock than I am."

"And why is that, Mother?" he asked before I could faint.

"Because she's decidedly middle-class! The middle class, they're just better at these things."

I started to laugh. There was no other proper reaction.

"What are the decidedly, sickeningly rich good at?" asked Tom.

"Being sickeningly rich, of course," said Amelia as Gerrit toddled to us and Peter cried louder. She intercepted him before he could get to me. "Also drinking. Guiding the gentle hand of man. Attending various functions. Singing. The rich are quite good singers. Oh, and we're excellent at having nervous breakdowns and affairs."

"Oh, Mother, anyone with genitals is good at having affairs."

"Do you have to be so crass?"

"I learned it all from my father."

"That part is true. Now, please, leave before I change my mind." She looked down at Gerrit.

"Guess what your grandmama has in her handbag? Another revolver!"

Tom gestured to the elevator and I followed. Three doors down from our apartment was an overpriced French bistro. He started walking toward it, but I suggested the bench across the street. The one that looked at the zoo.

"Why in the world is my mother in our apartment?" asked Tom when we sat down.

"I don't know. To talk about motherhood."

"Do you want to talk to me about motherhood? Or maybe just about our marriage?"

"Both," I said quietly, not the least bit ready for such a conversation.

"Then I'm going to ask you again. Are you having an affair?"

"I am not," I said, not able to meet his eyes. "I was involved with something. Someone, a man, asked me for a favor. Asked me to . . . interpret something. And it got a bit complicated."

"The interpretation or the man?" asked Tom, looking toward the park.

"The interpretation. Sometimes things like that can be very difficult."

"Is that what you want? Difficult? I've spent our marriage trying to ensure nothing was difficult for you."

"But I don't want to live that way, Tom. When life has no difficulty, it's like a coin with one side."

He nodded and crossed his legs uncomfortably, his body allergic to inactivity.

"And this . . . interpretation is why you've been acting so strangely. Skulking around, crying, lying, drinking—"

"No, Tom," I said clearly. "This interpretation is the only thing that has made me happy." I took a deep breath. "Perhaps I should have told you something about it, but you and I, we have grown so far apart that I can barely remember a time when our marriage was different. And, despite your best efforts, there actually *is* difficulty in our lives. Our children can be very difficult."

"But things change, Katharina. They're difficult now, but it will be much better soon, and then you'll miss them being babies. All women do. You just have to grit your teeth and get through this part. I wish you enjoyed it more. I wish you enjoyed *me* more," he said earnestly.

"I do enjoy you, but I don't ever see you, Tom. How can you enjoy someone who provides a life that he doesn't share with you?"

"It's a phase, Katharina."

"Fine. A phase. Then since we're speaking plainly, let me be frank. You no longer find any magic in me, Tom. You find it all at the hospital. And why should you find it in me? I have so little left."

"Katharina, life is not about magic. Not always. We grow up. We have responsibilities. Careers. Then there are moments of magic still. Aren't there?"

"What is my career, Tom?"

"This is your career," he said, swinging his arm toward our building. "Is there anything better than being tasked with raising your children?"

"In fact, there is," I said, thinking of how I felt getting off the bus at Lake Success.

"I'm sorry you feel that way. I want our life to make you happy. I want you to be happy."

"Do you?"

"Of course I do," he said quietly.

"When I was thinking about leaving the UN—well, when I was being pressured into leaving the UN—you said I could go back when our children were older. Well, they are older, and I'd like to go back."

"To work? To the UN?"

"Yes, Tom, to work! You're not the only one with a graduate degree in a subject you love. I want to speak to adults, I want to contribute to this world."

"You are contributing already, by raising two good boys, who will be two great men."

"That's not enough, Tom. Am I not great? Why do we have to waste me, and my mind, in the process?"

"I don't think I'm seeing things the way you want me to."

I shook my head in frustration. "That's because so much has changed since the day you put that Band-Aid around my finger. I have changed too much. And you. So have you."

Tom exhaled loudly, his frustration overpowering his poise.

"Why don't you understand that nothing is forever, Katharina? You know my goal. You know I'd like to be at the helm, not always at the bedside. You can't just leave the boys before that happens. We're all depending on you."

"And then what? Do you imagine that when you are Mr. Lenox Hill, we will see you more, and I will magically be more fulfilled? The hospital just received three million dollars from the Millses. Three million! Which I may have played a tiny role in, mind you, but you're still not satisfied. You're not working any less, nor do you have plans to work any less."

"I'm extremely thankful that you and Mrs. Mills got on so well. But it's not enough money to do all we've set out to do. We need at least—"

"Listen to yourself, Tom! You think you are so different from your father because you're going to a hospital instead of a hotel room, but the void in my life is not unlike your mother's."

"I am nothing like my father," he said angrily, practically clawing the bench.

"Except that, like your father, you are never home. It is you who should be sleeping in the guest room. You have become the guest in our house, not me."

Tom stood up. "I can try to change that. In the future. But you have to realize—"

"No," I said, interrupting him. "As I just said, you promised me before I had the boys that if I still cared about working for 'peace and security,' I could go back to the UN. That the Edgeworth name would help me attain my goals there. But lately, being Rina Edgeworth causes more panic than pleasure. Your family is so worried that I will sully your precious name by being anything less than their stifling version of perfection. And let's be quite honest, Tom, the only professional goal you want me to attain is the permanent shedding of my ambitions. So what *you* need to realize is that if you can't balance your devotion to Lenox Hill with your devotion to your family, there will be no future here. Our home will be short one wife."

He looked at me, and for the first time, he seemed to recognize that his loving wife had lost much of the loving. There was grief in his eyes. "If you want to learn to love me again, I can try to make it easier."

"I still love you, Tom," I said. "I do. It's me I have the problem with."

"Well, I love you enough for two, Katharina. I lovely smart love you."

I nodded. I knew he believed that. But how could it be true if he had failed to care that since the day I'd traded Turtle Bay for Fifth Avenue I'd stopped loving myself? I stood up. "You want me to be happier?"

He nodded.

"Then just let me leave. Just let me get off this bench and go," I said.

"Will you come back?"

"To an always empty house? No. But if that changes—"

"You know it can't right now. You know that—"

I didn't stay to hear the last of his words. I went back to the apartment, took the boys from Amelia, and got into a taxi.

"Where to?"

"The Brooklyn Bridge."

CHAPTER 41

I held Peter to my chest and let Gerrit stick his head dangerously far out the taxi window. "New York," he said gleefully.

"Yes, baby," I said. "And we're going to see one of the best things New York ever built."

It turned out that Gerrit was extremely passionate about the Brooklyn Bridge. He kept screaming about it and clawing at his stroller, wanting to get out so he could plunge straight into the water. Bringing him to a very large bridge was about as good of an idea as inviting your cat to bathe with you.

But I needed to see something big, to feel the wind against my face, to marvel at the city. The person who made me feel the most alive was gone. Nothing could replace Turner, but I needed to start finding moments of joy on my own.

As we reached the middle of the bridge I saw a very familiar man standing dead center. Lee Coldwell.

"Bridge!" Gerrit bellowed, waving his hands in the air wildly.

"Let me guess," I said to Coldwell. "You followed me here."

"Maybe," he said, gesturing for us to walk. We moved past a group of loud young men, then walked alongside some architecture student pontificating about the bridge to his exceedingly patient girlfriend.

"Can I ask why?" I said once we were alone. "I thought I wasn't supposed to be seen with you."

"These days, it seems that everyone is taking chances. Making very stupid decisions. Risking it all. I thought I'd join in."

I ignored the edge in his tone and kept walking. Lee Coldwell was no longer just an FBI agent, he was the man who had made Turner Wells part of my story. "What does that have to do with me?"

"You . . . Well, we don't think we're quite done with you." He paused. "That sounds very macabre. Let me try again. We have an opportunity and we think you're the perfect person for the job."

"You do?" Suddenly I couldn't even hear Gerrit's screams. All I could hear were those words.

"There's someone on the periphery of Nick Solomon's group. Robert Bolle. Heard his name before?"

I shook my head no.

"We don't have any evidence of him moving documents out of the Justice Department, where he's employed now—as a litigator of all things—but we've seen him with Solomon too many times to ignore. Now he's gotten himself a job at City Hall. As in New York's City Hall. And not just in any office. He's working on judicial recruits. Advising on candidates for criminal court, civil court. He's going to weigh in on who goes to the bench, and I'd bet my ass that he'll be filling it with sympathizers. We need someone on the inside to make contact with him. Become friendly with him. Observe him."

"City Hall?"

"Yes. Remember what Solomon told you? There's a door open in the governor's room? That's City Hall."

"Of course," I said, picturing the reception room in City Hall. That must have been what Nick was referencing. "So, you think I could be useful because I was once under the employ of City Hall?"

"That's a big reason," he said. "We could help ensure that you'd get hired again. Probably not with Judicial, but there's an office that does something with immigrants, which means they'll have translation work.

It's not sixty hours a week, not even half that. But the real reason we want you, Mrs. Edgeworth, is because you're pretty good at all this."

I didn't know how to answer. If the Soviets knew about Turner, perhaps they knew about me. Coldwell didn't seem to think so, and I was too scared to tell him I knew what Turner had done. Or what could be done to Turner.

"City Hall," I said, thinking of the way I'd felt running up those stairs. That memory was now forever entwined with my night in the subway station with Turner.

"Will you consider it?" Coldwell asked again.

The only place I had been dreaming of returning to was the UN. But sometimes another door opened. Perhaps City Hall would be the thing, the place that would allow me to thrive inside 820 Fifth Avenue instead of desperately trying to escape. Or maybe it would be the force that made me leave my keys there for good and start a new life without Tom. Either way, I needed to try.

"I would like to," I finally said. "But even if I'm getting paid by the city of New York, I still want your money. Forty dollars a week."

He nodded. "I wouldn't expect anything less from you."

By the time we walked across the bridge to the Brooklyn side, both boys had fallen asleep. We turned around and walked back toward Manhattan.

"Ava is dead. Jacob is dead. But I'm going to City Hall."

"Yes. Because you are very much alive."

"My best trait."

"Mrs. Edgeworth," Coldwell said when we once again reached the middle of the bridge. "You've been an incredible help. You can still be an incredible help, if you can figure out how to make it all work," he said, gesturing at the children.

"Mr. Coldwell," I said through the noise of the wind. "I'm sure as hell going to try."

"I knew you were the right person to ask."

When we reached the road on the Manhattan side, not far from where we'd first met, Coldwell lit a cigarette and blew out the match. He was about to put it in his pocket, but handed it to me instead.

"My version of flowers."

"Strange," I said, putting it in my pocket. "But charming."

"Most people tend to think I'm the former."

"Not me."

"Good."

He tipped his hat to me and puffed on his cigarette. "I'll contact you if it all goes through, Mrs. Edgeworth."

I watched him disappear into the crowd and then pushed the boys onto Lafayette Street. I needed to walk a few blocks, to allow myself to feel the high of again being the perfect person for the job—and the low of the job being short Turner Wells.

I pushed the stroller on the crowded sidewalk, accidentally touching the side of a man's leg. He whipped around, irate.

"Could you watch it!" he screamed, looking at the two sleeping boys like they were two-foot murderers. Then he glared at me. "You might as well just push a wheelbarrow around Manhattan."

I murmured an apology and tried to right the stroller, which had fallen halfway off the curb. With both boys in it, plus the metal frame, it was extremely difficult to lift. I tried and failed several times, with no one offering to help me. As I tried again, I saw a set of hands on the base of the stroller. An older woman was reaching down to assist.

"Maybe if we do it together. On three," she said, counting. When she reached three, we were able to lift it, but both boys woke and started crying.

She bent over them and patted their heads.

"Thank you so much," I said as she straightened back up.

"Of course. Having young children is very difficult."

I waited for her to say "But it gets better" or "But it's a blessing." Instead, she simply nodded firmly and walked away. I wanted to tell her how much I appreciated her candor. The ability to say "This is very difficult" and leave it be.

I looked down at my children. "Come on, darlings," I said in my brightest voice. "Let's get this wheelbarrow into a taxi and go home."

CHAPTER 42

The taxi turned onto Fourth Avenue, by Union Square, sped up to try to catch a yellow light, then braked hard just as it turned red. We all flew forward.

"Just a reminder that only passengers who are alive at the end of their ride can tip their drivers," I murmured.

I rolled down the window as the driver grumbled an apology.

We moved quickly up Park Avenue, traffic unusually light for the hour. Everyone was leaving town, in the worst of ways. Maybe it should have felt like there was poison in the water, but I still wasn't ready to jump ship. On my left, the Empire State Building watched over the city, watched over me.

Tom wasn't home when we arrived, nor by the time I put the boys to sleep. At nine, I went to the bedroom, took out the bronze Dunhill lighter, and stared at the telephone. I wanted to dial Turner's number, to hear the intonation in his voice rise slightly when he realized it was me. I flicked the lighter open and closed until I found the strength to dial another number instead.

It was only seven p.m. in California.

"Faye Buckley Swan," she answered with command.

"You really do have a movie star name," I said, trying not to burst into tears. "I think you went into the wrong business."

"Keep flattering me and I'll reverse the charges. How are you, Katharina Edgeworth?"

"You know, frankly, I've been better."

"Now, let me guess, did you pour gin on Elizabeth Taylor?"

"For the last time, it was a mere sprinkle," I said, grinning.

"Well, if Hollywood's brightest lights are still safe, to what do I owe the honor of your long-distance call?"

"I wanted to chat, of course. And I also wanted to hear more about a very modern divorce."

"Why, are you considering one?" she asked, her voice skipping up.

"I might be."

"Fascinating. Well, first, let's clear something up. Divorce is nothing new. Women have wanted to divorce for centuries, since marriage was invented. What's different now is that they can finally do it without getting completely screwed. Isn't that lovely?"

"Lovely."

"So that's the very modern part. The woman not being raked through the coals, thrown out to pasture with a few quarters to her name."

"The thing is," I said. "There are many discordant thoughts rattling around in my mind, but one of them is that I've been offered employment, at City Hall, where I worked during the war. I'd like to take the job, but my husband will refuse me. I'm sure of it."

"Have you asked?"

"Not in so many words. It's a mere ladies' job at less than thirty hours a week, but that's twenty or so hours I would not be tending to my boys' every need. Where I'd require a replacement Rina."

"How dare you even speak those words."

"It's frightening how much you sound like him."

Faye laughed and I heard a door close. "But that's not really why you're considering divorce, is it?" she asked. "Go ahead and give the long answer. I've already waived my hourly fee in the name of friendship."

"Well, no," I said. "It's a hundred reasons that have added up over the years without my even noticing until they all fell at my feet and then I noticed. Really noticed. And I suppose the icing on this very expensive cake is that lately I've had forces in my life, you included, that helped me realize I'm not quite dead yet. That I may have a lot of life and love left in me and that I want to share all of that with someone who enjoys it. Who enjoys me."

"This person is not your husband?"

"Presently? No. I don't think Tom Edgeworth enjoys me. He's convinced himself that he does, but it's out of habit."

"Maybe you should pretend to be a very sick child and wheel yourself into Lenox Hill."

"You know, that might just do it," I said, remembering that drawing of a sewed-together girl that had brought Tom back to himself all those years ago.

"Jokes aside, my advice to you is this," Faye said authoritatively. "Start building a new life for yourself, inside the constraints of your current life. Of your marriage. Maybe it will turn things around for you. If after six months—a year, if you're feeling very patient—it doesn't seem to make a difference, then, in my opinion, it's time for that very modern divorce. Sometimes women simply cannot be their fullest selves inside a marriage. There have been scientific studies, you know. Men become far happier after getting married, women much unhappier."

"These are not well-publicized studies," I said, thinking about all the women's magazines I'd read over the years that told me I'd be walking on rainbows once I was safely married.

"Of course they're not. All those magazine owners are men. Everyone who runs the world is a man. But you need to start running your own world. The person who runs Katharina Edgeworth is a woman, and a pretty smart one at that. You can't bring her anywhere, butterfingers and all, but she is wonderful. Try not to forget it."

CHAPTER 43

If I had not found the courage to call Lee Coldwell in Los Angeles, his number would have disintegrated into a memory I could not hold. What I was reading now, and would reread thousands of times, would never meet such a fate. I took the piece of paper out of my pocket again. A letter from Turner had arrived a week after I'd spoken to Faye, abruptly handed to me in Central Park by a woman who then disappeared into the crowd. There was no return address, no name on the envelope. Only a letter, which wasn't even signed. But I knew exactly who had written it.

> As I stroll down Massachusetts Avenue, that stretch where we walked together near Union Station, I find myself paralyzed by the tyranny of distance, of circumstance, of obligation. And I very much want to stand outside your window, even if you don't look down. The views in Washington leave much to be desired.
>
> This is not a city of windows. The people here hide secrets behind marble walls instead of in buildings that brush the sky. How I miss your New York window.
>
> How I miss our city. How I miss you.

As I had with Coldwell's phone number back in April, every morning I transferred the letter to another dress pocket.

Turner had disappeared, and I had no way of reaching him. But it had to be that way. I leaned back on my window seat and closed my eyes. I felt that New York afternoon on 110th Street. It was part of me, embedded in my skin. I looked out at the sidewalk in front of the park. It was empty. No loud coeds, no girl with a red umbrella, no Turner Wells. I'd have to let the memories carry me instead.

CHAPTER 44

"Over here, Peter!" I called out. "Kick the ball. That's right, darling. Kick!"

Peter's tiny foot moved the big red rubber ball just a few feet, through the door to the bathroom in the same Chinatown park where I had first met Coldwell.

"Your turn, Gerrit," I said, kicking the ball to him. He sent it flying through the door and then rolled through the dust after it. I opened my mouth to yell, then clapped instead.

He came over to me, quite thrilled with himself.

"Aren't you full of energy," I said, smiling. The second week of August had brought no relief from the heat, but as happened every year, my body had finally gotten used to it.

"I'm so glad Peter is no longer a cat," said Tom, watching both boys kicking the ball. "Look at him walking upright."

"*Pauvre petit chat,*" I said, smiling at my baby.

"Rina with her little languages," Tom replied, reaching for my hand.

"Actually, French has one hundred thirty thousand words in current use. I wouldn't call it little."

"Rina with her big languages, then," he said, laughing. Hand in hand, we watched the boys play with the ball. Our children were incredibly dirty, but Tom still smelled like antibacterial soap and responsibility.

Start building a new life for yourself, inside the constraints of your current life, Faye had said. *If it's a bust, then just give me a jingle for a very modern divorce.*

I didn't know what I was doing, but I was doing something. I had not yet told Tom about City Hall, but what I did do was gather the troops. I had flipped the calendar to August and realized that I had not done anything with my family in months. The place where I wanted to start was where the new Rina had begun, Columbus Park.

Tom had not fainted when I told him my idea. He had not said, "For an hour, then I have to go to work." He had looked grateful that I had asked, that I wanted to spend time with him, then he rushed to the five-and-dime and returned with a large red rubber ball.

I was almost sure Tom was going to say no to me going to City Hall. We had already covered that ground during our conversation in the park. But if it was offered to me, really offered, I'd decided that I'd take it anyway. I would start as I had with Sarah Beach. Make the decision first, change my life, and tell Tom afterward. It had worked with Sarah; maybe it would work with City Hall. And if it did, perhaps I could tell him more about what I was doing. About how of all the people in Manhattan, a very monotone FBI agent had chosen me for a simple conversation that became not so simple after all.

After an hour, we headed toward the iron gate, saying goodbye to way downtown. "Ball!" Gerrit screamed out, running toward it.

"No, darling," I replied. "Let's leave it here. Other children might like to play with it."

Later that afternoon, when I was in the kitchen with the boys, Tom popped his head in and said that he was just going to stop by the hospital. "Briefly," he said, smiling. "I'll try to be home for dinner."

I watched as he went off to take a shower, and to morph back into Dr. Tom Edgeworth.

While Tom was in the bedroom getting dressed, Gerrit escaped into the living room with a butter knife in hand. I ran after him, wrestled it away, and forced both boys into the playpen, turning on the greatest friend to any mother, the television.

As I passed the foyer, I saw Sam's silver tray was on the entry table with a telegram on it that I'd missed when we'd come in. I tore it open.

They're waiting for you and your five languages in the Office of Immigration. You start August 23. It's also the day Mount Vesuvius started stirring, going on to destroy Pompeii. Good sign, no?

I smiled, thinking of the day I walked arm in arm with Turner toward the Vesuvius Restaurant to reunite with Jacob. The day I again said, "'All City 'Let's Go'" and started running toward a new, exhilarating story.

"Is that for me?" said Tom from the living room. I hadn't heard him walk down the hall.

"No," I said brightly. "It's for me," I clarified, slipping it in my pocket.

"You're okay, Katharina?" he asked, looking at me, a flicker of concern on his face.

I pressed the elevator button for him, then put my hands in the pockets of my dress. One hand held Turner's letter. The other, Coldwell's note.

"I am," I said, smiling. "I really am." I turned away as the elevator chimed and walked down the hallway, to my window seat. I pulled my knees up until they were right under my chin and looked out at Fifth Avenue. I closed my eyes and suddenly I could see so much more. I could see the entire city, from Harlem to Battery Park, the steam and heat, the limestone and concrete, the place where I had been born and reborn. It was waiting for me.

Acknowledgments

I am deeply indebted to the following people:

My editor, Sarah Cantin. Of all the books, this book. Of all the years, 2020. You are brilliant, you are wonderful. I am forever grateful.

The entire team at St. Martin's Press, especially Katie Bassel, Jessica Zimmerman, Sallie Lotz, Brant Janeway, and Alexis Neuville.

Bridget Matzie. What a journey. I'm so thankful for the six books we worked on together, and for your intelligence and grace, wisdom and friendship.

My fantastic agent, Alyssa Reuben. Also Matt Snow, Cassie Graves, and their colleagues at Paradigm. Here's to the future.

Elizabeth Ward. Your early edits are so needed, and so appreciated.

Kathleen Carter. Thank you for all your work championing this book.

Emeline Foster. A gift in my life. Here's to the memories—in New York and around the world.

Amy Cenicola. You redefine the meaning of friendship.

Raia Margo. Every conversation, every word. They're such a part of this book. Thank you.

Those who helped me shape the details: Clarissa Atkinson and Kari-Lynn Rockefeller.

My gorgeous friends who became gorgeous mothers in 2020: Kheira Benkreira and Keisha Nishimura.

The ones who found each other during this difficult time: Rashida Truesdale and Michelle Barsa.

My wonderful family.

And to Mary-Alice Farina, a friend for the ages, and her beautiful baby sunshine.

1. Consider the opening scene of the novel. What does it reveal about Katharina's feelings toward motherhood and her daily existence? How does it set the tone for the unfolding narrative?

2. Discuss the moment when Tom says he doesn't want to marry someone like his mother, Amelia Edgeworth. What does this reveal about Tom and Rina's relationship? What does it reveal about Tom's relationship with Amelia? How did your feelings toward Amelia evolve over the course of the novel?

3. On page 38, Rina says, "But I'm still a woman in 1946." Consider the weight of this statement. What did you learn about the societal expectations for women during the 1940s and 1950s?

4. What did you make of the novel's title?

5. The novel's setting of New York City is so integral to the narrative, serving as a character in and of itself. What are some moments in the novel when you see this to be true?

6. Discuss the significance of the hallway in Rina and Tom's apartment ("the gallery") and the window seat. What does this spot represent for Rina?

7. Discuss the evolution of Rina and Tom's relationship over the years, from the beginning of their relationship to their marriage. What do you think the future holds for the two of them?

8. Examine the female friendships that Rina has in her life. How do Faye Buckley Swan, Ava Newman, and Marianne Fontaine influence Rina?

9. What did the novel teach you about the Red Scare and McCarthyism that you may not have known before?

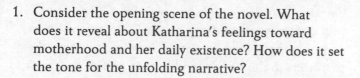

Discussion Questions

ST.
MARTIN'S
GRIFFIN

10. On page 346, Turner Wells says to Rina, "Don't let your circumstances extinguish you." Discuss the impact and meaning behind his words. In what ways have the characters in the novel—and Rina in particular—been affected by and/or overcome their circumstances?

11. Consider the role of Turner Wells in Rina's life. What does he mean to her? How does he change her? Did the racism regarding interracial couples in the 1950s impact them and their interactions?

12. Do you think our views on the roles of motherhood, a mother's identity, and postpartum depression have changed since the 1950s?

13. Discuss the end of the novel. How did it make you feel? What do you think comes next for Rina?

Tim Coburn

KARIN TANABE is the author of six novels, including *A Hundred Suns* and *The Gilded Years* (soon to be a major motion picture produced by Reese Witherspoon/Hello Sunshine). A former *Politico* reporter, she has had her writing featured in *The Washington Post, Miami Herald, Chicago Tribune,* and *Newsday*. She has appeared as a celebrity and politics expert on *Entertainment Tonight,* CNN, and *The Early Show* (CBS). A graduate of Vassar College, Karin lives in Washington, D.C.